# V.C. ANDREWS®

## Daughter of Darkness

POCKET **STAR** BOOKS

New York   London   Toronto   Sydney

Pocket Star Books
A Division of Simon & Schuster, Inc.
1230 Avenue of the Americas
New York, NY 10020

Following the death of Virginia Andrews, the Andrews family worked with a carefully selected writer to organize and complete Virginia Andrews' stories and to create additional novels, of which this is one, inspired by her storytelling genius.

This book is a work of fiction. Names, characters, places, and incidents either are products of the author's imagination or are used fictitiously. Any resemblance to actual events or locales or persons, living or dead, is entirely coincidental.

First Pocket Star Books paperback edition November 2010

V. C. ANDREWS® and VIRGINIA ANDREWS® are registered trademarks of the Vanda General Partnership

POCKET STAR BOOKS and colophon are registered trademarks of Simon & Schuster, Inc.

For information about special discounts for bulk purchases, please contact Simon & Schuster Special Sales at 1-866-506-1949 or business@simonandschuster.com.

The Simon & Schuster Speakers Bureau can bring authors to your live event. For more information or to book an event contact the Simon & Schuster Speakers Bureau at 1-866-248-3049 or visit our website at www.simonspeakers.com.

Cover design by Anna Dorfman
Cover photograph by John Ricard
Designed by Esther Paradelo

Manufactured in the United States of America

10  9  8  7  6  5  4  3  2  1

ISBN  978-1-4391-5501-1
ISBN  978-1-4391-8115-7 (ebook)

# First Taste

My sister Ava smiled at me. "Maybe you don't realize it yet, but the change has begun in you, Lorelei. Don't tell me you don't feel it in yourself."

"I do, Ava, but I'm not sure what it is I'm feeling exactly."

"You're feeling the power," she said.

"What is the power?"

"The gift that makes it possible for you to do for Daddy what your sisters, what I, have done for him. It's not just being attractive. You will mesmerize, capture, and fascinate. You'll get to feel like a goddess, like the puppeteer pulling the strings and making men dance. You had a taste of that last night, didn't you?"

"Yes."

She smiled and nodded. "I remember my first taste of it. It was truly like drinking from the Fountain of Youth. The energy, the strength, the confidence in yourself that you feel right now will never die."

"You make it sound as if we're immortal."

Ava smiled.

V. C. Andrews®
*Daughter of Darkness*

# V.C. Andrews® Books

**The Dollanganger Family Series**
Flowers in the Attic
Petals on the Wind
If There Be Thorns
Seeds of Yesterday
Garden of Shadows

**The Casteel Family Series**
Heaven
Dark Angel
Fallen Hearts
Gates of Paradise
Web of Dreams

**The Cutler Family Series**
Dawn
Secrets of the Morning
Twilight's Child
Midnight Whispers
Darkest Hour

**The Landry Family Series**
Ruby
Pearl in the Mist
All That Glitters
Hidden Jewel
Tarnished Gold

**The Logan Family Series**
Melody
Heart Song
Unfinished Symphony
Music of the Night
Olivia

**The Orphans Miniseries**
Butterfly
Crystal
Brooke
Raven
Runaways (full-length novel)

**The Wildflowers Miniseries**
Misty
Star
Jade
Cat
Into the Garden (full-length novel)

**The Hudson Family Series**
Rain
Lightning Strikes
Eye of the Storm
The End of the Rainbow

**The Shooting Stars Series**
Cinnamon
Ice
Rose
Honey
Falling Stars

**The De Beers Family Series**
Willow
Wicked Forest
Twisted Roots
Into the Woods
Hidden Leaves

**The Broken Wings Series**
Broken Wings
Midnight Flight

**The Gemini Series**
Celeste
Black Cat
Child of Darkness

**The Shadows Series**
April Shadows
Girl in the Shadows

**The Early Spring Series**
Broken Flower
Scattered Leaves

**The Secrets Series**
Secrets in the Attic
Secrets in the Shadows

**The Delia Series**
Delia's Crossing
Delia's Heart
Delia's Gift

**The Heavenstone Series**
The Heavenstone Secrets
Secret Whispers

My Sweet Audrina
(does not belong to a series)

# Daughter of Darkness

# Prologue

I know there are many my age who are ashamed of or embarrassed by their parents. Usually, it's just something annoying, like them babying us too much or being too restrictive and nervous, especially when we go off with friends or do something on our own, like driving for the first time. Instructions for raising a child, especially a teenager, are sort of like the instructions my daddy's fencing instructor once gave me when he described how to hold a sword.

"Hold it too softly, and it will fly out of your hand. Hold it too tightly, and it will suffocate and move as cumbersomely as a dying body."

Sometimes, however, our embarrassment and shame come from something quite dramatic and serious, as in stories in which young people discover their fathers or mothers did some terrible things in their youth. They love their parents, and their parents love them, but when they make the horrible discovery, everything changes, regarding not only what they now think of their parents but also what they think of themselves. They feel stained, tainted. It is as if evil is in their blood.

So it was for me when I forced myself to realize fully what and who my father was and who he, my older sisters, and my nanny were expecting me to become.

# 1

## In My Blood

"Stop that racket!" my older sister Ava commanded in the sharp, deep, stinging loud whisper only she could produce, after she had poked her head inside my bedroom door. Her words reverberated just under my breasts and shook my spine as if they had originated inside me and not inside her. Whenever she spoke to me like this, it sent a chill through my chest and into my heart. It was as if I had just gulped and swallowed a cup of ice water. Even my lips felt numb.

Minutes ago, our housekeeper and nanny, Mrs. Fennel, had ordered our thirteen-year-old sister, Marla, out of my room to go clean up her own. Cleanliness and neatness were as important in our house as they were supposed to be in a hospital. There was always a demand for tidiness and freshness that gave every home we lived in the appearance of being just created.

For us, time froze. We had new things, but we were taught that nothing became worn or out of style if it was cared for well. I grew up to understand that for the Patio family, days, months, years weren't locked up in some old chest and left to be forgotten. Nothing fell back or away or died in our world. It was as though everything Daddy touched became immortal. Memories swirled about us with the dazzle of colorful butterflies caught in rays of sunshine. Every one was precious and special. One of Daddy's favorite expressions was, "It's so old that it's new." That was because so many of the things we possessed people hadn't seen for some time, whether they were windup clocks and oil lamps or Victrolas and quill fountain pens.

We didn't relegate the antiques to some attic cemetery, either. Nothing was put away to sleep under a blanket of dust. A hundred-year-old music box sat side-by-side with an MP3 player. Daddy still had his Gibson and Davis piano, built in 1818.

"The piano's old, but the notes are new," he would say when I played it. "Life," Daddy told me, "simply means reinventing yourself every day. Every day is your birthday, Lorelei." He told that to Marla and Ava and our older sister, Brianna. He said it was something he constantly told himself.

We held on to the past, cherished it, but we certainly didn't dwell in it. The here and now and the future were always paramount. Maybe that was why, unlike other families, we had no family albums. There was little or no nostalgia. There were especially no early pictures of Daddy or Mrs. Fennel anywhere in our home and, of course, no videos of family events. Daddy never looked back at a time in history and said, "It was better then" or "I'd rather be alive then." There were individual things that were better, perhaps, but "Every generation, every age, has something to offer us, something to cherish," he said. "When you stop looking forward to the future, you begin to dig your own grave."

Although we were given new clothing and shoes regularly, we never threw anything out or gave anything away. That certainly wasn't because we were poor. We were far from it. The fact was, there was always a younger Patio daughter to assume some of what had belonged to the younger daughter before her.

And so my younger sister, Marla, had inherited many of my old things, some of which I had inherited from Ava. Most of them were barely worn. I grew out of them quickly, almost overnight. I took good care of everything I had, but Marla could be very sloppy, leaving a blouse on a chair, a skirt on the floor, or shoes in the doorway, which was the thing Mrs. Fennel hated the most.

Most of the time, Mrs. Fennel moved through the house as if she were on radar. No one could travel more confidently through the darkness. She seemed very proud of that, proud of all the things she could do and did efficiently, effectively, and gracefully, so stumbling over something one of us carelessly left in her way infuriated her.

Mrs. Fennel didn't have to raise her voice above a whisper to indicate her displeasure, either, and that indication was enough to move a herd of elephants. It was as if the air were filled with static and your ears were drowning in heartbeats that resembled the sound of thundering wild beasts.

Marla didn't dare protest or even appear upset when Mrs. Fennel came looking for her in my room. She avoided Mrs. Fennel's eyes just the way any of us would

and hurried to her room, chanting, "I'm sorry. I'm sorry."
It was as if she were trying to memorize it.

Mrs. Fennel hated that word. "Don't tell me you're
sorry," she would say. "Sorry doesn't mend fences well.
Something broken, something ruined, can't be restored
to what it was with an 'I'm sorry.' "

I certainly wasn't going to say "I'm sorry" to Ava. I
had just inserted my iPod into the player, speaker, and
charger, and it had barely begun to play. I had it so low I
didn't think I needed to listen on my earphones, so I was
genuinely surprised when she burst in on me. She frightened me, but as soon as I settled down, I was more annoyed than afraid. She looked half-asleep, even though it
was nearly noon. Of course, I knew why.

Almost always, whenever Ava slept this late or took
naps, so did Daddy. My recollections of my oldest sister,
Brianna, were the same. Anyone would wonder how she
could have heard anything through our walls when she
fell into that comalike sleep, but what amazed me about
both my sisters and my father was the sensitivity of their
hearing. I really believed my father and my sisters when
they were older could hear a pin drop, even when they
slept deeply. It was as if they had a sixth sense, especially
for danger. Would I inherit the same power? I hadn't yet.

In movies and on television, when someone's dog
suddenly growls or barks, the person pauses to listen and
doesn't hear anything but always in a dire whisper asks
the dog, "What is it, boy? What's out there?" Usually, it
turns out to be something evil.

I had seen Daddy do that many times. He would
suddenly stop reading or looking at something and listen

harder. His ears didn't go up, and he didn't growl, but his face changed into a dark, concerned expression. His eyes grew beady, and he moved his nostrils as though he were sniffing for some threatening scent. It was not fear, exactly. I had never seen him afraid of anything. I suppose it was more like suddenly being extra cautious.

Once, even though none of us was saying anything, he held up his hand and said, "Quiet." It was as if we were thinking too loudly.

My heart began to pound. Brianna's face mimicked his, and everyone froze. After a moment or so, Daddy nodded, relieved and satisfied, and returned to what he was reading. Brianna looked relieved and satisfied, too. I looked at Ava to see if she wanted an explanation as much as I did, but she didn't, or if she did, she was too frightened to ask. Ava was seven then, and I was four. Marla had not yet been born and brought to live with us.

If I asked what was wrong, why everyone looked so worried, Ava and Brianna would glance at me and then look to Daddy, who would simply shake his head and return to what he was reading.

Even at that young age, being so in the dark at times when it concerned my family made me feel like a total outsider, a visitor rather than another daughter. Eventually, I realized that something or someone was always pursuing us. I didn't know what or who it was yet, but, like all the information I was given, it would come when Daddy thought I was ready for it to come.

There were secrets sleeping in every shadow, secrets cloaked in whispers, and secrets implied in glances. Sometimes I thought they were like mold in the walls.

Not that we celebrated it, but I dreamed of a Christmas with packages of secrets under the tree, all addressed to me. All I had to do was open each one, and I'd learn the answers.

"Creepers, Ava," I said now in a mild protest, "I can barely hear the music."

"Stop thinking of only yourself," she snapped. Her eyes suddenly came alive, lost their sleepiness, and were luminous. It was as if matches had ignited behind them. Even her cheeks turned crimson. Ava could never be ugly, but more and more lately, I saw movements and incremental changes in her features that made them harder whenever she was upset.

"I'm not."

"Yes, you are. I don't know why no one else sees how selfish you can be. I was never that selfish when I was your age. You don't think of our family first. You think of yourself first."

I shook my head. Tears filled my eyes. In this house, there was no greater sin than selfishness. "That's not true!" I protested loudly.

Her eyes widened again. "Quiet, you fool. If you wake Daddy . . ."

"Okay, okay," I said, and shut off the iPod. I never had woken Daddy. None of us had, but the threat of his and Mrs. Fennel's anger should I do so was quite enough to make me tremble.

Daddy would have to sleep nearly the entire day at least once a month. Most of the time on those days, he didn't even come to dinner. When I was much younger and asked Mrs. Fennel about it, my nanny cryptically replied, "Digestion." She would say nothing more, and one look from her told me not to ask any more questions about it. She hated my questions anyway.

One time, she snapped at me and said, "Your questions buzz around my ears like annoying flies." She waved her hand near her head as if they were really there.

Brianna would be just as disturbed with my questions and either ignore me or say, "Stop pestering me. You'll know when you know. Try to be more like Ava. Be patient."

Despite how much Brianna watched over me when I was very young, I never had a close relationship with her. I thought I was closer to Ava, although getting close to her wasn't easy, either. With Brianna, at least I could blame it on age. She was too many years older than I was.

One day, she simply was no longer home. The way Mrs. Fennel, Daddy, and Ava behaved led me to believe there was nothing bad about her leaving even though it was so sudden, at least for me. On the contrary, they were pleased, happy for her. Of course, I wondered where she had gone and when she would return.

"She won't return. She has gone to fulfill her destiny," Mrs. Fennel told me.

When I asked Daddy why Brianna wouldn't return, he said, "Mrs. Fennel has already told you, Lorelei. There is nothing more for you to know right now. Just be as happy for her as we are."

How could I be happy for her if I didn't know where she was or what she was doing? What did that mean, "fulfill her destiny"? Would I have the same destiny to fulfill? And at the same age? Would Ava? Where Brianna was remained a mystery even to this day and, like other questions, was still not to be pursued, even though it was always on the tip of my tongue to ask. Less than a year later, Marla was brought to live with us, and I had a little sister to help watch, but my curiosity about Brianna's whereabouts never stopped. I wondered aloud about her often in front of Mrs. Fennel, who simply glared silently at me.

"You nag Mrs. Fennel at your own peril," Ava once said. "She has the patience of a trapped rattlesnake."

Right now, Ava herself resembled some sort of angry snake glaring back at me from the doorway, her head poised like a cobra's ready to strike. I sat back and folded my arms under my breasts. I was what anyone would call a late bloomer. My figure didn't really fill out until I was sixteen. Before that, I looked more like a twelve-year-old. I knew that was why most boys in my classes had barely given me a glance, that and the boring grandma clothes I was made to wear, mostly loose-fitting, in drab colors, with the ugliest shoes. I was sure I wobbled when I walked.

Strangely, enough, boys, and girls as well, assumed I came from a fanatically religious family, a family of Puritans. This was why I wore such clothes and no makeup and no earrings or bracelets. In their minds, it explained why I didn't participate in clubs and games or go to dances. Surely, they thought trying to be friends with me would be a total waste of time. I could see it in their faces. To them, my whole life was a waste of time.

Recently, however, I had become very aware of

my figure. Just as I had been told to give some of my clothes to Marla, Ava was now told to give some of her newer outfits to me, and these outfits revealed how I had blossomed. Lately, especially in the past week, I was even more self-conscious because of it, especially when boys now had that *Hello, what have you been hiding beneath those grandma outfits?* look. One boy, Tommy Holmes, asked me if I had been drinking our gardener's Miracle-Gro.

"Maybe it's plastic surgery," Ruta Lee suggested coyly, her face ripe with envy. If anyone needed plastic surgery, she did, with her long, pointed nose and doggy ears.

I said nothing, so she went ahead to spread the rumor like creamy peanut butter through the school. I could see the story smeared over the faces of my classmates. Ironically, it enhanced the interest some boys had in me. Had I had breast enhancement, something done to make my buttocks more curvaceous, my waist so small? Almost overnight, my baby face had morphed into a stunning cover girl's face, including a magazine model's complexion. Ruta began to regret her mocking. She would glare angrily at me in the hallways and classroom but had nowhere near the fire in her eyes that burned in Ava's right now.

"What is it, Ava? What else do you want from me?" I was sure she could stare down a charging tiger. "I turned it off!"

She smirked and then relaxed and brushed her silky black hair away from her face. It was shoulder length and never looked dull or dirty. My dark brown hair always felt coarse compared with hers, and I thought it was too curly. Maybe I felt that way because Daddy enjoyed stroking Ava's hair and rarely stroked mine. Lately, when I complained about my hair to Mrs. Fennel, she threatened to take out the ironing board and iron every strand.

"If you keep moaning about it, I swear I will do it when you sleep," she warned, "and if I burn some of it and you become bald, that will be on your head. Literally."

And that was that.

Mrs. Fennel, who had been with my father for centuries, it seemed, always spoke with staccato efficiency. When someone said, "That woman doesn't waste her breath," he or she was surely referring to Mrs. Fennel. Often she went all day without saying more than a dozen words, but she could speak pages with a look, an expression. Even as a toddler, I always knew when my questions were foolish to her and not worth her answering. Ava said Mrs. Fennel was a surgeon. She could cut the waste out of any day. She never said or did anything without purpose or meaning. She had the best IWPB—important words per breath—of anyone.

"You should be grateful she has been your nanny," Ava told me once after I complained about something Mrs. Fennel had said to me. "I'm grateful she has been mine."

"I am!" I claimed, even though in my heart, I didn't mean it. I dreamed instead of having a real mother.

"Spoiled," Ava muttered, under her breath but loudly enough for me to hear. "She lets you get away with too much. She never let me get away with that much."

I tried to be grateful, to appreciate all Mrs. Fennel did for me, but it was never easy. As an infant, I was forbidden to cry too much or too long, and I quickly realized that crying didn't get me anything anyway. Mrs. Fennel was never physically rough with me. She never struck me or spanked me; she didn't have to do that. Her stern looks, with those gold-tinted black eyes that were like laser beams cutting through me, were far more than enough to get me to swallow back a wail or a sob.

Tall and thin, with a hardness in her arms and body that had me believing she was made of iron until I saw her naked once, Mrs. Fennel radiated a firmness and confidence that gave me, Marla, Ava, and, I'm sure, Brianna, a sense of security. As long as she was there, nothing could harm us. Even germs feared her. No one ever got sick.

And yet she was so feminine at times, so concerned about our appearance, our looks, that I felt as if she had the power to sculpt us into beauties. She had bath oils (her own mixtures) that kept our skin smooth and soft, shampoos with one of her magical ingredients that, despite my unhappiness with my own hair, really did keep it soft and healthy compared with the hair of the other girls in my classes, and of course, she cooked and prepared the healthiest things for us to eat, which were mostly from her own herbal recipes. To this day, I don't know what she gave me to eat as baby food, but whatever it was, it was homemade. There was always a gentle tug of war between her and Daddy, who tried to give us something sweet or decadent from time to time when we were younger.

"Don't corrupt them. There's time enough for that," Mrs. Fennel might say, and that was that. Daddy would back off. Someday, I thought, I would know why Mrs. Fennel, who was supposedly our housekeeper and nanny, had such power over Daddy, who was supposedly her employer. Either jokingly or maybe because she knew more than I did, Ava once said, "She's Daddy's mother. He got his good looks from her."

Despite her hard, sculptured features, Mrs. Fennel did look as if she might have been beautiful once. Her gray hair was still long and soft. She didn't have any of those age spots elderly people develop, and her wrinkles weren't deep or long. Sometimes they seemed to be gone anyway. It was as if she could have days of returning to her twenties or her teen years. It gave me pause to wonder about her past. Until now, at least, she especially didn't like me or Marla asking her too many personal questions, and she wasn't one to volunteer personal information. Maybe she really was Daddy's mother and he had inherited his good looks from her. In our house, beauty seemed to be a fruit you could pluck when it was time to pluck it.

Ava was very attractive and very sexy. She could suck the eyes out of admiring men, young or old. I could hear them practically panting as we walked by, Ava seemingly floating, her head up, her eyes forward. She looked oblivious, as indifferent as some goddess might be, even though she was far from it. She always gave me the impression that she expected nothing less than admiration, even idolization. Walking with her was almost a sexual experience because of the way she flaunted herself. In their virtual-reality worlds, the men who saw her were already in the throes of heavy lovemaking.

Would I ever have Ava's self-confidence? Her arrogance? I knew I was expected to have it. I couldn't be my father's daughter if I didn't.

Ava stood there in her soft silk nightgown, her ample bosom firm, her neck curved smoothly into her shoulders. Even when she had just awakened, her complexion was vibrant. As long as I could remember, she had never had a skin blemish and certainly not a pimple. Even though she did use it, she really didn't need to put on lipstick. Her lips were naturally a rich ruby. She never went to a doctor or a dentist; none of us did, for that matter. When I asked Mrs. Fennel why none of us ever needed any sort of medical attention, she simply said, "Good genes."

Good genes? How could that be? From what I understood, I didn't share those genes, and neither did Marla, but we didn't go to a doctor or a dentist, either. Ava said it was because of the foods and drinks Mrs. Fennel prepared for us. She said Mrs. Fennel was better than any doctor or dentist. That was nice, of course. Who wanted to go to a doctor or a dentist? But it wasn't enough of an explanation for me. Why had Mrs. Fennel told me it was genes? What did she know about our genes?

Like Marla's, my origin was a mystery. All I really knew was that I had been plucked out of an orphanage, just as she was. Whenever I tried to find out anything specific about myself, I was always told not to think about it.

"Don't dwell on what makes you different and apart from this family. If you do, you'll be disowned," Mrs. Fennel warned.

I certainly didn't want that to happen, but my curiosity about myself seemed only natural, and my classmates often asked me personal questions. I ignored them or simply said I didn't know, which most of the time was true, but it was always uncomfortable to say it.

"How could you not know that?" they would ask, astonished.

Meg Logan smirked and said, "You're just a big mystery wrapped up in a secret. Enjoy yourself, but keep away from us. You're like someone with Alzheimer's."

That was painful to hear and did make me feel foolish. Why couldn't Mrs. Fennel or Daddy help me with some of these questions so I wouldn't look like such a freak in school? Goodness knows, I didn't want to feel different or in any way alienated from my father and my sisters. If anything, I wanted to be just like Ava. I was always trying to imitate her walk, the way she held her head, even her smile.

Was it wrong for me to be in such awe of my own older sister? Was it natural?

Right now, a quick movement in her eyes told me she saw how I perused her body the way some art student might gaze upon a statue in a museum.

"What else do I want from you? I want you to stop behaving like some lovesick teenager."

"I'm not."

"You're not?" She stared a moment and then shook her head and smiled. "Okay, what's your problem today, little sister? The boy you have a thing for at school won't look your way?"

"I don't have any problems, and I don't have any thing for any boys in my school," I said, realizing too late how defensive I sounded.

She laughed skeptically, sat on the edge of my four-poster dark walnut bed, and then threw herself back on my oversize pillow. We rarely had what I would call a close sister-to-sister conversation, from what I understood those conversations were like when I saw them on television or heard girls in my class talk about their older sisters. Ava had stepped too quickly into the surrogate mother's role Brianna had played, but maybe, now that I was older, she would be different, I thought. Her life was different. Why wouldn't mine be as well?

At Daddy's suggestion, Ava was attending classes at UCLA in Westwood, California, but she didn't seem to have any real interest in them. She did it because it was something Daddy told her to do. It was the way we were all raised. When Daddy spoke, everything stopped. Even the earth paused in its spinning.

We had been living in Brentwood, on a side street just off Sunset Boulevard, for three years now. It was quite rural, with surrounding woods and acreage. The nearest house was far enough away for us to feel as if we had no neighbors. Daddy liked to move every few years. I had gone to school in three different states since first grade: upstate New York; Nashville, Tennessee; and now California. We always attended private schools that Daddy carefully chose, no matter how expensive they were.

Daddy was wealthy through inheritance but also

because of what Mrs. Fennel said were brilliant invest-
ments through the years. Praising Daddy was at least one
thing Mrs. Fennel would do frequently and fully. It was
practically the only subject that interested her enough to
talk about: Daddy's wonderful qualities. She did sound
like a proud mother. According to her, there was no one
stronger, no one smarter, no one more successful than
my daddy. A day rarely passed without her telling us how
lucky we were to have him and how important it was for
us to please him.

She didn't have to do much persuading. Daddy really was the most charming, traveled, and educated man
I had ever seen or heard. He was elegant and handsome
in a very aristocratic way. People who met him for the
first time believed he was from a European royal family. There was something Old World about him, in his
demeanor, his manners, his way of speaking and eating. I often thought he could be a prince. I believed that
someday, he might very well inherit a throne or be called
back to occupy a castle in some exotic country. In my
daydreams, I saw myself being treated like a little princess because of Daddy. The sapphire ring he wore on his
right pinkie was set in gold and looked like the sort of
ring a king might wear for his subjects to kiss, the way
Catholics kiss the ring of a bishop. Ava wore a smaller,
feminine version on her pinkie, and I recalled Brianna
had one, too.

Daddy had friends everywhere, and all of them
seemed highly educated and wealthy. I was to call
some of them Uncle or Aunt when they visited, and
they always brought gifts for all of us. Some were as

young-looking as Daddy, but some looked more like Mrs. Fennel. What I observed and was proud to see was how deferential they were to Daddy, no matter how old they appeared. They did treat him as if he was royalty and they were his loyal subjects. Occasionally, one or more of these uncles and aunts were upset when they arrived and then were quickly ushered into a room away from any of us. Only Mrs. Fennel was permitted to be there. Regardless of how upset our guests might have been when they arrived, they left smiling and confident again.

It didn't surprise me. No matter what time of the day it was or what he was doing at the time, Daddy never seemed flustered. It was as if there was nothing in this world that could surprise him. He had a calm, even demeanor that impressed anyone he met and put him or her at ease almost immediately. No one, except maybe Mrs. Fennel, knew his exact age, not even Ava or Brianna. He really did seem to possess the wisdom of a man centuries old, even though it was difficult to believe he was more than forty-five or fifty.

*When was he born? Where was he born? Who were his parents?* Those were questions I thought Mrs. Fennel would never answer. I asked Daddy how old he was, of course, but he only smiled and said, "Guess," or "You tell me, and that will be my age."

When I asked him where he was born, he said he'd been too young to remember. He always joked but never revealed anything.

Ava didn't seem to care, and when I asked her what she thought, she looked at me as if it were a question that had never occurred to her. How could that be? I wondered. What made her so different from me? At times, she took on that expression Daddy had, that far-off look that made me feel as if he didn't know I was there.

As far as I knew, Ava was the only one of us who was Daddy's natural child. She claimed it was something she had learned only recently, and, contrary to how I would feel if I learned such a wonderful thing, she seemed angry when she learned that Daddy had fallen in love with someone and married her. It was as if love were a disease, Daddy had been infected, and she was the result. She made it sound as if she were a scar.

"What's wrong with falling in love?" I asked her when she complained.

"Love is poison for us," she replied, and would say no more about it, no matter how many times I asked.

If it had been responsible for my being Daddy's natural daughter, I thought, I wouldn't call it poison.

At times, Ava looked so much like Daddy that it was as if she were cloned. Rarely, if ever, did Daddy talk about Ava's mother, and Ava hated to talk about her. She would get furious with me if I made the smallest reference to her. All I knew was what I had gleaned from Mrs. Fennel and the tidbits Daddy revealed. Her name was Sophia. I was told she had died in childbirth.

"Were there any pictures of your mother?" I asked her once.

"If there were, I don't care to see them," she told me.

"Aren't you even a little curious about her?"

"No!" she said, practically shouting back at me. "Stop talking about her. For all I know or care, I was hatched, understand? Not born. You can consider me half an orphan."

How could she be even half an orphan? She at least knew who her mother was and who her father was, although Daddy was as real in my mind and in my affections as any daddy could be. Why was she so bitter about her mother, treating her as someone who had tricked or corrupted Daddy? How had he met her, anyway? What made her so different from other women he had known? Why couldn't anyone talk about it? Why did we all have to swim in so much mystery? Sometimes I thought I would surely drown in it. I was barely keeping my head above water with the little bits of information Mrs. Fennel threw in my direction from time to time as it was. I felt like some caged animal kept moments away from starvation.

Ava had one of those Mrs. Fennel impatient and annoyed expressions on her face right now.

"Come off it, Lorelei. Stop giving me that innocent look. You don't lie here in your room and just listen to your music," she continued, lying on my bed and looking up at the ceiling. "You lie here and fantasize about sex with one or another of the boys in your school, fantasize about wonderful kisses, their tongues on your tongue, their lips moving down your neck as they slowly undress you," she said softly, with such an erotic feeling I felt myself tingle.

She turned on her side to look at me. Her breasts ballooned, and her eyes brightened impishly. How could any man resist her, resist those inviting lips? Would I ever have her power? It both excited and frightened me to think I would.

"I . . ."

"Please. Don't bother denying it. I can practically hear your dreams through the wall, and I know the reason you're so flushed sometimes. It comes washing down over you, doesn't it? You feel like you might drown in your own sex, like your heart might burst because it's beating so hard and so fast, and all that simply from images, thoughts. You can't even begin to imagine what the real thing will do."

I nodded. No sense lying to her. It was that way exactly. Satisfied with my confession, she smiled again and lay back to look at the ceiling.

"Don't forget, I was your age, too, and went through exactly what you're experiencing. I will admit that I was doing it when I was younger than you, but it was the same, so stop trying to deny it."

"I didn't say I don't imagine myself with any of the boys. I said I don't have a crush on any of them. There's no one I would die to be with, Ava. I swear!"

"Crush? Do you teenagers still use that term? I don't care what you call it. You have it, this longing. Sometimes your body aches because of it."

She grinned like a cat and then turned back to look up at the ceiling again. The way she stared at it made me wonder if she saw something on it. I glanced at it, too. Daddy was asleep right above us. Was that what she was thinking? Was she saying these things to me knowing he could hear her? Daddy could hear us in his sleep, even if we spoke as softly as we were now. He once told me he didn't sleep. He drifted in the darkness, floated like an astronaut in outer space.

"Let me tell you something, little sister. Don't be so eager to give it away," she warned, clearly referring to my virginity.

"I'm not."

"No sense denying you want to, Lorelei. Daddy senses it, too. He's worried you might be at it like a rabbit and put us all in some danger."

I gasped. What had I possibly done to give him that impression? "Did he really tell you that?"

"Of course. He tells me everything he thinks about you and discusses every change he notices, no matter how small it might seem to be."

I expected that because she was older, Daddy would confide in her about things before he would confide in me, but not such an intimate thing about me. I always thought Daddy and I had a very special, honest relationship.

"You must always tell me exactly what you're feeling, Lorelei," Daddy once told me, "and I will do the same with you."

I was deeply disappointed, but I didn't complain. Even the smallest suggestion of dissatisfaction with Daddy or the smallest criticism of him could bring down thunder and lightning from either Mrs. Fennel or one of my older sisters. For them, that was blasphemy. Just as worshippers could be excommunicated from any religion, any of us could be excommunicated from this family. No one came right out and said such a thing, not even Mrs. Fennel, but I felt it. I had been plucked out of nowhere and could be dropped back into it, dropped into a world without any family, without any daddy, much less any mother.

Sometimes, maybe because of books I read or movies I saw, I tried to imagine how hard and lonely it must be for those foundlings who never find a family to take them into their lives. How cold it must be to have an institution for a home and paid bureaucrats substituting as relatives. I had no doubt that any of them would gladly trade places with me, no matter what the obligations and rules were here. Here there was at least a real home, where there was at least a daddy to show you real love and affection. I knew that as much as I needed Daddy, as much as we all needed him, he needed us, and that was too precious to surrender.

After a moment, I asked Ava, "How old were you when you did it with a boy for the first time? You said you had all these feelings when you were younger than I am."

She looked at me again, more of a coy smile on her lips now. "Who said I have even had a first time?"

"You haven't?"

She laughed. "Look at you. See how you're surprised? Aren't you more interesting, exciting, if men are not sure?"

"I don't know. I really don't know much about men and what they think or how they think," I admitted.

She lost her humor quickly. "Well, I'm telling you that you are more mysterious and that it is important. It is always the obvious girls who are the most uninteresting. It is essential to have a cloak of mystery about you, Lorelei, especially since you're one of us. You would think you would know that yourself by now, but I keep forgetting how immature you are sometimes."

"I'm not immature." I pouted for a moment and then added, "If I am, it's because I'm not permitted to do anything, to experience anything, when it comes to the opposite sex. I haven't been out on a date or even to a party, have I? Well, have I? Girls much younger than I am have been out on dates and gone to parties. Some of the kids in my class think I must have done something really terrible to be so restricted or that we're religious nutcases."

She laughed and then said, "Who cares what they think?"

"I do. It's hard, Ava. Don't tell me it wasn't hard for you, too."

She looked at me with an uncharacteristic softness for a moment. I knew that meant she was going to tell me something important. "Well, Daddy agrees with you about all that. He thinks you're just about ready to go out with me, but he's worried. He doesn't think you're as instinctively prepared as Brianna and I were. He wants me to start to teach you things you need to know, prepare you, and show you how to be more attractive, more sophisticated, and especially more cautious."

"He does?"

"We will go on some dry runs first so I can observe you in action and you can observe me and learn something. Consider it on-the-job training," she added out of the corner of her mouth. Then she sighed so deeply I thought her chest would crack. "Your sexual education is my newest obligation, but it's something I always knew would come."

"You sound upset about it. Didn't Brianna do the same for you? Was she upset about having to do it?"

"That was different."

"Why?"

"I just told you. I was instinctively better prepared."

"Well, maybe I am, too. It's not fair to think I'm not without giving me an opportunity to demonstrate whether I am," I protested.

"Daddy said you weren't. Are you questioning Daddy's judgment?"

"No. Of course not, but—"

She sat up quickly, brushed back her hair again, and got off the bed. "I have to get some more sleep," she said.

"Where were you last night?"

"Why?"

"I just wondered where you go to . . . I mean, what sort of man—"

"You will know when you know," she said.

"You weren't back until very late this time," I blurted before she could walk out.

"What, were you waiting up, spying on me to see if I was successful? You thought I was taking too long? You're judging me now?"

"No, I just . . ."

"Just were waiting up." She relaxed and thought a moment. "Maybe Daddy's right. Maybe you are ready. I was doing the same sorts of things, spying on Brianna, and thinking the same sorts of things when I was ready. That's why it's important you don't mess up with some teenage romance. You know what would happen to you if you ever got pregnant, Lorelei. You know how useless you would be to Daddy, even to yourself," she said sharply, her face reddening with an anticipation of anger.

"For the last time, Ava, I'm not having any teenage romance, and I'm not trying to have one!"

"Lower your voice."

"Well, I'm not, Ava."

"Uh-huh," she said, nodding with suspicious eyes. She could be so infuriating. She nodded at my iPod. "Use your earphones."

She left, closing my door quietly.

I put on the earphones, but I didn't play any music. Instead, I listened to my memories of the night before.

I had lied to her. I did spy on her, because it did seem to be taking her longer. I waited by the window in my bedroom that looked out on our driveway and saw her drive up with the young man beside her. The moonlight illuminated the front of the house just enough for me to make him out. He looked tall, with wide shoulders, like a UCLA football player, but I knew he couldn't be that. Daddy wouldn't let her bring anyone from her college here, not as long as we lived so close.

All the lights were out in the house. She had probably told him there was no one home. I was sure Mrs. Fennel was watching through a slightly opened curtain. I went to my closed door and put my ear against it. I heard the young man's laughter and then hers. He sounded so happy, probably thinking himself lucky to be making it with a girl as beautiful as Ava. It sounded to me as if they had paused just inside the entryway and were kissing. She wanted him to be excited. She wanted his heart to pound, his blood to rush through his veins.

Then I heard them going up the stairs. There was more laughter, although their voices were muffled now.

Ava sounded silly, actually. I opened my door slightly and listened. I was very interested in what she would be telling him at that moment. Instead, there was a long silence. Suddenly, I could hear the surprise in his voice, and then the door to Daddy's room slammed shut.

The young man had time to scream only once.

# 2

## Understated

"Look at how beautifully that fits her," Daddy said when I stepped into the living room.

I had just put on the dress he had brought back for me from France. He sat back in his Louis XV Giltwood armchair with Aubusson tapestry. Daddy was always very proud of his furniture. He told us that what was in a man's house was in his very soul. "His art, his choice of color, his very flooring and walls, reveal what's in his heart. They tell us who he is, how he was raised, what are his tastes in wine, women, and song," he added with a laugh.

He sat with perfect posture as always. Daddy never slouched, never looked tired or lazy. Often, when I saw him sitting alone and thinking, he reminded me of a Greek statue. He had alabaster skin, with the most intelligent yet warm black eyes that picked up the ebony tone of his hair. His eyes were truly like jewels, rich opals. He had a strong, straight mouth and a Romanesque nose. His cheekbones were high and his jawbone just prominent enough to give him a look of power.

Ava stood at his side with her hand on his shoulder,

as if she thought they were posing for a family portrait and she should have that important position. Marla was sitting at his feet, her face against his leg, her right arm around his legs as if she were claiming he was hers. Every time we touched him, every time he touched us, every embrace, especially every kiss, was coveted and collected to enrich our love bank accounts. None of us would come right out and say it, but each of us hoped and believed he loved us more than any of his other daughters.

He had brought back clothing, jewelry, and perfume for all three of us but specifically asked me to put on my new black sleeveless dress for dinner that night. It had a deep V-neck collar and a hem about midway between my ankles and knees. The material was something I had never seen or felt. He said he had had it specially made for me. It clung to my body like another layer of skin. I was braless and wore a pair of thong panties. He asked me not to wear any jewelry tonight.

"Real beauty is always understated," he told me. "Attractive women don't realize that they challenge their own natural attractiveness when they are ostentatious and wear too much valuable jewelry. There's too much unnecessary competition occurring on their own bodies. Why take attention from your eyes, your lips, your magnificent complexion?"

That sounded so right. Was there anything Daddy didn't know about women, about anything?

"Am I beautiful now, Daddy?" I asked him.

"I wouldn't have bought you this dress if I didn't think the time had come," he said.

I would be the only one of us girls wearing something

formal to dinner that evening. Marla was in jeans and a
school sweatshirt. Ava wore a pair of black jeans and a
white knit blouse. Daddy wore a dark blue shirt and white
slacks. Tonight he looked even younger. Time fell help-
lessly at his feet. He was shielded against the slings and
arrows of days, months, and years. They were like flies
on the skin of an elephant. I think that was why he was so
unconcerned about dates, even days of the week, unless
he had an appointment. No one seemed to notice that he
rarely wore a watch. He had beautiful rings, gold bracelets, and exquisite necklaces, jewelry from all over the
world, but usually avoided wearing a watch, even though
I knew he had a drawer full of them.

When I asked him why he rarely wore one, he said,
"What difference does one hour to the next make for me,
Lorelei? I always live in the moment and never waste my
time longing for tomorrow."

He seemed to have a built-in clock anyway and instinctively knew what time it was whenever it was important for him to know. We girls all had watches, and there
were all sorts of antique clocks in our house, remarkably
in sync, announcing the hour in perfect harmony. In the
living room, we had a pendulum clock Daddy claimed
was made in the eighteenth century and had once been
hanging in the palace of Louis IV of France. The way
he described it there, described the entire palace, in fact,
with such detail, I was sure he had been there and had
seen it there.

As he looked at me in the new dress, he smiled with
appreciation. I could feel his love as though it flowed in
soft, melodic waves from his eyes, his lips, and his heart.

How many of the other orphan girls had a daddy who appreciated them as much as mine appreciated me? Why shouldn't I do everything he wanted, get anything he needed, be anyone he wanted me to be? Maybe he wasn't my real father, but I existed because of him. That was what my heart told me every day.

"Ava?" Daddy said. "Look at our Lorelei. She's stunning in that dress. Wouldn't you agree?" Neither of my sisters had yet commented.

"Yes, Daddy, it does fit her well," she said rather flatly. She could have easily added, "Big deal."

He looked up at her. "It's more than just the dress. She's grown wonderfully. I'd say there's been a remarkable maturing, wouldn't you?"

"There has been, Daddy. Remarkable," Ava replied dryly. I saw how Daddy held his gaze on her. There was nothing in his face to reveal his displeasure, but just that extra moment was enough. "I mean, she's blooming into someone very beautiful right before our very eyes," Ava quickly added.

"Exactly," Daddy said, now pleased with her response. "I expected nothing less."

He put his left hand on Marla's head, stroking her the way he might stroke a dog. Maybe he could feel her jealousy through his legs. She clung to him as if her life depended on it.

"Don't worry, Marla," he said. "You're next. We will see similar beauty appearing in you as well when your time comes."

"When's that, Daddy?" she asked, looking up at him hopefully and excitedly.

"Patience," he said. "Everything comes to those who wait. Ava was the same way, weren't you, Ava?"

"I didn't have to be as patient. I bloomed a little bit earlier, Daddy," she said softly.

He glanced at her wryly, his lips pursed for a moment. "Our Ava," he said, "is a little insecure yet."

Insecure? Ava? None of Daddy's daughters could be insecure, especially by Ava's age and doing the things Ava was now required to do. I was more surprised than she was at the obvious criticism, but she took it harder. She looked as if she might break out in hysterical sobs. I almost felt sorry for her, even though a bigger part of me took pleasure in seeing her knocked off her pedestal.

"It's nothing," Daddy quickly added. "It's quite normal, in fact. It always comes with some sibling rivalry, and there's nothing wrong with some good old-fashioned sibling rivalry." He laughed and then added, "I have every confidence that Ava will prove to be one of my best little girls, if not the best."

That pulled her back from the cliff of dark sorrow, and she looked happy again. As if our lives were a play being enacted on some grand stage, right on cue, Mrs. Fennel came to the doorway that opened to the dining room before anything more could be said about who would be Daddy's best daughter and who wouldn't.

"Everything's ready," she announced. The manner in which she spoke and the way she stood there, her body stiff, her shoulders back, made it seem as if one of us was about to go to an execution and not our dinner.

"Well, then, let's go to the table," Daddy said, and stood. Marla leaped to her feet. Ava moved forward quickly. She expected him to put his arm around her shoulders, as he often did, and lead her into the dining room, but he reached out for my hand instead. I looked at Ava. Her eyebrows lifted, and her eyes flashed anger and disappointment in my direction, but then she quickly looked away and started for the dining room so she wouldn't see Daddy kiss my cheek. However, I was sure she heard him whisper, "You're a diamond now out of the rough. How complete and confident I feel just looking at you."

Could my heart be fuller? I glanced at myself in the wall mirror in our dining room and saw the glow in my face. The flame inside me that my happiness fueled could light a room, I thought. I was filled with the sin of pride but completely unconcerned. In our world, the deadliest sin was not pleasing Daddy. Everything else was more a misdemeanor than a felony.

"Tell us about your trip to France, Daddy," Marla said after the four of us had sat.

Mrs. Fennel never ate with us. She served our dinners, breakfasts, and lunches and ate by herself in the kitchen. Ava said we should be grateful about that. "Watching her eat is like watching a starving dog go at food."

"I visited friends outside of Paris near Versailles," Daddy began.

"Old friends?"

"Oh, yes," Daddy told her. "All my friends are old friends these days," he added with a smile. "But everyone was excited and energetic. It was a wonderful reunion. For us, no matter where we are, it's always as though we are there for the first time, and if you think as I do that every day is the first day of your life, it really feels like it is the first time. We were like silly tourists. We went to great restaurants, shopped everywhere, and of course, we all went to the Louvre in Paris. We had known so many of the artists. It takes days and days to really appreciate the Louvre. I expect all of you will go there eventually."

"I've been," Ava reminded him.

"Yes, but you were too young to appreciate it," he said.

"I remember going there," she insisted, "but . . ."

"But you don't remember anything you saw," he suggested with his soft smile.

She laughed like someone caught with her hand in a cookie jar.

Then all of us laughed.

"My girls," Daddy said. He reached for my hand and Ava's, and I reached for Marla's. The four of us held on to each other around the table. Daddy lowered his head and closed his eyes. This was the closest we ever came to any sort of prayer. There was a stillness around us; the lights seemed to dim.

"I see great things ahead for all of you, my lovelies," he said. "You will all go to wonderful places and see the world's most beautiful scenery, great art and architecture. You will walk with princes and kings and queens and all the rich and the powerful. Men will cherish a warm look, a warm word, from any of you, and women will always envy you."

"Will I be a movie star?" Marla asked excitedly. When Daddy made his predictions, they sounded as firm as any biblical prophet's.

He lifted his head and opened his eyes. "No, Marla. You won't be in anyone else's movie but your own."

"I don't understand," she said. The brightness left her eyes, showing her disappointment.

Daddy looked to Ava.

"What Daddy means, Marla," she said, glancing at me as well, "is you will be a star in the story of your own life. You will do things people dream of doing, pretend to be doing in movies. You will really do them. We all will."

Revived, Marla widened her smile.

"Well said," Daddy told Ava.

She beamed. Whenever Daddy flattered any of us, it was as if he had touched us with a magic wand. I could see both Marla and Ava had the same reactions as I did when he gave a compliment. They brightened as if a light had been turned on inside them. A warmth fell over them. Ava said it was a feeling better than sex. I had to take her word for that, of course.

"Let's eat what Mrs. Fennel has worked hard to make for us," Daddy said, "and then we'll listen to music, all of us together. I love nothing more than having my girls around me when I'm relaxing. I need to feel your warmth, your love, tonight. You make me feel truly immortal."

No one spoke for fear of shattering the wonderful moment. I looked at the food Mrs. Fennel had prepared. It was a sort of beef stew cooked in her herbal sauces. As I ate, I thought no one in my current class or even the whole school or any school I had attended had experienced or would experience the unique taste in the food Mrs. Fennel made. I was as sure of that as I was of anything.

From the moment I was brought to Daddy's world,

I ate things no one my age ate. Even as a small child, I knew instinctively that I was different and was living differently. Occasionally, I would ask why or complain, but in the end, I always did what I was told, and when something was given to me that I didn't like, Mrs. Fennel fixed it so I would like it.

"What does she put in our food?" I once asked Ava.

"Blood," she said.

"Whose blood? Cow's blood?"

She simply looked at me and walked away. I wondered, of course, if she had been teasing me, but I wouldn't dare ask Mrs. Fennel. I thought about asking Daddy, but then I worried that he would be angry at Ava for telling me that, and then she would be angry at me. It wasn't pleasant having Ava angry at me. It was actually a bit frightening. It was like having a ringing in your ears and a drill buzzing away just under your heart.

One of the consequences of the diet Mrs. Fennel prepared for us was that we rarely had an opportunity to enjoy the food other girls our ages enjoyed. We didn't go to restaurants very often, unless we were on a trip with Daddy. I could count on one hand how many times I had had a slice of pizza or a frozen yogurt, much less any candy. Why, we didn't even chew gum. We had a candy Mrs. Fennel prepared, if we could call it candy. It was hard, like a sour ball, but would soften almost immediately in our mouths and satisfy some urge. Once, when I was much younger, I gave one to a classmate. As soon as she put it in her mouth, she spit it out, claiming it burned her tongue. When I told Mrs. Fennel that, she went into a rage.

"You never, never give anyone else what I give you. Never!"

Of course, I started to cry and was sent to my room.

After tonight's dinner, as Daddy had said, we went into the living room and listened to music, beautiful music, especially waltzes. Daddy loved doing the waltz. He said it took him back to more elegant times, grander days, not that he wasn't having elegant days now, and he fully expected he would for many, many more years to come.

"And all because of you, my lovelies," he would say.

He would dance with each of us. Tonight he chose me first. It always was exciting to be in Daddy's arms, to move gracefully with him. I could feel my heart synchronizing with his, my blood moving as quickly or as slowly as his blood moved through him. Sometimes I felt as though I were floating and actually had to look down to see if my feet were touching the floor. Daddy's smile washed over me, and I wished the moment would go on forever and ever.

I thanked him again for buying me my dress.

"You really are quite stunning in it," he said, and kissed me softly on my forehead.

"I will wear it soon somewhere, won't I, Daddy?"

"Yes," he said, looking to Ava. "You will."

It was very exciting knowing that I would finally be permitted to go on a date or to a party, but before I could ask anything more, he reached for her. Instinctively, I knew that pushing Daddy to say or permit something was not wise anyway. Despite the affection he showed me, the gifts he gave me, I always had this nagging feeling that if I failed him or disappointed him in some way, even something simple, he would disown me. He would send me back to whatever nowhere place I came from, a world in which all discarded children lingered, hoping someday to be given a name.

I had no memory of it, of course. I was just born and hardly there, wherever it was, before Daddy and Mrs. Fennel came along. The little that was told to me was told the way a parent or guardian might tell a child a bedtime story.

"Once upon a time, you were born and lay in a cradle alongside other foundlings. You were crying in the chorus, but when we walked near you, you stopped, as if you sensed our presence and welcomed it. Mrs. Fennel picked you up and said, 'This one, Sergio.' I touched your cheek, and you turned toward me, and I knew she was right."

I had the story memorized. Ava, whether jealous of my joy in hearing the story or simply skeptical, always mocked me when I recited it.

"It's a fairy tale, you fool," she would say. "Mrs. Fennel didn't tell Daddy that. He told her, but that was after someone dumped you on the front steps."

"Is that what they told you happened to you?" I fired back. When I was brave enough to challenge her, she would suddenly take on this impish grin. Unlike other sisters, we didn't break out into vicious shouting arguments and fights. She could whip me with her words from time to time, and when it was something serious, I would shrink back or close myself off like a clam, but when it wasn't, I would throw something back at her.

Usually, she would surprise me and act as if she were pleased I had the backbone.

Recently, when I asked her about it, she paused and then after a little thought said, "Like all older Patio sisters, I have to share the responsibility of shaping you into someone Daddy will appreciate. You have to develop some backbone, Lorelei. Without it, without confidence, you'll fail, and if you fail, I fail, too. Not to mention how you will fail Daddy, how we will both have failed him."

"I won't fail Daddy," I said quickly.

"Maybe," she said, and then warned me again about doing something stupid with one or more of the boys at school. I had to listen to her warnings. She was more of my guardian now than Mrs. Fennel was.

Marla looked up to her for guidance as much as I did, but after that night when Daddy asked me to wear the dress and made so much of it in front of her and Ava, Marla began to look up to me more, asking me many of the questions I had once asked Ava. I suppose it was because I was closer to her in age than Ava. Marla was very pretty as well, with sea-blue eyes and soft light brown hair, just a shade or two darker than blond. She had dimples in her cheeks and perfect features, but, like me when I was her age, she had not yet matured enough to be popular with boys. I knew she yearned for it but, like me, kept it to herself.

I hated having to tell her I didn't know the answers to many of her questions or that it wasn't for me to tell her these things, but there wasn't much more I could say.

"Maybe you should ask Ava that," I would tell her.

She thought I was deliberately or jealously guarding something.

"You could tell me, Lorelei. You just don't want to," she complained. "And you know I won't ask Mrs. Fennel or bother Daddy."

"That's not true. I would tell you anything you wanted to know if I could. Believe me, I wasn't treated any differently from the way you're being treated when I was your age, Marla."

"You just don't want me to know," she insisted.

Frustrated, she complained about all the mystery in our lives. I couldn't disagree, although I couldn't do much to help her. It was as if every shadow had a voice whispering, every dark room had someone in it before the lights were turned on, every window had someone looking into our home before I turned to look out. Every creak was a clue, a letter, and a word to a sentence that would tell me something I didn't know. It would be the same for her. The fact that I couldn't satisfy her added to my own frustrations.

Later that night, when I was in my room getting ready for bed, Ava came in. She came in the way she often did, silently, as if she walked on air. Many times she had told me we had to practice being soft. We had to catch people, especially young men, unaware. It added to the mystery when we suddenly seemed to appear beside them as if what they were fantasizing about had come true. Those sorts of little things, she said, were important. "Nuances of your sexuality," she called them. "We finesse men, turn and twist them about like puppets on a string."

She certainly caught me unaware. I was in the

bathroom, gazing at myself naked before the full-length mirror beside the tub. I didn't know whether it was normal for someone to be so fascinated with her own body. Most of the girls I knew at school seemed to complain constantly about their bodies. They were too fat or had noses and ears that were too big. They were jealous of this one or that one. No one seemed to be satisfied. Sometimes I thought they hated me because I didn't voice similar complaints or envy.

"You think you're so damn perfect, don't you?" Meg Logan snapped at me one afternoon in P.E. All the girls were running through their litany of complaints about themselves, and I remained silent as usual. She realized I was just listening and not offering anything in common. Maybe it was the slight smile on my face that annoyed her.

Actually, I was so curious about them, how they thought and what they said, so I just wanted to listen, almost the way someone from another country might. I couldn't help wondering if I really was dramatically different from them in ways I was just beginning to understand.

"No," I told her, annoyed with how she had come at me so viciously. "Just not as imperfect."

"Huh? You're weird," she said. "No one knows who you really are and why you're so damn secretive, slinking around here like some ghoul and guarding your precious privacy. Frankly, I don't want to waste my time finding out anything more about you. I know enough to disgust me."

The others agreed, shook their heads at me, and moved away. I couldn't argue with what she had said, although I wasn't secretive in order to guard my precious privacy. I really didn't know as much about myself as I would have liked to know. Sometimes I felt like someone inhabiting the shell of someone else, wearing my body and face like a costume and mask.

Now, when I looked at myself in the mirror, I felt as if I were looking through a window at another girl, one who had just emerged from within. The tightening of my waist, the curve at my hips, the lift in my rear, and the soft lines now in my neck and shoulders made my heart race. I brought my hands slowly to my breasts, in awe of how they had filled and firmed. The excitement shot down to my thighs, and I moaned with pleasure.

"Not bad," Ava said, and I spun around, my face reddening. She nodded. "Daddy's right. You're looking more and more like me every day now. No wonder my clothes fit you so well. For a moment, I thought I was looking at myself when I was your age."

"Really?" I asked, reaching for my bath towel.

"I wouldn't say it if it weren't so, Lorelei. I don't flatter." She sounded as if she wished she didn't have to say it. "Stop fishing for compliments, anyway. You're way past that need now, or should be."

"I'm not fishing for compliments. I'm just so happy about . . ."

"Okay. I get the point. I came to tell you that you're going out with me this coming weekend, but as I explained before, it's just to observe and follow my orders. Consider it a field trip."

"I am? Oh, that's terrific, Ava." I clapped my hands and bounced on my heels.

She shook her head and made a ticking sound with

her lips the way Mrs. Fennel sometimes did. "I don't remember being as naive and as innocent as you are. When Brianna took me with her for the first time, I didn't gawk and gape and squeal like a tween or something."

"I won't do that. I promise."

"We'll see," she said, and turned to leave, but then she paused to look at me again. "Daddy doesn't see it in you, but I do."

"See what?"

"Fear," she said.

"Fear? Fear of what?" I asked.

"Yourself," she said. I watched her walk out.

*Fear* wasn't a word we used in this family. As far as I could see, there was nothing either Daddy or Mrs. Fennel feared, and Ava acted as if she could face down a stampede of elephants. Was I that different from her, from everyone else? How could I be afraid of myself, anyway?

I thought a moment, worried, and then I shook my head. No, she was wrong. To claim that she could see something Daddy couldn't see was ridiculous. If Daddy didn't see it, it wasn't there. It was just jealousy, I concluded. Lately, Daddy was spending more time with me and giving me more of his attention, and I could tell she didn't like that. It was the sibling rivalry at work, just as he had described it. It flattered me to think that Ava could ever be envious of me, but if anything also could frighten me, that might be it.

Happy again, I put on my nightgown and slipped under the blanket. Just as I was about to reach for the light switch, I heard a gentle knock on my door.

"Yes?"

Daddy entered. He hadn't come to my bedroom for quite some time. As far back as I could remember, no one really tucked any of us in. There were no bedtime stories. Mrs. Fennel certainly wasn't going to do anything like that. One thing we were taught especially was never to fear the dark. Even when I was a very little girl, Daddy told me the darkness was our friend.

"We exist because of the darkness," he told me. "All of you are daughters of darkness."

I wasn't sure what he meant by that back then, but I was sure now. Darkness, secrets, and anonymity were tools that helped keep us alive and safe.

Maybe that was why Ava thought I was different, why she thought I might be afraid of myself or for myself. She knew that I was never completely comfortable in the dark, or at least as comfortable as she and, apparently, Marla were.

"How's my new beauty?" Daddy asked, and sat at the foot of my bed.

"I don't know if I'll be able to sleep," I said.

"Why not?"

"Ava just told me I'm to go out with her this weekend. Only to observe, but at least I'm going out, going to exciting places, and I'll be able to wear the beautiful new dress you bought me. Do you think I'll do all right?" I asked, this time admitting to myself that I was fishing for a compliment.

He laughed. "I know you will. When I first set eyes on you, I knew you were one to drink deeply of every pleasure this world has to offer us. When you were an infant, I saw the way you ate and drank, enjoyed a bath or simply being comfortably wrapped in a blanket. Even the way you slept told me you were soaked in pleasure."

"Really?"

"Of course, but none of this will be anything close to what you will be experiencing in the time to come, Lorelei. In fact, consider it all to be nothing more than a taste."

"A taste? Now that you've told me all that, I surely won't be able to sleep, Daddy," I said, and he laughed.

"You're a delight, Lorelei. You are, in fact, one of the brightest little girls I've ever had. You were precocious at the age of two. I see how well you do in school, and I see how curious you are about everything. Just be patient and never frustrated with time or the care taken to educate you properly, okay?"

"Yes, Daddy."

"Don't worry. I'm sure you'll fall asleep," he said. "Mrs. Fennel always includes something in our food to help my little girls sleep and grow more beautiful."

"What does she put . . ."

He put his finger on my lips. "Don't ask for details. Just enjoy," he said, then leaned over and kissed me on the cheek. The aroma of his cologne filled my nostrils and made my head spin. Like almost everything in a bottle in this house, it was surely something Mrs. Fennel had prepared, some magical scent that would stir any woman's libido. Where did she learn how to do all these things? Where did she live when she was my age? Who taught her all that she knew?

Sometimes I wondered if she was ever my age. Maybe she was created in some laboratory like Frankenstein's monster. I knew I could think these thoughts, wonder, but never voice them unless Ava voiced them first. Daddy certainly wouldn't. It was because of how much he obviously respected and depended on Mrs. Fennel that I did all I could not to cross her. It certainly wasn't because I had great affection for her. I did everything for Daddy. Sometimes I thought I was breathing only for Daddy.

He rose slowly. I held his hand until it slipped softly from mine. His smile fell on me like soft, warm rain, and I snuggled in my blanket. I watched him leave the room. He slipped out as if he walked on the darkness itself and softly closed my door.

There was no moonlight tonight, but the sky was clear and the stars as brilliant as a full moon. I listened to the breeze licking at the windows and closed my eyes. He was right; I did fall asleep. But sometime later, I woke with a shudder and listened. It sounded like howling right outside my window. It didn't stop, so I rose slowly and went to my window.

When I looked out, I saw what looked like dozens of young men. They were all looking at my window, and they weren't just howling some horrendous sound.

They were howling my name, stretching it out as if the sound of it were caught on the wind. Their faces were pale yellow, their eyes black, tears spilling out and down their cheeks like streams of tar.

"Loreleiiiiiiiii."

In unison, they all reached out toward me and then took a step closer, slowly turning their heads to show me their opened necks, as if they hoped I would do something about it, something to help them.

I gasped and quickly stepped back from the window, my heart pounding. After I caught my breath, I waited and listened hard. The howling stopped. Slowly, I returned to the window and looked out again.

There were no young men there.

I looked as far to the right and the left as I could, but there were just shadows, twisting and turning as if the wind were toying with them.

Was I in a dream? Was I walking in my sleep? Was my imagination running wild?

I hurried back into bed and listened for the howling until I was too sleepy to keep my eyes or my ears open.

I remembered it all when I awoke, but I dared not mention it to anyone.

It was another mystery, another secret to add to the dozens and dozens in this family. Only for now, it would be my own.

# 3

## Best Daughter

Of course, I knew why I had that nightmare. Its origin went back years. It had been festering inside me like a bad boil, and its time to burst had come, perhaps because I was so close now, so close to being Daddy's best daughter.

There was never a doubt that I was not supposed to learn the first and most important secret of all as early as I had learned it. From what I understood, none of Daddy's daughters had ever learned it as early as I had. No one had time to prepare me for it as his other daughters had been prepared, and later, because this happened when it did, Daddy was furious at Brianna, blaming her. It was practically the only time I could remember him losing his temper and raging at any one of us until then. I think it was because of what happened that night that Brianna was really not as friendly or as loving as a sister should be toward me. She blamed me for Daddy's reprimanding her so vehemently. I know it frightened her as much as it frightened me.

I was only four at the time. We were living in upstate New York. Brianna was assigned to tutor me, give me what was called preschooling. I remember she wasn't happy about having to do that, but making progress with me pleased Daddy so much that she tried very hard. She didn't have to try that hard, actually. I was always a good student, eager to learn new things even at that young age. But I saw how important it was for her to take credit, to collect Daddy's compliments and approval. I saw the pleasure it gave her, and I knew that pleasure was awaiting me.

Back then, she would have me recite math problems and solutions, word meanings, and scientific information before we all sat to have dinner. She gave me piano lessons and taught me songs to sing and play. She wanted me to look at her when I recited something or sang, but I always looked at Daddy, for it was his approval I sought, not hers.

Ava would sit with a smirk on her face, obviously displeased with all the attention Daddy was giving to me. I could almost hear her thinking, *What about me? What about my singing, my playing the violin?* The problem was that she didn't have as good a singing voice as I had even at four years old. She didn't play the violin with as much passion and enthusiasm as I had playing the piano. I had the impression, even at that young age, that Brianna didn't sing or play the piano as well as I did when she was my age, either. Even back then, I had the suspicion, the hope, that Daddy might love me better than any of his other daughters because he saw that I was truly the special one in our family.

I wasn't all that surprised at what Daddy had said about sibling rivalry the night I wore the new dress. I always had the feeling that he encouraged it. He wanted us to be jealous of each other and especially covet the compliments he might give to one or the other of us. It was truly as if we were being taught to resent, to dislike, even to hate each other, just so we would be more competitive when it came to gaining his compliments, but then he would have his warm family moments during which he would remind Ava and me that we were sisters and had to look out for each other.

"You're both very special," he would say. "No one will appreciate you out there as much as you will appreciate each other. Never forget that. In the end, you must be willing to die for each other."

I saw the way Ava looked at me. Fatal sacrifice? *Not hardly,* her eyes said.

"You will never die for each other," he said. "It will never be necessary."

Ava relaxed.

"But you must live as if it could be necessary," he warned, losing his smile quickly. "We have no one but ourselves. Never forget that."

Whenever he made pronouncements like that, it felt as if he had stamped the words on my brain and in my heart. I could feel the way they thundered inside me and quickly became part of who and what I was to be. I fed on his words the way most people fed on food. Nothing made me feel more special than Daddy talking directly to me and to me only.

When I attended a private elementary school, I listened closely to other students to see how different their family lives were from my own, especially girls with older sisters. I was interested in how much sibling rivalry went on in their houses and what their fathers or mothers did to encourage or discourage it. From what I had heard, no other parents wanted such resentment or competition between their children. They did their best to keep one or another of their children from feeling favored, but it seemed natural that sisters and brothers felt that their parents treated one or the other more favorably. It was inevitable, so maybe it was inevitable with us as well.

Eventually, I decided that Daddy was being more honest, perhaps, by admitting and even encouraging sibling rivalry. Why pretend that it doesn't exist in all families? Some of us might not know all of the secrets another one knows, but lying to each other was a form of betrayal, and betrayal was as big a sin as any in our world. We had our own religion, our own holy trinity: obedience, loyalty, and sacrifice. So when it came to facing the truth about each other, Daddy was most encouraging and continued to stress why sibling rivalry was a good thing in our world.

"Not wanting it is like not wanting one or the other horse to win in a race," he said. "How foolish is that? Someone, something, always has to be at least a little better, a little stronger, a little faster. It's what nature teaches us and expects us not only to accept but to cherish and to embrace."

Who among us, then, would be a little better, a little stronger, a little faster? Who would indeed be Daddy's best daughter? Who would serve him best? Who would give him the assurance he needed that he would live on? For our whole purpose in life was to do just that.

I had no idea that was the reason for my being

brought to live in Daddy's home, even after I accidentally made that first discovery. I was too young yet to appreciate the full meaning of what I had seen and heard and how it all related to me. Even now, I didn't think I understood it completely, but that would come. There was no doubt. That would come.

Something had awakened me that night. Usually, I fell asleep easily. Maybe, now that I knew about it, it was because of what Mrs. Fennel put in my dinner. Maybe it was her fault. Maybe she had forgotten to do it that particular night. However, even back then, I couldn't imagine Daddy ever getting angry with or reprimanding Mrs. Fennel. Whatever the reason for it, my eyes just popped open, and I felt wide awake. I tried to go back to sleep, but suddenly, I heard Brianna's laughter. It was obviously very late, but she was very loud. It sounded as if she was right outside my window. What was she doing right outside my window? And what was so funny so late at night?

We were living just outside Rhinebeck, New York, at the time, in an old Queen Anne–style house with more than fifty acres. The house had been refurbished without losing its character. Daddy had moved in his furniture and paintings, and as all of it would in houses to come, it seemed as though all of it was made just for this house. Everything fit perfectly; every color coordinated. When I commented about that after we had moved into our Brentwood home, Daddy cryptically replied, "All our homes were built especially for us."

It did seem as if nothing happened accidentally or by coincidence. Everything Daddy did was well planned, and there was a network of support, not only in America but seemingly all over the world. All our needs were always anticipated and fulfilled, no matter where we were or when we were there.

The Queen Anne house was, of course, the only family home I had known. I had been brought there directly from the orphanage. Mrs. Fennel, who didn't look much different to me then, had a large herbal garden just behind the house, and when I was old enough, I often had to work with her, weeding and nursing her plants. As far as I could tell, they were the only things toward which she showed any affection. I was actually jealous of the plants and sometimes wished I had been planted in a garden. She spoke to them as though they really were her children, encouraging them to grow and be healthy and complimenting them on their maturation. She'd stroke their leaves lovingly and even kiss some. Nothing was worse than my accidentally stepping on one of her newly placed plants. Her rage made me tremble and start to cry.

"Don't drop your tears in my garden," she would tell me, her whole body poised and slightly tilted, giving me the impression that she would turn sharply and slice me in half. She made me feel I could contaminate the earth and kill her plants with my tears, and that feeling more than anything, perhaps, had me suck back my sobs and stop crying quickly. Apologies didn't satisfy her back then, either, even from a small child.

"I don't want to hear it," she would say, sweeping the air between us as if my words were as clearly visible as soot to her. "Just be more careful."

I would look back at the house to be sure Daddy

hadn't been watching from some window and seen my blunders. Of course, I hoped she wouldn't tell him. He never said anything, but that didn't mean he didn't know. There wasn't much about me, what I did or what I said, that he wasn't aware of, just the way an omnipresent deity might be. Other children might hear their parents say, "God hears and sees everything." Mrs. Fennel told me, "Your daddy hears and sees everything."

Ava was in school and didn't have these chores to do with Mrs. Fennel, and of course, neither did Brianna. Afterward, I would go into the house with Mrs. Fennel, wash up, and have my lunch. Then Brianna would take control of my day, and I would be at the piano or learning words and other important basic information. All the toys I had seemed to have some educational purpose, whether they were coloring books that taught me about animals and geography or little plastic dining sets to teach me how to sit at a table properly and eat properly. The dolls I had were mainly there to serve as props for my education in social graces. I was never permitted to develop any sort of relationship with or affection for one particular doll and take it to bed with me. When I tried that once, Mrs. Fennel smashed the doll's head.

No, the security and comfort I would find had to be found inside myself. There was never any hesitation about closing my bedroom door at night. If something frightened me and I screamed or cried, Daddy was the only one who would come to comfort me.

"You're one of my precious little girls," he would tell me. "I won't let anything bad happen to you. Why, it would be like letting something bad happen to myself."

Little did I know how true that was to him.

But I got my first hint of it that particular night, when I woke suddenly and heard Brianna. After her laughter, she sounded as if she was pleading with someone. My room was at the corner of the house closest to the driveway that led to the unattached garage. I slipped out from under my comforter. It was the beginning of fall, and although we hadn't yet had a night with temperatures below freezing, it was cool enough to justify sleeping with a heavy but soft comforter.

Because of the foliage and the trees surrounding our house, it was always in a blanket of shadows and dark inside. Those windows that faced the east in the morning and the west in the afternoon were shuttered. Neither Daddy nor Mrs. Fennel liked it to be too warm in the house anyway, and the heat was turned up only during the coldest winter months. Mrs. Fennel told me we would all sleep better that way. I liked the early fall, the colors of the leaves and the crisp air. I wasn't permitted to wander far from the house, but because of the proximity of the woods and the foliage around us, I could see and watch the squirrels and often deer and rabbits that seemed as curious about me as I was about them.

I thought the moon was a deeper shade of yellow in the fall so it could match the color of leaves. This particular night, we had a full moon with a cloudless sky. The glow fell like a great spotlight over the house, the illumination threading itself through the leaves and branches, twisting and turning shadows into new shapes as if they were made of black clay. One of my bedroom windows had been left open enough for me to be able to hear Brianna's laughter and then the voice of a stranger, a young man.

When I peered out at them, I saw he had driven Brianna home and was dressed formally in a jacket and tie. Brianna had gotten out of the car and was on his side now, urging him to get out, too. She was actually pulling on the door handle and tugging at his arm through the opened window. For some reason, he was resisting.

I pushed my window up a bit higher so I could lean out and hear what they were saying more clearly.

"Stop being such a coward and a jerk," Brianna told him, and let go of his arm.

"I'm not being either. I'm just being sensible. All the lights are out. We'll wake them up."

"I told you. My father's away," she said.

Why was she lying? I wondered. Daddy wasn't away. He had just come back yesterday.

"The only ones in there are our housekeeper and my younger sisters, who are both asleep. We can easily slip into my room unnoticed, and I don't plan on making a lot of noise anyway, do you? I mean, I should be the one moaning with pleasure. You can grunt."

He laughed, but he didn't get out of the car. Frustrated, she put her hands on her hips, glanced up toward Daddy's bedroom, and then turned back to her date as if something new had occurred to her, something that would get him to do what she wanted him to do.

"I didn't think you were this shy. You didn't act shy earlier tonight. What was that back at the bar? All some macho act for your friends or something?"

"No. I've been accused of a lot of things but definitely never of being shy."

"Right. You're really hesitating because you're worried about waking up my housekeeper."

"Look," he said after a momentary pause, "I do have a confession to make."

Brianna took a step back. "Oh, no, don't tell me you're gay."

He laughed. "No. But I am married."

Brianna just stood there looking at him. "You're kidding," she finally said. She stepped back up to the window. "Married? You're not wearing any ring."

"I don't usually when I go to the Underground looking for some action. I asked you to let me take you to a motel, didn't I? I don't understand why you want to go into your own house. Why would you want to do that?"

"I like making it in my own bed. Call me kinky. I'm better in my own bed," she added. "You'll see."

"I don't know. I mean, if someone does wake up, you have to explain, and then, I mean, one thing can lead to another, and I don't need to get involved with a costly divorce right now."

"You're very deceptive. That's very dishonest. What kind of a marriage do you have?"

"Obviously not the best, but . . ."

"But you're disgusting," she said, and turned away from him for a moment. I saw her look up again at Daddy's bedroom, and then she turned back to him.

"Listen. There isn't any problem and won't be any. My room is away from everyone else's rooms. The walls are thick. No one will hear us, and even if anyone did, she would ignore us. My maid certainly wouldn't care. You're not exactly the first guy I've brought home, you know."

He didn't reply. I could see Brianna was getting very agitated. She turned away again, looked up at the house again and then back to him. "I don't know," he said.

"Please come in for a little while," she pleaded.

"What is with you? How could someone who looks like you be so desperate for a lover?"

"I'm not desperate," she snapped back at him. "I don't like being teased, and I don't like my time and energy wasted."

"Hey," he said. "I'm not teasing. We can still make use of your time and energy, too. Get back into the car, and we'll go to this motel I know. I don't see why you . . ."

He stopped talking. I could see that something had captured his attention.

"Who's that?" he asked her. She turned toward the house.

"It's my father. Thanks a lot. You woke him up."

"But you said he wasn't home."

"I didn't know he was home."

"I'd better go."

I didn't blame him for being frightened. I was sure Daddy was unhappy about being awakened at that time of the night. I held my breath, anxious to see what would happen to Brianna.

"No. You can't just go," she moaned, and actually opened his car door. "You'd better get out and at least let me introduce you. If you just drive away, he'll think I'm trying to hide something, and I'll be in big trouble."

"Speaking of big, he looks . . . pretty big."

"Will you just say hello? Please? Don't worry, I won't tell him you're married. It will just take a minute or so, and you can go."

With obvious reluctance, the young man got out of the car. Brianna took his hand, and they walked toward the front entrance. I couldn't see around that far, but I waited by the window, expecting that he would come back to his car. I wondered if Brianna would walk back with him and maybe go to the motel he had suggested. But instead of that, I heard the young man shout and then scream like someone in great pain or danger.

My curiosity got the better of me, and I leaned too far out my window to try to see around the corner. I lost my grip on the windowsill and fell to the ground. Luckily, I wasn't that high up. I brushed myself off, but the shock of falling and the pain in my shoulder caused me to call out for Daddy and then cry.

I started for the front entrance and saw Daddy backing up into the house with the young man in his arms. The young man was unconscious, his arms dangling, his legs dragging. He looked like a big doll. Daddy paused when he saw me.

"Brianna!" my father shouted, his voice deeper and louder than I had ever heard it, and he did look bigger than I had ever seen him. His shoulders were wider, his neck much thicker, and his arms and hands longer. His eyes glowed.

He closed the door. Brianna spun on me, a look of panic and shock on her face, her eyes almost as luminous as Daddy's were in the moonlight. It was as grotesque an expression as I had ever seen on her.

"Lorelei! What are you doing out here?"

"I fell out of my window," I said, moaning and rubbing my shoulder.

She hurried down to me and seized me at the back of my neck. "Why would you fall out of a window?"

"You woke me up, and I wanted to see what was going on. Who was that man? Why did he scream? Why was Daddy carrying him into the house? What happened to him?"

"Quiet," she ordered.

She marched me forward, waited a moment at the front door, and then opened it: She pushed me in, but as we turned toward our bedrooms, I looked up toward the top of the stairway. Daddy was leaning over the young man. He looked as if he was kissing him on the neck and shaking his body the way I might shake a rag doll.

"What's Daddy doing?" I asked Brianna.

Daddy heard me and started to turn our way.

"I told you to be quiet," Brianna said. She lifted me at the waist and hurriedly carried me down the hallway and back to my room, where Mrs. Fennel was waiting at the door. The sight of her standing there looking even more furious than Daddy had looked frightened me even more.

"You fool," she told Brianna. "How could you let this happen?"

"I didn't let it happen. She leaned too far out of her window and fell."

She ripped me out of Brianna's arms roughly. "Go to your room."

"But what about the car?"

"I'll do what has to be done," Mrs. Fennel said. "As always. I'm the one left to look after the messes you and your sisters cause."

"I didn't do anything. I . . ."

"Go," Mrs. Fennel said. Then she took me into my room and slammed the door shut on Brianna. I was able to glance back at her before it closed. She looked even more terrified than I felt.

I started to cry. Mrs. Fennel ignored that, as usual, and slammed me onto my bed. It was always hard for me to believe that anyone who was as slim as she was had such strength in her arms, but I often caught her lifting heavy things, things I imagined most men would have trouble lifting.

"Stop that crying instantly."

"I didn't mean to fall out the window. It just happened. What . . . who is that man? Why is Daddy carrying him on the stairway? Daddy looked so big and angry."

She stared down at me for a long moment. There was something about her look, her posture, the way her anger subsided, that told me she wasn't just going to leave me wondering about it. I quickly caught my breath, flicked the tears off my cheeks, and sat up a bit, folding my hands in my lap.

"You must never tell anyone about that young man or any young man who is brought here," she began.

I was afraid to ask why not, afraid she would simply turn and walk out, but how could I tell anyone anything anyway? I had no friends.

"I can't tell anyone. I don't know anyone," I said.

Very rarely did I see her smile, especially at something

I had done or said, but she smiled that time. "You're very intelligent for your age, Lorelei," she continued. "Obviously more intelligent than your older sister, maybe both older sisters."

That took my breath away. A compliment from Mrs. Fennel? And now, when it seemed I had done something terrible? I wasn't sure how to react or what to say.

"I expect you will be able to understand a little more at an age younger than your sisters were able to understand, so I'll tell you more." She then did something she never had done. She sat on my bed and took my hand into hers. "You're all very special, because you and your sisters can keep your daddy strong, healthy, and alive. You want to do that very much, don't you?"

I nodded, still afraid to speak, to utter a sound that might stop her.

"From time to time, your Daddy needs something young men have. For him, it's only young men, virile young men. What that means exactly is something I'll explain to you when you are a little bit older, but for now, you must understand that your sisters will bring him what he needs, and someday you will, too. Your daddy will love you even more than he loves you now. That would make you very happy, wouldn't it?"

I nodded.

"When you go to school, you must never tell anyone about this. You must never talk about us at all, in fact. Don't worry," she said. "I'll remind you."

"I wouldn't tell," I said.

"Good. That will be enough for now. Let's get you back to sleep."

She rose, and I crawled back under my blanket. She leaned over to tuck me in, which, again, was something she rarely had done.

"Is Daddy angry at me?" I asked. Despite what she had told me, whether Daddy was angry at me now was still the most important thing to know as far as I was concerned.

"No, not you," she said. "Tomorrow, he will be sleeping most of the day, so don't disturb him."

"Why does he have to sleep so much tomorrow?" I asked, and that was when she told me, "Digestion."

I wondered if the commotion had awakened Ava and if she would be asking me questions tomorrow. I also wondered why Mrs. Fennel and apparently Daddy would be so angry with Brianna. What had she done? It wasn't her fault that I fell out of the window. It would be a while before I would learn and understand all of it, of course, but I was able to pick up something more when I heard Brianna talking to Mrs. Fennel about it the following day.

They didn't know I was listening. It was morning, and I was working on the math problems that Brianna had given me to do. Mrs. Fennel came in, and the two of them looked at me and then stepped into the hallway just outside the living room. I moved closer to the door. I knew they were going to talk about something very important. Whenever they looked at me first and then moved farther away from me, I knew some secret was possible to pluck from the tree of secrets that grew at the center of our lives.

"How could you bring someone like that to your father, Brianna? A married man?"

"He wasn't wearing a wedding ring, and he came on to me so fast and furious that I thought he was an easy catch. I don't see why Daddy's blaming me for not knowing he was married."

"If he was married, he must have had a wedding ring."

"I guess he took it off when he went whoring. The creep. Now I'm glad he was the one I brought here last night."

"Sometimes, when they take off their rings, they still have that white band on their skin," Mrs. Fennel said. "You should know that."

"The Underground doesn't have what you would call a well-lit bar."

"You don't need a well-lit bar to see what you have to see," Mrs. Fennel retorted.

Brianna was quiet for a moment. "So what if I saw it? That didn't necessarily mean he was married. He could have been recently divorced," she said. "Daddy will realize that, too, right?" She sounded so afraid.

"That doesn't matter. You should have found that out first. You know as well as I do, better even, that it makes everything more complicated when you take a married man."

"I know that," Brianna said.

"Apparently, you didn't last night," Mrs. Fennel said.

Brianna was quiet again.

"Anyway, you shouldn't have had him pull up so close and argue where you could be heard and wake Lorelei."

I knew now that they would be talking about me, so I listened even harder.

"I didn't think she would be awake and hear enough

to get out of bed. Who could imagine she would fall out of a window?"

"Why did you bring her into the house so quickly?" Mrs. Fennel asked. "She saw your father with him on the stairway."

Brianna sighed deeply. "I was just . . . so flustered," she said. "She fell out of a window!"

"Stop whining about it. You'll wake your father."

Brianna lowered her voice. "Talk about stupid. How could she be so stupid, even at four?"

"How could she be so stupid? Why didn't you wait longer, give your father the time he needed, before you brought her back into the house?"

"I was flustered. I never saw Daddy in such a rage," Brianna said. I'd never heard her sound so frightened. "I didn't think clearly. My brain was a blur. All I could think about was getting her back into her room."

"Did Lorelei ask you anything this morning?"

"Nothing," Brianna said. "I think she was still too afraid to ask me about anything."

"You can thank me for that. I spoke to her last night and calmed her down."

"What did she say she actually saw?" Brianna asked.

I drew closer. What did I actually see? Would Brianna explain it now?

"Enough," Mrs. Fennel said. "Too much, for now I guess you won't be your father's best daughter after all."

Brianna was silent. I heard Mrs. Fennel walk off, and I moved back to where I had been, but Brianna was in the room too quickly. She seized me at the shoulder and spun me around.

"Were you listening to my conversation with Mrs. Fennel, Lorelei? Were you eavesdropping, spying on us?"

I just looked at her.

"You'd better not say anything more about this to Daddy, or we'll both hate you, Lorelei, both me and Mrs. Fennel. Forever."

I didn't have to say anything to Daddy. He could keep hundreds of secrets from us, but it was very hard for any of us to keep one from him. Brianna knew that better than I did, especially back then. As Mrs. Fennel had said, Daddy was furious at her about the man she had chosen to bring home to him. A day later, I overheard him telling her that she had been very careless. He didn't yell, but he warned her that she couldn't make another mistake like that. I was surprised to hear her crying. I had never seen either her or Ava cry.

For nearly a month afterward, Brianna was more than just sorry and sad about Daddy's being angry with her. She moved about as if she was constantly terrified. I saw the way she avoided Daddy and Mrs. Fennel whenever she could. She was like a whipped puppy. She spent more time alone in her room. Still blaming me for everything, she would give me stabs of fury when she was teaching me, but they were instants, and she was very careful not to get me crying. She was just as frightened of failing to do for me what she was supposed to do as she was of anything else. I was tempted to complain about her nasty looks, but I sensed that would make her more furious with me. Anyway, I had learned early on that sisters like us didn't tell on each other. Loyalty.

I tried not to look at or speak to Daddy any differently,

but Daddy could easily read my thoughts and tune in to my feelings. One day not long afterward, he decided to take me aside and tell me more. Whenever Daddy isolated one of us for some special time with him, the rest of us were jealous. I was sure that was true for Ava and Brianna, even though Brianna had less reason now. Daddy was doing this only because of the mistake she had made.

He held my hand, and we walked out to the gazebo behind our house. It was a much colder afternoon than the previous one. I wore my winter coat, but Daddy wore only his turtleneck black knit shirt. Neither the cooler air nor the sharper breezes bothered him. He was comfortable and relaxed.

"Let's just sit here a while and talk," he said when we stepped into the gazebo. He buttoned the top button on my coat. "Warm enough?"

"Yes, Daddy."

"Good." He smiled at me and looked out at the woods. "Most of the leaves are already gone. Earlier this year," he muttered, and shook his head as if someone had made a great mistake.

"The trees died again?"

"No, not died. They're just hibernating like bears."

"Did you see ever see a bear here, Daddy?"

He smiled. "A few times."

"You weren't frightened, though, right?"

"No, it was the bear who turned and fled." He took my hand and held it between his as he leaned forward, his eyes seeming to grow larger as he gazed into my face. "Now, I want to talk to you a little bit about what happened the other night."

"It wasn't Brianna's fault that I leaned out of the window too far," I said quickly.

"You're under Brianna's wing right now. It's always the fault of the person in charge."

"Even accidents?"

"Even accidents. Everything is preventable if enough thought and preparation are committed. Don't worry. She's learned an important lesson. You did her a favor."

"I did? What favor?"

"Never mind all that for now. Let's get back to what you saw, Lorelei, okay?"

I nodded.

"Remember when I brought you out here with me in the spring and we watched a robin plucking worms and bringing them up to her nest?"

"You boosted me up, and I saw the baby birds."

"Right. The mother was bringing them what they needed to live and grow."

"I remember."

"Well," he said, keeping his hands tightly around mine. Mine were a little cold, but his were so warm that mine quickly felt better. "I'm not a baby, but I need what I need to live and grow brought to me periodically, too. Periodically," he continued before I could ask, "means once every month in this case." He smiled.

"Mrs. Fennel told me. Virile young men," I said, and he laughed.

"She said that? Yes. I need what's in their veins, only what's in their veins. It has to do with hormones, too, but don't concern yourself now with what it all is exactly. Just know that it has to happen once a month.

You'll learn that's like a woman having her period once a month."

I shook my head. Brianna had shown me what periods were when I wrote my first sentence.

Daddy laughed again. "I see I'm confusing you. Usually, my girls are much older by the time they make this discovery, learn all this, Lorelei. Maybe I should have had Mrs. Fennel continue explaining things to you."

He saw the disappointment on my face. This was the nicest, most private talk we had ever had, and I didn't want it to end. I certainly didn't want to learn it from Mrs. Fennel.

"But I think it's better we have this little talk after all," he quickly added, and I nodded, happy again. "You know I will do everything I can for you, don't you? You know how much I love you."

"Yes, Daddy."

"Good. You and your sisters love me, too, and you know your sisters would do anything they could to help me."

I nodded.

"You will, too, won't you, when your time comes to do it?"

"Yes, Daddy."

"That's what it means to have a family, why your family has to be the first and most important thing to you. We're a family. We're not like other families, I know, but that doesn't mean they are better than we are. You will have more. You will be happier than any other girl you know, Lorelei. I will make sure of that. I'm so happy we have you as part of our family," he added.

My eyes filled with tears of happiness. He kissed my

cheek and lifted me to hold me in his lap. The afternoon was folding into night. Shadows began to grow around us, but I wasn't afraid. Right then and there, I thought I would never be afraid. Daddy was too strong. Even the shadows seemed to stop before they could get too close to us.

We sat there without speaking until I saw the first star. My head was against his chest. I could hear his heart beating strongly. I tried to make my heart beat exactly in sync with his. I wanted to breathe when he breathed, eat and sleep when he did. If I could have his love forever, I would never be unhappy, I thought. I would bring him what he needed to live forever, too. I would never want to see him sad or weak.

And nothing was more terrifying to me than the thought of him dying. Who would watch over me? I'd probably be returned to some orphanage.

No, I vowed. I would be his best daughter. I would do anything he needed or wanted.

I thought that then, and I thought it still today.

The real question was, would I think so tomorrow?

# 4

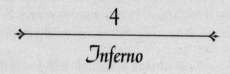

## Inferno

"Ordinarily, I would never go to one of these places," Ava began as she drove us away from the house Friday night. I was so excited and happy that I could barely breathe, much less talk. I could see she wanted me just to shut up and listen anyway.

First, I was up and out later than I had ever been. We didn't get started until nearly ten. Second, she made surprising changes to my hair and my makeup. From eight to ten, she oversaw my dressing and preparations. At the start, I thought my curly hair bothered her as much as it did me, but she showed me how to get it more fluffy, so that it had what she called "the bedroom look." After that, she taught me how to do my eyes and, for the first time, let me wear some glitter. I thought we'd never get off the choice of lipsticks. She had brought in a good part of her own makeup kit. She didn't want me wearing anything she was wearing, however.

"We want to stress differences between us," she said, "not similarities."

"Why?"

"It's most important that none of the men we meet knows we live in the same house and are sisters."

"Why not?"

"You'll learn all this very quickly," she began, "but when a young man chooses whom he will come on to, he thinks about the girl who's with her."

"Why?" I really felt like a little girl driving her parents crazy with the *why* questions, but I couldn't help it.

"She could be something to overcome, an obstacle. He's wondering, will these two separate tonight? Can I go off with one? Will she be willing to leave her girlfriend behind? Most girls feel guilty about that sort of thing. They make it almost mandatory that the guy find someone for their girlfriend first, and most times, that proves to be very difficult, if not impossible. While many men come alone to these places, almost no girls do. When one does, and when she's attractive, she's like a stronger magnet."

"That's why you always go out alone?"

She grimaced and shook her head. "Think about what you ask and say, Lorelei. How can I, can you, really ever have a girlfriend going out with us, much less have a girlfriend, a girl pal?"

I nodded.

I knew in my heart that we couldn't, but I asked the question more out of hope that there was some way to have a trusted companion. So many girls in my school had best friends, and just watching them together made me jealous.

"I guess there's no one else out there like us," I said. I couldn't help it. It came out like a complaint.

"I didn't say that," Ava replied. I looked up quickly. "There's no one else like us around here. We have our territory; others have theirs."

"We can't ever be friends with them?"

"No. It could be very dangerous for all of us."

"Do they ever get too close to us or we to them?" I asked. I felt I could get some answers from her now, now that we were going out together. I sensed I had reached a new plateau, one that would be filled with new trust and new answers.

"Sometimes." She turned. "And that's not something we want to happen."

"That's something Daddy senses occasionally, right? He can tell when they get too close."

"Yes," she said.

"Is that why we move so much?"

"Sometimes, yes. Never mind all that," she said, back to her characteristic annoyance. "You're getting us sidetracked with all these questions. Concentrate only on what I'm telling you. I'm telling you that if you think about what I just said, two sisters are more formidable for a guy. It's one thing to separate friends but quite another to separate sisters."

"Choosing one over the other would cause sibling rivalry," I said.

"Yes, that would play into it, too. Now you're thinking. The one left behind might be so upset about it that she would say something at home, something that would get her sister in trouble."

"How do you know all this?"

"Some of it Brianna taught me the way I'm teaching

you. Some things I read. Most of it will come naturally to you, just being out there among them."

*Among them,* I thought. That really did make us sound as if we had come from another planet.

She started to go through some of my earrings and necklaces.

"Daddy didn't want me wearing any jewelry with this dress," I said.

"When did he tell you that?"

"When I put it on for dinner. He thought it would take away from my natural beauty."

"That was then. This is for now. There's understated and overstated. Daddy doesn't keep up with the youth scene out there. That's why he needs us. This would be all right," she said, plucking a pair of teardrop diamond earrings out of my jewelry box, "and this matching necklace. You need some color, some glitter," she added, before I could voice any protest.

"But Daddy knows style," I blurted, still not taking the jewelry from her.

"Is Daddy taking you out for this field trip, or am I? Well? Make up your mind. He put me in charge of this for a reason. He has faith in me. I think I know what I'm doing. I don't fail out there, do I? Well?"

I took the jewelry from her, but I couldn't help feeling I was disobeying Daddy. Even something as small as this seemed like a great defiance, a possibility of disappointing him. But then I thought that if Ava wasn't afraid of getting him angry, I shouldn't be so timid about it. I couldn't imagine her taking any such risk.

"Okay, finish up," she told me, and went to do her own makeup and get dressed.

When she was finished and came for me, we stood before my full-length mirror and looked at ourselves standing together. She was wearing a light pink silky one-piece dress that was tapered at her waist and a little shorter-hemmed than my dress. Her collar didn't go as low as mine, but she had put on one of her uplift bras. She looked as if she could fall out of her dress at any time.

We had different looks entirely. Ava, despite what she had wanted me to wear, was not wearing any jewelry. Her hair was straight, down around her shoulders. I thought I looked like a young lady dressed for a formal dance, and she looked as if she worked in a strip club.

"You're not even wearing earrings," I said.

"Don't worry about what I'm wearing and not wearing," she said. "I know what I'm doing, what has to be done tonight. Let's go."

I followed her out. I half expected to see Mrs. Fennel standing at the door waiting to inspect us, inspect me, but she was nowhere in sight. Daddy had left earlier in the day to meet some business associate and wasn't home yet. I was happy about that. No matter what Ava had said, I still felt he would be disappointed in my appearance. Marla heard us, however, and came hurrying out of the den, where she was watching television.

"Oh, you both look so beautiful," she said, dripping with envy.

"Relax. As Daddy told you, your day will come, Marla," Ava said. "Don't be in such a rush to grow up. It's not all fun and games. There's more responsibility."

Marla grimaced and then muttered to me, "I don't care what she says. You're lucky, Lorelei."

She retreated with her shoulders sagging, her head lowered.

"She's lonely," I said. "I usually spend this time with her."

"You want to stay home?" Ava snapped. "Go ahead. Sit with your little sister, and watch some cartoon."

"I didn't say I wanted to stay home, Ava. I just felt sorry for her. Didn't you ever feel sorry for me? Even a little?"

"No," she said. She held her gaze on me a moment, as if she were searching for some sign, some proof, that I was indeed too different.

"Okay, okay," I said. "Let's go. She'll be all right. You're right."

She opened the door, and we went out. I looked back once, but Marla was probably already curled in close to a fetal position on the sofa. I was confident that, like my situation when I was her age, one or more of her classmates had invited her to go somewhere to do something, whether it was to a movie or just to hang out at someone's house, and she had had to say no. You could refuse these invitations just so many times before they stopped coming altogether. It didn't much matter how you refused them, either. Your excuses could sound quite plausible, but the result was always the same. You weren't going to be there. You weren't going to embrace someone's attempt at a closer friendship.

I used to think, *I know we're different, but can't we just pretend we're not once in a while? Can't I do the things other girls my age do?* Finally, one day when I was about Marla's age, I asked Mrs. Fennel just that, and she said, "No," but with such an accompanying angry, biting look that I dared not even think it again.

Ava said we didn't need school friends. We had each other, and we had Daddy.

It was true that Daddy did his best to occupy us. He took us to shows and on trips and even permitted us to attend his parties sometimes. If he ever invited a woman to dinner, we were all there at the table as well. Whoever she was, she was always impressed with our manners and our polite and informed conversation. More than one of his dates said something like, "You're raising them by yourself better than most couples raise their own children."

"You simply nurture what's already in them," Daddy would tell them. "You give it room to grow, to breathe. You have patience. It's like this wonderful wine," he would say, looking at the decanted wine. "If you don't rush it, it will be smooth, the flavors full."

Of course, I didn't realize it when I was very young, but now I knew that whenever he spoke to one of his women like that, in his silky soft voice, she was practically having an orgasm. I remember looking around the table and seeing the sly, almost smirking smile on Brianna's face. She would look down the whole time Daddy spoke. Ava was mesmerized and was just as curious as I was about the women Daddy had brought to our table and later would bring to his bedroom. We could see his power unfold right before our eyes, and that made us idolize him even more.

"We're taking the convertible?" I asked Ava as she headed for the Mercedes. Daddy had three cars: two sedans, one of which I used for school, and this convertible.

"Of course. We want to look the part. We're on the prowl," Ava said.

"Like wolves."

"Better than wolves," she replied, and finally laughed at something I said.

Now that we were on our way, I was feeling as if I had fallen into a blender. A variety of emotions were swirling around inside me. I was frightened, nervous, excited, and even a bit numb. I waited for her to continue talking and explain why she didn't go to these places normally. When she didn't follow up, I asked her why not.

"This sort of a place is a college hangout. College boys are usually too immature for me and too gregarious."

"Gregarious? What do you mean?"

"They hang out in clumps to give each other moral support. The worst are fraternity guys with their rah-rah, boom-bah. Those pins and sweaters and hats drive me nuts. And these sorts of young men gossip more than women do. Take my word for it. When they return from a date, they have to give a blow-by-blow account, and they usually exaggerate to make their buddies jealous. They are, in a word, too dangerous for us. So, as I told you, Lorelei, nothing will happen tonight, not in the sense we mean, understand? This is really and truly just a field trip, an experimental little journey."

I nodded, but she didn't see it. We rode on.

"That's not to say there isn't a great deal to learn

from these college boys. You want to know what to say, how to say it, and when to say it. You want to know when you return a gaze or a glance or when you fish with your eyes and hook with a smile. This isn't like some harmless flirtation in class, either. These young men aren't at this place to find little high school romances. They're not there to find a girl they can go steady with and write home about. Most of them, anyway," she added. "There are always the dreamers."

"Dreamers?"

"Why shouldn't there be some of them looking for their miraculous soul mates? You've got to be able to recognize them and, for the most part, stay away from them. The men we want are those who want no lasting relationships. They won't care if they don't learn all about you in one or sometimes two nights. They want to go to bed with you, have a laugh, and go back out there with no promises left on the table. Some men," she said, smiling, "give women they're with promises the way people leave tips for the maid in a hotel. So," she continued, "what you want to telegraph to them, sometimes like breaking news on television, is the fact that you, too, are not looking for anything lasting. You want a good time. And boy, does that work fast."

"How do you mean?"

"They drop all caution, Lorelei. They'll go practically anywhere you tell them you want to go and do whatever you want to do. Like puppies you feed little tasty tidbits after they go outside to pee."

Something struck me about the way she was talking about men, something I hadn't thought about, even though this wasn't the first time I had heard her speak about them in this mean, disrespectful manner.

"You don't like men, do you, Ava?"

I could see my question gave her great pause. She even slowed down a bit, her face darkening, tightening. For a moment, I thought she was teetering between turning to me to shout something nasty and suddenly breaking out in tears herself.

"It's not a question of our liking them or not liking them the way you mean. We don't have that sort of freedom."

"Freedom?"

"Lorelei, tonight, if you learn anything important," she said, "you will begin to learn that being so attractive to men is our particular curse, while at the same time being our particular blessing."

"I don't understand. How could it be both?"

"We can get who we want when we want him."

"And that's bad? How is that bad?"

"You will understand," she said with Daddy's confidence. "I promise. You will."

We drove on in silence for a while after that. My mixed emotions of excitement and nervousness had suddenly settled into a pool of dread. This was certainly not the first time I had had this feeling, but right now, it seemed stronger than it ever had been.

When Daddy had decided we were moving after I had begun my first years at school in New York, I had dreaded starting a new school. I was in fifth grade by then. Having friends was something everyone wanted and pursued. Friends invited friends to their homes and to birthday parties. One or two friends were important companions, to help each other get through any difficult challenges. They shared homework, stories about funny and sometimes sad things that had happened at their homes. They trusted each other with their emotional baggage, invested in each other in small but significant ways.

No matter what school I attended or where we were living at the time, it didn't take long for my classmates to learn that I had been adopted and had only a father. Few had older sisters who bore so much responsibility for them as mine did. Many differences, such as differences in race and religion, even family wealth and importance, usually don't matter as much to younger children. They concentrate more on the similarities, but my being an orphan and the way I was made to stay aloof from the rest of them caused them eventually to ignore or avoid me.

So when I began again in a new school, I knew I would hate the strangeness of it. I would hate having to get familiar again with all the small but necessary things every new student has to learn. But most of all, I knew what would soon happen. I knew how the other students would treat and see me, and that filled me with dread. I hated that feeling. I often wanted to cry when I was alone at home, thinking about the world I was missing, but nothing was more frightening to me than Daddy believing even for an instant that I was unhappy having him as my father and living in his home with my sisters, that I was in the smallest way unhappy about our lives. If I cried or in any way showed my disappointment and dissatisfaction, he would see it and be terribly hurt, I thought.

Besides, and this was most important, I could see that my older sisters were not upset about the way we lived, so I thought that would soon be true for me as well. I would get over these feelings. I must be patient. Brianna, before she left home, had seemed very happy to me. Ava never complained and really seemed to enjoy being who she was and what she was. How could it be any different for me? The ecstasy that came with being a daughter of darkness was just ahead, waiting for me to claim it.

Obedience.

Loyalty.

And sacrifice.

Worship the three, and, as Daddy promised, all would be well.

Ava turned sharply onto a city street. Just ahead of us on the right was a neon marquee that read "Dante's Inferno." There was a small crowd of young men trying to get in and obviously failing. We could hear their protests and pleadings.

"This is it?" I asked. "Dante's Inferno?"

She laughed. "Yes. They toy with the idea of being in hell. Little do they know how easily we can take them to it."

Her comment made me wince, but I guessed that was what we did.

"Now, listen to me, Lorelei. When we get inside and the men start to approach us, let me do all the talking first. In fact, you want to get used to letting them do most of the talking. Volunteer no information. Act as if you're a secret agent, undercover or something. Wrap your mystery around you like armor. Most men will be nervous, too, no matter how they act or try to impress you with their savoir faire. You'll learn quickly that it's the quieter ones, the confident ones, who are more impressive and in some ways more dangerous for us."

"Dangerous? Why?"

"It's like any competition. They'll be more qualified to play the game. The danger for us is they might sense danger and pull back. You can spend just about all evening with such a man and come home empty-handed, and you don't ever want to come home empty-handed. That's a disappointment Daddy can't tolerate. I have never returned empty-handed, and neither did Brianna, but both of us wondered, and you will wonder, what would happen if we did."

"What would happen?"

She just looked at me, and in that look, every possible nightmare seemed to show its ugly head. What if Ava's subtle accusations about me were right? What if I was too different? What if I couldn't do what she and Brianna could do? What if I failed the first time I was on my own? Would Daddy send me away? Should I fear something even worse?

"Don't worry about it," she said, as if she could read my thoughts. "You'll be a success. Daddy and Mrs. Fennel don't choose girls who won't be."

"How do you know that?"

"Mrs. Fennel told me, and you know Mrs. Fennel. She doesn't make excuses for us or for herself. There's no 'Oh, you'll do better next time,' or 'Don't worry, you'll understand next time.' None of us is ever coddled, Lorelei, and we're stronger for it. You're stronger than you realize you are right now."

"Really?"

"Yes. Now, remember, let them talk more. Use your eyes, your shoulders, and your whole body to speak to them. It's enough."

"What do we tell them about ourselves?"

"Nothing, Lorelei. We're not looking for a relationship. There's no reason for us to tell them anything."

"Not even our names?"

"Oh, you can tell them your name."

"I can?"

"Let's see. Tonight your name is Diane. No last name."

"Diane?"

"Right. And I'm Elsa. I haven't used that one recently. Elsa. Okay, Diane, here we go," she said, pulling up to the entrance.

The valet stepped forward eagerly to take our car. Ava seized my left arm when I opened the door before the valet had a chance to get to it.

"You're being too anxious. Don't step out awkwardly like some high school teenager, Lorelei. Slowly, slowly, always move as if there are a hundred pairs of eyes on you. Sex and grace go together well. The men will see immediately that you have some class, experience. Think about your posture. Concentrate on your figure. Always be aware of yourself. Do nothing by accident, no matter how small and insignificant you might think it is."

"Okay," I said, but let her get out first so I could mimic how she moved, turned, paused, and started toward the entrance to the club.

She smiled at me to indicate I was doing it right, and

I felt confidence transfusing from her body into mine. Maybe the men in here wouldn't think of us as sisters, but they would surely think there was no innocence poured into our clothes and shoes. The two men at the door practically leaped out of their own clothes to get the rejected young men to make a path for us, and they opened the doors quickly for us to a few choruses of catcalls and whistles. Ava ran her hand over the cheek of the door guard on our left and then down under his chin, holding her hand up as if she had an invisible wire tied to him and she were inviting him in with us. I thought I could hear his quickened breath and small moan of pleasure. His companion on the right smiled hopefully at me, but as Ava instructed, I touched him only with my eyes. It looked as if it had the same effect.

"Very good," Ava said. "Feel the power? You're the puppet master, and they are the puppets."

We stepped in and then paused like two divers on a cliff about to dive into the sea.

Now, anyone judging my reaction to Dante's Inferno would have to take into consideration the fact that I had never even been to a house party or a school party. I had never gone on a date or been alone with a boy. The only dancing I had ever done was in our house with one of my sisters and my daddy. I was up on the music and the dancing, and I had seen movie scenes shot in such places, but until that very moment, I never fully appreciated the effect such a sight would have on me.

My heart began to race as it never had, and I felt the blood rising through my neck and into my face. For a moment, I thought I might simply explode. My eyes couldn't swallow what they drank in fast enough. And my ears felt as if they were opening wider and wider to take in all the music, laughter, giggles, and screams of joy and excitement before us. I felt Ava's hand on my arm.

"Easy," she said. "Remember. Slowly, slowly. Let it all come to you."

We walked toward the bar. Wouldn't they check to see my age? A small panic started at the base of my stomach. I could be terribly embarrassed. Why wouldn't Ava think of this? I turned to signal my concern, but she didn't move her gaze from the men who were standing between us and the bar. Instead, she just squeezed my hand hard, which I knew meant *relax*. I tried. The men separated, none of them taking their eyes off us.

"Ladies," one tall, dark-haired boy wearing a pair of wire-frame glasses said. He bowed and gestured at the seats that had been quickly vacated for us. I thought he had a gentle, sweet face and warm hazel-brown eyes.

"Thank you," Ava said, and took one seat, nodding at the other for me.

"What would you Miss Americas like to drink?" a shorter, blond-haired boy on my right asked us. He looked much younger, too. Maybe he was someone's younger brother visiting.

"We're just having Shirley Temples tonight," Ava said.

One of the bartenders, a good-looking brown-haired man with the sort of sculptured male-model look Ava called face candy, stepped up quickly.

"Shirley Temples?" another young man asked, pushing his way between the other two. He was stouter and the least good-looking, with large lips and a nose that looked as if it had been broken a few times. His dull brown hair was uneven and stringy. He was very muscular, with thick forearms and shoulders, and looked as if he might bust out of his tight red shirt. "What the hell's a Shirley Temple?"

Ava looked at the bartender for the explanation.

"It's a nonalcoholic drink," he said. "Lemonade, Seven-Up, or something like that with a touch of grenadine and a cherry on top."

"Huh? Nonalcoholic? That's no fun," the bigger young man said, grimacing. "I'll buy you a real drink."

"Look at it this way," Ava told him. "I can keep my wits about me in this den of sin and still keep my cherry, too."

All the men laughed, especially the bartender, who set out to make our drinks.

"I'm Buddy Gilroy," the boy with the glasses said. "You guys go to a college here or something?"

"Something," Ava said.

"Maybe this is their college," the bigger man said. "You can learn a lot here." He laughed at his own joke.

"Why, are you teaching?" I asked. It just came out before I could think if I should say it. Ava had said she wanted to do all the talking first, but I didn't like the way he was elbowing the others out of his way, especially Buddy.

All the men cheered and teased their big friend. Ava raised her eyebrows. I held my breath, but she smiled at me. *Don't get overconfident,* I told myself.

"Yes, Professor," Ava followed up. "What is your subject? And don't tell me sex education."

"He needs to go to that class himself," someone behind him said. There was more laughter.

"Oh, yeah. Listen, if either of you needs lessons," the now red-faced big man said, "I'd be happy to volunteer."

"What if it turns out your friends are right and we know more than you do?" Ava asked him as the bartender brought our drinks. "You might have to go to the back of the line."

All of them laughed again. His face reddened even a darker crimson. He struggled to think of an appropriate comeback.

"In this case, I'd be happy to learn more, and if you're the teacher, I'd gladly stand there and wait my turn," he said, and his friends cheered.

Ava smiled. "That's fine," she said. "As long as you know your place."

They all roared again. More young men broke off their conversations nearby and hovered behind the small group that had greeted us. I could see the envious, even angry faces of the girls to whom they had been speaking.

"So, really, where are you guys from? I haven't seen you before. Anybody see them before?" another boy asked.

"I have," Buddy said, looking directly at me. "Every night in my dreams."

They all laughed.

"That's all he ever does is dream," the bigger young man said. "So, where are you from?"

I looked to Ava.

"Well," she said, "we kiss, but we don't tell."

There were more roars. I sipped my drink. Buddy smiled at me and then asked if I wanted to dance. I looked at Ava. She gave me a short *yes* smile, and I nodded. When we got onto the dance floor, the music was so much louder it was nearly impossible to talk. I looked back and saw how Ava was holding court, none of the boys who had been around us leaving. I was torn between being there to hear her banter and learn and remaining here on the dance floor with Buddy, who seemed unable to take his eyes off me. Actually, I was having trouble taking my eyes off him as well. It also felt good to be out there, to dance in a crowd with other girls and young men who at times seemed to be in a frenzy.

What was it they were all celebrating with the same energy and abandon they would have on New Year's Eve? Was it just the weekend, their freedom, or their youth? Were they celebrating or fleeing from sanity, from rules and supervision? What was it exactly that everyone was trying to prove to everyone else about himself or herself?

As I looked around, I thought many were saying, *Look at me. Don't you want to be with me more than anyone else?* Here and there, I saw some shyer girls and even some shyer boys, but on the whole, everyone looked ready to cast off every restriction, every warning, every bit of advice on how to live moderately, sensibly. The room reeked of sex, bodies rubbing against bodies, lips close to lips, and hands sliding over rears and thighs. Every gyration, turn, and twist looked like a move in some mating dance.

"You're a great dancer!" Buddy shouted. He drew closer. "You make me look good."

"Thank you."

"Where are you two from, really?"

"Around," I said, and he laughed.

"What's your name? Will you at least tell me that?"

"Diane."

I saw Ava break away from the crowd with the young man on her right. The others watched them head to the dance floor, each one regretting he hadn't asked first, I imagine. She threw me a smile and went at it. The young man she was with seemed immediately overwhelmed. He waved back at his friends lingering at the bar to indicate that he was drowning. There was more laughter, and the night began.

We danced most of the time. Other boys asked us both, but I favored Buddy and was able to dance with him more than with anyone else. He never stopped asking me questions about myself. I hated not being truthful with him. Was it simply my inexperience, or was he really as honest and sweet as he appeared? My instincts told me yes, but I was afraid they made me too vulnerable. I had to keep my wits about me and not make a mistake and tell him more than Ava would want me to tell him.

She and I were constantly offered something stronger to drink and even something to take or smoke, but Ava refused.

"We don't need anything to get high," she told them. "We're high on life."

No matter how hard any of them tried to learn more about us, we avoided having to answer any questions. In between dances, Buddy asked me to step out with him on a small patio. I saw that he wasn't drinking as much as his friends and asked him about it.

"I hate having hangovers, and most of those guys

need to drink before they have any courage when it comes to women."

"But not you?"

"I don't have that much courage with or without a drink," he said. "I have the nerve to say something to you, however. If I don't, I'll regret it all night."

"What's that?"

"You're absolutely the most beautiful girl I've seen here, or anywhere, for that matter."

"How do I know you don't tell that to all the girls you meet?"

"You don't. Tell you what," he said. "Let me take you out next weekend and see if I say it again."

I laughed. Maybe I wanted to see it, but what I saw in his face was the sincerity and honesty of a young boy, someone who either hadn't learned how to deceive or couldn't live and be comfortable with deception. He was close to me, his lips tempting mine.

"We'd better go back in," I said.

"Sure."

He followed me back. Ava saw us and looked suspicious.

"What went on out there?"

"Just talked," I said. "He talked. I didn't say anything."

"I hope not. I think it's time to leave."

When the boys who had been hovering around us saw we were going, they protested. They still knew only our first names. Buddy practically begged me to give him my phone number, give him something. Of course, I didn't. Two things began to happen even before we started out. Most of the boys simply gave up and moved on to approach other girls. The ones who had tried hardest to get to first base became belligerent as we gathered up our purses. Their remarks were nasty, crude.

"What, do you have some tricks to throw on the street?"

"Going to the dyke club?"

"Last chance to experience a real man, girls, or are you really both virgins and saving it for marriage?"

"Leave them be," Buddy said. He nearly got into a fight with one boy mouthing off, but I could see the frustration was defeating him as well.

"Let's go," Ava whispered.

"Hey," the big young man who had been with us from the beginning called out. "Your car turning into a pumpkin?"

There was lots of laughter trailing behind us.

"I'd love to bring him home to Daddy," she muttered, but we continued out.

"Hope I see you again," Buddy called.

I smiled back at him. I would never tell Ava, but I hoped I'd see him again, too.

"How do you feel?" she asked me when we got back into her car.

"Like I could go on and on for hours."

She laughed. "That's good. We have the energy," she said. "You did well. You had that one hooked and could have reeled him in anytime you wanted. And he knows nothing about you, right? You didn't talk too much out there on that patio?"

"No. Nothing but the name you invented," I told her.

But in my heart, I thought, *He knows my smile. He'll see me in his dreams.* Actually, I thought I would see him in mine.

As soon as we were home, Ava went to speak with Daddy. I knew she was giving him a report about me. I was nervous, of course. I couldn't help worrying that despite what she had told me, she was going to tell him I hadn't done well. It was the old sibling rivalry at work.

I didn't know it then, but Ava was more concerned now about her own future than she was about my rising above her in Daddy's eyes. Her destiny was calling.

Before I went to sleep, Daddy came to my room. I didn't hear him come in. I was in the bathroom washing off my makeup. When I stepped into the bedroom, he was standing there, smiling.

"Ava tells me you passed your first test with flying colors," he said.

*What test?* I wondered. All I did was go to a dance club and flirt with some young college men, maybe one in particular.

"You followed your orders well," he added, perhaps seeing my thoughts on my face. "You understand how you must behave. That's important, Lorelei. You understand restraint and the importance of guarding our personal lives."

"I'm glad you're happy, Daddy."

"Oh, I'm happy, but I always knew I would be," he said. He embraced me, kissed me at the top of my head, stroked my hair, and then held me out at arm's length. I could feel the power in his arms, but also I could see the love in his eyes. He looked at me with such intensity

I felt as though he really could look into my thoughts. I couldn't help wondering if he could see how much I had been attracted to Buddy. "I can see how alive this has made you. You can feel the power inside you."

I hadn't thought about it as being a power, but I knew what he meant. I nodded. "I do feel different, Daddy, older."

I wanted to add that I felt what it could be like to like a boy, maybe even love one, but I knew that would not make him happy. Most fathers felt ambivalent about giving up their daughters, but in Daddy's case, that would be tragic, probably for both him and me.

"You are different now, Lorelei. You're closer to being one of us, and I have the best daughters any father could hope to have," he said softly. He kissed me on the cheek and then turned and smiled just before he left, closing the door softly and leaving me standing in the afterglow of his enormous love.

Maybe my instincts weren't as sharp and developed as Ava's were, but instinctively, I knew I would either grow because of that love . . .

Or drown in it.

# 5

## Morning After

Had something really happened to change me? Was I different now, older, almost overnight?

I knew I felt different, even though it seemed silly. Surely, one night out with Ava wasn't enough to make me feel more mature, and what had I actually done, anyway? Danced, flirted, enjoyed some repartee with college boys, stayed out later than any other time? But older was just how I felt. Could it be that when I went out with Ava, something magical did happen, that I not only looked older but had grown more sophisticated? After all, it was true that my body had matured quickly after what had seemed to be a body on hold forever, so why not my mind and personality?

"Surprising things will happen to you because of the way you are being brought up, the way we live," Daddy once told me. "But I promise you, it will all be good, all wonderful."

I believed him. As I observed other girls in school, I did believe that all of us Patios, all of Daddy's daughters, were truly special in so many ways. It wasn't only our physical beauty, either. We seemed to move in and out of another dimension and wore looks on our faces that had others believing we knew very interesting and mysterious things.

One of my fifth-grade teachers, Mr. Foggleman, told me one day that I looked like someone who knew the future. I had no idea what he meant. He tried to explain by telling me I never seemed surprised by anything. "It's as if you always know something's coming, expect it, Lorelei. Your father's not a fortune-teller, is he?"

"He's everything to me. Why not a fortune-teller, too?" I said, and Mr. Foggleman laughed. He thought I was joking, but I meant every word.

I thought about all that while I stood in front of my full-length mirror and studied myself. Today I was wearing an ordinary cotton short-sleeved red blouse and a dark red skirt. Except for a little lipstick, I wore no makeup, and I had pinned my hair back, more or less so I wouldn't have to deal with it.

As I looked at myself, I concentrated on my eyes. There really was something new about them. The color hadn't changed, but I could see a wiser, calmer look. The maturity appeared to radiate out of my eyes and through my face. I felt like a young girl realizing that once she had been cute and now she was on the threshold of real beauty. Dare I think it? Was I even prettier than Ava?

I always felt there was something cheap about Ava's look. Her sexiness was more obvious. She was attractive in a more movie-star-glamorous sort of way. She had to wear enticing and revealing clothing. She had to do what she told me I had to do, be constantly aware of and employ her attributes, titillate with her nearly bare breasts and very tight skirts, whereas I was becoming a classic beauty, someone whose loveliness couldn't be surpassed. In short, I didn't think I had to try as hard as she did.

I expected I would be the more confident one and yet not the more arrogant one. In my heart of hearts, I hoped this was what Daddy saw in me, why, to me at least, his eyes always said, *No matter what I tell the others, you will be Daddy's best little girl.*

Recently, I had gotten my driver's license, and Daddy assigned one of our sedans to me. All I did was drive myself and Marla directly to school and drive us home after the last classes of the day. I was still forbidden to join any teams, go out for any stage productions, or become a member of any clubs. Without explaining exactly why it might be dangerous at the time, Daddy told me it was better for us not to have too high a profile. It was more advantageous for us to have less exposure.

"We come and go so quickly, Lorelei," he did tell me as an initial reason. "It's better if we're easily forgotten."

Of course, he meant only us daughters when he said "we." I couldn't imagine Daddy ever being easily forgotten. And yet I supposed that was part of his magic. He could swoop down on a new community, very quickly impress those he wanted to impress, and then slip away like a dream.

This particular morning, Ava surprised me by getting up before me and being at breakfast. She had no early classes to attend at UCLA and usually slept until hours after I rose. That didn't bother me in the least. I was happy to miss her in the morning. Most mornings, she was angry at everything, even the sun for having the audacity to rise so early. *Why couldn't night be longer?* she would petulantly ask.

"Ava will have to move to Norway," Daddy would joke, "or perhaps the North Pole and room with Santa Claus."

"Fine with me," she would reply. "They are the luckier ones."

At the time, I didn't realize she was talking about families like ours who really did live in Scandinavia. She saw it as some sort of a reward.

"Once you spend a full winter there, you will change your mind," Daddy told her. "I remember being stuck there for a few months during winter."

Was there anywhere on this earth where Daddy hadn't spent some time?

Contrary to her usual morning misery, Ava looked bright and cheery, babbling on with Marla about the fashions teenage girls wore these days. I was hoping to see Daddy at the table, but he had apparently left early on one of those secret missions Mrs. Fennel covered with the words "business trip." Usually, Ava hated it when she was up and I said "Good morning," but she said it before I could even think of it.

"I'm taking you and Marla to school today," she told me immediately. "And I'll pick you both up at the end of the day."

"Why?"

She glanced at Mrs. Fennel, who was putting out my bowl of her warm cereal, but Mrs. Fennel didn't look at her or speak. She barely glanced at me, but when she did, I saw she had a softer, more pleased expression. Her eyes confirmed that there was something very different about me, and whatever it was, it very definitely pleased her. Had Ava given her a report on our night out as well?

"I need to spend more time with you," Ava said. "Especially after last night."

Marla looked at me enviously. Ava wasn't up this early talking to her because of her. She was up talking to her because of me. "What happened last night?" she asked.

"Never mind," Ava said.

"I'm old enough to know," Marla moaned. If she was looking to Mrs. Fennel for any help, she might as well look at the wall, I thought. Neither she nor Ava responded. Marla sulked, but when Mrs. Fennel glanced at her, she quickly returned to her breakfast.

I sat and started on my cereal. Like everything else Mrs. Fennel made, it was different from anything my classmates would eat. From what I understood, many of them didn't even eat breakfast, and if they did, it was some sweet cake or some supposedly healthy morning drink their mothers made them drink. Of course, they were starving at lunch. Mrs. Fennel always prepared our special lunch drink for Marla and me. We drank it with one of her unique crackers, which were always a dark gray color, nothing that appeared too appetizing to the other students who saw us drinking and eating.

Recently, Meg Logan, pretending to have a change of heart about me, had sweetly asked me what I ate and what skin cream I used. As difficult as it was for her to admit it, she envied me for my complexion and my figure. Of course, I couldn't tell her, because I really didn't know exactly what I was eating or what Mrs. Fennel put into her recipe for our skin creams. I couldn't describe the flavors, either, at least not in ways she or any of the others would understand, and Mrs. Fennel had made it very clear, frighteningly clear, that we must never let anyone else taste our food.

"Nothing unusual," I replied, which she took as a blowoff.

She pulled her head back and her nose up, as if she had suddenly smelled something horrible. "Well, excuse me for asking," she said. "You might not eat anything unusual, but you're certainly weird."

"Is that the only word in your vocabulary, Meg? Try 'different,' 'strange,' 'peculiar,' and give 'weird' a day off. In fact, shut up for a day, and give the English language a break."

She muttered something under her breath and hurried away to tell her friends what I had said. They all glared angrily in my direction. Although I wouldn't show it, I would have to admit that all of this bothered me. When I told Ava about the looks they often gave me, she said, "Ignore them. They're meaningless," but I was having trouble doing it—more trouble, I believed, than she and Brianna had had when they were my age. Neither had ever expressed the unhappiness I felt at school and at not being part of anything girls my age were a part of. Why didn't they long for these things as much as I did?

Of course, I was very curious about what Ava wanted to discuss. It had to be important to get her up this early. She began the moment we were all in the car and leaving for school.

"I told Daddy that I had a really good feeling about you last night. I don't have to tell you, Lorelei, that I've had my doubts about you."

"Why?"

"That doesn't matter right now. What matters is I saw things going on in you last night that were positive, things that reminded me of myself when I first went out. You're a quick study, maybe even quicker than I was."

"Really?"

Was this my sister Ava talking? Giving me compliments? Was I really the reason for this new bloom about her face, this pleasantness and happiness? I couldn't help but be suspicious. When would the famous second shoe be dropped? What was the catch here? Where was all of this flattery taking me?

"Yes," she said, smiling at me. "Maybe you don't realize it yet, but the change, as Daddy likes to refer to it, has begun in you and, I might add, is going gangbusters. Don't tell me you don't feel it in yourself."

"I do, Ava, but I'm not sure what it is I'm feeling exactly."

"You're feeling the power," she said.

"What is the power?"

"The gift that makes it possible for you to do for Daddy what your sisters, what I, have done for him. It's not just being attractive. You will mesmerize, capture, and fascinate. When the expression *He lost his head over her* is applied to you, it will have real meaning." She laughed. "You'll get to feel like a goddess, like the puppeteer pulling the strings and making them dance. You had a taste of that last night, didn't you?"

"Yes."

She smiled and nodded. "I remember my first taste of it. It was truly like drinking from the Fountain of Youth. The energy, the strength, the confidence in yourself that you feel right now will never die, Lorelei."

"You make it sound as if we're immortal."

She smiled and then lost the smile quickly as her real purpose for getting up early and driving me returned. "The reason I wanted to drive you to school today and talk to you, something Daddy insists on, by the way, is that you're going to see the change reflected in the way the boys in your school look at you today. You're going to lay down a direct path to their libidos."

"What's a libido?" Marla asked. For a while, I had forgotten she was with us, I was so lost in the things Ava was saying.

"You want the technical definition?" Ava asked, winking at me.

"Okay."

"It's what Sigmund Freud called the generalized sexual energy of which conscious activity is the expression. I'm taking a course in human psychology," Ava told me.

She never discussed or even mentioned her classes at UCLA. I always thought it was an unpleasant experience for her but something she had to do because Daddy asked her to do it. In fact, she complained so much about doing it that I was afraid to ask her anything.

"Daddy thought I needed the class," she added. Then she turned to Marla and said, "It means getting them hot, Marla. You know what that is, right?"

"Yes, of course," she said. "I know when boys are hot."

Ava laughed.

"I do."

"She'll be right on your heels, Lorelei. Be happy about it."

"Is that why you're so happy this morning, Ava?" I asked. "I'm right on your heels?"

"Exactly. See, you are getting smarter, wiser, more perceptive."

"Why does that please you so much, Ava? Not that I'm upset about it. I just want to know why."

"Why? Why?" She shook her head. "Simple, Lorelei. You'll be taking over that much faster."

"And what about you?"

"I'll leave to fulfill my destiny," she said, and drove on, her face filled with such pleasure and delight it was truly as if she could see her destiny right before us.

"What is this destiny, exactly?" I asked. "I never understood when Mrs. Fennel said that was what Brianna was pursuing, her destiny."

She looked at me and smiled. "When your time comes, Lorelei, you'll know. Believe me, you'll know," she said, and left it at that, another secret still wrapped tightly in mystery.

After we arrived at school, Ava asked me to wait until Marla had gotten out to go into the building. She looked more serious now, more her old self, her eyes filled with warning and threat.

"From now on, you have to be even more cautious than before," she began. "I know what you've been through up until now. I know what it was like for you to remain so aloof, be such a loner, with no apparent interest in making close friends, joining anything. Even though you were somewhat attractive, boys gave up on you, right?"

"Yes," I said, although I wasn't convinced they had entirely given up on me. Some still smiled and said hello occasionally. A few even tried to start conversations, but I knew where those conversations would lead, so I discouraged them.

"That doesn't mean you weren't in their fantasies, Lorelei, and now you're going to be in them even more. It's because of the gift, this glow that's around you."

"I don't understand, Ava. Where did it suddenly come from? Just going out with you?"

"No, it started before that. Neither Daddy nor I wanted to mention it until you had gone out with me, been tested in the field, so to speak. You don't quite realize it all yet, but you're like a race horse that, if not kept under control, would gallop so hard and fast it would burn itself out. *Control* is now the key word. When I told Marla you had laid a path to their libidos, I left out that yours is eager to charge forward, too. Remember how I've been constantly warning you about your urges, how I teased you about having a crush on a boy or giving away your virginity too quickly? Well, I was preparing you for this," she said. "This is what Daddy saw coming."

"The gift?"

"Exactly. It's the reason you are so special, why we are all so special."

"I don't understand why I am special, Ava. I've never understood that."

She nodded. "You will."

"Why do you keep saying *you will, you will*? Why can't you just tell me?"

She was silent a moment and just stared ahead at the school building. "You're going to be late," she said.

"No. Answer me," I said, taking a sharper tone than I had ever taken with her. "Why can't you just tell me things and not have me go around guessing and wondering?"

"Don't start regressing on me and acting like a child. No tantrums, now, Lorelei."

"I'm not having a tantrum. You say I have this special gift, that I'm older. Well, treat me that way. Why can't you just tell me?"

Her eyes grew smaller, not hateful and not even angry. They were more full of mystery than rage. She looked as if she could see something in me that I couldn't. I felt as if I were under an X-ray. I actually sat back.

"Why?" I repeated more forcefully.

"For the same reason Mrs. Fennel or Brianna couldn't come right out and tell you what Daddy needed. Remember how shocking it was for you?"

I just stared at her, my heart suddenly thumping. "I still don't understand. Are you saying I'm going to be shocked about myself? Is this what you meant that day when you said you saw fear in me, fear of myself?"

"Oh, Lorelei," she said with an air of exhaustion. "You've always been at the questions far more than any of us."

"Didn't you have this sort of curiosity about everything, Ava?"

"No. I understood I had to be patient. Forget about it for now, Lorelei. I've already said too much. Just remember my warnings, and don't do anything stupid. Go on," she urged. "I'll be here at the end of the day."

I heard the first warning bell.

"This is what you meant that day you said you saw fear in me, fear of myself," I insisted. "You still see it in me, glow, gift, power, or not, right? Right?"

"Go to school, Lorelei," she ordered. "Beware of pushing too hard and moving too quickly. Remember the myth of Icarus, the one Daddy likes to tell us. He flew too high when he was warned not to, and his wax wings melted. For now, stay on the ground, Lorelei. You'll have plenty of time to fly later. Go on. Go to class. Go!"

I got out and watched her back up and drive off. I had been so happy when I rose that morning, so full of energy and eager to start the day, even in school, where I felt so alone and under attack daily. If Ava's intent was to slow me down, to lower the flame burning inside me, she had succeeded. Suddenly overcome with a dark depression, I entered the building and moved so slowly toward my homeroom that I was a little late. My homeroom teacher, Mr. Burns, was surprised, but instead of the chastisement and warnings he gave other students, he just gave me that look of surprise and then, to my surprise, a nice smile.

*After all,* as Ava might say, *he's a man, and he sees the gift that has unfolded inside you.*

When I looked around, the girls in the classroom looked angrier at me. I saw them start their whispering.

The boys, however, wore smiles not unlike the one Mr. Burns had given me. When I first began to feel and see the changes in my body, the maturing that finally had begun to show, I felt a little like Cinderella. Something magical was happening to me, but because of who I was, who we were, I could have only moments at the ball. My midnight came quickly, and I had to shut down all the attention I was starting to get. There would be no parties, no dates, and no dances. I accepted and was obedient, always wondering why I had to be.

Ava had been right to take the time out that morning to lay heavier warnings on me. I felt the new Lorelei within me strain against those chains, but I also wondered why I couldn't smile back at the boys who interested me. Why couldn't I come out of the shadows and enjoy being there? What would be so terrible if I had a date? I wouldn't go too far. Daddy had often told me I was the smartest daughter he had ever had. Ava didn't realize how smart I was. I was beginning to think that just because she couldn't do these things, she didn't want me to do them. If I really did have a gift, a power, why did I have to wait to enjoy it? I would never lose sight of how important I was to Daddy.

The bell rang to start the day, and everyone rose, some moving faster than others, chatting with that shotgun energy that took them in all sorts of directions, what Ava called wasted energy. I did suddenly feel even more aloof, but not arrogantly so. I simply felt wiser, older, and more mature. I held myself back, because I didn't want to fall in with them, be part of them. Mr. Burns smiled again and nodded at me.

"Have a good day, Lorelei," he said. He was one of the younger high school teachers, probably only in his early thirties. Besides homeroom, I had him for English literature, my last period of the day. We were doing Shakespeare now, and he taught it by playing recordings of professional performances. He said the school didn't pay him enough to have him endure us reading Shakespeare aloud.

Most of the other girls had a thing for him. I hesitated to think *crush* ever since Ava had mocked the word. He was good-looking, with dark brown hair, a little less than six feet tall, with impish green eyes. He had a tennis pro's physique, lean and fit. I wasn't part of the Gossip Broadcasting System here, but I knew that he was going hot and heavy with an intern at Cedars-Sinai Hospital. There was supposed to be breaking news soon on his engagement announcement.

"Thank you," I said. "Sorry I was a little late."

"First time, I ignore," he said. I knew he didn't. "You did something different with your hair today, didn't you?"

The students for his first-period class were streaming in. He stepped closer to me.

"Not really much," I said.

"Whatever you did looks very nice."

I held his eyes with mine for a moment, smiled softly, and then walked out, feeling his gaze still on me. When I looked back, he was in the doorway, smiling in my direction.

*Ava, help me,* I thought, feeling I should think that after it had become clear that a teacher was flirting with me. But the truth was that I didn't want her to do anything, not even give me those warnings. I wanted to explore, test myself and my power. More than anything, now more than ever, I wanted to be myself, even if it meant playing with fire.

Would I be sorry?

# 6

## Play with Fire

"As a recent new student myself, I've been appointed to welcome all the new students to our school," Mark Daniels said. "The concept is that I know more about what it's like to start somewhere new like this in the middle of a school year, especially your senior year. So welcome."

I finished my cracker and looked up at him. Lately, I found myself sitting alone in the cafeteria at a far right corner table that enabled me to watch everyone else. It had been a while since any of the boys had spoken to me. I had noticed Mark when he first entered our school. He was one of the better-looking seniors. He had a rugged, early Robert Redford look, the same almost messy dirty-blond hair, the same sexy smile. He had barely smiled at me since he arrived or said much more than "Hey" in passing through the hallways. He always kept moving, never expecting an answer. It was almost something he saw as his duty, to say hello to all the girls. That struck me as kind of arrogant, so I didn't reply.

Ava, in a rare moment when we were talking about high school boys, told me the thing they feared the most was rejection. "It's why most of them aren't very original or exciting, Lorelei. They practically want guarantees before they'll risk approaching you or asking you on a date. Here and there, a rare one came along, and I was tempted, but only for a moment," she added quickly. "Our lives begin after high school."

"Why?"

"It's the way it is," she said, and would say no more.

When I looked up at Mark and recalled Ava's comments about high school boys and our restrictions, I thought her answer hadn't been good enough then, and it certainly wasn't good enough now. It wasn't easy just to ignore the attention of someone as good-looking as Mark.

"I'm not a new student," I said.

He pretended great surprise. "Are you kidding?" He sat across from me and then, in an overly dramatic display of amazement, glanced back at the other students and said, "Those bastards. They just told me you had to be a new student. No one recognized you. Are you saying you've been here all this time and I didn't notice? What, have I become blind or just plain stupid? I thought I knew all the girls in this school backward and forward. Some look better backward."

I couldn't help myself. I laughed, and that encouraged him.

"I know I should know your name," he said, and then pretended to be running through some possibilities. "Lois? Laura? Lauren?" He snapped his fingers. "L . . . Lorelei, Lorelei Patio, right?"

I looked past him at the other students in the

cafeteria. Many had stopped talking and had turned our way. They looked frozen, anticipating. What did they expect I would do? Get up and charge out?

"Okay," I said. "You've got my attention. What's your point?"

"My point? My point?" He thought. "Oh, yeah, my point. My point is that you are without doubt the most beautiful girl in this school and maybe in the entire city. And," he continued with an amusing air of seriousness, "I find it downright rude of me not to have acknowledged that fact long before this. Can you see it in your heart to forgive me?"

I was laughing inside, but I kept myself from even smiling. It was as if Ava were right there, looking over his shoulder at me and grimacing, just waiting for me to do something wrong or say something wrong.

"I'll try," I said. "You're forgiven."

It took a lot of self-control, but I turned to look at my opened English literature textbook as a way of dismissing him.

"Oh, great. Thank you, thank you. Now that we're past that, can I ask you if you are free this Friday night?"

"What?"

"Friday night. A few of us are going over to party at Gavin Murphy's house in Malibu. You know the Murphy family, right? Very respectable. His father's an important movie producer, did that film *Deadly Verdict*."

"I don't know him," I said. "And I never saw the movie."

"No problem. Their house is right on the beach. We'll have a campfire, good stuff, and lots of music, plenty to eat. The weather promises to be terrific, and there's no better view of the stars."

"I . . ."

"Don't say yes or no right now," he said, holding up his right hand. "I don't want you to regret you said yes too quickly. And I certainly don't want you to regret you said no, because I'll have to regret it, too. Let the idea just settle in your mind. Examine it from every angle. Turn it about like a precious diamond. Think of questions to ask me during the week. You know, like time, what to wear, who all's coming, and all that. Oh, here is a list of references for me," he added, and handed me a slip of paper that said, "Moses, President Lincoln, Buddha, Jesus, and Allah."

"You left out George Washington," I said.

"Didn't know him."

He got up, which surprised me.

"I'm not going to pressure you. Don't worry about me haunting you the rest of the week. Just turn around whenever you come up with a question. I'll be right behind you, at a discreet distance, of course. Enjoy the remainder of your lunch," he added, and walked away.

I knew I was smiling now, and I also knew Ava would be furious. I stuffed his list of references into my book bag and left the cafeteria a little before the bell rang. I didn't look back at him, either, nor did I glance at any other students. I felt their eyes on me, however. Curiosity only grew stronger and more intense about me the remainder of the day. Everywhere I looked, every time I turned, some girls and some boys were talking and looking my way. Mark Daniels was true to his word, too. He was always nearby, smiling, shrugging. I tried to concentrate on the schoolwork and get him out of my mind, but it seemed impossible. His smile and his sexy eyes were frozen across my vision.

He tapped me on the shoulder at the end of science class and handed me another slip of paper. "I forgot these two."

I looked at what he had written: "Albert Einstein and Mahatma Gandhi."

"But no pressure, no pressure," he added, holding up his hands and backing away.

I laughed. Maybe I shouldn't have. Maybe it was wrong, but I couldn't help it. He was funny, handsome, charming, and certainly what Ava would have described as original. Even she would have had trouble rejecting him out of hand, I thought.

By the time I reached Mr. Burns's class, I sensed that everyone was talking about me and Mark. I thought even Mr. Burns was looking at me with greater interest. Whether it was my imagination or not, the effect was the same. I felt myself blushing and tried to keep my eyes down. We were studying Shakespeare's sonnets, and suddenly, after a discussion of one, he had us turn to Sonnet 18 and then moved down the aisle as he read, stopping right before my desk. He liked to be the one to read them completely before we talked about them. I felt his gaze on me and looked up.

"Shall I compare thee to a summer's day?" he began. It did seem as if he was speaking only to me. I felt like getting up and running out of the room. "Thou art more lovely and more temperate . . . But thy eternal summer shall not fade, Nor lose possession of that fair thou owest; Nor shall Death brag thou wander'st in his shade, When in eternal lines to time thou growest . . ."

When he finished the sonnet, he held his gaze on me. I held my breath. What was he doing? He was drawing all the attention to me. I thought it wasn't only embarrassing for me but also for him. He was a grown man. Why didn't he realize this?

"So," he said, finally pulling his eyes from me, "who wants to try to explain this in more modern terms?"

Mark raised his hand quickly. Mr. Burns looked surprised.

"You're inspired, Mr. Daniels. What could have made our most recent new student more inspired than my old crows?"

"Such is the power of real beauty on me and you," Mark replied. I glanced at him and saw he was staring right at me. The other girls in the class looked as if they would chorus in a deep, heartfelt sigh. Some of the boys were grinning from ear to ear. Mr. Burns seemed lost for words for a moment but quickly regained his composure and started to ask his usual questions about the imagery and meter.

Never since I had begun in this school had the sound of the bell ending class been more welcome. I practically leaped up to lunge for the door before anyone could say anything to me. Mr. Burns shouted out the assignment. I barely heard him. I didn't look back.

Marla was waiting for me at the entrance to the parking lot. Even my little sister, unsophisticated, still more boyish than girlish, looked up with surprise at what she saw in my face.

"Something wrong?" she asked. "Some boy say something sexy to you?" She looked hopeful that it was true.

I shook my head. "No, c'mon."

"Oh," she said with disappointment, and followed me out.

Ava was waiting in the car. I moved as quickly as I could toward it, but heard Mark shout out, "But thy eternal summer shall not fade."

"Huh?" Marla said, looking back. "That boy is talking to you, Lorelei."

"Forget about him," I said, and turned her toward the car. I had hoped somehow to escape Ava's scrutiny, but she was already gaping at me through the passenger-side window, her face a portrait of disgust and disappointment.

"It's not my fault," I said, getting in quickly.

She hesitated, continued to look toward the school entrance at Mark Daniels and some other boys who had joined him, and then put the car in drive and headed away. Her silence was a deception.

"What did you do?" she finally asked.

"Nothing. I followed your advice, your orders. It really wasn't my fault."

"You're not telling me the truth," she said, nodding. "Who is that boy, and what was he shouting?"

"It's a line from one of Shakespeare's sonnets. He's a relatively new student. I hadn't said a word to him until today."

"So you did speak to him," she said, practically leaping out of her seat.

"I had no choice, Ava. He came over to me in the cafeteria."

"What did he say? What did he want?"

"He wants me to go to a party with him this weekend."

She glanced back through her rearview mirror and then looked at me with a scowl on her face. "You obviously didn't shut him down firmly enough."

"Before I could say no, he got up and left," I said. I didn't think it was necessary to tell her about his joke, using famous people as personal references. In fact, saying anything positive about him would be a disaster.

"I don't like this," she said. "If he approaches you again, shut him down clearly enough, even nastily enough, to end it firmly, Lorelei. Did you hear me?" she asked when I didn't respond.

"Yes. I just thought . . ."

"What? What did you think?"

"That maybe a little more experience with boys would help me later on, help me become more like you."

"What? That is such a load of crap," she said. "I'm going to have to tell Daddy about this."

"Why? For heaven's sake, Ava, didn't boys approach you for dates in high school? You said you were tempted a few times. Why make a big deal of this?"

"Yes, I told you I was tempted, but I quickly shut that down and afterward never entertained thoughts of going out with any of them like you're doing."

"Yes, you did," I said, and tightened my arms around myself. "You're lying. You just want to make me look bad in front of Daddy."

"If any boy asked me out, I'd tell him where he could get off," Marla piped up.

I spun around on her. "No, you wouldn't, Marla. Don't tell us that now. You were all excited in there that some boy might have approached me. You couldn't wait for the details."

"I might be interested in the details, but I wouldn't think of doing something Daddy told me not to do," she replied, now looking more like Ava to me.

Ava nodded. "She has more sense than you do already."

Marla smiled smugly at the compliment. I could feel it coming, the day Marla would be breathing down my back to become Daddy's best girl. She was different from the way I was at her age. She was more sophisticated, sharper, more intent, and, despite her sloppy ways at times, more anxious to please Mrs. Fennel. It wouldn't be long before sibling rivalry would be spelled in all capital letters when it came to what went on between her and me.

"Don't worry. I'm not going to do anything wrong," I said.

"Oh, I'm not worried," Ava said, "but that doesn't mean you won't."

We drove on in silence. I felt all the conflicts raging inside me. I would never say it now, but I was more than just tempted to say yes to Mark. I really wanted to go with him, to be part of something people our age were doing. Why wouldn't it be good for me to have these experiences now? Wouldn't it make me smarter, wiser for the future?

Even thinking these thoughts created a battle within me. I tried to chastise myself, to make myself feel bad about thinking of doing something that would displease Daddy and in some way endanger the family. I could feel the tug of war going on in my brain, thoughts wrestling with thoughts.

Why was any of this surprising, anyway? Daddy said I was stunning now. Ava taught me how to flirt and be attractive. Where did they think I was going to school, a nunnery? *This is just Ava's jealousy again,* I concluded. *Daddy won't be angry. He knows she's been even more jealous of me these days. Let her go tell him. She'll be disappointed in his reaction.*

She was frustrated when we arrived at the house, because Daddy was still away. I thought she would tell Mrs. Fennel as a consolation, but she apparently said nothing to her, because nothing was mentioned at dinner. Just after ten, when I was thinking of going to sleep, Daddy arrived. I could hear he had brought a woman home with him, so I thought Ava surely wouldn't trouble him with her complaints about me tonight, but to my surprise, she did. When he came to my room, he didn't look angry, however. He looked more concerned than anything.

He was still wearing his tie and jacket and looked as handsome as ever. I had just gotten into my nightgown and sat on my bed when he entered.

"I must speak with you, Lorelei," he began.

"I don't care what she said, Daddy. It wasn't my fault, and I didn't do anything."

"I know." He sat next to me and took my hand. I felt like a little girl again, sitting with him on the gazebo in New York, hanging on his every word, his every look. "It's my fault this has happened."

"Your fault? Why?"

"I pushed you a little faster than I have the others," he said. "Usually, I wait a little longer before I unveil one of my daughters, but I thought, and still think, you're a little different, Lorelei, wiser in some ways, and certainly one of the most intelligent. From your questions, the way you look at things, I could see you were going to be . . . how shall I say . . . more complete. And you are, you are."

He paused and took a breath.

"Of course, I would expect boys to pursue you, and vigorously, too. The feelings you're having and the desires you have are natural but also dangerous. Oh, I don't mean dangerous the way other fathers might feel it was for their daughters. You know that. I don't believe you would lose yourself in some love affair and get pregnant or anything. But if you developed even a small romance now, you would have far too much to explain. You understand, right?"

I nodded.

"You'll have plenty of time and plenty of opportunities very soon to enjoy yourself out there, Lorelei. Just be a little more patient and listen to your sister. She's been through it."

"I'm not sure she has," I said, perhaps too quickly.

"Oh? What do you mean?"

"Ava's a harder person than I am. She seems almost angry all the time, especially at men."

He didn't laugh or smile. The look he gave me instead put icicles down my back. It was as if he was learning more about me than about Ava from what I was saying.

"Well, then, try to be more like that," he said. He rose. "I don't want to hear any more talk about this boy at school, Lorelei."

"Okay, Daddy," I said quickly. His look and his tone were frightening me and causing my heart to thump.

I think he saw that in my face and softened his expression without quite smiling. "It will all be fine. Just be patient," he said. He started to turn away and then stopped and turned to my window. The look that came over him now reminded me of the times he would stop whatever he was doing and listen hard.

"What . . ."

He put up his hand for me to be silent. I barely breathed. And then he surprised me again by returning to sit next to me on my bed.

"Tell me about this boy," he said.

"There isn't much to tell, Daddy. I don't know much about him. He recently entered the school but quickly has become very popular. He is very good-looking and different."

"Different? How?"

"He's more mature, I think. I barely spoke to him today and never before today."

"He never approached you before today?"

"No. He acted barely interested in me, no different from how he acted toward most of the girls. He'd grunt a hello in the hallway but never waited to hear me respond or try to have a discussion."

"Until today?"

"Yes."

He looked out the window again and was silent.

Then he turned back to me and said, "I want you to tell me exactly what he says and how he responds tomorrow when you tell him you can't go with him on any date."

"What should I tell him is the reason, Daddy?"

"Don't give him any reason. No excuses. A simple 'no, I'm sorry, thanks for asking.'"

"And if he asks why not?"

"Tell him you don't want to go with him. If you say it strongly and firmly enough, he should be quite discouraged. He'll be angry, of course, but he'll not bother to ask you out anymore. If he does bother you, annoy you, you let me know that, too. Understand?"

"Yes, Daddy."

"Good." He rose again.

"Daddy?"

"Yes?"

Maybe it was the wrong time to ask, but the way he had looked at me when I complained about Ava made me think more about myself, more about the differences between us.

"Why can't I know more about myself, about where you found me and who my birth parents might be?"

"What for, Lorelei? What difference does any of that make now?"

"I read this story about an adopted girl who accidentally meets her real brother when both of them are in their twenties and . . ."

"And they don't know they're brother and sister and they fall in love?"

"Yes."

He smiled. "Don't worry about that. You have no brothers."

"How can you know for sure?"

"Your birth parents died right after you were born and had no other children. Okay? Put that to rest. Go to sleep. I'll be here tomorrow when you return from school. You'll drive Marla and yourself. Ava has other things to do for me and then has to attend her own classes at college."

"Okay, Daddy."

"Good night, my sweet and beautiful daughter," he said. He kissed me, touched my cheek, his eyes lingering on my face a moment, and then left.

I thought about what he had told me. It wasn't much, but at least he had told me something about myself. Maybe I would get him to tell me more about my birth parents now. Even though they were dead, I'd like to know what they were like. What would be so terrible about that? Surely, now I was old enough to understand it all.

I gazed at my window. Why was he looking out there so hard? What else wasn't he telling me?

And what could any of this possibly have to do with Mark Daniels and an innocent invitation to a party?

# 7

## Sibling Rivalry

I was both surprised and happy that Ava had gotten up ahead of me in the morning and had gone to do whatever Daddy wanted her to do for him. Had she been there at breakfast, I thought my first words to her would have been "Thanks a lot, Ava. Are you satisfied now?" But knowing her, I was sure that would have led to more bitter words and perhaps brought Daddy downstairs. That would have displeased him. He was still upstairs with whomever he had brought home. Worried that I might go knocking on his bedroom door for something, Mrs. Fennel told me immediately that he was still entertaining a guest.

"Daddy's not a slam-bam thank-you-ma'am kind of guy," Ava once quipped when I commented on how long a particular woman had been with him in his room. "Most women are amazed at his stamina."

"How do you know all this?" I asked her.

"A little bird told me," she said, and laughed at the expression on my face. "You have a lot to learn, Lorelei, a lot to learn."

She made it sound as if every little new tidbit of

information was as sweet and wonderful as a ripe grape, especially anything new that I learned about Daddy.

Marla looked sullen and disappointed at breakfast when I stepped into the dining room. What had she been expecting to see? Me sour and tearful? Was she hoping I'd be sent away and she'd move up the ladder toward a bigger place in Daddy's heart ahead of me?

"I bet Daddy was very angry with you last night," she began. She made it sound like the first line of a song. Mrs. Fennel looked disinterested as she moved about the table, but I sensed she was listening closely.

"No, not really," I said as casually as I could. Clearly, Ava had said something to her. "We had a wonderful conversation last night after you went to bed, in fact, and he told me things about myself, about my birth parents."

Marla looked devastated. "He did?"

"I wouldn't say it if he hadn't, Marla. We don't lie to each other, especially in this house, and we certainly don't plot against each other," I reminded her sharply with one eye on Mrs. Fennel. I saw her smile.

This pleased her? Did she like me to be snippy and more like Ava? Maybe in her way of thinking, I was too soft and easy and not, therefore, made of the steel and grit necessary to be one of Daddy's daughters. However, I didn't care what pleased her. I didn't like being this way, but Marla's attitude drove me to these darker places in myself.

"Well, what are you going to do about that boy? I'm sure Daddy doesn't like the idea of your seeing him, right? Right?" she repeated to force an answer.

"Don't worry about it, Marla. It's not of any concern to you. Just look after yourself."

"We are all supposed to worry about each other and look out for each other, because it's the same as looking out for ourselves," she said, wagging her head at me. "Isn't that what Daddy has told us often?"

"I said I would take care of it. I don't need you to remind me of anything, either."

She smiled a bitter little smile at me. "You'd better take care of it and take care of it fast," she said. She sounded as if she were the older sister now and not me.

"I don't need you threatening me, Marla."

"I'm not threatening you. Am I threatening her, Mrs. Fennel?"

"Stop!" Mrs. Fennel snapped at us both. "I will not have this sort of behavior in my house."

Marla constricted like a balloon losing its air. I stared back at Mrs. Fennel. Her house? *This is Daddy's house,* I thought. She saw the defiance in my face but didn't challenge it or get angry. She didn't look surprised as much as she looked more interested in me. It was as if she saw something in me she was afraid I didn't have, like the killer instinct or something.

That frightened me more. Did I have it? I felt as if I was being introduced to myself by myself in quick, sharp ways now. Every revelation would open my eyes wider and wash away the childhood fantasies to which I had clung. Ava once told me she carried Daddy inside her wherever she went. It was truly as if he saw what she saw and heard what she heard. She said she was happy about that, too. It helped her make sure she always made the right decisions.

I was happy to finish breakfast and get us off to school, despite what I knew awaited me there. Marla was still smarting from my sharp comeback at breakfast and sat sullenly as I drove. Then she suddenly smiled and turned to me to say, "Ava told me something very secret about Mrs. Fennel a few days ago."

"Is that so?"

"Yes. It's something I bet you don't know."

"Stop it, Marla."

"Stop what?"

"This childish tit-for-tat. You don't know anything I don't know."

"Oh, really?" She sat there with that smile frozen on her face.

"Okay, what is it?" I reluctantly asked.

"I don't know if I'm supposed to tell you. Maybe Ava will get angry."

"Please, will you," I said, grimacing. "You're behaving like a spoiled little brat."

"Mrs. Fennel is Daddy's older sister," she blurted. "I bet you didn't know that. Well?"

I smiled. "Ava was just teasing you, Marla. She once told me Mrs. Fennel was Daddy's mother."

"No. She was teasing you. She wasn't teasing me. She trusts me more than she trusts you. She told me so."

"You had better stop this lying, Marla."

"I'm not lying. She said she and I have more in common. You can ask her yourself."

"Right. I might just do that, and then you'll be really sorry."

"I won't be sorry. Ava and I talk more than you know lately."

I didn't say anything, but I had a sick feeling at the

base of my stomach that she was telling the truth. My silence gave her more courage to continue her little taunting. She was more like Ava, all right, I thought. She had Ava's mean streak, especially whenever she was checked.

"I know something else you don't know," she sang. I didn't respond. "What do you think happened to Mrs. Fennel's husband, Lorelei?"

"You know?"

"Maybe," she said. "Yes, I do," she quickly added. "If you're nicer to me, I'll think about telling you."

"I'll hold my breath," I said.

When we pulled into the school parking lot and I shut off the engine, she turned to me and in her most whiny voice said, "I don't care if you hold your breath all day, Lorelei, but you'd better do exactly what you're supposed to do with that boy today."

Then she got out and walked ahead of me to the building.

How could Daddy ever think sibling rivalry was a good thing? I wondered, and got out.

When I reached the entrance, I was surprised to see Mark Daniels standing there. He opened the door quickly for me.

"Your majesty," he said, bowing. "I am at your royal service. Your wish is my command."

I looked past him and saw Marla standing near the corridor she was to take to homeroom. She was watching us, looking like an evil child spy.

"In that case," I said, walking past him, "I command you to leave me alone." I paused and looked back. "In short, forget about me."

I walked on, glaring back at Marla, who looked disappointed again. I was sure she had been hoping she would see something bad about me to tell Daddy.

She still had an opportunity for it, I thought later. Mark didn't scare off easily. Right after homeroom, he was beside me in the hallway. I tried to walk faster, but he stayed alongside me.

"What do you want?" I muttered.

"What you're asking for is impossible. It's against Mother Nature."

"Mother Nature?" I said, stopping and turning to him. The students around us paused as well because of how abruptly I turned and how loudly I spoke. "What stupid thing are you saying now?"

"The command to leave you alone, forget you," he said in a very calm voice. He shook his head and looked sad. "Can't be done. Every cell in my body, every beat of my heart, every corpuscle of my blood, is drawn to you the way nature intended. Even if I tried to forget you, my body wouldn't listen. You're like a beautiful magnet."

I stared at him. He had a soft smile on his face, but his eyes were full of deep, serious feeling. If Daddy saw this boy, I thought, he'd understand why doing what he asked me to do was so difficult. In fact, if Daddy had a son, his son would surely look and act like Mark Daniels.

"Listen to me," I said, imitating his soft tone but still speaking firmly. "I don't want to go out with you this Friday. I don't want you asking me to go out any Friday or any Saturday, ever. I would like you to leave me alone. Do you need that translated into any other language, or do you get the point?"

"That's very good," he said.

"What's very good?"

"Your performance, for I know it's a performance. You want to go out with me. I can see the struggle going on inside you. You're saying these things, but you're hoping I won't listen."

"Believe what you want," I said, and walked away, but my heart was pounding so hard I thought I might faint. The truth was he was right, but how would he know that and be so confident knowing it?

For most of the day, I assumed that was that. Despite what he hoped he saw in me, he had gotten the message loud and clear. I had turned him off, and he would leave me alone. I avoided looking at him, and whenever I did see him, he appeared to avoid looking at me. He didn't approach me again before lunch or in the cafeteria, but I could see that my outburst at him was the talk of the school. Some of those girls who I knew had been jealous of me from the start saw another chance to pounce. In P.E. class, Ruta Lee and a clump of her friends accused me of being gay.

"No one can come up with any other reason why you would blow off Mark Daniels," she said. "You don't date anyone. You refuse any other boy's invitations. This clinches it. It's all right if you want to be gay. We just want you to know we know and don't appreciate your staring at us when we change clothes in here."

All of her friends were grinning from ear to ear. I could hear Ava's words: "Daddy sees through my eyes, hears through my ears."

I nodded and stepped toward her. "Ruta," I said

softly, sympathetically, "we both know that you're saying this in front of your friends just because I rejected your advances in the girls' room. I'm right, aren't I?"

"What?" She turned red.

I looked at the others. The tone of my reaction and comment took them all by surprise. "Has Ruta approached anyone else? If so, you know what I'm talking about. I couldn't stop her in the bathroom. It was embarrassing." I looked at her again and shook my head, my face locked in a sad-serious expression. "The way you came at me, complimented me on my clothes, my makeup. Really, Ruta, you should return to the therapist you said you were seeing."

All the girls looked at her.

"I never saw any therapist. Shut up."

I sighed and shook my head at the other girls. "I thought she was having an orgasm in the toilet stall beside me. I was so afraid Mrs. Gilbert would walk in on us. Ruta hasn't noticed it, but Mrs. Gilbert has been very suspicious. She sees when you touch my hand in class, Ruta. I've asked you to stop."

"You're disgusting!" Ruta cried.

I didn't smile. One thing about accusations, I thought. You could always depend on them to ruin or weaken someone else. I could see the possibilities swimming in the eyes of her friends. Had she ever touched any of them in a suggestive way or talked about homosexuality, maybe even wondered aloud what it would be like? She wasn't very popular with boys. Would they think this might be why? She was the one who had used that to strengthen her accusations about me. As the

Wiccans warn their own: do evil to someone, and it can come back at you three times.

Ruta seemed to shrink back, her eyes revealing a new sense of desperation. "I wouldn't turn down Mark Daniels," she claimed, searching for a strong comeback. She looked at the other girls. "No one here would. That's for damn sure."

"That's not the issue here, is it? Now that you've brought it up, let's talk about it. Why wouldn't he or any other really good-looking boy in this school be after you? I'll tell you why, Ruta. Boys can sense when a girl's gay," I said, looking at the others and nodding. "It's instinctive."

I saw Ruta's eyes begin to tear. She looked as if she would turn and run.

"After all," I delivered as a final killing blow, "why would being gay be the first thing to come into your mind when you thought about attacking me just now? Anyone else think that?" I asked the others. One or two actually shook their heads. Ruta's lips began to tremble.

"That's ridiculous," Meg Logan said, stepping up to her defense.

"Is it? Haven't you slept overnight at Ruta's, Meg? Ruta told me how hot and heavy you two can get," I said. "Did you put her up to this? Was it because you were jealous of how strong her feelings have been for me?"

"What?"

Some of the other girls looked shocked.

"You bitch!" Ruta cried, and swung at me. I caught her wrist in midair and turned it sharply. She screamed, and I stepped forward, my face in hers so closely that, as Shakespeare would say, our breaths did kiss.

"Don't you dare make up any more stories about me," I said in a cold, gruff whisper. I felt more like Ava, the rage in me rising to the top and spilling out like milk boiling over in a pan. Ruta wilted with the pain. "If I hear that you are, I'll come see you in your sleep."

I let go of her and returned to my locker. No one spoke. Ruta turned away, rubbing her wrist. Meg started to put her arm around her to comfort her, but Ruta threw it off.

"Stop!" she cried.

I smiled to myself. How quickly an innocent gesture would look telling to the others. She had tried to poison them against me but only poisoned herself. I couldn't wait to tell Daddy all about this and how well I had handled it and Mark Daniels.

But Mark Daniels wasn't as discouraged as I had thought. He was right, though. Despite myself, I still felt a longing to be with him, to have fun together. Pressing all that down was like smothering a starving baby.

"Okay," he said, stepping up beside me as I made my way through the halls at the end of the day. "This is my final offer. Maybe they're more to your liking and you'll reconsider."

He handed me a slip of paper and walked faster. I watched him head toward the exit to the parking lot, and then I looked at the paper. He had listed four more personal references: Elvis Presley, the Beatles, the Rolling Stones, and Madonna.

It was certainly difficult being hard with him, I thought, laughing to myself, but one thing I knew for sure, I couldn't let Daddy know that.

"Well, what happened with him?" Marla asked me when we got into the car. "I saw him talking to you even after you told him off at the school entrance this morning."

"What, were you spying on me?" I thought for a moment. "Ava didn't tell you to do that, did she?"

"Maybe Daddy told me to do it."

"You're lying. I'm going to ask him, and he'll be enraged. You said it yourself. He wants us to look out for each other, not hurt each other."

"Nobody told me to do it. I'm just trying to be a good sister and help you," she whined. I had frightened her. "I'm sorry. I'm sorry."

I felt myself calm down. "It's over, Marla. Stop asking me about him."

"Good, but you don't sound happy," she said. "I'm just telling you as a good sister would. You'd better be careful."

I didn't speak for the remainder of the trip. When we arrived at home, Mrs. Fennel told me my father was waiting for me in the living room.

"Marla, you go to your room," she added. Marla's shoulders sank. She had so hoped to listen in on any discussion. Maybe she was afraid I would still tell Daddy what she had done and said.

"Tell me everything," Daddy said when I entered the living room. Dressed in his ruby velvet robe, he was sitting in his armchair. He put down the book he had been reading while waiting for me and folded his hands.

I told him what I had said to Mark and his reaction

and then how he had continued approaching me. "He kept kidding around about it, but I didn't smile or laugh at anything he said."

"Very persistent. Are you sure you were stern enough?"

"Oh, yes, Daddy," I said. I repeated the words I had used and then told him what had happened in the girls' locker room and how I had turned the tables on Ruta Lee. That brought a smile to his face.

"Very clever of you, Lorelei. But," he added with concern, "I don't want you getting into trouble at school. None of my girls gets into trouble like that and brings unpleasant attention to us. Ignore them from now on. Your days at that school are limited."

The way he said that made me think we might be moving again very soon.

"Are we moving?"

"Soon, yes."

"How soon?"

"I'm not sure yet, but don't worry about it, Lorelei. Moving at short notice is not a problem for any of us," he added. "Okay. You can go do your homework if you'd like."

"Is Ava back yet?"

"Not yet," he said. "She won't be at dinner, either."

*She's hunting,* I thought, and mentally counted the days. It was time. I didn't see or hear her until the middle of the night. Apparently, she had gone much farther for her catch this time.

To my surprise, Daddy wasn't at dinner, either. When I asked why not, Mrs. Fennel said he had things to do and wouldn't be home until late in the evening. Usually, she would just say, "He had things to do." I was sensitive to the fact that she was speaking to me more now. Something had changed between us. She wasn't sniping at me, and I thought I even saw her smile occasionally. There was no change in how she spoke or acted toward Marla.

Marla was quiet and solicitous at dinner. I thought she was still afraid I would tell Daddy how she had behaved and even some of the things she had said. It was clear also that Daddy was not unhappy with how I had handled things in school with Mark. She knew that eventually, as Ava had been my mentor, I would be hers. I saw how frightened she was now of my holding a grudge. I was pleasant to her but took advantage of her timidity and bullied her a little. It made me feel more and more like Ava, and I wondered if I was tumbling headlong into her persona. Perhaps it wouldn't be much longer before she would feel usurped and move on to fulfill her own destiny, whatever that was.

After dinner, Marla went right up to her room. She asked me to stop in to listen to some music with her after I had done my work, and I said I might. I lingered in the dining room for a few moments longer, and when Mrs. Fennel came in to start cleaning up, I rose to help her. She never tolerated any help unless we had company and she wanted us to make a good impression. Since my younger days helping her in her herbal garden, I had always been timid about doing anything to assist her. We were responsible for our own things and our own rooms, but she guarded the rest of the house as if it were her special kingdom. No one was to move anything ever and certainly we were never to touch the very valuable antique artifacts.

Most girls my age would have loved not having to do kitchen and housework. A number of them in my class came from families that had permanent maids, and some even had cooks. Ava never minded our arrangements, and Marla, who was often too lazy to care for her own things, loved not being asked to do anything else, but I had a different feeling about it. As strange it would sound to my classmates, being so unattached to caring for our home made me feel more like a tenant. I wanted to cherish our possessions, feel that they were part of who I was. Sometimes I felt as if I were in some shop or model home, looking at things the way customers might look at merchandise.

Mrs. Fennel glanced at me when I started to pick up plates to follow her into the kitchen, but, unlike after my other attempts, she didn't say, "Just leave it." She went into the kitchen and let me follow her. I put the plates down on the counter and went back into the dining room to bring in the rest. She was quiet and worked as I cleared the dining-room table. And then, in a very uncharacteristic soft tone of voice, she turned to me, smiled softly, and said, "You want to talk to me tonight?"

"Yes," I said, holding my breath.

"Return to the dining room," she said.

I did, and a few moments later, wiping her hands with a dish towel, she returned as well and sat in Daddy's seat.

She leaned forward and said, "Go ahead."

"Marla was being a little brat today," I said.

"Oh," she said, sitting back with a look of disappointment. "Is that what this is about?"

"No, no," I said quickly. "I'm not here to complain about her. I can handle Marla myself."

She smiled at that. "So, what is it?"

"She claimed Ava told her things, things about you."

"Did she?" She twisted her lips and then nodded. "Ava can be spiteful. She was like that with Brianna, too. None of you is perfect or as perfect as I would like."

"She said you were Daddy's sister."

She stared at me a moment and then nodded. "Your father has been moving you along a little faster than the others, so your learning what Ava learned when she was older than you is appropriate."

I held my breath. I had been waiting for this so long. How much would she tell me?

"Yes," she began. "I am your father's sister, but I am considerably older than he is."

"What are your ages?" I asked in a low, meek whisper.

She smiled at me, and it was one of the few times I had ever seen a warm, truly humorous smile on her face. It made her look younger, too. "You know what, Lorelei? We've lived so long that after a while, we lose track. Time isn't the same for us, anyway. We don't look for it on watches and on calendars. It doesn't move in increments. It all seems to stream, flow. It's like trying to find a single drop of water in a stream. Just know we've both been around a very long time. You'll understand someday."

It was going so well, I thought I would continue. "Ava knows who her mother was. She's angry about her. I'd almost say she hates the thought of her, blames her for dying. Is that true? Was her dying her own fault somehow?"

"No," Mrs. Fennel said. "A man like your father can have children with an ordinary woman, but she will always die in childbirth. He knew this. I don't want you talking to Ava about this anymore. Understand me?"

"Yes."

"Good. That's enough for now. Thank you for helping. Now, put all this away for now. You have a ways to travel yet before you can handle what more there is to learn and to do," she said.

I didn't get up immediately. I was trembling. My legs felt weak. Then I heard the door open and close and turned to see Daddy standing there.

"Why are you sitting by yourself in the dining room, Lorelei?"

"I . . ."

"She helped me with the cleanup, and then we had an important conversation," Mrs. Fennel said. I supposed I should be thinking of her as Aunt Razi, I thought, but I wouldn't, nor would I call her that until she told me it was okay to do so.

"Oh? That's good," Daddy said. I thought he looked tired. His shoulders sagged, and his face was darker. "We'll talk more tomorrow," he added, and headed upstairs. I looked quickly at Mrs. Fennel.

"Tend to your own duties now," she said, and returned to the kitchen.

I rose and went to my room. I heard Marla watching television in hers and started toward it but stopped. I really didn't feel like talking to her. I certainly didn't want her to ask me about any conversation I might have had with Mrs. Fennel. Instead, I went to my room and started my homework. I fell asleep once while I was reading and decided just to go to bed. There were so many different thoughts troubling me, but I did doze off.

The sound of a car door slamming woke me. I sat up to listen and, hearing nothing, went to my window. There was a strange car in the driveway. I saw no one near it, however, and went to my bedroom door. What surprised me was the sound of Ava's voice. She wasn't pleading so much as complaining. Her voice began to sound more strident. I stepped into the hallway and looked toward the entryway.

The young man Ava was with was obviously stoned. He was trying to get her to go right down on the floor with him. At one point, he simply sat at her feet and pulled on her arm to get her to join him. He was that out of it.

"I'm not climbing no stairway," he said. "This rug's about as soft as my bed."

"Stop it!" she cried.

He laughed, and then he paused as Daddy stepped forward. I hadn't heard him come down the stairway, either.

"What is this?" Daddy asked.

"Huh?" the man said. "Who's this?" He blinked his eyes and wiped his face.

"Is he on drugs? You brought me someone stoned?"

"I couldn't help it, Daddy," Ava said, sounding years younger. "He took something on the way up here. I didn't realize it until we were almost here."

"This is spoiled food, Ava. I can't feed on this tonight."

"What? What the hell's he talking about?" the young man asked, and struggled to get to his feet.

I never saw the blow. Daddy's hands could move that quickly. He struck him on the back of his neck, and the man folded to the floor. Then Daddy kneeled down and lifted him in his arms as if he were a child, when he looked to me to be more than six feet tall and easily more than two hundred pounds.

"I'll have to put him in storage until nearly morning," Daddy said sharply to Ava.

"I'm sorry, Daddy. We were just drinking earlier. I told him I didn't want to take anything, and I thought he understood, but . . ."

Daddy didn't wait for any further explanation. He turned and carried the young man toward the stairway. Ava stood there with her head down. She looked up when Daddy was nearly to the top, and then she started toward me.

"What happened?" I asked.

She glared at me for a moment. "You saw it. Why ask?"

"I don't . . ."

"Let me tell you something," she said, looking as if

she might actually cry. "If you thought you were moving too quickly and magically before, it will be nothing compared to how he'll move you along now."

"What do you mean?"

"I'm not little Miss Perfect anymore. You are, or you'd better be. The writing's on the wall, Lorelei, and it's in blood," she told me, and walked on to her room.

# 8

## Daddy Knows Best

The young man's car was gone in the morning. I didn't have to ask Mrs. Fennel why Daddy was still asleep, either. Even Marla looked tired that morning. I wondered if she had overheard anything or seen anything the night before, but as it turned out, she had simply stayed up too late watching television. Actually, I hadn't slept that well myself.

Ava's remarks to me had left me trembling. I tossed and turned, hearing her words echo in my head, and didn't fall asleep for hours. It left me depressed, and I wasn't very talkative in the car. I knew Marla thought I was still angry at her or that maybe I was worried about what might happen with Mark Daniels in school now. After we parked, she told me to come looking for her if I needed anything.

"I'm all right, Marla. Don't worry about me," I said.

"I'm not worrying about you. I'm worrying about us," she reminded me. So much for that sisterly feeling I had been hoping would develop between us.

Mark wasn't waiting for me at the door again and in fact, he was nearly late to school himself. All day, I anticipated him approaching me with some funny remark, but when I looked at him, he appeared depressed himself, walking with his head down and not volunteering any answers in any of our classes. I noticed that he wasn't very talkative with his friends, and he left lunch early. Just before the last period of the day, one of the boys who did hang with him, Jeff Kantor, came up beside me and said, "Mark's really taking your rejection hard. Don't look for him in class. He went home."

He continued walking past me.

I looked back to see if Mark was there and this was just another one of his jokes, but he wasn't anywhere in sight, and when class began, his desk remained empty. Could this be true? Would my rejecting him really disturb someone like Mark so much? Was I simply a failed conquest, or did he really have strong feelings for me? On the way home, I told Marla about it, simply because I was truly amazed.

"I can't help feeling a little sorry for him," I said.

"That's stupid, Lorelei. Maybe now he'll leave you be," she said. "Good work."

Good work? I had blown off the best-looking, most charming and delightful boy in the school. How could I make her understand? What would it have been like if I could have had a little high school romance? What would it have been like to be picked up for dates, go to movies and dinner, hang out together at the beach, or just take long rides? What would it have been like to have a date for a dance, go to parties at other kids' homes, talk on the phone, always be together in school, and maybe say dramatic things to each other?

Could I explain to her how I would be excited every morning and look forward to seeing him? I'd really care about what I wore and what I looked like, how I fixed my hair, what makeup and nail polish I used. I'd look and act like everyone else. Other girls would be envious of our relationship and be dying to ask me questions or just hear me talk about us. He'd invite me to dinner at his home, and I'd invite him to mine. We'd see the world through four eyes and not two, hear the world through four ears, feel it through twenty fingers, and smell it through two noses, all of it merging into one feeling, one reaction. We'd giggle about anything and everything, comfort each other whenever one of us was unhappy about something. I'd be beside him at school ball games. In short, we'd be an item, the perfect couple, instead of two separate souls meandering awkwardly through our lives as if we had lost our senses. Everything wouldn't be about only me.

Most of all, I'd feel even safer, more secure, knowing there were two strong arms ready to embrace me whenever I needed to be embraced when Daddy wasn't around. He wasn't with us every minute of the day, was he? I would have Mark's shoulder to lean on whenever I needed comfort.

*No, Marla,* I thought. *Although I can't explain it to you in a way you might appreciate, believe me, it wasn't good work. I did what I was told to do, but it didn't make me happier.* In fact, for the first time in my life, I wasn't happier that Daddy was pleased with me. It was a feeling I had never expected. It frightened me, because I thought Mrs. Fennel would take one look at my face and know.

She would tell Daddy, and they would have a serious discussion about me, about whether I was good enough to be one of his daughters after all.

I did my best to avoid her eyes without revealing that I was doing it. She didn't seem to notice any difference in me. Daddy was still sleeping, of course. Ava had gone to class. Marla asked me to help her with some homework. I was happy to, because it kept me from thinking about everything. She started to ask me about Mark again, expecting to hear how happy I was now, but I cut her off.

"It's better if we both just forget about him, Marla. It's not good to bring him up. Daddy wouldn't like it," I added to put a firm period to my sentence.

She nodded and returned to her work. I had shut Mark out of her mind, but I hadn't been able yet to shut him out of mine. I wondered what he was doing now. Had his parents noticed how upset he was? Did they ask him about it? What sort of a relationship did he have with them? Would he confide in his father, perhaps, tell him about this beautiful girl in school who completely rejected him? Look for sympathy, advice? Would his father tell him something that would renew his hope, and would he try again if and when he returned to school tomorrow? What would I do then? Would Daddy tell me to go to the dean? Would some invisible circle be drawn around me that Mark was never to cross? How stupid would all of this make me look? How much more difficult would it be for me to continue at the school? Ultimately, would Daddy take me out, and if he took me out, wouldn't he have to take Marla out as well? It was all so troubling.

Just before dinner, Ava came to my room. She had a

no-nonsense look on her face, as if she had come to the end of her patience.

"What happened with this boy?" she demanded.

I told her everything, except, of course, how I really felt about it.

"That's such a crock of crap," she said. "It's another ploy to get at you. He's playing for sympathy. Don't even acknowledge that you realized he was gone. That will drive it home like a stake through his heart."

She sounded so bitter, so angry. I wondered how she would feel if she saw him, met him. Would she at least understand why I wasn't happy?

"You really and truly never regretted not having a boyfriend in high school, Ava?"

"No. They were all too immature for me. And where was I going with it if I started a high school romance? What was true for me is true for you, Lorelei. Don't you realize that yet?"

"I do. I just wondered."

She gave me one of her scrutinizing looks again, the sort that made my insides curl.

"What?"

"Maybe . . . maybe you should ask Daddy about all this," she suggested. The threat and implication that lay beneath that idea were clear. "Maybe he should know you have these thoughts."

"You mean you won't go running off to tell him?" I shot back at her.

"No need to," she said with a crooked smile. "You know Daddy can see through you, can see through all of us."

Why was she being like this? Was she taking out on me what happened to her last night, how she had angered Daddy? Did she think because I was able to do what Daddy wanted and she had blundered that now he would favor me even more? As long as I could remember, she had been afraid of that. She was even afraid that Mrs. Fennel would like me more, if that was possible. Now I was the one who felt a little impish.

"Mrs. Fennel told me things yesterday," I said spitefully. "Without my asking."

"Oh? What things?"

"Things about herself, mostly."

"Oh," she said, as if that wasn't anything.

"And about your mother."

Her eyebrows nearly jumped over her forehead. "What did she say?"

"Only what you know, Ava. Her dying wasn't her fault. Daddy knew what would happen to her. Now I know the truth as well."

"Good for you," she said. "Now you know."

"She told me she was Daddy's older sister."

"Did she?"

"You knew that. You told Marla. Why didn't you tell me?"

"Didn't I?"

"You know you didn't, Ava."

She shrugged. "What difference does it make?" She started to turn away to leave, paused, and turned back. "You know why you're learning more things now, don't you?"

I didn't want to say it, but I knew, deep down I knew, but was still trying to keep it buried.

"It's coming soon, Lorelei. Your time is coming soon. This is what happened when my time was coming, too. You'll be graduated, licensed, turned loose to be Daddy's most cherished daughter, just like I was. Only," she added, "I think I was more ready when my time came than you are." She shrugged. "But Daddy knows best," she said, and left.

Every religion, practically every culture, had rituals to mark the maturity of a young person, the entrance to adulthood and more responsibility. Parents and other adults would look differently at them, look at them with more respect, and expect more from them. While a young girl or boy might be nervous about it, she or he certainly didn't fear it. Ava made my coming of age sound more like a threat. There would be no party, no celebration of any kind. We'd have no cake, no friends to share in the special moment.

One morning, I'd wake up and discover Ava was gone. The great weight of responsibility for Daddy's life would be on my shoulders. I'd be the one thrust out there in the darkness. I'd be the one who would work her sexiness and charm like some deep-sea fisherman working his line and reel. I'd cast myself into the waters and land some great catch, some unsuspecting young man lusting after the hook, completely unaware of how sharp and deadly was its point.

Instead of feeling that she was being rushed along because I was being rushed along, I wished Ava would be more sensitive to my feelings and fears. I wished she would really be my older sister and spend time with me, talking to me, reassuring me, convincing me I was ready.

Wasn't that what Daddy would want her to be doing? Should I complain to him? Would that do any good?

There was no talk of any of this at dinner. Marla went on with a nonstop description of her school day and how boring the kids in her class were. I knew she was doing the same thing I had been doing before now. She was trying to justify not having anything to do with any of her classmates or participating in any of their events by denigrating them, making them sound like complete un-desirables. Maybe it made her feel better for a little while, just as it had made me feel better, but that wouldn't last. I wanted to tell her, but I knew that would bring down thunder and lightning, especially from Ava.

After dinner, I watched some television with Marla, both of us putting off doing any more schoolwork. Ava had shut herself off in her room. I had no idea what she was doing, what she was feeling after what had hap-pened to her last night. She had no best friend to talk to on the phone, and even if she had one, she certainly couldn't have talked to her about any of this. There was only me now. Why didn't she see that? Why was she so hard? I certainly would go to her, even now, even after the nasty things she had said.

We were different in many ways, and not all of them made her better than me or more equipped for whatever futures awaited us. She wasn't anywhere near as good a reader as I was, nor was she as interested in reading or art and music. I never heard her talk about a movie she had seen or a television show. Despite the act she put on for me, for everyone, I thought, Ava was the loneliest person I knew.

Was that what awaited me, loneliness? If ever I had wanted to talk with Daddy, to hear him say comforting, wonderful things, it was tonight. Every once in a while, I looked out toward the stairway, expecting him to come down, but he hadn't by the time I decided to go to my room to finish up what work I had left. Marla lingered behind me for a while. I heard her go to her room. All three of us had our doors shut, each of us locked away as if we enjoyed solitude. I knew I didn't.

Although I wasn't tired enough to sleep, I went to bed and just lay there staring up at the ceiling, listening for any creak in the floor above, any sign that Daddy had awakened. The house was so quiet. I was reminded of so many nights like this when I was much younger. Marla wasn't here yet, and Brianna was still with us. Neither she nor Ava would spend many nights doing anything with me. Now that I thought about it, I had never realized how lonely I already was back then, how much I depended on Daddy to come by or ask me to do something with him. No wonder he had become my whole life. Our talks, the gifts he gave me, the clothing and jewelry, the books he told me to read, all of it made up the foundation of what I had in the way of family events and pleasure. Later, when I attended school and saw and heard how much other girls my age were doing and enjoying, I did feel my isolation more, but Daddy seemed always to be there to help keep me from sinking too low.

Could he help me now, now that I was older and needed him even more? At least, I thought I did. According to Ava, I would soon be so independent I would need no one and nothing I didn't get for myself. There was that moment coming for her, the same moment that had come for Brianna, when she would break away, leave us, leave Daddy. Brianna had not come back for even a day. Would that be true for Ava as well? Could I do that, leave and never see Daddy again? Right now, I didn't see how.

These depressing thoughts weighed heavily on me. I grew tired. *That's good,* I thought. I wanted to go to sleep and forget. Mornings always made things look better. Tomorrow, I hoped, would be no different. *Good night, Daddy,* I thought, looking up at the ceiling.

Just as I reached to turn off the lamp on my side table, I heard what sounded like scratching on one of my bedroom windows. At first, I thought it might just be the branch of an untrimmed bush caught in a twisted wind, but when I looked, I saw the clear outline of someone standing in the shadow just outside. He was in darkness, so I could not make out anything else about him. Was he a ghost or one of those young men I had once seen in a nightmare? When he tapped on the glass, he brought himself closer, and I gasped.

It was Mark.

How had he found out where we lived? I had told no one at school, and Marla certainly wouldn't have told anyone. It was one of the most forbidden things to do. He tapped again, much louder this time. I got out of bed quickly, fearful that he would draw someone else's attention. He stepped back as I opened the window softly. He was wearing a black leather jacket and black pants to camouflage himself in the darkness. I looked past him and didn't see any car.

"How did you get here?"

"I walked, miles."

"Why? What are you doing here?"

"I was rereading *Romeo and Juliet,* and I thought I'd come to plead at your balcony, but you're on the first floor," he said. "How can I be dramatic if you sleep on the first floor?" He looked up as if we had a balcony and reached toward it. "Lorelei, Lorelei, where art thou?"

"Shut up, you idiot. How did you find out where I live?"

"A determined lover would find ways," he replied. "Come out with me for a little while."

"Are you crazy? You're going to wake my family and get me into big trouble. Go away, Mark."

"I can't," he said. "Your beauty has paralyzed me. I can't even move, especially now that I see you in your nightgown, your face glowing with the starlight."

"How did you know which room was my bedroom?"

"The heart knows exactly where to go, Lorelei. Lorelei. Your name is magical, melodic. I'm drunk on the sound of it. Come out with me. Just for a little while. Give me a chance to win your heart."

"No," I said. "You'll get me into very big trouble now. Please leave before it's too late."

"It's already too late," he said, moving closer. "I'm no longer in control of myself. I can't help myself. I can't leave unless you come out and spend a few minutes with me. Come." He beckoned. "Come out, Lorelei. Enjoy the night air, look up at the stars, and dream a little dream with me. Come out. I promise I'll leave, but you won't want me to leave. Parting, remember, is such sweet sorrow."

His words were suddenly mesmerizing. He reached in and gently took my hand.

"Come," he urged. "Please."

I felt myself moving toward him. His eyes were suddenly luminous, a soft blue. He brought his left hand to my shoulder.

"I'll lift you out. In my arms, you will be as air," he said, and his hands went to my waist. I could feel his fingers tightening. He brought his face closer, his lips inviting mine, and then, just slightly at first, I saw his teeth, sharp, pointed, growing.

What happened next happened so quickly that I questioned whether it had happened at all. A darker, thicker shadow fell over Mark and then metamorphosed into Daddy. He was bigger and wider than I had ever seen him, even when I saw him that time when I was only four. He enveloped Mark as if his body had turned into a great cape and lifted him away from my window. Mark's grip around my waist loosened quickly, so quickly I thought his fingers had turned into water.

I didn't hear a groan so much as a muffled scream. I stood there captivated by the struggle that went on in front of me. It didn't last long, I'm sure, but it seemed to go on and on. Daddy's grip on Mark was too iron-clad. He gave up trying to break out of it and instead pushed against Daddy's face in a desperate attempt to keep Daddy's teeth from reaching him.

It was as if Daddy were struggling with a clump of butter, however. He moved swiftly, undeterred, until he was on Mark's neck. Then I heard the scream, the piercing sound that vibrated everything around them, made trees tremble, woke sleeping birds, and seemed to shatter the stars. Mark folded just the way a punctured balloon might. He seemed to lose all his bones, his skeleton crumbling into dust under his skin.

Daddy held him in his arms like a bag of clothes, turned, and glanced at me. I was unable to move. Daddy's face was so distorted, every feature widened and stretched. Although there was no anger in it directed at me, it was still terrifying to see. I tried to swallow back the gasp that was stuck in my throat, but it wouldn't move. He said nothing. He simply turned and walked into the darkness.

Moments later, the door opened, and Ava came in. She turned on the lights. Never had I seen her look this frightened, this close to tears. She stood there in her nightgown, staring at me and the window, seemingly unable to move. Before I could say anything, Mrs. Fennel came in behind her, glanced at her, and then walked over to the window and closed it.

"Go back to bed, both of you," she said.

I started for mine, but Ava didn't move.

"Ava!" she shouted. "Go!"

Ava woke from her trance. She looked at me and then turned and left the room.

"You won't be taking Marla to school tomorrow," Mrs. Fennel said.

"What happened?" I asked. Was I awake? Was this a nightmare?

"You'll learn everything tomorrow. It's over. Don't worry. Just get some sleep."

"Get some sleep?" I almost laughed. "How do you expect me to go to sleep now?"

She didn't answer. Instead, she went into my bathroom, got a glass of water, and returned, handing me a tablet. "Take it. You'll sleep enough. Go on," she ordered.

I plucked it out of her palm and swallowed it with some water.

"Is Daddy all right?"

She turned off my light.

"Is he?" I cried out.

"Yes," she said, and left me in the dark. I gazed at my closed bedroom window. She hadn't seen it or didn't care right now, but there was a splatter of blood on the glass. I turned my back to it and closed my eyes. I pressed on my eyelids to keep them from springing open. It was still too terrifying.

There was no one in the room, no one to hear me, but I asked anyway.

"What just happened?"

# 9

## Nightmare

When I awoke, I just lay there looking up at the ceiling. I wanted everything that had happened last night simply to be a nightmare. As with any nightmare, it would linger a while, but it would soon dissipate like smoke and even be hard to recall. I would go to school and see Mark winking at me in the hallway, pretending to be suffering because of my rejecting him, and later find him passing me a note full of additional personal references. I would laugh at it. I would continue to obey Daddy and keep Mark at bay, of course, but that didn't mean I couldn't enjoy the game, the tantalizing and dangerous game that, despite all the restrictions, filled my day with some excitement.

I would tell no one about the nightmare, because that would only keep it alive. I didn't want to see those images ever resurrected, but it wasn't easy to push them aside. He had looked so gallant, exciting, and romantic to me. His voice had been softer, his lips so inviting. And when he put his hands on my waist and began to lift me out of the window, I felt myself softening, losing all forms of resistance, and eager to be taken.

Every sexual impulse that had tantalized me and

drawn me toward a deeper longing and desire had come alive and was now full blown, screaming to be acknowledged and served. I so wanted to be a slave to my sex and let it, like some invisible strong hand, seize my spine and whip me about until it had shaken any and all restraint from my body, reluctance pouring out of every cell until I was completely lost in Mark's kiss.

Surely, no young woman was ever mesmerized more quickly and then more willing to give herself completely. A look across a room, a glance with an accompanying sexy smile, a kiss blown through pursed lips, a soft whisper caressing her ear, sent a tingling from her breasts to her thighs and made her weak and hungry for love, but none of that came close to the power of Mark's voice, Mark's magnetic eyes.

I wanted him in me, part of me, absorbing and controlling me. I wanted him to put me on like a glove and hold me against his chest and heart for as long as he liked. No warnings, no lessons in prudence, could withstand the onslaught of wave after wave of his sex growing harder and deeper inside me. And not once during all of this did I think I was losing anything of myself. Not once did I feel the slightest abuse or imagine the slightest regret. *I am where I was meant to be, longed to be,* I thought. *Take me. Take me now.*

I was lost in the fantasy for a few moments, but happily lost. It filled me with warmth. I felt as if I were snuggling in my large comforter, even though I had begun to roll it away. I thought about remaining in bed longer, but then I turned slightly and saw the blood on the window again. It was as if a rock had been thrown through it, the shattering shards flying all about. Cold air came charging in behind it, pouring over my warm, sensual thoughts and feelings, drowning them, extinguishing them the way a fireman's hose would extinguish a fire.

I heard my door opening. Mrs. Fennel stood there looking in at me.

"Still in bed? Your father is waiting for you in the living room," she said. There was nothing in her voice to indicate anger or sadness.

"Is everyone else up?"

"Dressed and waiting," she said, and left.

I got out of bed quickly, went into the bathroom to rinse my face in cold water, and then barely ran a brush through my hair before hurrying to slip on a pair of panties, get into my jeans, and throw on a school sweatshirt while sliding my feet into a pair of sandals. I stepped into the hallway and paused, realizing how very quiet it was. Usually, by this time, I would hear Marla talking or some sounds coming from the kitchen. I practically ran toward the living room. When I entered, I found Ava sitting on the sofa with Marla. Mrs. Fennel was in Daddy's favorite chair, and he was standing with his arms folded, gazing out the window, his back to everyone. Rarely was Mrs. Fennel there with us when we sat with Daddy. Daddy turned when I entered. They all looked quite glum.

"I'm sorry, Daddy. I didn't mean to oversleep, but I didn't sleep that well, and . . ."

Ava groaned at my frantic explanation.

"Just sit, Lorelei," Daddy said, nodding at the sofa. Marla moved over a little to make more room for me. I looked up at him with anticipation. Mrs. Fennel was staring ahead as if she were lost forever in a trailing thought. She didn't blink. Not a muscle moved in her face. For a moment, I thought her face was shattering and crumbling away.

"All right now," Daddy continued, stepping closer to us. "Ava knows most of what I am going to tell you about all this. Normally, I would wait with both of you until your times had come, but . . ."

"But this is the first time we've been attacked at home," Mrs. Fennel added, looking impatient.

"Exactly," Daddy said. "He was quite emboldened."

"It's her fault," Ava muttered, nodding in my direction. "She must not have ended it sharply and firmly enough."

"We don't have time for that right now," Daddy snapped at her. "And anyway, last night can't be her fault if she didn't know what to watch for, can it, Ava? Can it?"

"No. I guess not," she said, but she didn't look as if she believed it.

"I don't understand, Daddy. Who was Mark Daniels?" I asked. I had been going to ask *what* was Mark Daniels?

"He was a member of a renegade family," he said. "That's a family like us who do not follow the rules. Every family has its own territory. These things are decided in advance. There's good planning here, careful planning. No other family must set down in the territory claimed by another. For two families to be there, to operate there, would do much to bring more and possibly fatal attention to us. There are other rules. No daughter is ever to be chosen to be a victim. Once something like that occurs, there are power struggles. We end up destroying ourselves. The renegades don't care."

"There's something wrong with them," Mrs. Fennel said, her teeth clenched. "They have a ruthless bloodlust. One feeding a month is never enough."

"I've called some of the elders to meet here today," Daddy continued. "You will tell them how this boy pursued you. Describe it in whatever detail you can recall. They have to understand that this was a justifiable act of self-defense, and everyone must be warned. Normally, we don't do to each other what he was out to do to you and I had to do to him."

"And we like to keep track of their movements," Mrs. Fennel said. "To warn the others."

I glanced at Marla. She looked terribly confused. She hadn't seen any of it and wasn't sure exactly what Daddy meant by all of this, although she sensed we had all been in some terrible danger last night.

Was it my fault? Was Ava right? Had I endangered us all somehow? But how? What could Ava possibly point to that I had done? I had never told him anything specific about us. The truth was, I never had a conversation with him that was more than a few minutes long.

"I never saw anything in him that would lead me to believe he would . . . that he was . . . what he was, Daddy. There were no hints, nothing in what he said or how he looked at me, that would have revealed such a thing."

"I would have seen it if he had approached me in school," Ava said.

"You are a lot more advanced than she is, Ava," Mrs. Fennel said.

"I'm not talking about now. I'm talking about when I was her age," Ava said, taking a much sharper tone with Mrs. Fennel than I had ever seen her take.

"Well, we don't know that to be true, since it never happened to you, now, do we?" Mrs. Fennel insisted.

I raised my eyebrows. I would never expect Mrs. Fennel to retreat, but it did surprise me that she was coming to my defense so strongly.

"None of that is the point now, Ava!" Daddy shouted. Ava wilted and lowered her head. "The point," he continued in a much calmer tone, "is that we'll have to be a lot more aware now, a lot more alert. They know by now that he failed last night. They'll either move on or return for revenge."

"You can never tell what renegades will do," Mrs. Fennel added, nodding. "Usually, they are a cowardly bunch. Whenever they're discovered where they shouldn't be and they're threatened, they retreat. That's what makes what happened last night unusual. He had the courage to come right to our door, practically."

"Window," Ava muttered. "Her window."

"I swear, I never told him where we live, Daddy."

"He didn't need you to tell him."

"Maybe he followed us home one day," Marla said. Even though she didn't know all the grisly details, she was eager to make a contribution.

"Maybe," Daddy agreed. She smiled, pleased that she might have made some significant input to the discussion.

"What do we do now, Daddy?" I asked. "I mean, what do we look for in the people we meet?"

"I'm afraid Ava's right when it comes to that," he said. Ava had that self-satisfied expression on her face. She looked redeemed. "It's something that grows inside you, this instinct for survival, our special survival. I'm sure you'll develop it soon, but in the meantime . . . well, I don't want you to become paranoid, of course, but . . ."

"Trust no one," Mrs. Fennel said. "Assume no one is innocent."

"How did he know to target me, Daddy? I'm not that much different from the other girls at school."

"Is she kidding? Are you kidding?" Ava asked me. Ava looked at Daddy as if she expected he would elaborate more on what she was saying.

"Let's not go into this any further right now," he said. Ava looked disappointed. "I am expecting our people in about an hour, so have your breakfast and relax. I don't want to hear any bickering," he warned, looking more at Ava. "We're united, one, when it comes to this sort of thing."

Mrs. Fennel rose. "Everything's been put out for your breakfast," she said.

The three of us got up to go to the dining room. Daddy lingered, turned, and went back to the window. If they were going to seek revenge, did he expect they would come this soon? Had what happened last night been what he was always worrying would happen? Was this the sort of thing he would pause to listen for? Were these so-called renegades always after one of us? Why was it my luck to have it happen to me? Why hadn't it happened to Ava? Maybe then she wouldn't be so damn arrogant, I thought.

None of us talked much at breakfast, even though

Marla wanted to know more details. Daddy never came in. I returned to my room and waited until Mrs. Fennel came to get me.

"They're here," she said. "You know some of them, of course. Just do what your father said. Tell them what happened."

I nodded and followed her out to the living room. Four of the elders had arrived. I recognized Mr. Biggi and Mrs. Everstreet. They had both been here many times before and brought both me and Marla presents. We called them Uncle and Aunt. Mr. Biggi was as kindly to us as any grandfather would be. He had a full head of thick white hair, a robust complexion, and a firm, self-confident posture. Like Daddy's age, his was impossible to determine. Despite the soft, light wrinkles around his eyes, his eyes were as bright as a newborn baby's.

Aunt Everstreet, on the other hand, looked more like Mrs. Fennel, tall and slim, with a habitual hardness in her face. Her nose was not as pointed or her chin as pronounced as Mrs. Fennel's, but she seemed to have the same eyes and spoke with the same sharp confidence, projecting that no-nonsense demeanor. She was always happy to see us, however. This morning, she looked more serious than ever.

I was introduced to Mr. Taggert and Mr. White. Both looked younger than Mr. Biggi and Mrs. Everstreet but much older than Daddy. I thought I had seen Mr. White before, maybe when I was only five or six. He looked more nervous than any of the others.

Daddy sat in his chair. "This is Lorelei, you'll all remember," he said.

Mr. Biggi was the only one who smiled at me. The others nodded and quickly sat.

"Okay," Daddy said. He wanted me to remain standing in front of them. He turned to me. "Begin with the first day he approached you."

I didn't know how detailed I should be, but I even described what he had been wearing. I told them the things he had said as best as I could recall, and I even told them about his joke with the personal references.

Mrs. Everstreet asked me to describe his face in as much detail as I could. I didn't want to say it, but his eyes drew my attention so hard and fast that it was almost as if I didn't notice the other features. She asked me about his hands, too, which I thought odd. There was nothing unusual about them that I could recall.

"I didn't hold hands with him ever," I said when she asked if his palms were soft and smooth.

They were all silent for a moment.

"The Ilks had a son who fits that description," Mr. White said. "Remember that incident in Pittsburgh?"

"Yes, but that was some time ago. In fact, I haven't heard anything about them for more than fifty years, I think," Mr. Biggi said. "Tell us exactly what happened last night," he told me.

I was a little hesitant, afraid that they would all see how weak I was, how I had almost been drawn out of my window. When I was finished, they were all quiet a moment. Then Uncle Biggi looked at Daddy.

"That was very close. Do you think you might want to move on, Sergio?"

"Absolutely not immediately. I've never run from any

of them before, and I'm not about to now. I'll consider when things calm down," he said. "Lorelei has farther to go in her education," he added.

No one had to tell me that he didn't mean my school education.

"Everything's been going fine here until this incident," he continued. "You'll all get the news out. It's important that everyone understand that what was done had to be done. No one here is trying to do or be anything more."

"I strongly doubt anyone would suspect you of that, Sergio," Mr. Biggi said. He looked to Mr. Taggert, who had yet to say anything.

"However, if they farm here," Mr. Taggert said, "it will be very bad, Sergio, very difficult for you to continue."

"Well," Daddy said, softening a bit, "not right away. It's a city, a huge population, from which we draw."

"You're not saying there's room for them, are you?" Mrs. Everstreet said. "Remember what happened in Paris just ten years ago."

I looked at Daddy. What had happened in Paris?

He glanced at me. "Thank you, Lorelei. You can go do what you like now," he said.

I rose.

"You're looking quite beautiful," Mr. Biggi said. "You're surely going to be one of your father's favorites."

"Quite striking, Sergio. Don't risk losing her," Mr. Taggert said.

"I won't," Daddy said sharply. He looked at me with an expression that said, *Go.*

I returned to my room. Ava was waiting there for me, standing by the window and staring at the bloodstain Mrs. Fennel had not yet washed away. Maybe she wanted it to be there forever as a reminder for me.

"What happened?" Ava asked.

I told her about the questions and what I had told them.

"I think Uncle Biggi wanted us to move," I said.

"Really. What did Daddy say?"

"He was adamant that we wouldn't."

"Good. Uncle Biggi is a wimp. Brianna never liked him, either." She looked at me harder for a moment, and then her eyes softened. "I've got to spend more time with you now, and you with me, Lorelei. Some of this is my fault."

I didn't say anything. Lately, I thought we were becoming more and more estranged and I thought that she resented me. I was happy to hear that she wanted us to spend more time together.

"We'll do something together this weekend. Just something sisterly," she quickly added.

"Okay. I'd like that."

"I'm taking you two to school and picking you up on Monday. It might be a strange day there."

"How do you mean?"

"How do I mean?" She rolled her eyes. "Mark Daniels won't be there, Lorelei. He doesn't come back."

"Oh. Right. I wasn't thinking of that."

She shook her head. "I'm not criticizing you," she said, "and I'm not speaking like some jealous sister, but you either are ignoring your powers of foresight or you don't have them. Later," she said before I could respond, and left.

What she said brought back a fear I'd had ever since I could remember. I didn't have the same confidence she had and, from what I could remember of Brianna, she had as well. Even Marla had more confidence than I had. They were all secure in their faith in themselves, in their belief that they would please and satisfy Daddy. They would live up to his expectations. I looked for some self-doubt in Ava but never found it. I was simply more afraid than they ever were that I would not be the daughter Daddy expected.

Nothing more was said about Daddy's meeting with the elders or what had happened the night before. We all went about our business as if nothing unusual had happened. Only I seemed to be thinking about it, but perhaps that wasn't unusual. I was the one he had come after, and I was the one who was almost lost. A few times, I approached Daddy with the intention of apologizing, but I didn't know for what. I wanted to thank him as well, but he didn't look as if he wanted to hear any more about it, so I retreated from that idea.

On Monday morning, as she had promised, Ava drove Marla and me to school.

"What you do now," she told me as we drove, "is be just as surprised as anyone else that Mark Daniels isn't there. If asked, you just say that you don't know anything. He never called you, nor did you ever see him anywhere but in the building. Don't say anything else or encourage any further discussion, understand?"

"Yes, Ava."

"However, if you overhear anyone else speak about him, especially his family, you listen carefully. Daddy would want to hear about that."

Mark's absence wasn't really noticed until the third day. Chatter had begun lightly but really broke out into full interest by then. From what I overheard, no one really knew that much about his family. Curtis Simon, an African American who was probably going to be the class valedictorian, seemed to know the most about Mark and his family. I sat close enough to him and his friends at lunch one day to overhear him say that while he had never met anyone else in Mark Daniels's family, he had once been at his home in Westwood.

"Actually," he told the others, "it looked like no one else lived there. He never talked about his parents much at all."

I saw him look my way.

And then, in a loud voice, he added, "He was probably so brokenhearted he couldn't go on attending school here."

Everyone laughed.

Later that afternoon, Curtis approached me in the hallway and asked me if I knew anything about Mark's disappearance.

"Did he call you or anything and tell you he would be leaving?"

"Mark never called me," I said. "I never gave him my phone number. Maybe his father lost his job or something. I couldn't care less," I added, and walked away.

"Well, pardon me, Miss Hot Ass!" he shouted after me.

If anything, all this did was alienate me more from

the rest of the student body. The only one who seemed to notice, however, was Mr. Burns. He asked me if there was anything wrong, anything he could help me with.

"I'm fine," I told him.

"You come to me if you need anything," he said. "Anything at all, Lorelei. You wrote a very good paper on Lady Macbeth," he added.

I thanked him but tried to avoid his eyes and his interest in me the rest of the week. Word finally spread that Mark Daniels's family had moved away. When I arrived home, I immediately told Daddy. He was in the kitchen talking with Mrs. Fennel. They both looked at me and were quiet for a moment.

"Well, maybe it's over, then," Daddy finally said. He smiled. "Let's just continue as if none of it ever happened."

I looked at Mrs. Fennel. She was studying me so hard my heart began to race.

"Okay, Daddy," I said.

When I stepped into my room, I looked at the bedroom window through which I had almost been pulled into oblivion.

The bloodstains were finally gone.

# 10

## Back to Normal

Ava was true to her word. Suddenly, she wanted to include me in everything she was doing. We went shopping together to keep up with some of the latest fashions. Ava was far more of a fashion guru than I was, but in her way of thinking, it was all work-related.

"Daddy places no limits on our budget because he wants us to be walking sticks of dynamite out there," she said, half kidding. She looked at me and added, "Neither of us really has to depend on clothes, though, Lorelei. But why not take advantage?" She laughed. It was good to hear her laugh and, more important, to have her include me in everything she thought for herself.

Sometimes we just took rides with no particular destination in mind. She would pop her head in my doorway and say, "Let's get some fresh air."

I loved that, because just cruising was conducive to talking, to exchanging thoughts and ideas the way sisters should. I learned a lot about her youth during those rides, how she had always been so envious of Brianna, until that night when Brianna made the mistake with the married man. She had often questioned me about it when I was younger, acting as if she was unhappy that she had not been the one to have actually seen it all. I would have gladly changed places with her.

"I told myself I would never disappoint Daddy like that, if I could help it," Ava said. "Of course, I did with that stoned man," she sadly admitted.

"He's forgiven you," I told her.

"Maybe. In any case, Lorelei, Daddy forgives only once. Remember that."

I didn't want to ask her what that meant, what would happen if she or I seriously upset Daddy more than once. At this point in my life, I couldn't imagine Daddy ever being so angry at me that he would disown me. When I was younger, I had had those fears, but I felt closer to him now, and although I wouldn't say it to Ava, I did still feel that I was his special daughter.

We continued to have these good, intimate talks. Sometimes we just sat on the beach in Santa Monica and watched people sailing or simply sunned ourselves. She became more and more open about her own feelings while growing up with Brianna still in the house.

"I learned a lot just watching her, despite my young age. That's what I mean by instinct," she said, but she went on to describe her own days of doubt and difficulty, especially when it came to Mrs. Fennel, whom she now admitted she obeyed more out of fear than respect.

"I mean, I respect her because Daddy has such high regard for her, but I won't miss her when I leave."

"When will you leave, Ava?"

"When Daddy says it's time," she said. She turned to me. "And that depends on you."

I didn't say anything, but I nodded.

"Don't worry. You'll do fine," she said. She reached for my hand and smiled. For a while, it was as if we were no different from any other two young women, young sisters opening up their intimate thoughts and feelings.

We continued to spend time together. We went to movies, flirted a bit with boys in the malls, and enjoyed our shopping sprees, sometimes just buying silly hats or purses. Marla was upset that she wasn't included, but Ava got around that by telling her that I would do exactly with her what she was now doing with me. Once again, she heard that familiar expression, the one I had grown up with: "Your time will come. Be patient."

Daddy stayed home more, too, and soon he was doing more things with us, things that included Marla anyway. When spring break came, he took the three of us to San Francisco. We had a wonderful time doing what he called the "Tourist Polka," and we had some fun food for a change, without Mrs. Fennel looking over our shoulders. We spent a day in Carmel and then drove down the coast and saw Big Sur. Daddy also decided we would go to the Hearst Castle on the way home. He had been in many, many castles and made comparisons for us, sometimes with very descriptive details about the art, the interiors, and the grounds, including the plants and trees.

"How can you remember so much?" I asked him.

"I don't know, Lorelei. I just do. There are many things I don't understand about myself," he revealed.

Ava overheard his answer. I saw her eyebrows lift. I understood why. Daddy never admitted to any weaknesses or flaws. This sounded a bit as if he was doing just that, and for us that was extraordinary.

The vacation flew by too quickly. I had never felt more like part of a family and hated to see it end. Although Daddy was sweet to all three of us, he once again singled me out to take me for a walk on our last night of the vacation. We had driven down to Santa Barbara, and after dinner, he had come to Marla's and my room in the hotel. Ava had her own room. Marla was already in her pajamas in bed watching television.

"Step out with me for a while," he told me, and I did. We were staying at a hotel right across from the beach, so it took us just a few minutes to be there.

He reached for my hand, and for a while, we just walked quietly, the two of us. I imagined that people seeing us might think we were lovers instead of father and daughter. Maybe that was wishful thinking. The moon painted a silvery sliver of light over the ocean. I remarked about it, and Daddy said it reminded him of an old Japanese haiku, a three-line poem about a butterfly that died on the water but thought it had died on the moon.

"You understand?" he asked.

"Yes. It died on the reflected light. Fish out there probably think they're swimming on the moon tonight," I added, and he laughed.

"You are brighter than any other daughter I've had, Lorelei," he said. I blushed with pride.

To the right and left of the moon, the stars blinked, and the lights of a commercial jet flickered as it crossed the sky to head east. Toward the horizon, we could see an oil tanker moving so slowly that it seemed painted on the ocean.

"When you were little, you told me the night sky was a dark blanket with tiny holes in it. You said that behind it was this second sky of bright light."

"I did?"

"It made sense to me," he said.

We never spoke about heaven and earth, God and the devil, or anything religious that other families discussed or believed. It was part of Daddy's philosophy that everything just is, and it's futile for us to try to explain it.

"We don't need to go to a house of worship or read a Bible to learn what is important to us. There is only one place to get your morality," he said. "The family. All comes from that. What you do for the family is good. What you do to hurt the family is bad. I am the family," he quietly added. "It all comes from me."

"I'm happy with the way you handled our recent crisis, Lorelei," he said as we walked farther down the beach. "It gives me the faith in you that I need. Soon all responsibility for our survival will be in your hands."

"Ava will be leaving us," I said. I was resigned to it now.

"Yes. Her time will come very soon."

"Where will she go?" I asked. "To join Brianna?"

Was he finally going to tell me that?

"In a way, but that's thinking too far ahead for you right now, Lorelei. Think only of the near future."

He paused and turned toward the ocean.

"There is so much out there," he said. "So much that awaits you. It's important, however, that you never think of yourself as less than anyone or anything, that you never think of yourself as evil. Everyone out there does things others disapprove of, but they have to battle for their own survival. Everything living does.

"In fact, Lorelei, everything living feeds on something else that lives. No living thing on this earth is above doing that. If that's wrong, then all that lives is wrong. We all participate in survival of the fittest. We didn't decide that was to be our overriding rule. We were born into it. Every nation, every people, every tribe or religion, struggles to survive and in the end will do whatever is necessary to protect its own existence. They may pretend to care about some higher morality, but when it comes right down to it, it's every man for himself. Understand?"

"Yes, Daddy."

He looked at me. The moon made his face look as if it was on fire, with his eyes two hot coals simmering within the flames. Just as a candle flame could hypnotize a moth, I was hypnotized by his glow.

"Do you love me, Lorelei?"

"Oh, yes, Daddy, very much."

"Do you want me to go on?"

"Yes, Daddy."

"Is your heart big enough to conquer anything and anyone who stands in the way, then?"

I nodded.

He didn't speak. He stared at me and then started to walk again in silence, holding my hand. I walked along, but I felt as if I were trailing behind, caught up in the soft light that came from him and followed us along the beach, to take us quietly back to our beds and our comfortable and contented sleep.

Later the following day, I thought about our conversation on the beach and his questions. Was I wrong to be so confident about myself and what I was capable of doing? Ava didn't know about my private walk with Daddy. I was tempted to tell her, because I wanted to hear what her answers were when Daddy told her these things and asked her similar questions. Then it occurred to me that he might not have felt the need to ask her these questions. Maybe he was more confident in her. Although he didn't say it, I also felt he wanted what we discussed and how we discussed it to be something only between us, so I said nothing about it.

Our lives fell back into our regular daily activities. When I returned to school, the other students appeared to have lost all interest in and curiosity about Mark Daniels and, perhaps by proxy, me as well. Very few students said anything to me. I began to feel invisible. When I told Ava, she said I was lucky. She admitted to having had similar feelings and being grateful for it.

"You've outgrown them," she told me, "and they know it, too. When they look at you, they don't see themselves or someone who cares about the same things anymore. The boys are probably intimidated, and you've done a good job of driving the busybodies away. Good for you," she said.

I didn't feel the same way about it, but I didn't disagree with her. The truth was, it was still quite lonely for me, and I hated that I was still someone looking through a window at everyone else. I was like the poor waif who stood outside the ice cream parlor watching the other, more fortunate kids lick their cones and eat their whipped cream. In class, in the hallways, or in the cafeteria, whenever I heard a conversation about parties or dances or dates girls had, I either moved away quickly or tried to close my ears by thinking hard about schoolwork. It got so I hated getting up in the morning to attend school, and some days, if it hadn't been for Marla having to go, I wouldn't have gone.

I think Ava either saw the turmoil going on inside me now or felt it. One morning, she decided to come to my rescue. I knew there were many reasons for Ava to concern herself with my happiness and well-being, not the least of which was her concern that I wouldn't be able to step into her shoes and give her the freedom to leave and fulfill her own destiny. Then, at minimum, she would have to wait until Marla was capable of becoming the daughter Daddy needed.

When Mrs. Fennel left the dining room at breakfast, Ava whispered, "I'm taking you two to school today, but you're not going."

"What?"

"You'll cut a day and spend it with me. I have a class in nineteenth-century American literature we'll attend, and then a big break until my biology class. We'll have lunch in Westwood, just enjoy the day, and you can see what it's like to be in college, not that it's anything I want to do much longer," she added. "Daddy thought I needed more background, whatever that means."

"That's great," I said.

"Just keep your mouth shut about it," she said, watching the door.

I pretended to zip my lips, and she laughed. Marla, who was straining to hear us whisper, looked annoyed.

"Don't say it," she quipped when Ava turned to her. "I know. Be patient."

We both laughed at that, so loudly that Mrs. Fennel popped in again to see what was happening. We quickly returned to our food. She stood there full of suspicion but then retreated. We smiled at each other. It really felt wonderful to have Ava finally thinking of me as a real sister and the two of us being little conspirators.

Later in the car, when Marla heard I was going to cut school and go with Ava, she pouted. "It's not fair," she moaned. "I hate school just as much as Lorelei does."

"I don't hate school, Marla."

"Lorelei will promise here and now to do something similar with you after I'm gone," Ava told her. It wasn't enough to satisfy her, but she didn't moan and groan about it anymore.

Every time Ava talked about her leaving and my stepping into her shoes, I had a creepy feeling in the base of my stomach. It was as if hundreds of little wires inside me had snapped and were pinging. I knew that any night now, she might decide to take me out with her on a monthly hunt. The time after that, she might accompany me, but it would be my job, as Daddy liked to say, to "bring home the bacon."

I didn't know if I would be better off knowing the exact night we would go out together on her regular monthly hunt or not. I didn't ask her about it, and she still hadn't said anything specific. I tried to put it out of my mind and enjoy my day with her at UCLA. It was a spectacular California morning, with barely a wisp of a cloud violating the sea of light blue. The breeze was cool and refreshing. It carried the sounds of other students' laughter as they went to and fro on the campus, and the music from nearby car radios.

Maybe it was because of my excitement about being with her and being on a college campus, but everything looked sparkling and fresh. There was a different energy there. The students were buoyant and loose. Perhaps it came from their being on their own. That sense of freedom was infectious. There were bells for classes and rules to follow, of course, but no one was standing in the hallways ready to pounce on them for not wearing something proper or for talking too loudly. The teachers I saw seemed to be just as casual, too. Why wasn't Ava happier about being there? I would be, and I hoped Daddy would send me to college, too.

"Let's get this over with," she said, referring to her class.

"Aren't you getting anything out of it, enjoying anything?" I asked.

She tilted her head and looked at me askance. "You're kidding, right?"

I shrugged. Was I missing something? Was I supposed to feel the same way about my education? It was clear to me that I didn't, but ironically, every difference between myself and Ava only made me feel more insecure, even frightened. Were these differences big enough to cause me to fail Daddy?

"The real school is out there," she said, nodding toward the street.

"The more you know, the better you'll be out there," I said.

"Who told you that? Did Daddy tell you that?" she asked, pouncing on me.

"No. I just thought it was true."

She smirked. "Get real, Lorelei. Ninety percent of what these people learn and do here has nothing to do with survival, and survival is the only graduation I want to attend."

Daddy had stressed the importance of survival, too, when we were together on the beach, but wasn't there more to all of this than just survival? Despite what he had told me, Daddy enjoyed music and art and being with his old friends. What would Ava have after she left us? Where were her old friends? How would she fill her days? What did Brianna have? Was she closer to Ava or to me? I was so tempted to ask her, to continue the conversation, but I just nodded and walked beside her into the building.

One of the reasons I was happy to come here with her was my interest in how the other students reacted to Ava and how she reacted to them. Would it be different from the way things were for me in high school? The moment we entered, I saw how the boys were looking at her and smiling. To my surprise, she smiled back and even said hello to some. Although she didn't introduce me to anyone, there was no avoiding anyone, either. She could tell that I wondered why she hadn't introduced me.

"Let them all wonder who you are," she said. "Mystery is an aphrodisiac."

The class in nineteenth-century American literature

was in a small theater, so there were plenty of seats. Nevertheless, she had us sit away from most of the others. I looked around and saw how so many of the students were staring at us, especially the boys.

"How do you keep those boys from asking you out on dates?" I asked her.

She smiled and showed me her left hand.

"What is that?"

"An engagement ring," she said. "I slip it on before I come to class."

"Did you think of doing that?"

"No. It was Mrs. Fennel's idea," she said. "I had the feeling it was something she once did, too."

"I can't imagine her our age."

"Oh, she was," Ava said. She smiled and added, "And for a long time, too."

Her teacher entered and went to a lectern. He wore a light blue sweater and jeans and had a dark brown goatee, but he was mostly bald with two even strips of hair just above his temples. From where we were sitting, they looked painted on his head. He was giving a lecture on Mark Twain's *Huckleberry Finn.*

"Did you read it?" I asked Ava.

"The first ten pages," she said. "Boring."

"Boring?"

I had read it in eleventh grade and thought it was one of the most fun and interesting novels taught that year. How could she call it boring? Despite her attitude, she looked as if she was listening attentively but took no notes. Others were either writing in notebooks or typing on little portable computers. The point of the lecture was what exactly the importance was of Huck saying, "All right, I'll go to hell."

The teacher encouraged some discussion then. A tall, very thin girl, with glasses thick enough to be called goggles, raised her hand and pointed out that Huck believed slavery was right because his society told him it was. In his heart, he didn't think so, and because of that, he was willing to help the slave Jim escape, even if it meant he would go to hell. I had known that and even had the urge to raise my hand.

"Exactly. And so you see," the teacher concluded, "why I call Huck Finn the most courageous literary character."

The bell rang. Although she looked as if she had been listening, Ava jumped as if the sound had woken her.

"Is it finally over? What did I miss?"

"A very important point."

"Really?" she said.

"Yes. What your teacher means is that what's right and wrong isn't something for a government to decide. It's for you to decide inside yourself."

"I didn't need him to tell me that. Didn't Daddy ever tell you that?"

"Yes."

"Thought so," she said. "C'mon. I'm hungry, and I don't want to eat what Mrs. Fennel made for our lunch."

We followed the other students out. Some paused to talk to Ava. She was as normal as anyone else, talking about her vacation, the class, whatever subject was mentioned. How different it was for her, I thought. She was relaxed and not on any special guard, and all because she wore that engagement ring.

"I'll give it to you when I leave," she muttered as we continued to walk out.

"What?"

"My engagement ring."

"How did you know I was thinking about it?"

"Your face is better than a flashing billboard. At least to me," she added, laughing.

We had started toward the parking lot when I suddenly heard someone just behind me shout, "Diane? Hey?"

Even though my name wasn't Diane, I turned and stopped walking.

The young man hurried to catch up. For a moment, I thought he was going to join someone else, but he came directly toward me. I recognized him immediately. Ava stepped up beside me. She either didn't remember him or wanted to get me to ignore him, but he was too close.

It was the young man from Dante's Inferno, Buddy Gilroy.

"Hi," he said. "Remember me? Buddy Gilroy. You go to school here?"

"No," Ava said. "We're Jehovah's Witnesses delivering the *Watchtower*. C'mon," she said, tugging my arm.

"Very funny," Buddy said, walking along. "I had a feeling I had seen you before when we met at Dante's," he told Ava.

She glanced at him. Suddenly, she stopped us, looked at me, and then turned to him. "What do you want?"

"Hey, I'm just saying hello. I didn't mean to blow

your cover or anything," he replied, holding up his hands.

"You're not blowing any cover," she said. She thought a moment. "Where are the rest of your bosom buddies, Buddy?"

"Around," he said. "Where are you heading?" he asked me.

I was afraid to speak.

"We're going to Papa's for some pizza."

"Honest to God," he said, raising his right hand. "I was heading there myself. Can I walk along with you?"

"Did you get your flu shot?"

"Huh?"

"Never mind," Ava said. "Walk along."

"Thanks. So what year are you?" he asked me.

"She's only auditing today," Ava answered for me.

"You're not enrolled?"

"No," I said.

"You didn't tell us where you were from, Buddy," Ava said.

"You didn't ask."

"Let me guess," Ava said, pausing again. "Hemet or some other small California town?"

He laughed. "No. Born and raised in Long Beach."

"Keep talking," Ava said, continuing to walk. I realized what she was doing. She was making sure Buddy Gilroy was no renegade.

"I'm the oldest of three boys. My father is a dentist, and my mother works as his receptionist now. My father was a dentist in the navy."

"How patriotic," Ava said. "Drill, drill, drill."

"Are you two related?" he asked, his questions always directed at me. I was still afraid to answer before Ava, however.

"Do we look like we're related?" she fired back at him.

He shrugged. "You're both beautiful," he said.

Ava finally smiled. She glanced at me, an impish twinkle in her eyes. "We're blood related," she said.

"So, that's like sisters, right?"

"Just like sisters," she said, and we crossed the street.

"I can't believe I ran into you," he told me. "Ever since that night, I've been thinking about you."

"Just thinking?" Ava asked him. She smiled as we headed for the restaurant. "Or did you fantasize?"

"Guilty," he said.

She laughed and gave me another knowing look. What was it she was trying to tell me? She further surprised me by inviting him to join us at our table in the restaurant. After we ordered, she once again did most of the talking. Buddy tried to start a conversation only with me, but Ava interrupted frequently, finding out more about him and his family. He finally reacted.

"This is beginning to feel like a job interview for the CIA," he told her, and looked to me.

"It's been our experience more often than not that men lie to us," I said. I saw how much that pleased Ava.

"Well . . . I'm Buddy Gilroy. I'm not all men," he said with a little indignation. He looked from Ava to me. "Fact is, I'm getting vibes from you two that tell me you're the ones speaking with forked tongues."

Ava laughed, but I was sure he saw the truth in my face.

"Except for your name and that you are auditing a class or two here with your blood relation, I don't know anything about you."

"You know we like pepperoni on our pizza," Ava said. "Don't be in such a rush."

He laughed and looked around.

"None of your friends show up?" Ava asked him.

"No."

"Little white lie, Mr. Gilroy?"

"Huh?"

"When you said you were heading here," Ava practically sang.

He looked from her to me and then back to her and laughed. "Am I that obvious?"

"Hopefully," Ava said.

He shook his head, ate some pizza, and smiled warmly at me. I had a strong urge to tell him the truth, to tell him that my name wasn't Diane, but with Ava right beside me, I kept my feelings under lock and key.

Ava excused herself, took her purse, and went to the ladies' room.

"C'mon," Buddy begged. "Who are you? Where do you live? When can I see you again? You and I had a great time that night. Don't say you didn't."

"I'm not," I said.

"So?"

Something in me wanted me to be reckless, to be a little rebellious, and it wasn't only his good looks and sweet personality.

"My name isn't really Diane," I admitted.

"Oh. What is it?"

"Lorelei."

"Why did you tell me it was Diane?"

"Caution," I said. "We've been stalked."

"Oh. Well, I won't stalk you if you don't want me to, but boy, I want to very much."

I smiled. Surely, he was too sweet and innocent to be dangerous. He didn't have Mark Daniels's cocky attitude, either.

"Why don't you give me your phone number, and maybe I'll call you?" I told him.

"Really?"

"Really," I said, and he wrote it out quickly on a slip of paper and handed it to me.

"So, are you coming back here tomorrow?"

"No."

"Why did you come today?"

"Maybe I'll go here someday," I said.

"So you're not in college? You're in high school?"

I realized I had already said too much, but as Mrs. Fennel said many times, you can't unring a bell. Before I had to reply, however, Ava returned.

"Let's get the check and go," she said. "We don't want me to be late for my next class."

"Hey, let me take care of the check," Buddy said. "That's the least I can do for telling a white lie."

"Yes, redeem yourself," Ava said.

I stood up. "Thank you," I said.

"My pleasure."

We started out.

"He's telling the truth," Ava whispered. "I checked him out on my BlackBerry. His father is a dentist in Long Beach. No renegade there."

"Good."

"I'll speak to Daddy, but I don't think he'll want him."

"What? Want him? What do you mean?"

"You know," she said, smiling.

I looked back at Buddy, and then I tried to get my heart to stop thumping loud enough for everyone to hear.

# 11

## Love

I sat in my room and stared at Buddy's phone number.
What Ava had said frightened me for a while, but then I
comforted myself in the knowledge that Daddy forbade
Ava from involving herself with any young men from
her college because of the obvious greater possibility of
being discovered. Nothing was more important to him
than her being careful about this. I recalled how angry he
had been when Brianna had brought home the married
man. He had almost moved us away from where we lived
in New York immediately. No one, not even the best and
most intelligent fugitives, could disappear as quickly or as
well as Daddy and his family could. As I had nearly very
painfully learned, the only ones who had any chance of
finding us were the renegades.

Why was I so concerned about Buddy, anyway? I had
never thought much about any of the young men either
Brianna or Ava had brought home to Daddy. Maybe I
just never wanted to think about them. I didn't want to
know their names or anything else about them. As long
as they remained vague, I didn't have to think of them as
actual people. Except for the time with the man Brianna

had brought home and the time with the stoned man Ava had brought home, I had never witnessed Daddy with anyone else all these years. Those occasions plus the way he had attacked Mark Daniels were the only violent incidents I had witnessed in my life. For someone else, that might sound like enough, but considering what we daughters were responsible for, it wasn't very much. After all, it went on at least once a month for all our young lives.

But recurring and troubling visions in which I saw Buddy Gilroy on that stairway were beginning to haunt me all times of the day and night. There were other boys in school and young men I had seen who were attractive, Mark Daniels being the most attractive, perhaps, but there was something special about Buddy, something different. He wasn't simply handsome and sexually interesting. There was something gentle, soft, caring in his eyes. As trite as it certainly would sound to Ava, he struck me as sincere in a very human sort of way. To put it simply, I didn't feel he was only eager to get into my pants. I thought he really and truly wanted to know me, to spend time with me, and might very well be satisfied spending a day just walking and talking with me.

Oh, we'd want to kiss, to touch, even to go farther and be completely intimate, I was sure, but there wasn't that frenzy about him, that rush to score and then move on to another female target that I had seen in other young men. Maybe that was why I had singled him out at Dante's Inferno. Maybe he saw something sincere in me as well, and that was why he was so attracted to me. Surely, Ava wasn't right. Not every single young man out there was out for one thing only and couldn't care less about you as a person. I was convinced that she thought that way to justify what she had to do. It helped insulate her conscience, if she had a conscience. I couldn't recall either Ava or Brianna demonstrating even the slightest regret or guilt.

I put the slip of paper with Buddy's phone number on it back into my purse and tried to forget about it. I succeeded in keeping all the ugly visions out of my mind and thought maybe I was past it. He would soon drift out of my life as quickly as he had drifted into it. But when I returned from school the following day, Ava was waiting for me in my room. I almost jumped out of my skin when I opened the door and saw her sitting on my bed, wearing one of her angriest looks.

"What are you doing here? What's wrong?"

"Just close the door and lock it," she said, speaking through clenched teeth. "Do it quickly, before Marla decides to burst in on us."

I did as she asked. "What is it?"

"How could you be so stupid? After all the time I've spent with you, the things we've discussed, the confidences I took you into, and what's happened here recently, you do this?"

"Do what, Ava?" I asked, trying to appear undaunted. "Or am I supposed to guess?"

"You don't have to guess. You know. You went and told that Buddy blue-eyes your real name?"

"Oh," I said, and put my books on my desk.

"Why, Lorelei? Tell me why you did that."

I sat at my desk. "I just . . ."

"Just what? What?" she screamed.

"I just felt like having one normal relationship. A real friendship," I quickly corrected, avoiding her eyes. "And the only way to do that was to be honest."

"Honest? What does that mean, Lorelei? Honest about what? Everything?"

"No, not everything. It's not important to tell someone everything, is it?"

"I'll tell you what's important. What's important is to tell someone outside of this family, someone who is not our kind of people, nothing. How could you not know that? You've grown up following the rules, being careful. What is more astounding is that you do this after what almost happened to you, almost happened to all of us here." She leaped to her feet.

"I know all that, but you told me that you were positive he wasn't a renegade," I said.

"So? What does that mean? That gives you permission to get involved with anyone else? You'll bring him around, maybe? Invite him to dinner, to spend time with your family?" she asked, wagging her head.

"Daddy brings women here who aren't one of us," I said.

"That's Daddy. You're comparing yourself to Daddy now? You and your seventeen years compare to his decades, centuries, of experience?"

"I'm not saying that, Ava."

"Then what are you saying, Lorelei?"

"Didn't you ever just want . . ." The words were stuck in my throat. It was as if my whole body was rebelling against my tongue.

Ava sighed deeply and shook her head. "Want what, Lorelei? Spit it out or swallow it."

"Want to have a real relationship with a man, maybe fall in love? I see the way you look at couples on the street or in the mall when they're holding hands or embracing. I see the look in your eyes. I know that look, because I see it in myself when I look in the mirror."

She stared at me for a few moments, her eyes softening. "I thought we had this conversation once," she said in a calmer tone.

"I know, but I liked him. He was different, Ava. Maybe he's someone I could love and who could love me."

"Never."

"Is that really impossible, Ava?"

"Of course it is. I told you that love was poison for us," she said.

"I remember, but I didn't think you meant it. Or at least meant that it was true forever."

"Why not?"

"You've never been in love, never had that feeling?"

"Been in love?" Ava said, laughing. Then she grew serious, even angry. "Of course not. Think, think, Lorelei," she said, poking her temple with her right forefinger so hard I thought she'd drill a hole. "How can we fall in love? What, do you dream of Daddy giving you away at a big, beautiful wedding? Damn your stupidity. I hate that you make me think of this now."

"Why? Why can't you at least think of it?"

"Why? Why? What is it I do?" she asked, more of herself than of me. She rose and went to my bedroom window to look out for a moment. I thought she wasn't going to say anything else. "I'll tell you what I do and what you will do," she said with her back still to me. "I make Daddy happy.

"I keep Daddy alive.

"I ensure my own survival and my own happiness and pleasure.

"I participate and will continue to participate in the most exciting adventures and travel and see things few young women my age see and always in the most luxurious style.

"I serve lustful, arrogant men a platter of just deserts.

"I grow more beautiful every day, and that beauty gives me more power.

"What is it I don't do?" she continued, now turning to me. "You may have noticed, Lorelei. I don't have or make any lasting friendships.

"I don't think of a career for myself or think about the future much beyond tomorrow.

"And yes, Lorelei," she added, "I don't fall in love with anyone. And all this is and will be true for you as well."

"But shouldn't we be sad about that?" I asked softly. Even during these past few weeks, I had never heard her sound so intense, so revealing about her own thoughts and feelings.

"Sad about it? Ha," she said. "You make me laugh. Like we have the privilege of being sad, ever."

"How can sadness be a privilege?"

"It leads to other things, things that will be very destructive."

"I thought Daddy was in love once."

"Yes, and what did it bring him?" She thought a moment and shrugged. "Actually, I thought about these things, too. I once asked Mrs. Fennel about love."

"What did she say?"

"'Love,' she said, 'is an unnatural attachment to another living thing. It's the root cause of most personal problems people have. From this egg is hatched jealousy, which you will learn is the green-eyed monster that mocks the meat it feeds upon.

"'Also hatched from this egg are unrelenting passion and a drive toward possession. Men and women of high intelligence will do the most foolish things in pursuit of passion. Because their passion is so all-consuming, they will want to possess the object of that passion. It will drive them to sell out their own family, their own children, in fact, and it will motivate them to steal and to kill, to lie and deceive, to connive and reject their other basic needs.

"'Love, in short, is the most dangerous emotion humans can experience. But,' our Mrs. Fennel added, offering me one of her infrequent slight smiles, 'you will use it as a fisherman uses his bait.' That's exactly what she said, and as you can see, I not only never forgot it, I memorized every word."

"How did that make you feel?" I asked, and held my breath. Would she keep talking, keep telling me these most intimate things about herself?

"I remember I didn't understand most of it at the time, but I did understand enough of it to feel sad. It did sound as if the world was a treacherous and unmerciful place. Flowers, blue skies, lakes, and mountains, as well as beautiful birds, were then all deceptions. To survive in such a place, one had to be good at being false."

"Be good at lying?"

"Exactly. I asked Mrs. Fennel about that, too, and she said truth was quicksand. Once you step into it, you have to stay with it, and it will bring you down. 'If you're honest, you're naked,' she added, and laughed. Yes, our Mrs. Fennel actually laughed.

"As you can imagine, as you know from your own experiences out there, this wasn't exactly what everything and everyone else would preach to me.

"Maybe I thought I was being cute or smart, but I asked her about all those romantic greeting cards lovers sent each other. 'Postcards from Satan,' Mrs. Fennel said. 'Touch them. They're still hot.'

"The next day, I went to a greeting-card store and felt them. They did feel hot. Power of suggestion or some truth only our kind could know? That wasn't hard to believe. After all, what was the primary thing I had been taught about myself and the primary thing you're being taught about yourself?"

"What?"

"What? That you're special, of course. There are only a few selected to be what we are, Lorelei."

I didn't feel special, not in the way she was thinking, but I didn't tell her that. I looked down for a moment and then slowly raised my head. She was staring at me but staring as if she were in pain. "Daddy loves us, doesn't he, Ava?"

"That's a different kind of love, Lorelei. That's love to survive."

"But you love Daddy, too."

"For the same reason, and you'll see, that's true for you as well. It will always be true for you. Love to survive, nothing else, no sweet music, no glorious summer days, no moonlit nights to embed in your brain forever and ever. In short, no poetry, just survival. We've been chosen for it."

She made it sound more like a tragedy than a blessing. I looked away so she wouldn't see the tears coming into my eyes. I knew she would mock them. "How did you know I told him my real name?" I asked her after a moment.

"How did I know?" She laughed. "He's become my shadow over there now. It was like he was lying in wait for me. I didn't even realize it. Suddenly, there he was walking beside me, but only to talk about you. He practically fell to his knees to get me to tell him where you live. The only way for me to get rid of him was to come on to him."

"Come on to him? What do you mean?"

"I'm sure you know what that means, Lorelei. I started to flirt with him in order to get him to forget about you. I think I'm capable of doing that, getting him to forget you. It worked, of course, so shake him out of your head. He's just like any other man who stands when he pees," she said, rising. "Nothing more, nothing less."

"What about your engagement ring?" I asked, challenging her story.

"I took it off. It does come off, Lorelei."

"What exactly happened?"

"What exactly happened? I had him eating out of my palm. I kissed him, and I mean really kissed him like he'd never been kissed. He practically had an orgasm on the campus grounds. If someone mentioned Lorelei to him now, he would say, 'Who? Lorelei? Who's that?' "

I didn't believe her, but I wasn't sure if that was because I didn't want to believe her.

"Fortunately for you, I have him dangling on a string out there. I don't think it's necessary to tell Daddy about this, but you can't return to the campus with me ever again," she said, moving to the door.

"What are you going to do with him now?" I asked.

She opened the door but stood there thinking. "Nothing. What can I do with him? You know the rules we must follow. I won't think about him any more, and I advise you to do the same. We have other things to think about now. Daddy is moving closer to a decision."

"What decision?"

"A decision about how much longer he wants the family living here. I overheard him talking about it with Mrs. Fennel. I have the feeling it's in the works."

"Soon?"

"Don't look so devastated," she added as she stepped out and turned to me. "It's not good for you, for any of us, to grow too fond of a place and especially the people living there."

"I know. It's just that . . . I thought Daddy liked living here."

She laughed. "Daddy likes wherever he lives. That's the point, Lorelei. He doesn't live anywhere he doesn't want to live. For a while," she said. "Besides, don't you enjoy starting new? I always did. Of course, I was never so susceptible as you seem to be."

"Susceptible to what?"

"Friendships, boyfriends. Get over it," she said, and left.

I sat there staring after her. If I had ever felt I was very different from her, it was right then, but was I really any different? Wouldn't I soon be just like her, just as hard as she was? Would it matter if I tried to fight it?

*If I only knew more about myself, more about my origins,* I thought. Maybe, just maybe, mine were different from hers and from Brianna's, and that was what accounted for my feelings. Maybe this was why Mrs. Fennel and Daddy wouldn't tell me very much about myself. Maybe they were afraid of how I would feel or react if I knew.

I sat in my room for a while, just thinking about it all, and then I went out to the living room, expecting to see Daddy, hoping, now that I was older and closer to the maturity he expected, he would tell me more. I wouldn't let him tell me to be patient. If I had to, I would beg him to be more forthcoming. He wasn't there, but I heard Mrs. Fennel in the kitchen and went in to ask her if he was home.

"No. He won't be back until morning," she said. There was no point in asking her where he had gone or why. She wouldn't tell me. She would act as if she didn't hear me. I stood there for a moment, thinking, and then turned to return to my room. But I paused at the bottom of the stairway. I looked up and wondered if I dared. I could hear Mrs. Fennel still in the kitchen. Quietly, my heart pounding, I walked up the stairs.

Normally, it wasn't often that any of us were in Daddy's bedroom even in our other homes. Besides a bathroom in the hallway on the second floor, there was Mrs. Fennel's bedroom. She always slept near him. Her bedroom and his had en suite bathrooms. The hallway bathroom was there for the guest bedroom that had been incorporated into Daddy's before we moved here. The wall between them had been removed, and this grand suite had been constructed.

The flooring of Daddy's entire suite was a very soft, fluffy white carpet. The walls were covered in velvet with black trim. His bed was a dark cherry wood with a headboard that had what he told us was his family crest embossed. It looked like a crown wrapped around a shape that resembled a human heart.

"Don't ask me to tell you exactly what it means," he told us. "It's so old that no one really remembers, but it is striking, isn't it?"

His suite had double dark cherry-wood doors, both lightly embossed with the same family crest. I once told him I thought it meant "the king of love." He liked that very much and told everyone who visited what I had said.

"She's so imaginative," he said, and then shrugged and added, "Who knows? Maybe she's right. Even if she isn't, I like it, 'the king of love.'"

It always brought laughter and smiles and pats on the head to me whenever Daddy told his friends. Naturally, both Marla and Ava were jealous.

There were many artifacts in Daddy's room, very old portraits of relatives in gilded frames, ivory carvings from the Far East, framed scripts or letters written in Gaelic and some Slavic dialects, beautiful jeweled boxes, statuary from Greece and Italy in wall niches, some old clocks, wall tapestries from the Middle Ages created in France and England, and a marble table on which were many interesting things he had collected or had been given through the years—lockets, small pearl-handle knives, and, strangely enough, some bones encased in glass. He never spoke of them, and I never asked him about them, but we all understood they were the bones of his ancestors.

A part of his suite was a sitting area furnished with nineteenth-century French settees, foot rests, tables, and embroidered chairs. Daddy had a very valuable collection of original recordings of great opera singers as well as popular American, English, French, and Italian singers. When he was relaxing in his room, he was content to play those rather than use the tapes and MP3 players we girls had, even though the sound was scratchy. It was his way of recapturing some sweet memory or another.

The other pieces of furniture in the bedroom matched the bed. There was a large chandelier above the bed. He had bought it in France at some auction and claimed it had once hung in Marie Antoinette's bedroom.

"I tell any of the women who've slept here to eat cake," he said, joking about Marie Antoinette's famous response when told the people were starving and had no bread. "Let them eat cake," she supposedly said. "I so admire anyone who will not permit the misery around us to interfere with his or her pleasure," Daddy said.

I opened the doors slowly, as silently as I could, and

stood there for a few moments, just looking at everything. As always, the suite was pristine, not a spot of dust
on anything. The chandelier was dimly lit, even though
it was still quite bright outside, and the sunlight streaked
through the open curtains, making crystals glitter.

What had brought me up here was the thought that
maybe, just maybe, somewhere in his suite, in a drawer,
in a box, somewhere, there was something about me,
about my origins. Just contemplating going into Daddy's
room without his permission was terrifying, but here I
was, driven by this overwhelming need to know myself
better.

I took off my shoes so I would leave no trace on his
immaculate rug. Even so, I was convinced Daddy would
enter his suite and know I had been there. No matter
how careful I was, he would know. I had to risk it. I took
a deep breath and crossed into the suite.

As if it sensed someone there, a clock in the sitting
area bonged the hour just as I entered. I froze in place
and then slowly looked around the bedroom. Where
would I begin to look? Mrs. Fennel kept Daddy's dresser
drawers so neat. Just moving a pair of socks seemed forbidden. I couldn't imagine him keeping any paperwork
under clothes, anyway. Why would he hide it like that?
He had no fear of anyone going through his things, least
of all me, I thought. But where would he keep papers?
He had no office up here, no file cabinets.

I continued to circle the room, not touching anything. I didn't think he'd leave anything out in the open,
even though he would not expect any of us to come in
here without his permission. And even if he had, Mrs.

Fennel would certainly put it in its proper place. Just one look at this suite would tell anyone that it was kept as reverently as a shrine.

My gaze went to his closet. I knew he had a large walk-in with all of his clothes neatly arranged, but I recalled that toward the rear was a small desk and a chair against a wall mirror.

I started toward it but thought I heard footsteps in the hallway and hesitated, my heart pounding. I waited, and the footsteps died away in the opposite direction. That was surely Mrs. Fennel going to her own bedroom. I had to be sure not to make the slightest sound.

As quietly as I could, I opened the closet door and entered. For a few moments, I stood there studying the small desk. It had two drawers, but both had locks. I tried them anyway and discovered they were locked. This was probably a futile venture, I thought. He surely carried the key to the drawers on him always. Nevertheless, I looked around the closet and focused on his velvet robe. He wore it practically every day. It was worth a try. I searched the deep pockets and felt the keys on a small ring. Excited, I hurried back to the desk to try them, and they fit.

Still, I hesitated. If he realized I had opened these drawers, I would have no possible excuse. I couldn't say I had come looking for him to tell him something or bring him something. Anyway, Daddy could look into my eyes and know when I was lying. Why worry about it now? I had come this far, risked this much. There was nothing to do but look. Even if I retreated, he would know I had come this far. If he was going to be angry at me, it might as well be for something worthwhile, I thought. I would tell him the truth, tell him how much I needed to know about my origins. Maybe he would understand, I decided, and opened the first drawer.

I was surprised. The drawer was filled with pictures of beautiful women. Why would Daddy keep pictures of women? From the clothing and the hairstyles, I could tell that some of these women had lived years and years ago. There were even some sepia photographs that suggested the late nineteenth century. Daddy was in none of the pictures with any of the women, but I knew each of them must have meant something special to him, or he wouldn't have kept their photographs. I sifted through them slowly, studying each one. Then it occurred to me to look on the backs. There were only first names. I sifted through a few: Alexandra, Tia, Penelope, Thalia, Leah, and Kyla. How unique some of these names were, as unique as mine and Ava's, I thought, and looked at some others. I paused when I saw Brianna.

Daddy knew a woman named Brianna? I stared at her picture. She looked a lot like my oldest sister. From her style, I thought she probably was someone Daddy had met in the '70s. I turned over the next picture and froze. The name here was Ava. Was this Ava's mother, Sophia? These names, I realized, were not the names of the women but the names of their daughters. With trembling fingers, I turned over the next picture and stared at Lorelei. Daddy knew who my mother was? But . . . I had thought I came from an orphanage.

I stared at the woman who was very possibly my mother. Did I want her to be? Was I seeing resemblances that weren't really there? There was only one more picture. I lifted it slowly. It was a more shocking discovery than the picture of the woman who was possibly my mother. It was a picture of Brianna. Why? I turned it over slowly, the answer unfolding in the darkest part of my brain even before I read the name Marla. For a moment, I thought I couldn't breathe. My lungs were filled with burning hot air. Did this mean Brianna was Marla's mother?

I separated the picture of the woman who might be my mother from the rest and dropped them back into the drawer as close to the way they had been as I could. Then I closed the drawer, locking it again.

I couldn't take my eyes off the picture I held in my hand. Questions exploded in my mind. What was her name? Where did she come from? Why did Daddy have her picture and the pictures of the other women? Did she die, or did she simply give me up to an orphanage?

Dare I open the second drawer? Maybe the answers to some of these questions were in there, especially something about my father. I had to look, but I was trembling so much I couldn't get the key properly into the lock and dropped it. I held my breath. Had Mrs. Fennel heard that? Would she be charging in here at any moment? I waited nearly a full minute, but she didn't come.

I closed my eyes, took a deep breath, and tried again, this time opening the drawer. There was a very old-looking, cloth-bound book in it and nothing else. I plucked it out very carefully and opened it slowly. It reeked of age, the pages yellow and fragile. I was afraid to turn any, but I did.

The words were written in perfect script, the first

pages done with what was probably one of Daddy's quill
fountain pens. Each page contained one of the names
I had seen on the backs of the photographs. Under the
names were dates and addresses. There was a physical
description of each as well, hair and eye color, length and
weight, and any particular birthmarks.

I had a birthmark just under my left breast. It wasn't
quite round and looked more like an unfinished circle.
Still turning the pages delicately, I found the page with
my name on it and quickly went to the birthmark. It was
mine; this was my page. I looked at the address: Lost Angels, An Infant Sanctuary, 8 Dunning Road, Heartsport,
Oregon.

Was this where I came from, and was this woman
my real mother? I looked back at Ava's picture. She had
the same address in her small biography, Lost Angels.
Brianna did as well, and so did Marla. Before Brianna, a
girl named Raine had as her address of origin New Creation Home for Foundlings. It was in Ukraine. Flipping
back, I found homes in Russia, France, India, Thailand.
Carefully, I closed the book and set it back in the drawer.
Then I closed the drawer softly, relocked it, and returned
the keys to Daddy's velvet robe.

My discoveries didn't make me feel better or explain
why I felt so different from Ava. Instead, they created
more mystery, dropped me deeper into the well of secrecy
from which we all drank. Why was I always told my parents were unknown if my mother was known? Did this
mean my father was known, too?

How did all of this fit the story I had been told and,
to my knowledge, Ava had been told? Ava had been

told that Daddy had fallen in love with her mother and had died in childbirth, as would any normal human woman who carried his child. Did Ava know of this book and these pictures? Should I tell Ava what I had discovered? Wouldn't she tell Mrs. Fennel, if not Daddy? Wouldn't I be in very big trouble then? How would I handle the burden of carrying this secret, knowing what I had discovered? Was I as bad at hiding my thoughts as Ava claimed? In no time at all, Mrs. Fennel would know what I had discovered, and Daddy would know soon afterward. Would they see my foray into his suite and into the closet and desk drawers as a kind of betrayal?

As quietly and as softly as I had come up the stairway, I descended. When I reached the bottom, I hesitated. I had a cold feeling at the back of my neck telling me someone was behind me, but when I turned to look, I saw no one, not Mrs. Fennel or my sisters and certainly not Daddy. He wasn't home, but it really felt as if something was following me. Maybe he was able to leave his spirit here to watch over his things. I hurried on to my room and quickly shut the door behind me. Then I went immediately to my desk, and on a pad, I wrote the address of the orphanage from which I had been taken so I would not forget it.

After that, I sat on my bed and stared at the picture of the woman who could be my mother, looking again for any resemblances between us and trying to figure out what she was like from the way she held her head, from her eyes and her mouth. She looked happy in this picture. Had she been with my father when it was taken?

Had I been born yet? What did her voice sound like, her laugh? How could she leave me behind? What if she saw me now? Would she recognize me?

I had gone upstairs, snuck into Daddy's suite in order to satisfy my desperate need to know more about myself, and all I had done was create more mystery, more dark places. It was like unwrapping one of those boxes I dreamed would be under a Christmas tree and finding only another wrapped box. Frustrated, I put my mother's picture inside my English lit textbook and set it aside on my desk. Then I went to my bedroom window and looked out.

Twilight was passing into night. A cloudless sky was beginning to reveal the brighter stars. A tiny cyclone of emotions was spinning up from the pit of my stomach. I felt myself begin to breathe faster and harder as my heart went into a gallop.

When Daddy had swooped down on Mark Daniels just outside this window, I had seen the fear and terror in Mark's reddened eyes. He had resembled a child struggling against a powerful adult. Before he was swallowed up in the darkness, he had turned toward me, and for a fleeting moment, he once again looked like the Mark Daniels who had charmed me at school, who had tempted that part of me that longed to be like everyone else. Had he been pleading for my help?

But I saw his fangs again, too, and a wave of rage overtook any sadness I had felt. Something hard and muscular unfolded and awoke in me. I hadn't admitted it to myself until this very moment, but I had had the urge to go through that window and help Daddy destroy what

Mark had become. It had flowed through me with such heat I thought my skin had begun to melt.

And then later, after it was over, when I had finally closed my eyes again, I had sunk into my bed like a body in a coffin, reaching up to pull the lid down over myself and shut out the world outside.

It struck me that, like Daddy and Ava and Brianna, I was welcoming the darkness. I was no longer afraid of the darkness. The darkness had become my friend, too. It made me think of the most important question of all.

That question still echoed down the long corridor of my sleep and into the morning light and still reverberated and haunted me, which I feared it might do forever and ever. Even now, perhaps more than ever before, because of the mystery I had begun to unravel, I could hear it clearly. Only now, I heard it in a voice unlike my own, an older female voice, but one with a sweet and concerned tone, a loving voice, asking more questions.

*Who are you, Lorelei?*
*Really.*
*Who are you?*
*And what are you becoming?*

# 12

## Who Are You, Lorelei?

If Daddy knew I had gone up to his suite, he didn't come down in the morning to confront me about it. Mrs. Fennel said nothing to me, either. Only Ava seemed to sense something different about me. I could see it in the way her eyes followed me about this morning, how thoughtful and studied she was. Suspicion fell from her eyes like tears. Unfortunately for me, this was the one morning she had an early class, so she was there at breakfast.

"What's wrong with you today?" she asked me.

"Nothing. I'm just a little tired, I guess."

"We don't get a little tired," she said. "You have no reason to be tired at all, Lorelei. I hope you're not still thinking about Buddy."

"Who's Buddy?" Marla asked.

"Never mind," Ava told her. "Well?"

"No," I said, but I was sure it wasn't firm enough of a no.

"Right," she said out of the corner of her mouth reserved for skepticism. "You let me be the one who thinks about him."

Her words were like tiny knives sticking into my

stomach. I avoided her eyes and hurried Marla along so we could leave for school, but my mind was never free of the thoughts she had deposited there.

"What's Ava talking about? Who is Buddy? Why does she want you not to think about him?" Marla asked. "I thought we were sisters. Why are you keeping secrets from me?"

"It's nothing, Marla. Ava is overreacting. He's just some college boy I met when I was with her at UCLA the other day," I said, trying to sound as casual as I could. "I made the mistake of telling her I thought he was good-looking, and you know how Ava gets when you mention a boy is good-looking."

"As good-looking as you thought Mark Daniels was?" Marla asked. I glanced at her. Already, at her age, she could look as mean and angry as Ava.

"He's different," I said.

"Oh, you can tell the difference now? That's a relief. I won't have my life at risk because of your romantic notions," she said. She not only looked more like Ava now, she also sounded more like her.

Why was Ava having more of an influence on Marla than I was having? I was the one with whom she spent most of her time. After school, she was usually in my room, not Ava's. Maybe I shouldn't have been so flippant with her when she started asking me more questions. Maybe I shouldn't have been so eager to get her to go to Ava. I wondered if she thought I didn't like her or want her around me. Now that I thought about it, she had been avoiding me more and more in the house. These suspicions were about to be elevated.

After a few moments of silence between us, Marla suddenly said, "Don't look for me after school today."

"What? Why not?"

"Ava is coming for me."

"When?"

"Before the final period. She has permission to sign me out, you know. Daddy made sure of that."

"Where are you going?"

"She didn't say exactly. She just thinks we should spend more time together."

I was silent. Why was Ava doing this now? Were things going to move this quickly?

"You know," Marla said, almost as if she had developed the ability to listen in on my thoughts, "she'll be leaving us sooner than we think."

I turned to her.

"In fact, we'll all be leaving Los Angeles," she continued.

"How do you know this?"

"A little bird told me. How do you think?"

"No, really, Marla. Do you know anything about that?"

"I heard Mrs. Fennel and Daddy talking this morning."

"Daddy didn't come down this morning."

"No," she said. "You have that wrong. Daddy didn't come home until this morning."

"Oh. What did they say?"

"Maybe I shouldn't be the one telling you this. Maybe you should go to Ava," she said spitefully.

"I never told you to go to Ava with your questions

unless I really didn't know the answers, Marla. Don't be a little bitch."

She laughed. "I heard Daddy say the arrangements were being completed. He thought maybe another two months or so at the most, and most likely sooner. That's what I heard."

"You're sure? He said another two months or so at the most?"

She shrugged. "We'll have a family meeting, and he'll tell us everything when he's ready to tell us. But you know what I think now?"

"What?"

"I think Ava will be leaving before we move." She smiled. "And then you'll be my big sister. That's why she wants to spend more time with me."

Another two months or so? That meant possibly two more hunts before we left.

Was that my heart thumping, or had we gotten a flat tire?

The commotion that had begun in my mind didn't stop all morning. I don't think I heard more than a few words my teachers spoke. I know I did poorly on a quiz in math. I couldn't stop thinking about Buddy. He had such a trusting smile, such innocence in his eyes.

Even when I sat eating my lunch in the noisy cafeteria, I couldn't get myself to stop thinking about Buddy. I opened my purse and found his phone number. For a while, I just sat there looking at it. It felt hot in my fingers, as hot as the greeting cards Ava claimed lovers sent each other. The scribbled numbers were a way of connecting myself to him, resurrecting his face, his smile, and his trusting eyes. I had not come as close to kissing any boy as I had come to kissing him that night at Dante's Inferno. His lips haunted me now.

When I rose and walked out of the cafeteria and out of the building, I knew that what I was about to do could be the beginning of the end for me as far as my family went. Ava's recitation of Mrs. Fennel's warnings about love replayed in my mind. "Men and women of high intelligence will do the most foolish things in pursuit of passion. Because their passion is so all-consuming, they will want to possess the object of that passion. It will drive them to sell out their own family . . ."

I took out my cell phone. Was I terribly afraid? Yes, so frightened my fingers wouldn't work the tiny buttons. I had to sit on a bench and take deep breaths to try again. Slowly, I brought the phone to my ear and listened as the call went through. It rang twice, and I flipped the phone closed.

*I can't do this,* I thought. *Once I do this, Daddy will hate me forever. I can't.*

I stood up to go back inside the building, but my feet felt glued to the ground. There was a tumultuous battle going on inside me, my heart against my mind.

*Why call him?* my mind was asking. *What can you say? Where do you expect it to lead, anyway? A date? It would be like playing with fire. You would be teasing him, giving him hope that something could come of a relationship.*

I didn't trust Ava. I had nightmares about what she might do, regardless of the restrictions Daddy placed on her. I could call Buddy to warn him.

*But how? Would he believe what you told him if you*

*dared to tell him? You'd be betraying your family, betraying Daddy.*

*But what if you don't tell him anything?* I thought. *What if one night, you heard Ava's car drive up and you saw Buddy Gilroy step out of it? Would you just watch in silence, or would you cry out? And what would you cry out? "Run"? "Watch out for my daddy"? What?*

*Wouldn't it be better to avoid that scene, and what better way is there to avoid it than to go to him, to warn him ahead of time?*

I sat on the bench again, but before I could decide, my cell phone rang. It was not outside the realm of my thinking to imagine that Ava or even Daddy knew I had tried to call Buddy. I let it ring again, and then I flipped it open and said, "Hello."

"Who is this?" I heard. "Huh? You called me, but I couldn't answer it in time. Is this Elsa?"

"Elsa?" I asked.

He laughed.

Who was Elsa? Then I remembered. That was Ava's phony name the night we went to Dante's Inferno. He must have given her his cell-phone number, too. Otherwise, why would he even think it was Ava calling me? She wasn't lying to me, then. She had come on to him, and she had him infatuated with her. I felt like hanging up and really trying to forget him, but I didn't. I couldn't.

"No," I said. "It's Lorelei."

"Lorelei? Really?" The excitement in his voice encouraged me.

"Yes, although I guess you were expecting someone else."

"No, no. I wasn't expecting anyone else. What a great surprise. Please. Where are you? When can I see you?" His eagerness made me smile.

"What makes you think I want to see you?" I teased.

"Hey, when a prayer is answered, I never question it," he said.

I looked at my watch. Since Ava was picking up Marla, I didn't have to return directly home after school. If I left early and Marla found out, she would surely tell Ava. No, I had to tolerate the rest of the school day, although it was going to be as useless for me as the morning had been.

"I'll meet you at three-thirty on the Santa Monica Pier," I said.

"Three-thirty?"

"Is that all right?"

"I've got to cut a class, but that's fine. I hate the class anyway," he said. "I'll be there."

Another thought occurred to me. "Really, Buddy, was Elsa supposed to call you today?"

"Sometime soon," he said. "Why?"

"If she calls, please don't mention I called you or that you're seeing me."

"No problem."

"It's very important. If you do mention it, I'll never be able to see you again."

"Okay. How's this? Elsa who?"

I smiled to myself. That was the reaction from him that Ava had expected if my name was ever mentioned.

"Great. See you then," I said, and hung up before I could change my mind.

What had I done? At least four times before the school day ended, I paused to step outside and call him again to cancel, but every time, I resisted. When the final bell rang, I hung back so that Ava and Marla would leave the parking lot before I appeared. I stood by the doorway and watched Marla get into Ava's car. As soon as they pulled away, I hurried out to my car. Just as my fingers had trembled when I had gone to insert the keys to Daddy's desk drawers, they trembled again. When the car started, I sat back for a moment and took deep breaths.

Every teenage girl in that school behind me surely had done something in defiance of her parents, whether it was drinking alcohol, smoking pot, going places that were forbidden with other girls or boys who were forbidden, or merely staying out too late. There was probably a list of defiant acts that would fill a few shelves in the school library. No matter what act she committed, the first thing she had to have felt was fear. I wasn't thinking of those girls who were so bad, so defiant, that they couldn't care less if they were caught. The girls I was thinking of were more like me, girls who had made promises, who had been obedient and responsible, girls who were always trusted. In their hearts, they dreaded being discovered and seeing that look of deep disappointment on their parents' faces. After all, these were the only people in the world who loved them more than they loved their own lives.

What bound a family together, especially one like ours, if it wasn't trust and promises? You could betray your teachers, your school, and your friends, even your country, and it wouldn't come close to the depth of disappointment after you betrayed your own family. Every breath you took, every ounce of nourishment you consumed, was a family gift. Once you broke that tie, you truly drifted at the mercy of impish winds and capricious fate. Who cared if you were injured or hurt? Who suffered disappointments with you and helped you recover? Who was there to share your success with as much joy? Who was capable of being as proud of you?

Schoolgirls like myself would risk their parents' anger and disappointment because deep in their hearts, they believed that no matter how deeply they had hurt their parents, there was always going to be a reservoir of forgiveness. I recalled a line in a poem we had read in English class last year, Robert Frost's "The Death of the Hired Man." In it he wrote, "Home is the place where, when you have to go there, they have to take you in."

Where else would such a thing be true?

For the girls like me who risked their parents' wrath, there was always that thought, that hope to cushion the danger, and wasn't it the danger itself, the excitement of defiance, that usually won out in the end and got them to light that joint, take that ride, be with that forbidden boy?

The great difference was that I had no cushion. For me, home was not someplace where I would have to be taken in. I was a trapeze artist without a net, a skydiver with no second parachute, a first-time swimmer with no nearby dock or shore, no lifeguard, no rope, nothing to save me from sinking into the dark depth awaiting with open arms and gleeful smile.

*No,* I thought as I drove out of the parking lot, *I am*

*not simply another defiant teenager.* I wasn't taking this risk to enjoy the accompanying rush of excitement and adrenaline. I wasn't charging forward with a shield on which was inscribed "Life's unfair. I resent all unreasonable restrictions and rules."

And when I thought more deeply, questioned myself more closely, I also had to admit that I wasn't doing this simply because I was attracted to a handsome, sincere young man. It was greater than him, greater than both of us. There was something in me that wasn't in Brianna and Ava and Marla. It wasn't something I could neatly wrap in the word *conscience,* either. Neither Daddy nor Mrs. Fennel ever had mentioned God in a positive way in our house. There was never any talk of prayer or its power. I couldn't recall Daddy driving us past a church or a synagogue or even a mosque and not smiling disdainfully. If any of us mentioned anything whatsoever to do with any religion, Daddy would say, "Smoke and mirrors. More people are killed in the name of religion than anything else."

"What do we believe in, then, Daddy?" I once asked. It was at holiday time, and all the other children were preparing for services and celebrations.

"Believe only in yourself," Daddy replied. "Believe only in your own power."

And although he didn't come right out and say it, he clearly implied that we should believe in him because from him came our power.

No, neither conscience nor fear of punishments for doing something evil was what gave me the strength to make that phone call and drive off. Surely, my need to find another kind of love was part of it, but what I couldn't understand or identify yet was that part of me that now didn't fear being different from Brianna and Ava and Marla. In fact, it was drawing me in stronger ways. If anything, this was the most frightening thing of all, because if I wasn't truly my daddy's daughter, then who was I?

And what would happen to me?

Somewhere out there lay the answer, I thought as I looked west toward the Pacific, where I could see the clouds moving up from the horizon. As on most afternoons in Los Angeles, the marine layer had burned off, and a soft blue sky ceiling joined forces with warm breezes to put more energy into the legs of the joggers, more light in the smiles of the tourists who were already bright with the excitement that accompanied something special and new, and even more hope in the faces of the homeless I saw camped out along Ocean Boulevard. It helped me relax a little, too.

I found a place to park and walked out to the pier. There was already a good-size crowd enjoying the Ferris wheel and games. I overheard a variety of languages from Chinese to Russian being spoken. Young children were charging forward in all directions, only to be pulled back by a parent's words. They were like human yo-yos, because they'd start in a new direction almost immediately. It brought a smile to my face and then memories of Daddy bringing us here and to other fun parks. We were always well behaved and proud to walk with him, to be seen beside him, to share some of the admiration we saw in the faces of other people.

"It's important that you are out here," he said. "It's important that you feel the ebb and flow of human emotions and energy, that you, like me, draw your own essence from it. It's like dipping a cup into a cool stream and then, after you drink, feeling revived and alive and immortal."

His words mesmerized us. We soaked in the glow of his smile and, like kittens, purred in his arms. Daddy could explain anything, could meet any challenge, and could keep us forever safe. Anyone looking at us could read the words on our lips. *We are his daughters. We are the Patios. Step away. Don't touch. Just enjoy what you see.*

"Hey," I heard, and broke free of my reminiscences. Buddy was right behind me.

"I thought you might not find me easily in this crowd," I said as he approached. He was wearing a light blue jacket, a darker blue shirt, and jeans, and he looked spry in his bone-white sneakers. I hadn't noticed before, but his light brown hair was long and floated over his eyes. He swept it back.

"Are you kidding? You would stand out in any crowd," he said. He looked around. "And it is kind of crowded here. Want to take a walk on the beach?"

"Okay," I said. He reached for my hand, and we started off the pier.

"So, what made you decide to make this my lucky day?" he asked.

I nearly laughed aloud, thinking, *You have no idea how true that might be.* "How do you know it's your lucky day?"

"Hey," he said, leaning closer to lower his voice, "don't you see those envious guys watching us?"

I looked around. Once I had dreamed of drawing attention the way Brianna and Ava did. Had my dream come true? They certainly never revealed being as self-conscious about it as I was as we stepped off the sidewalk and onto the sand. I paused to slip off my shoes, and he did the same. The sand was warm, but not so warm that we couldn't walk barefoot, and as we drew closer to the water, it cooled.

"Where do you go to high school?" Buddy asked.

"It's a private school in Bel Air."

"Sounds expensive."

"It is."

"What do your parents do?"

"I have only my father," I said. "My mother died when I was born."

"Oh, sorry. What does he do?"

"He buys and sells very expensive things all over the world."

"Jewelry?"

"Anything expensive."

"Elsa is really your sister, then, right? This business about blood relation was just some nonsense."

"Yes, she's my sister."

"Is there just you and Elsa?"

"No. I have a younger sister, too."

"Oh, your father remarried?"

"No."

"But how did you get a younger sister?"

"He didn't marry her mother. She deserted him after my younger sister was born."

"Oh. Sounds like your father's had it rough."

"Yes. That's also why he's so protective of us."

"Sure. I understand. Well, you and Elsa don't look that much alike, you know." He leaned in toward me again to whisper, "You're much better-looking."

"Flattery will get you anywhere," I said. I remembered that line from a movie I had watched with Marla.

"With you, I'll settle for anywhere," he replied. We walked quietly for a while, and then he took off his jacket and spread it on the sand. "My lady," he said, offering it to sit on.

I did, and he sat beside me. We looked out at the waves. Two California brown pelicans were circling over the water to our right. Suddenly, one swooped down and came up with a small fish.

"Wow," Buddy said. "See that?"

"Yes. Everything living feeds on something living," I recited.

He looked at me. "Deep," he said. "Tell me more about yourself. Are you guys originally from California?"

"You've told me nothing about yourself," I countered.

He laughed and sprawled out, leaning on his left elbow to look up at me. "Not true. I told you I was born and raised in Long Beach, and my father's a dentist. We're almost even."

"I was born in New York. We moved a few times. We lived in Nashville for a few years."

"Can you sing country?"

"Hardly," I said, smiling. "I play the piano, mostly classical pieces. Daddy loves classical music."

He just stared up at me.

"What?" I asked.

"You're so beautiful. I think I'd be content just lying here and looking up at you for the rest of my life."

"Now you're embarrassing me," I said.

"I'd rather cut off my right hand than embarrass you."

"So, what do you intend to do with your education?" I asked, trying to get him off the topic of me.

He laughed. "You mean, what do I want to be when I grow up?"

"Think you ever will?" I said, and he shrugged.

"Maybe. When I get around to it," he said. He rolled onto his back. "I'm leaning toward medical research of some sort. Ever since I was a kid, I've been fascinated by what we can't see. There are worlds upon worlds swirling around inside us." He turned back to me. "You weren't far off when you said everything living feeds on something else living. There are bacteria living inside us, feeding off us. Even the bad guys feed off us."

"Bad guys?" I held my breath. He couldn't mean anything close to what I knew.

"Germs, viruses, you know."

"Oh. Yes, of course. I imagine you're a good student," I said.

"Straight A's. That was my nickname in high school, Straight-A Gilroy. And you?"

"I've always made the honor roll."

"You'd always make mine," he said. "Now, tell me really, what made you decide to call me? I gave up on the idea when you wouldn't give me your phone number."

"It's not a big mystery, Buddy. We had a good time at Dante's Inferno. I thought you were different from your friends, so I decided to see if I was right."

"Any decision yet?"

"Too soon to tell."

"Great. That means you'll give me more time, which might mean you'll give me your home phone number."

"Let's leave it the way it is for right now," I said. I embraced my knees and looked down at the sand.

"Boy, why do I have the feeling there's a ton you're not telling me about yourself?"

"Can't imagine," I said, smiling.

"Your sister Elsa is, please pardon the expression, a piece of work."

I was quiet a moment, and then I turned to him and said, "Her name is not Elsa."

"I know," he said.

"You know?"

"Yeah. I was just waiting to see how long you would keep up the lie."

"How did you find out the truth?"

"I checked with someone in one of her classes. Her name is Ava Patio. I pretended to believe her, because I didn't want to get her angry with me or something. I thought as long as she spoke to me, I had a chance of meeting you again. I searched the Internet to find your phone number. I called more than twenty Patios, but no one named Patio had a daughter named Ava."

"That's why you spend time talking to her and being with her at school?"

"That's it, solely it," he said. "Why, does she think otherwise?"

I smiled.

"What?"

"Let's just say Ava has no cracks in her wall of self-confidence."

He laughed. "Will you go out with me this weekend?"

"I don't know our schedule yet."

"Our schedule? What are you, a private jet pilot?"

"I'll go out with you one night if you promise me one thing."

"I'm ready to sign my name in blood," he said, sitting up.

"I don't want you talking to or having anything at all to do with Ava. If she asks you to go somewhere with her, say no, especially if she wants you to go out with her. Will you promise me that?"

"Sure, but what is this, some kind of sibling rivalry?"

I smiled. "You can call it that. Do I have your solemn promise?"

He raised his right hand. "I, Buddy Gilroy, do hereby swear not to have anything to do with Ava Patio. If she's walking easterly, I'll go westerly. If she's within ten feet of me, I'll immediately make it twenty feet. If she speaks to me, I'll be deaf. If she looks at me, I'll be invisible, and if she touches me, I'll scream like I was burned and walk or run to the nearest exit." He lowered his hand. "How's that?"

"It's fine if you really follow it," I said. I looked at him with steely eyes. "And I'll know almost immediately if you don't."

"Okay," he said, losing his joking smile. He looked down the beach. "You want to walk a little more?"

"Yes," I said, rising.

He picked up his jacket, and we walked silently on the darker, harder, cooler sand. The wind combed the waves and hit us with some spray, but it felt wonderful. We both laughed and trotted a little farther from the water. He took my hand again, and for a moment, we just looked at each other. Then, very slowly but smoothly, he brought his lips to mine. It wasn't a quick, friendly peck on the mouth, either. His lips lingered as if he were a bee drawing nectar from mine. Neither of us spoke. We walked along, silent again, but somehow hearing each other's voice, each other's heartbeat.

"Are you an only child?" I asked. "You never mentioned any brothers or sisters."

"I have a younger brother. He's in tenth grade. He's a jock's jock. Ask him about any football player who played during the past ten years, and he'll give you all his statistics. He's currently the second-string quarterback for the team, but he's breathing down the starting quarterback's neck. Helluva baseball player, too. Hit two-eighty last year, which is pretty good for a high school kid. My father's convinced he'll go to college on a sports scholarship."

"You sound proud of him."

"I am. We're so different that there's no sibling rivalry. That's why I was somewhat surprised at your request."

"What's between Ava and me has nothing to do with sibling rivalry, Buddy."

"What does it have to do with, then?"

"Let's forget it for now," I said. "Maybe it won't matter."

"Whatever you say. I'll play by whatever rules you want. But believe me," he added quickly, "this isn't a game with me. No girl I've met has ever had the effect on me that you had after just a short time together. You know what that means, don't you?"

"What?"

"You're magical. And you don't fool with magic."

I laughed. We walked on. I was so content just holding his hand and talking to him that I didn't think of the time. When I looked at my watch and saw how long we had been together, I felt a small bird of panic flutter its wings under my breast. Ava and Marla could be home by now.

"I have to go," I said.

He nodded, and we hurried back up the beach to the sidewalk. He decided to walk me to my car.

"I don't want to lose a possible second of being with you, Lorelei. If you will just . . ."

I put my finger on his lips. And then I kissed him.

"I'll call you," I said.

"Promise?"

"As long as you keep yours."

"Then you'll call me," he replied.

He stood there while I got into the car, started it, and pulled away. I looked at him through the rearview mirror. True to his word, he coveted every moment with me, even his last glimpse of me before I disappeared around a turn.

No one, not even Daddy, had told me how wonderful I would feel.

*This is surely love,* I thought. *Forbidden or not, it's what I want.*

The question hovering was clearly, what would I be willing to do to have it?

I had no idea, but worse, I was terrified that I would soon find out.

# 13

## Destiny

Ava and Marla were not home yet, which both pleased and bothered me. I was happy I didn't have to explain my late arrival to Ava, but I couldn't help but wonder where she had taken Marla and why it was so important all of a sudden to be alone with her for so long a time. Until recently, and only after Daddy's orders, Ava had never taken me anywhere special. We had never spent quality time together away from the house when I was Marla's age. With Daddy often fanning our sibling rivalry, it was difficult in this house not to think in terms of conspiracies. More and more lately, I found Marla resembled Ava and not me. She had Ava's temperament, certainly, and not mine.

The house was very quiet when I arrived. Neither Mrs. Fennel nor Daddy was downstairs. We usually didn't announce ourselves when we returned from school now, so I went directly to my room. I tried to do some homework and get my mind off my afternoon with Buddy, but his face, his smile, our kiss, wouldn't take a backseat to anything. Would Ava or, more important, Daddy take one look at me and know I was having strong feelings for a boy, and this after the near disaster with Mark Daniels?

When we had first gone to Dante's Inferno, Ava had told me that it was both a curse and a blessing that we could get whomever we wanted. She had said that someday I would understand how it could be both. As I sat there in my room, enjoying my reminiscing about Buddy and at the same time frightened that Daddy, Mrs. Fennel, or Ava would see that enjoyment in my face, I thought I understood what she had meant.

A real relationship between any of us and some boy was a threat to Daddy and therefore the family. Buddy was very attracted to me. I wanted him to be, but Ava was right. How could I afford to fall in love? What would come of it? How could I, like any other father's daughter, ever have a serious relationship, ever get engaged, marry, and move away to have a family of my own?

If I had had a close friend, and she had been there with me, she would surely have asked how I could put my love for and loyalty to my father so high above my own wishes and dreams, even my own needs. After all, didn't everyone need to have someone love him or her, someone other than a father or a mother, a sister or a brother? Or was it just romantic drivel to believe that someone out there was meant to be your life partner, your soul mate?

From reading, from history class, and even from stories Daddy had told me, I knew that there had been a time when young women lived in such a confined and restricted world that it was impossible for them to find soul mates, real lovers. Their parents arranged their whole lives. Those young women became wives and mothers and never experienced the thrill of romance, the excitement of self-discovery. Did they die because of it? Did they suffer and go crazy? Here and there, there were probably some who did, but on the whole, they lived full lives, had and loved their children, and although they didn't fall in love, at minimum, they developed cordial, respectful, and maybe even deeply devoted relationships with the men they were forced to marry. They lay beside each other in cemeteries just like passionate lovers who married, spent their lives together, and passed away.

So, too, my sisters and I could not have boyfriends, go to proms, press flowers and pictures into albums, write love letters, carry on endless soft and loving phone conversations, get engaged to someone we loved and who loved us, or have a wedding that fulfilled our hearts. Our destinies had been prearranged as well. Would we, like those young women ages ago, put all of those romantic ideas in some closet and forget them, or would they haunt us forever? Was that part of the destiny that awaited me?

I stared at myself hatefully in the mirror. Suddenly, everything that was attractive and beautiful about me annoyed me. If I had been born plain, if I had no more sexual power in me than someone like Ruta Lee or Meg Logan, wouldn't I be better off? If I hadn't cried out when Daddy and Mrs. Fennel were walking past my bassinet, would some ordinary childless couple have adopted me and soaked me in their love? I'd have probably fallen in love with some likewise ordinary young man and had a wedding and children. I'd have no other destiny than the destiny most young women had. I would grow old without any illusions about myself. I'd probably not battle against age, either. I'd accept it and be satisfied with an epitaph that read, "She was a good wife, a good mother, a good woman, who made friends easily and never knew the meaning of real unhappiness."

But would I have really been happier never to have known Daddy, never to have traveled in that first-class world that we lived in, a world of glamour and wealth, music and elegance? Would I have really been happier never to have lived in a world in which I never had a sick day, in which youth, energy, and beauty were forever? Would I really be happier sitting in my comfy little living room watching romantic movies or reading books about love and settling for the vicarious experience?

"When you stand on the cliffs of Capri or feel the wind in your hair as the yacht surges forward toward Mykonos, when you have dinner on the Eiffel Tower looking out over Paris or have lunch in Eze on the Riviera and look out over the bluest sea, when you have your cocktail on the rooftop of the Hassler in Rome and look out over the lights of the Eternal City, when you share hors d'oeuvres with the richest, most powerful people in the world, people who can clap their hands or snap their fingers and change the lives of thousands, you will feel the full glory of who you are and what you are," Daddy had promised. "It's out there, waiting for you to claim it, my darling daughter, like some ripe fruit for you to pluck and enjoy. You will have many affairs that are as passionate as any possible. You will miss nothing and have everything."

His kiss had sealed the promise.

I stared at myself in the mirror. *Yes, now I understand what you meant, Ava,* I thought. *Now I know why Mrs. Fennel called love our poison. I must try to fight back all these thoughts and feelings for Buddy Gilroy. I must try to become more like you. Loyalty, obedience, and sacrifice must replace this craving for love and self-fulfillment. I am,* I declared to myself with new resolve, *my father's daughter, too. I can be no one else.* Perhaps that was what Daddy and Mrs. Fennel meant by fulfilling our destiny. In the end, we really had no choice, nowhere else to go. Could I convince myself of that? If Daddy or Mrs. Fennel even suspected I had these doubts . . .

I wrapped my secret thoughts into a neat package and put them away as deeply as I could in the closet of my memory just as my door opened and Ava stepped into my bedroom. She looked about my room and then at me, as if she could literally search the air for traces of my innermost secret thoughts. Then she nodded at the textbooks I had open on my desk.

"Don't waste too much time on all that," she said, moving suspiciously about my room, her eyes going everywhere.

"What do you mean? Why not?"

She shrugged. "Your days at that school are numbered. Why bother to worry about your grades?"

"We're close to the end of the school year. Surely, Daddy wouldn't move us before I finish."

"Do you think that matters at all to Daddy?" she asked, and smiled. "Don't be ridiculous, Lorelei. Others, them," she said disdainfully, waving at the window to indicate any and all who lived outside our world, "need good grades to be the keys that open doors for them. We don't. Daddy arranges everything for us forever."

"I don't do it to get doors open for me, Ava. I do it because I enjoy it."

"Oh, please," she said, and sat at my vanity table. She primped her hair and studied herself in the mirror.

"Where did you take Marla?" I asked. She was so lost in herself that I didn't think she heard me. Then she stopped looking at herself and turned to me.

"To practice," she said.

"Practice? Practice what?"

"I don't know if you've noticed lately, probably not, because your head is in the wrong places these days, but our little Marla is surging into maturity. Daddy says there is something quite remarkable about her, even more remarkable than you or me. For the first time in, what should I say, centuries, he thinks he might have two daughters mature and skilled enough at the same time." She laughed. "Imagine being able to take turns every month. What a relief."

"I don't understand. How can that be? She's not quite fourteen. She doesn't have the mature figure, the—"

"Daddy says he can sense that she will soon look more like eighteen, nineteen. In less than six months, matter of fact, she'll probably be breathing down your neck." She widened her smile.

"My neck?"

"Of course, Lorelei. Just think of the competition, the real sibling rivalry then. Each of you trying to outdo the other when it comes to bringing Daddy what he needs as quickly as he needs it. Who will catch the better prize? Which one of you will do it better, easier?"

She turned back to the vanity mirror, took my brush, and swept her bangs back.

"That way, should one of you have to be replaced, there'll be no problem for Daddy, either," she said. She stopped brushing. "It's exciting, isn't it? I almost wish I could trade places with you, that you'd be the one leaving and not me."

"How can that be exciting? It sounds horrible to think of two sisters trying to outdo each other."

She nodded at herself. "I was right about you. Daddy's beginning to see it, too."

"Right about what?"

"You're missing something the rest of us have. It's a kind of hunger, a driving desire, a need that makes you harder, sharper, and more self-confident. Daddy thinks, hopes, you'll grow into it, that perhaps I'll inspire you, but I have grave doubts, and Daddy has grown to trust my instincts. You think he'll ever feel comfortable trusting yours?" She looked at herself again with pleasure. "I doubt it," she muttered.

"You never really liked me, did you, Ava?" I asked. "All that time we recently spent together was just part of some plan, wasn't it?"

"Don't be juvenile. This has nothing to do with whether or not I like you, and whether or not I like you has nothing to do with what must be, anyway. It's not me you have to please. It's Daddy and Mrs. Fennel, and whether you feel it or not right now, you have to please yourself, too. I must admit," she added after a pause,

"Marla is certainly growing more and more pleased with herself. I'm actually a little jealous of her, and I never thought I'd be jealous of anyone, ever."

"Where did you take her today when you took her from school?"

"Why? Are you suddenly feeling jealous, too?"

"Maybe."

She laughed. "That's good. Maybe there is hope for you. I took her down to Laguna Beach to let her get the taste of beach boys. She was quite a hit. I had to pull them away. I was very impressed with how mature she acted. It's easy to see that Daddy's right about her. I don't remember him saying such things about you at her age. Maybe that's why he babied you more than he babied any of us."

"He didn't baby me, Ava. He loved me."

"Call it what you want." She stood up, turned to look at her figure in the mirror, and smiled at me. "But don't worry, Lorelei. You'll be getting your chance to prove yourself to Daddy very soon now."

"When?"

"Soon." She suddenly looked younger herself, the happiness lighting her eyes. "It's exciting how fast things happen when you're ready, isn't it? I'm ready to leave, and you're ready to begin."

"Yes," I said quickly to cover up any self-doubts. "So, after you leave, will you be like Brianna and never have anything more to do with us?"

"Don't ask questions about my destiny, Brianna's, or even your own right now," she warned. Then she smiled again, her mood changing once more. "Daddy has another surprise to announce at dinner."

"What is it?"

"If I tell you, it won't be a surprise, will it?"

"Why isn't it a surprise for you, too, then?" I asked.

"Haven't you figured it out yet, Lorelei? I've moved to another stage in my development. I'm what you might call one of Daddy's inner circle now." She stepped closer to me and narrowed her eyes. "Think you'll ever get there?"

It was as if she had put her lips to mine and sucked the air out of my lungs and throat. I couldn't speak for a moment.

"I'll be just as good a daughter to Daddy as you've ever been," I said as firmly and as defiantly as I could.

"I hope so. For your sake, I hope so," she said. She walked to the door and opened it before turning back to me. "I guess we'll know soon enough, won't we? See you at dinner." She closed the door softly, but the sound of it, that sharp click, felt like a pin in my heart.

I was all pins and needles as I headed to the dining room for dinner. When I reached the living room, I heard Daddy's laughter and stopped to look in. Marla was demonstrating something that struck him as funny. From the way she was parading in front of him, it looked as if she was showing him how she walked, turned her shoulders, and flirted with her eyes. He clapped his hands, and then he saw me in the doorway.

"Ah, Lorelei. Come in. Marla was just demonstrating something she calls the Dance of the Honey Bee. Isn't that a cute name for it?"

"I don't know, Daddy. I didn't see her do it."

"Well, you will," he said, rising. "Now, where's our Ava? I'm getting hungry. Marla has stirred my appetites."

"I'm here, Daddy," she called from behind me.

"Okay, girls," he said. "Let's go in before Mrs. Fennel calls us for a change. I have some important announcements to deliver."

He reached for Marla the way he had reached for me that night when I wore the dress he had brought back from Paris. He kissed her, too. I looked more closely at her when she turned gleefully to me. There really was something older, more mature about her, especially in her eyes. I hadn't seen it that morning, but maybe that was because my mind was on other things. Or perhaps I was not able to see it emerging. Perhaps only Daddy could see that.

We sat at the table and joined hands, anticipating Daddy's opening remarks.

"My darlings," he began, "for life to hold any interest for us especially, it must from time to time provide surprises. Think of how boring it must be for a clairvoyant to know exactly what lies beyond the next minute, the next hour, the next day. If there is indeed a God and he is all-knowing, he must be as bored with his eternal existence as we would be. Never be afraid of the unknown. Cherish it, in fact, the way you cherish the darkness. I like to think that our lives have a rhythm, just the way our hearts have a rhythm, and when it changes for one reason or another, we know something different is coming or has come." He nodded at Marla.

I looked at Ava. She wore that smile of superiority, which right now I felt like slapping off her face.

"Changes require changes," Daddy continued. He brought his hands together and held them against his chest. "I've decided that in two weeks' time, we will be leaving this house." He paused and nodded at Ava. "Ava will not be leaving with us. She'll be leaving, but she won't be going where we're going. In this new home," he added, now looking at Marla and me, "you will eventually have a new baby sister."

"Oh, that's wonderful, Daddy," Marla said before I could make a comment. "I was just dreaming that I would have a baby sister to help care for."

"Were you? How prescient. That's a very good indicator of good things to come for you as well as for us," Daddy told her.

She practically went up in flames with her burst of pride.

"Why are we leaving so soon, Daddy?" I asked just as Mrs. Fennel entered. She paused with our food on a tray and looked at me angrily. Couldn't I even ask that?

"We're not running from anything or anyone, if that's what you think, Lorelei," he said. "It has nothing to do with what happened here."

"No, I wasn't thinking that. I just wondered."

"Your father knows instinctively when it is best for us to go," Mrs. Fennel said.

Even Ava and Marla were surprised that she had answered for Daddy.

"I know. I just wondered why," I said.

"It's not for you to wonder why," Mrs. Fennel replied.

"I can't wait to leave this place and this school, Daddy," Marla said. "There's nothing like starting somewhere new. Like you've told us often, live as if each day is the beginning of your life."

"Exactly," Daddy said, pleased. He looked at me with concern.

"I have no reason to want to stay," I said quickly, thinking that might be the right thing to say. "Do you know where we'll be going yet?"

He smiled, but it wasn't as warm a smile as I usually received from him. "Of course I do, Lorelei. You need not worry about anything."

"Lorelei is the worrier in our family, Daddy," Ava said, keeping her eyes fixed on me.

"A little worry is a good thing," Daddy said. Mrs. Fennel began to serve our dinner. "But you mustn't ever let anything take control of you or interfere with what you must do and who you must be. The road is littered with those who do," he added. He smiled at all of us and then at the roast Mrs. Fennel had prepared in her own special way.

Never before had Daddy's words frightened me, but there was something in his tone that sent a chill down my spine. That plus Ava's intense study of my every move, every reaction, stole away my appetite, but I ate anyway to hide it.

I was actually relieved to hear that Daddy was going out after dinner, and we wouldn't, as we often did, spend a few hours with him listening to music, talking, and dancing. I was afraid of anything else Ava might say about me, and it did bother me that Daddy was looking at Marla with more interest and love than he had when he looked at me.

All three of us went to our rooms, but not before I saw Marla and Ava whispering in the hallway. I tried to read to keep myself busy and not think about all the changes that would soon be thrust upon me, but I did not stop. Ava was right. I was the worrier in the family. I even worried that worrying too much would, as Daddy warned, prevent me from doing what I had to do and being who I had to be.

A few hours later, as I was beginning to prepare for bed, Ava came to my room. She rarely knocked on my door, but this time, she seemed to slip in with deliberate silence, as if she had expected to catch me doing something wrong. I had no idea how long she had been there staring at me when I looked up and saw her.

"Must you sneak up on me like that, Ava?"

"I wonder why you don't sense me there. I certainly would have sensed you when I was your age," she said instead of apologizing. "Your mind must be otherwise occupied."

"Maybe I'm just tired," I said. "What is it now?"

"You and I are going to plan our next catch. You're being accelerated. You'll make the actual delivery. It should occur a week from this Saturday," she said. "Daddy and I have discussed it, and he is convinced I'm right."

"Right about what?"

"The choice," she said. "It's best you have it a bit easier the first time you lead. We'll be together, but you'll bring him home."

"Who?" I asked, even though I knew the answer.

She smiled. "You know who, Lorelei. Don't pretend to be innocent with me. Sleep tight, and don't let the bedbugs bite," she teased, and left me.

Only hours before, I had made a vow to try to put away my feelings about Buddy. I was hoping I could be as cold about it as Ava was. Was I fooling myself? Was this impossible for me to do, and if it was, what would happen to me? I couldn't fail Daddy. What I had thought was worrying before was nothing compared with what went on my head nearly the whole night. I fell asleep but woke up hours later, only to struggle to sleep again. When morning came, I was disappointed. I had finally gotten myself to sleep again.

Compared with Marla at breakfast, I was like some nun who had taken an oath of silence. Mrs. Fennel looked at me suspiciously, but Marla was so into her own excitement about the things Daddy had told us that she didn't notice or ask me why I was so quiet. Ava had slept late, fortunately. She had no reason to get up as early as we did and wasn't there at breakfast to torment me with her smiles and wry remarks.

Finally, on our way to school, Marla asked me why I was so quiet that morning. Did I dare ask her questions to see if she felt any of the things I felt? Would she rush to Ava to report them?

"Like me, you haven't made any friends at school, Marla, so I guess it doesn't bother you at all that we're leaving, right?"

"Not in the least. Why? Does it bother you?"

"I know you've been unhappy sometimes, having to stay home while the other girls in your class go to parties or the movies together on dates. You've told me so."

"It doesn't bother me anymore," she said.

"When did it stop bothering you?"

"I don't know. Recently. Why, does that still bother you?"

"Sometimes," I admitted. I looked at her. "You don't have to tell me what you tell Ava," I said.

She laughed.

"What's so funny?"

"That's what Ava says about you. I don't have to tell her what I tell you."

"You and Ava talk about me?"

"Just like you and I talk about her and like you two talk about me," she said. "Don't start acting hurt or anything, Lorelei."

"I am a little hurt, Marla. I thought you and I were closer," I said.

"We're as close as Daddy wants us to be, needs us to be," she said. "Don't try to get me to feel sorry for you, Lorelei."

"I'm not."

"Right," she said. After a moment, she added, "Ava warned me you could be like this."

"Like what?"

"Afraid of me," she said, glaring at me the way Ava might.

"What? Why should I ever be afraid of you?"

"You will be," she said confidently. She smiled and looked forward, as if she really could see the future. "You will be."

"That's not a very sisterly thing to say. I thought we were supposed to look out for each other," I told her.

"And we will. At least, I will," she said.

I was happy to arrive at school and get away from her.

She was acting more cocky than ever. I was furious with myself for even trying to get closer to her, to share my feelings. Both of my sisters were making me feel more and more like an outsider now. It put me in a bad mood all day, and even those who always treated me as if I were invisible were obviously affected by it. They kept an extra foot or so away from me and hurried to get out of my way when I walked.

The truth was that the intensity of the anger and resentment I was feeling that morning surprised even me. It had a strange physical effect on my body, too. My arms and legs felt harder, my grip on things tighter. I felt my shoulders harden, and whether it was in my imagination or not, I thought I could hear more clearly, hear things said by students all the way across the hallways, as well as smell things more sharply. The bells that rang to end one period and begin the next reverberated in my bones.

And then the strangest feeling came over me when I was at lunch and sat close to Meg and Ruta. They were both fawning over Tommy Holmes, each probably dreaming of him asking her to the upcoming senior prom. It wasn't simply the sight of them, the obvious ways in which they pressed their bodies against his or touched his hand or even wagged their shoulders and pushed out their breasts to catch his eye. As strange as it seemed, it was the sound of their heartbeats and the scent of their very sex. It nauseated me, and I had to get up and leave. Neither probably noticed. They were too involved in their effort to get Tommy interested in them.

I calmed down when I went outside, but my reaction to what I heard and saw was a little frightening. I felt as if all my feelings and thoughts were twisting around one another. My insides were in turmoil. I was never sick. I never had to leave school or go to the nurse's office. I didn't even recall being uncomfortable at the onset of a period. I knew nothing of the cramps other girls had. Was all of that finally catching up with me? Why wouldn't Mrs. Fennel have mentioned such a possibility if it did exist?

I flipped open my cell phone and called home. She answered immediately. "What is it, Lorelei?" It was as if she had been standing near the phone, anticipating my call.

"I don't know. I'm not sure. I feel hot and then cold, angry and then sad. My body feels as if it's turning to stone and then suddenly is normal again."

"Come home," she said. "Ava will pick up Marla today."

"Is there something wrong with me?"

"No, nothing is wrong, but I'd rather you were home right now." She hung up before I could ask or say anything more.

I went to the office and checked myself out. Before anyone could ask any real questions, I was gone. Mrs. Fennel was waiting for me when I arrived home. She was standing in the kitchen doorway and holding a glass of greenish liquid.

"I want you to drink all of this and then go to your room to rest," she said.

"I don't understand what happened to me. What is that?"

"Just do what I say," she snapped back, and thrust the glass at me.

I took it, looked at her, and drank it. It didn't taste as terrible as it looked, and when it went down my throat, it made me feel warm, but it was a soothing warmth.

"Now, go to bed for a while," she told me.

"Is Daddy here?"

"He is not," she said. "Go to bed."

She turned, and I went down to my bedroom. I got undressed and crawled under the blanket, resting my head softly on the pillow and closing my eyes.

In moments, I was asleep. When I awoke, it was dark out. I rose slowly and looked at the clock. I had slept for hours. It took me a few moments to stop feeling numb and groggy, and then I began to dress. It was too late for dinner, but I imagined Ava, Marla, and Daddy were in the living room. Suddenly, however, my door burst open. Ava stood there glaring in at me.

"What?" I asked.

"Did you say anything to him?"

"Who?"

"Don't play games with me, Lorelei. I'll ask you again. Did you say anything to him?"

"You mean Buddy Gilroy? No," I said. "Why do you ask?"

She studied me a moment and then relaxed and entered, closing the door behind her. "Something is wrong," she said, sitting on my bed. "He avoided me all day, and I deliberately went looking for him."

"Did he ask about me?"

"What? No, of course not. Maybe he's really gay," she said. Ava could not stomach any rejection. It pleased me to see her suffering so.

"Maybe he is," I said. "I read where some gay college guys try to look like heterosexuals in front of their friends because they're ashamed of what and who they are or they're afraid of being ridiculed."

She considered. "Maybe," she said. "If that's true, he won't be good for Daddy, anyway. I'll have to rethink it all."

"Whatever you say, Ava."

She looked at me as if she had just realized I was there. "What happened to you today?"

I described my symptoms.

She listened and nodded. "It's normal," she said.

"It happened to you?"

"I just said it was normal, didn't I?" She rose. "Daddy's with someone tonight," she added, "so don't rush out there."

"Oh."

"I don't understand him. I can usually sense men who wouldn't be of any value to Daddy."

She looked at me, and I shrugged.

Then she walked out, closing the door sharply behind her.

Had I just saved Buddy Gilroy's life?

And maybe my own?

# 14

## Saved

It occurred to me almost immediately that Buddy had lived up to his promise and surely expected me now to live up to mine. If I didn't, he might very well go back to Ava, either to spite me or because he wanted what she offered. At school the following day, I stepped out between classes and called him. He didn't pick up, but I left a message that I would call when I was free. Right before lunch, my phone rang. If anyone's phone rang in class or even in the hallway, the principal would take away the phone privilege for the rest of the year and suspend the student for at least two days. Before anyone could hear it ring a second time, I charged into the girls' room.

"Hello," I said, thinking it might be Daddy.

"You called me," Buddy said, his voice rich with excitement. "You lived up to your promise. I wanted to believe you, but I couldn't help being skeptical."

"How did you get my number?"

He laughed. "Don't you know that it registered on my phone? Mine probably registered on yours."

"Oh."

"You don't use yours much, do you?"

"No."

"So, does this mean I have earned our night out? What about this weekend?"

"Things are a little hectic at home. I don't know exactly when or where we can meet again yet, but I wanted you to know I was happy you did what you promised."

"I can't even think of breaking a promise I make to you, Lorelei. How about meeting after school again? I'll go anywhere you say."

"I can't. I have to take my younger sister home today."

"What about afterward?"

"I can't today," I said.

"Bummer. You're not going to break your promise now, are you?"

"No. I'll call you as soon as we can meet."

"I'm going to sleep with this phone," he said.

I laughed. Two girls from my class, Shirley Fox and Patti Jonston, came in giggling about something. They stopped when they saw me.

"I have to go to class. I'll call you," I said quickly, and flipped my phone closed.

"You can get suspended for doing that," Patti said.

"I was suspended last year," Shirley said, "and all I did was text my boyfriend. It didn't even make any noise."

I thought about it a moment and then smiled. "Thanks for the advice," I said. They both smirked when I smiled and left them.

Right before the late bell rang for my next class, I pretended my phone had rung, and I stood outside the classroom doorway, listening and whispering. The late bell rang, but I did not go into the classroom. Moments later, my teacher, Mr. Trustman, stepped into the doorway and looked out at me. There was no doubt in my mind that one or more of the other students had told him I was outside on my cell phone.

"Lorelei Patio!" he shouted.

I acted surprised and flipped the phone closed. "Sorry," I said.

"So am I, and very, very disappointed in you. Not only are you late, but you're on a cell phone? Go directly to the principal's office right now," he ordered, holding his long arm out with the same stiff forefinger he used to make his points in class.

I lowered my head and hurried down the hallway. Because of the intercom system, the principal's secretary, Mrs. Winters, knew exactly why I had been sent to the office before I arrived. She was a plump five-foot-two-inch woman with dark gray hair and a cherubic face. Most of the time, she acted as if she was everyone's surrogate mother, gently chiding those who violated rules and praising those who had received some accolade. She had a personal bulletin board on which she pinned any student's outstanding achievement, from sports to spelling bees. She was shaking her head as I entered.

"What a disappointment," she said. "You of all people. What a disappointment. Dr. Phelps is waiting to see you. Go right in," she told me, and shook her head again.

Our principal was a tall, thin, forty-five-year-old man with brown hair and a habitual look of distress and fatigue. Normally, he spoke so quietly, it was difficult to hear him if you didn't give him your full concentration.

I had seen him in action when it came to discipline. No matter what the violation, from chewing gum too loudly to defacing a part of the building, he always had the same initial reaction, taking it very personally and feeling sorry more for your parents than for you or even himself. It was always "We've been let down. What are we to think and do?"

With some students, it worked, and they were sincerely remorseful, but most saw it as getting off easy, despite what punishment followed.

"I have met your father only a few times," he began when I entered his office, "but I know how much we'll both be disappointed by your actions, Lorelei. Up to now, you have been a model student, doing very well in your work, behaving like a little lady in and out of your classes. No one has anything but good things to say about you. How could you suddenly turn like this and so blatantly violate one of the most important rules of our school?"

I didn't respond, but I tried not to look too remorseful or apologetic. I was afraid he might lift the punishment and give me a second chance. However, this was a private school, with everyone sensitive about anyone else getting special treatment simply because outside the school, it was the norm. The kids were generally from well-to-do families with some influence. I had often heard students bragging about how their parents got them out of traffic tickets or into places from which they would normally be barred. Special favors resulted from financial or political muscle. No one was more sensitive to this than Dr. Phelps.

"You might as well leave that phone home from now on. If you should use it again in this building or on this property, you will be expelled from school," he said.

His long pause had me worried that he would do nothing more.

"As per our regulations," he added after he had obviously mulled over what he would do, "you are suspended for two days. I'll count today as one of those days, even though it is half over. You are to leave the building. A call will be made to your father, of course, so my advice to you is to go right home."

I nodded. My failure to say I was sorry or to say anything that sounded remorseful obviously annoyed and hardened him.

"Perhaps we have misjudged you." He narrowed his eyes. "We'll be watching you a bit more closely from now on, missy," he said, his taut lips revealing the anger stirred up inside him. I nodded again. "You're dismissed," he said.

I rose and walked out slowly, but the moment I stepped into the hallway, I hurried toward the exit. As soon as I had left the building, I took out my phone and called Ava. Even though she was at college, she sounded as if she had been sleeping. It took her a few moments and a second explanation from me to get her to understand.

"Suspended? For answering your cell?" I could practically see her suspicions exploding. "Who called you?"

"I thought it was you," I said. "Otherwise, I wouldn't have answered the phone."

"I didn't ask you who it wasn't. Who called you?"

"It was someone calling the wrong number. She

spoke in Spanish, and it took me about a minute to get through to her that I wasn't Lourdes or someone, but by then it was too late. One of my great new friends, or maybe two of them, told my teacher, and he sent me to the office. I have to leave the property. You'll have to pick up Marla at the end of the day."

"I don't know why we ever gave you that phone."

"Daddy gave it to me," I reminded her.

"Yeah, well, you lucked out there, Lorelei. He and Mrs. Fennel are gone for two days. She left our dinners to be warmed up. You can have that privilege."

"Where did they go?"

"Probably to see about your new home."

"Where is it?"

"I don't know. I don't run around here imitating you and asking questions all day."

"When will there be a new little sister living with us?"

"Didn't you hear what I said? I don't cross-examine Daddy, and especially not Mrs. Fennel. Does Marla know what happened to you?"

"No. I had to leave the building immediately. You have to pick her up today and tomorrow."

"Why didn't you just wait for her?"

"For three hours in the parking lot? Besides, the principal wanted me off the grounds," I said, exaggerating. "It won't be a problem. If you're just in the parking lot at the end of the school day, I'm sure—"

"Yeah, thanks. I have to go somewhere first. Now I have to rush," she said, and hung up.

As soon as she did, I called Buddy. It was clear to me from his whispering that I had caught him in a class.

"Hang on," he said. Moments later, he was able to speak louder.

"Sorry. I didn't mean to interrupt your class. Did you get into trouble?"

"Are you kidding? No. You did me a favor. You interrupted my sleep. This guy could bore a charging bull to death. I think he was put here to test our powers of concentration. He works for the CIA or something."

"Don't make me laugh," I said. "I'm in trouble and can't look or be happy."

"You're in trouble? What happened?"

I told him, and he immediately got onto the same train of thought I had been riding.

"You have about three hours before your sisters get home?"

"About."

"We're wasting time," he said, and described where we should meet in Brentwood. "I'll be there before you," he promised, and described his car.

"Are you sure? Won't you be missing other classes?"

"I'm walking toward the parking lot as I speak," he said. "Call me if you get lost."

I got into my car. My heart was thumping like a flat tire. There was a civil war going on inside me. A part of me was screaming warnings, sounding alarms, while another part was raging with new excitement and defiance. Less than a half-hour later, I turned onto a residential side street and saw Buddy standing and leaning against his parked car in the driveway of the address he had given me. It was in a cul-de-sac. I pulled up beside his car and got out.

"I feel like I just walked into my own dream," he said, his face beaming like a little boy's. "I had this dream last night, this hope, I guess you could call it, that we would meet here."

I stood while he approached me, put his hands on my shoulders, and leaned in to kiss me softly. I said nothing when he lifted his lips from mine, but he kept close enough to kiss me again easily. I felt the tingle of his kiss travel through my body as if it were floating on my blood and through my veins, electrifying my heart.

"Did I tell you how beautiful you are?"

"You mentioned it," I said. I looked around. "Whose house is this?" I asked. "Should we be standing here like this?"

"It's my uncle Frank's house. He's my father's youngest brother. He got divorced about two years ago, and as part of his settlement with his wife, he kept the house. He travels a lot, and since I'm close by, I sort of watch over it for him when he's away." He smiled mischievously. "He's away now, and when the cat's away . . ."

He reached for my hand, and I walked with him to the front door. He smiled again, opened it, and stood back for me to enter. Yesterday, I thought, I had been determined to stay away from him, and today I was entering a house to be alone with him. Had I lost my senses or gained them? I knew I should have been more frightened, more nervous, and certainly more reluctant, but I walked in quickly, and he entered and closed the door behind us.

"It's a comfortable old house," he said, gazing around the entryway. "It's probably only about an eighteen-hundred-square-foot ranch, but in this neighborhood, it's worth about three, maybe four million."

I looked at the living room. It was half the size of ours, and the furnishings looked as if they came from a department-store sale. I could just hear Daddy disdainfully calling the decor "Imitation Tasteless." To him, most modern furniture lacked class, style, and a sense of history. "A house without any antiques is a house without any soul," he would say. "Heritage is the life blood of character."

Buddy took my hand again, and we entered the living room to sit on the small brown sofa. The pillows were worn so thin we sank quickly and both laughed.

"It's like sitting on marshmallow," he said. "So, you got into trouble at school. First time?"

"Yes."

"Was it my fault?"

"Oh, yes," I said, and he looked surprised.

"When I called?"

"No, not then. That's what gave me the idea."

"You mean you . . . let me understand. Are you saying you deliberately got yourself suspended?"

I nodded.

"Why?"

"To see you," I said.

"But . . . why couldn't we see each other later or even tomorrow or, better yet, this weekend?"

"I don't know if we'll ever be able to see each other again," I said.

He recoiled. "Huh? You're not making any sense. I thought it was your sister who was wild and crazy."

"She's more than that, Buddy. She's dangerous. You keep your promise to me and stay away from her."

"Dangerous? How could she be dangerous, unless sex is poisonous?"

"Just take my word for it. She's dangerous."

He stared with a half-smile of incredulity on his face. "What's happening here?" he asked. "Are you and your sister playing some sort of game with me?"

"No, no, absolutely not."

"I remember how the two of you teased the guys at Dante's," he continued, the suspicion lingering. "You're kidding me, aren't you? I mean about deliberately getting suspended just so you'd have an opportunity now to see me?"

"No. I'm telling you the truth. I . . . my father is very strict about my socializing."

"Huh? Wait a minute. Your father is strict about your socializing, but he let you and your sister go to Dante's?" He shook his head. "You're not making any sense now, Lorelei. In fact, you're scaring me a little. You sound wacky."

"I know," I said. "I don't mean to sound that way."

He laughed. "C'mon," he said, leaning toward me and bringing his lips close to mine again.

"Wait," I said. "Let me explain. The night you saw me at Dante's really was the first night I was ever out without my father."

He studied my face to see if I was kidding him, and then he sat back. "You certainly didn't act like any girl out for the first time, at least any girl I've ever met or seen," he said.

"I had a good instructor that night," I said.

He squinted. "And who was that?"

"My sister," I said.

"Well, why was your father so lenient with her and not with you?"

"It's complicated," I said. I paused. Every word I uttered now had to be well thought out first. "I'm adopted."

"Adopted? You didn't tell me that. You told me your mother had died."

"That's why I was adopted. I don't reveal that. I don't like the effect it has on other girls and boys."

"Oh." He thought a moment and then smiled. "I didn't think you and your sister looked that much alike, but now that you've mentioned it, why does your being adopted make any difference in the way your father treats you as compared with Ava?"

"There were promises made," I said. I thought that was safe and somewhat logical even though a bit cryptic.

"Oh, so your father did know your mother?"

"Yes, he knew her."

"Well, what about your real father, then? Where was he at the time?"

"I don't know."

He nodded. "I see. This is a little complicated." He was thoughtful again.

I hated making all this up, but I saw no other way. "I'm all right with it. I love my father very much, and he's very devoted to me, to all of us."

"That's good. Maybe if your father met me, he would see I'm a decent guy and—"

"No," I said, perhaps too quickly and vehemently.

"No," I added softly. "Not yet. For now, I'd like to keep everything as it is."

"Okay. Whatever you say. I'll do whatever you want, as long as I can be with you, Lorelei. Besides," he said, smiling again, "we're wasting precious time."

He leaned in to kiss me again. His lips moved off mine, to my cheeks, my chin, and my neck. Any girl doing this for the first time had to feel anxious and even a little afraid. She wouldn't want to seem cold and awkward, so innocent and unsophisticated that she would make a fool of herself. I was sure that just as I was caught in an emotional tug of war for my own special reasons, any girl would be pulled in opposite directions.

One half of her would want to test her own passions, discover whatever wonderful surprises her body had waiting for her. She could read about it, imagine herself as a character in a romance novel or in a movie, but to feel a boy's lips actually on hers, moving over her body, his hands touching her in places never touched by anyone other than herself, in short, to enter her private space, her private places, and stir whatever wonderful part of her had been in waiting since she first felt she had stepped into maturity, was impossible to dismiss or belittle. Could a girl really ever be a woman without bringing all that to life?

But there was also that second part of a girl, the part that resisted, that pulled her back, that system of alarms her parents, her teachers, and other adults planted in her mind and heart, those warnings that told her not to go too far, not to surrender herself too quickly and risk losing all those years of joy that lay ahead. How confusing it was to think that something that brought her so much pleasure, made her feel so much like the woman she was meant to be, could at the same time destroy a significant part of her, steal away her most precious years, those years before she had to be sensible and responsible. Surely, a part of life was meant to be carefree. The laughter was different then. Even the air she breathed seemed different. Mornings and nights were certainly different. She felt immortal, capable of doing anything, going anywhere. All of that was at risk.

And it wasn't simply solved by taking a birth-control pill or having any other protection. They weren't perfect, and besides, even with that, a girl was giving up what Ava had called "the mystery of you." Even if it was cool and defiant to be intimate with any boy or man a girl was with, at the end of the day, she made something special into something ordinary. In her rush to be her own woman, she might have given away the one thing that made her so.

I had spent many hours thinking about all of this and especially listening to other girls talk about it in school. Most thought I wasn't paying any attention to them, that I didn't care what they had to say, but I very much did. Where else would I learn about it? My older sister had a different agenda, a different goal and objective for sex, and although that was going to be mine as well, I was, after all, the daughter who asked too many questions, thought about too many things. Ava didn't care one iota what other girls thought or felt about themselves and sex. She had made that clear to me many times. But I did. Was that another thing that made me different, dangerously different?

All of this raced through my mind as Buddy's kisses became more passionate, his breathing hotter and faster, and my own heart began pounding. I heard his tender expressions of love, his promises and admiration for me. The sound of his voice and all that he was saying did embellish the excitement raging inside me. Yes, I wanted him to touch me, to turn up the heat inside me, to drive me to the point when I would demand more and more from him, causing him to have that sweet and passionate desperation that made him whimper with desire.

Sex, I discovered, could also fill you with agony, an agony that intensified until you surrendered to it. Although I wasn't quite there, I could feel that he was. I could hear it in his now more desperate-sounding pleas for me to accept him, to be more compliant, more willing.

He began to undress me.

"You're so beautiful," he said. "So beautiful you bring tears of joy into my eyes."

When he began to undress himself, Ava's furious warnings began to echo in my head: *You'll be of no use to Daddy. He'll hate you. You won't be part of our family anymore.*

I couldn't help but think of Daddy's loving caresses, his soft kisses. Buddy thought my moans were moans of pleasure, but they were moans of fear and sorrow. And then, just as he was lowering his head to kiss my stomach and move down even lower, I looked past him and thought I saw Mrs. Fennel's face in the living-room window. She was glaring at me with those fiery eyes. I screamed and pushed him away.

"What's wrong?" he asked as I rushed to dress.

"I can't do this, not now."

He looked devastated. "I didn't mean . . . I couldn't help myself, but I really love you, Lorelei. Thoughts of you have taken over my brain. I can't sleep. I can't eat. I hear other people talking, but I don't hear their words or make any sense of them, or anything for that matter. It's as if you've possessed me, only I'm not complaining. I love that I'm possessed by you."

"It's all happening a little too fast," I said. "Don't be angry."

"Oh, I can't ever be angry at you."

"Don't say that so fast, either," I told him. I continued to dress.

"Are you upset with me? I just thought . . . I mean, since you agreed to meet here, that . . ."

"No, it's not your fault. I guess I'm just too nervous about what's happened. I did want to be with you, Buddy. I do. Maybe I'll be able to meet you again tomorrow," I offered. "We'll see."

"Isn't there any way that I can get your father to feel better about your being with me, so I can take you out on a real date?"

"Maybe later. Let me think about it," I said, hoping that would satisfy him.

He looked at his watch. "You still have a little time, don't you? Let's just talk, then. Tell me more about yourself. What happened to your real mother?"

"Cancer," I said. How convenient and all-encompassing that word could be.

"Oh, sure. Well, what about your current father?

Where's his wife? How was he able to adopt you if he didn't have a wife?" he asked.

"His sister lives with us," I said. "She's been . . . she's been our mother."

"That's weird. Your father never married?"

"Yes, he did. His wife died."

"Oh. And so he didn't give you back afterward, since his sister was there?"

"Something like that," I said.

"Something like that? Funny way to put it."

"It's not something I question, Buddy. Imagine asking 'Why did you keep me?'"

"Yeah, I see your point. You said you have a younger sister. So he legally adopted her, too?"

"Yes."

"So, Ava is the daughter your father had with his wife before she died?"

"Yes."

I looked at my watch. "I had better go. If I'm not home when Ava returns with my younger sister . . ."

"Okay," he said, rising. "Should I call you tonight?"

"I'll call you," I said. "It's very important that Ava not know about us, Buddy."

"You do make her sound dangerous. What is she, some kind of psychotic?"

"She's . . . a very jealous person. She can be very mean, yes, and she would do something to get me into big trouble."

He nodded and walked me out. We stood by my car for a moment. He just looked at me.

"What?" I asked.

"You're so full of mystery and contradictions. I'm frustrated, but I'm also even more attracted to you." He pretended to look around. "You sure we're not on some kind of reality show here?"

"Hardly," I said, laughing. He was so cute, his passion for me so obvious. I leaned in and kissed him. He kept his eyes closed after I pulled back.

"I want to savor every kiss," he said. "Pack it tightly into my memory so I'll be able to relive it while I'm away from you. Suffering, I might add."

I got into my car.

"You'll call me later? You promise?"

"Let's not turn everything into a promise," I said. "Too much opportunity for disappointment."

"Hey . . . that's deep. You are a woman of mystery. Okay, I'll keep my cell phone in the pocket next to my heart."

I smiled, started the car, and backed out of the driveway. He stood watching me. I waved and drove off. In my rearview mirror, I could see him still watching me, like someone who wanted to memorize every moment.

I knew that I did.

# 15

## Outsider

Because of a sudden rainstorm and heavy traffic caused by an accident, I reached home only fifteen minutes before Ava and Marla arrived. I was anxious the entire way and even more so when I got home. I hurried into the house, afraid they were right behind me. To keep myself occupied and contain my nervousness, I changed clothes, set the table for dinner, and checked on the food Mrs. Fennel had prepared. When I heard Ava and Marla enter laughing, I stepped out of the dining room.

"What's so funny?" I asked.

"You," Marla said. "Getting suspended. Little Miss Perfect with the perfect grades and perfect social graces. Wait until Daddy hears about it, how you messed up and brought unnecessary attention to us."

"You don't have to be so gleeful about my misfortune, Marla," I said.

"You would be if it happened to me," she countered, her face as full of venom as Ava's could be.

I looked at Ava, who stared at me as if she was waiting for my reaction. "I don't think so," she said when I didn't respond. "I don't think Lorelei would be as gleeful." The way she said it made it sound like a terrible fault.

"Well, I do," Marla insisted, and marched off to her room. Ava remained.

"Everything's ready for our dinner," I said, hating the moment of silence between us. "What time do you want to eat?"

"The same time as always, Lorelei. Why should tonight be any different?"

"I just thought you might have had something to do."

"I do. Watch over you two," she said, "like some babysitter."

"You don't have to worry about me."

I started back to the kitchen, but she followed me.

"Of course I have to worry about you. Guess what?" she said. "I went looking for Buddy Gilroy after you called me and couldn't find him. He cut his classes, apparently, all of his afternoon classes. Don't you think that's odd?"

"Maybe you scared him off and he withdrew from college," I said, unloading some dishes from the dishwasher.

"You sure it wasn't Buddy who called you at school today?" she asked.

"I'm sure." I spun on her. "Stop talking about him, Ava. I know it hurts your ego that he didn't fawn over you, but you've got to get over it."

"What? Me get over it? Please. He's a boy. I've been with men. I was obviously too much for him," she said, but my sharp comeback was enough to get her to walk away without another word about Buddy.

I remained in the kitchen to pretend to do something more for dinner. My whole body was shaking, and I didn't want her to see.

Later, at dinner, Marla insisted that I give her a blow-by-blow account of what had happened to me in school. I tried to sound bitter about it, even though I had deliberately arranged to get caught, but I was afraid that Ava saw I was overdoing it, so I stopped explaining and blaming the other girls.

"Why keep talking about it? None of this school stuff really matters to us, anyway," she said. "We go through the motions to please Daddy. And Mrs. Fennel, of course. Can't say as I've always pleased her," she added with a laugh, which raised my eyebrows.

"What did you do to make her unhappy?" I asked, seeing an opening into one of the darker hallways in our lives. It wasn't only Mrs. Fennel and Daddy who kept the keys to our vault of secrets. Each of us inherited some of that, Ava the most right now, since she was the oldest.

She laughed. "I guess it's all right to tell you now. Once I brought a boy home to play a video game with me."

"You did?" Marla exclaimed before I could.

"You don't remember that, do you, Lorelei?"

"No."

"I was only in the sixth grade, but I invited this boy, and his mother brought him over. Actually, in the back of my mind, I thought I was doing a good thing."

"How would that be a good thing?" I asked. I was interested to see if anything had been different for her when she was growing up with Daddy and Mrs. Fennel.

"Helping Brianna find someone new. He was big for his age and very strong. Boys in seventh, eighth, and even ninth grade were afraid of him. I didn't know our rules about whom to choose and not to choose for Daddy back then. I thought I'd bring him around for Brianna's consideration. Boy, was Mrs. Fennel angry. Neither of you have ever seen her that angry, and I hope for your sakes you never do."

"What did she do when the boy was brought over?" Marla asked.

"She let him stay, of course, but as soon as his mother came for him, she pounced on me. Daddy was away at the time. I thought she was literally going to kill me and bury me in the backyard or something. I went to sleep shivering that night."

"What happened when Daddy found out?" I asked.

"He was angry, too, but nothing like she was. He came to my room the next morning and woke me to tell me more than I knew about our lives up to then, so I wouldn't make the same error again. I cried, and he held me and told me it was all right. When Daddy forgives you, you feel forgiven," she said. "I wasn't as terrified of Mrs. Fennel the next day, but I swear, she glared at me with fire in her eyes for at least a week afterward. It was like two hot coals cooling down. I complained, but Daddy told me not to be upset with her. He said she was only being very protective and had gone through her own difficulties."

"Is that when Daddy told you what happened to her husband?" Marla asked.

I looked at her resentfully. Why was Ava growing

closer to her, telling her things at her age that she had never told me?

"Not exactly then but not long afterward," Ava said. She was quiet for such a long moment I thought that was it, but then she said, "She had made the nearly fatal mistake of falling in love with someone." She turned to me quickly. "That's why she has the thoughts she has about love."

"Why was it nearly fatal?" I asked, holding my breath. Would she tell us more?

"She told him too much about us and herself and put not only herself in danger but Daddy, too, and the others, of course."

"I can't believe Mrs. Fennel would have done that," I said.

"Love," Ava said out of the corner of her mouth. "Just because she's very old doesn't mean she can't keep learning things, too, you know."

"So, what happened then?" Marla asked.

Ava smirked. "Try to guess."

"I can't guess," Marla whined.

"She brought him to Daddy," she said, again looking at me. "It broke her heart forever, but it was the right thing to do. As a reward for her sacrifice, Daddy let her keep his name. This happened a very long time ago, but she still smarts over it, and that's why she hates being questioned about herself and why she says love can be poison for us."

*Mrs. Fennel,* I thought, amazed. I'd never in a million years have guessed she was someone with a broken heart. Was Ava telling me these things deliberately now?

Did she know about me and Buddy? Was it meant to be a lesson I should never forget?

"Well, I'm never going to fall in love," Marla said. "Just the idea of being with only one man forever makes me sick to my stomach."

Ava laughed and put her arm around her to embrace her and kiss her. "Our lovely, perfect little sister," she said. "Don't you agree, Lorelei?"

"Yes," I said. "She surprises me more and more every minute of every passing day." Although I didn't like being this way, I know I sounded bitter and sarcastic.

"Remember what Daddy told us," Marla said, wagging her head. "Surprises can be wonderful. It makes every day seem like the first day of your life."

"None of us quotes Daddy better or more accurately than you do, Marla," Ava said.

Why was she heaping compliments on our younger sister? She should be heaping them on me. I was the next in line, not Marla.

"So, what are you going to tell Daddy when he finds out you were suspended from school?" Marla asked me.

I looked at both of them, at the way they were both waiting for my response. It was as if they were testing me. It made me angry to see them ganging up on me, but I knew that losing my temper was just what Marla would enjoy seeing.

I shrugged as nonchalantly as I could. "I'm certainly not going to lie about it. I'll tell him the truth."

"What is the truth?" Ava asked.

"What do you mean, what is the truth? I told you exactly what happened. It was an accident. I answered the phone before I thought about it, but if those girls weren't so hateful—"

"Why was your phone on, anyway?" Ava pursued, leaning toward me and bearing down on me like a prosecutor in a courtroom. "Daddy and I know never to call you during school hours. Why would you think it was either of us?"

"I just told you. I wasn't thinking. I didn't realize it was on. I don't do everything as perfectly as you do, Ava."

She sat back, lapping up my backhanded compliment. "You'd better be as perfect as I am," she warned. "We have a great many wonderful things, and we'll each have more. But there are many tests ahead of you to pass, Lorelei. Failure is not an option for us, either. You had better think more than twice about everything you do from now on. If Daddy forgives you, that is," she added, and shifted her eyes toward Marla.

I felt Marla's eyes stinging me. Ava had been right about her. There were differences in her, mature changes happening almost right before our eyes. It was not hard to imagine her breathing down my neck as Ava had predicted. My changes didn't occur as rapidly. I didn't think they had for Ava, either, and of course, I couldn't recall anything about Brianna's maturing, but I had never heard any stories about her to illustrate these sorts of quick changes. Maybe of all four of us, Marla was the special one, after all.

As I looked from Ava to Marla and back to Ava and saw the steely cold in their eyes, I thought this was more than the simple sibling rivalry Daddy had described.

It was one thing to be competitive with your siblings, to seek to gain your parents' approval faster than your brothers or sisters and maybe even become their favorite, despite their insistence that they didn't favor one of their children over the others. But it was quite another thing to be absolutely ruthless about it, to wish actual harm on your brothers or sisters. Although my experience with other girls and boys as I had gone through school was very limited, I had learned and sensed enough to know that what was happening here among me and Marla and Ava was unusual, despite the lessons taught from the biblical tale of Cain and Abel. At least, I hoped it was; otherwise, what was the value of family? Where were the love, affection, and concern? Didn't we owe any loyalty to one another as well as to Daddy? Was the fable of Cain and Abel the truth? Were we Cain's descendants and not Abel's? Was this to be forever our truth?

Ava decided that since I was the screw-up that day, I would have to clean up after dinner while she and Marla went off to watch television and chat. When it was time to take out the garbage, I took my cell phone with me so I could call Buddy as I had promised him. The rain had stopped, but it was misty and cool. Even though both Marla and Ava were in the living room, I had the eerie feeling that I was being watched. I hovered near the door and made the call.

"Did you get into a lot of trouble at home?" Buddy immediately asked.

How easy it would have been for me to say yes and that I had been ordered to stay home until my suspension from school was over. But all I could think about when I heard his voice again were his soft eyes, his tantalizing kiss, and the way my body reacted to his touch. It was as if his fingers on my breast could literally touch my heart. Even though we didn't go that far, I could feel him inside me. Now, every quiet moment I had since I had been with him was filled with him. I heard his loving words and smiled at the vision of his smile. Everything I had read and seen on television and in movies about love reinforced what I was feeling. Surely, this was different from anything my sisters had experienced. Even Ava, if she felt the way I felt now about Buddy or any boy, might question having to forget him.

"Not yet," I said. "My father and his sister are away until late tomorrow."

"Does that mean . . . can we see each other tomorrow at the same place?"

"I don't know, Buddy. I'll call you in the morning." I looked back at the house. "Ava was looking for you today," I said.

"What for?"

"I don't know, but she will probably look for you again tomorrow."

"She won't be happy if she finds me. I can't see any other girl but you, no matter who I look at or who I hear talking."

"Ava's very clever," I said. "She'll know immediately if you and I have met. She'll get me in deeper trouble. Don't dare mention me. She'll tell my father."

"This is nuts. I don't want to keep hiding from your father," he said.

"It has to be this way for now. If you can't—"

"Okay, okay," he said quickly, afraid I would end it then and there. "I'll wait for your call, and if I see her, I'll be careful. I promise. Will you call?"

"Yes," I said. "Good night." I quickly shut the phone. I heard movement in the house and hurried inside.

"What a good little housekeeper you are," Ava said when she saw me enter. She was already in the kitchen, and I was afraid she had heard me make the phone call. "Mrs. Fennel will be so pleased with how you kept her kitchen. But don't think that will get you off the hook with her or with Daddy," she quickly added. Since she didn't mention hearing me, I assumed I was safe.

"I know it won't do that, Ava," I said, sounding as remorseful as I could. "I can't think of anything else." How good could I be with this performance? I wondered. Could I be the student who matched the teacher? "I'm scared, Ava. I really messed up."

She studied me a moment and then shook her head. "It's not that tragic. Daddy won't be pleased, of course, but considering that he's planning on a move quite soon, he won't be as worried as he would have been if you were staying here longer. I'm leaving, of course."

"I don't want to do anything to spoil your plans," I said.

"Don't worry. You won't. You'll live up to your responsibilities, I'm sure."

I glanced at her to see if she were being sarcastic, but she wasn't. If anything, she wore that face of utter self-confidence that shared a seat with arrogance.

"After all, you're my prodigy, aren't you?"

"Yes," I said. "I guess I am. Do you know when they'll be back?"

"Daddy said late in the day tomorrow but early enough for Mrs. Fennel to prepare dinner. I'd say around four, maybe five. You'll just have to be on pins and needles all day. I'd hang around and hold your hand, but I have to be at college. I've cut too many of the classes I have tomorrow and could bring some unnecessary attention to us. See? I think about that all the time. You'll have to get so you do as well, Lorelei."

"I will."

"Maybe. You'd better. After my classes, I'm scouting a new hunting ground for us, the setting for your full initiation. It's a club about fifty miles away near San Bernardino. I'll be with you, but it might be my last outing for Daddy in California, or anywhere, for that matter."

"You'll really be on your own after that?"

"I'll be on my own," she said.

"And that doesn't frighten you?"

"Frighten me? Hell, no. It's my destiny, and the same will someday be true for you."

"I still don't understand that."

"I've told you. You will. Okay, if you want me, I'll be in my room showing Marla how to fix her hair and put on makeup. I'm turning her into a little femme fatale."

"Why are you doing all this with her so soon? She's years younger than I was, and I thought it would be my responsibility to prepare her."

"Daddy's orders," she said. "Don't look so worried

about it. Everything will be just fine if you do what you were meant to do and nothing else." She flashed a cold smile and left.

Maybe it was my experience with Buddy or simply something newly born inside me, but whatever it was, it enhanced my sense of loneliness. I had never felt more like an outsider than I did at that moment. When I walked through our home, everything suddenly looked strange to me. I felt as if I had entered someone else's home. It occurred to me that except for the old piano I played, there was nothing in the house that called to me and only me. There was nothing I cherished and would want to bring with me when I left. What were my possessions, really? My clothes? Hardly. Most of them were handed down to me from Ava, and the things Daddy bought for me I was expected someday to hand down to Marla. What was mine, really mine?

There was only one thing that came to mind, and that was the picture of the woman who could be my mother. No one knew I had it, and that secret felt good to hold and to keep. I owned something of my past, something that told me more about who I was. It was my icon, my most religious possession.

I returned to my room and took the picture out. For a while, I simply stared at her face, as if I hoped it would somehow come to life and she would tell me exactly what I was to do. How I wished and hoped she was truly my mother. I needed her. I knew exactly what I would ask her if she were really there.

*Should I see Buddy again? Can I fall in love?* I imagined a conversation with her.

*Had you fallen in love, Mommy?* I loved the sound of
the word *Mommy.*

*Yes.*

*Was it poison, Mommy?*

*Oh, no, no. It filled me with hope and made every sunny
day brighter, every color richer, everything I smelled and ate
vibrant. It was truly being born again. I never felt so young
and alive, Lorelei. It was far, far from poison.*

*That's the way I feel right now when I think of Buddy,
when I'm with Buddy, Mommy.*

*Then that's good, Lorelei. Don't lose it.*

*Where are you, Mommy? Why did you let me go? Did
Daddy do the same thing to you that he did to Ava's mother
and the others? Will I ever see you, talk to you?*

There was no reply. She became simply a photograph
again, flat and cold. There was nothing to hug, no cheeks
to kiss, no scent of hair to smell, and no lips to feel on
my cheeks. Yet I embraced the photograph and held it
against my heart.

The sound of footsteps jolted me. I quickly hid the
picture and turned just as Ava opened my door.

"Who are you talking to?" she demanded.

"Talking? No one. Who's here to talk to?"

"I was sure I heard you talking," she said. I should
have remembered how keen her hearing was now.

"I was probably thinking aloud," I admitted.

"You weren't on the cell phone?"

"What? Hardly," I said.

She continued to stare suspiciously.

"Ava, I left it in the kitchen," I said. "Thanks for
reminding me."

"Why was it in the kitchen?"

"I went right to the kitchen when I returned from school to check on what had to be done and left my jacket hanging on the pantry doorknob. It's still there. I'd better get it. Mrs. Fennel would have a fit."

"Yes, she would," she agreed. She stepped back for me to go out. "When you return, come to my room to see how beautiful I've made Marla. She looks ten years older."

"I'll be right there," I said.

I hurried off. This was like living in Orwell's *1984,* I thought. Or Nazi Germany. Every word, every move I made, was under scrutiny. My sisters would rat on me in a heartbeat. There was only one person to trust: myself.

After giving it sufficient time, I went to Ava's room. Marla was sitting at her vanity table. When she turned to look at me, I nearly lost my breath. She did look years older and somehow even more sophisticated and cunning than me.

"Well?" Ava asked.

"I'm stunned. You performed a miracle," I said, hoping to please her.

"It wasn't my miracle. It was hers," she said, nodding at Marla. "Everything is already there inside her. I'm just bringing it out the way I recently brought it out of you."

"Maybe I should go with you and Lorelei on the next hunt," Marla said.

Ava laughed. "Ambitious, isn't she? I'm afraid not, little sister. You don't go out there until Daddy says."

"Maybe he'll say I should," she insisted.

Ava laughed again. "If you only had her edge,

Lorelei, this wouldn't all be such a struggle for you. Stop that damn thinking and worrying all the time."

"I'll be ready when Daddy calls me," Marla said, turning back to look at herself in the mirror. She did have Ava's vanity and ego.

"I'm going to read and go to sleep early," I said. "I'm tired tonight."

"You're just terrified," Marla said, talking to me through the mirror.

I looked at Ava, who widened her smile. "She's so precious," she said.

She wasn't so precious to me, but I had to admit she was right: I was terrified. Was I on the verge of losing Daddy's love completely? Why was I toying with it, endangering myself so much? It was clearly something neither of my sisters would do. And hearing the story about what Mrs. Fennel had done years ago didn't comfort me. In the end, she had destroyed the one she loved and then didn't blame it on who and what she was but on love itself. Was that what awaited me?

I was tormented with indecision and conflicting emotions all night. I couldn't read. I couldn't watch television. There was nothing that would shut off the turmoil inside me. I slept in spurts, waking and finding myself trembling as if I were freezing. I closed the window and put another cover over me, but I couldn't shake off the chill. Something dark and very cold was in my room with me. I was drawn to the image of Daddy enveloping Mark Daniels just outside my window. I could hear Mark's scream. If a renegade could be swallowed up so quickly and violently, what would happen to Buddy?

*I must not call him tomorrow,* I told myself. *I must fight off the urge. That is the solution; that is the only solution.* It gave me some comfort to think so, but when I closed my eyes and tried to sleep again, I saw his face. I heard his voice, and I felt his lips on my lips. I conjured him up so vividly it was as if he really were in my bed beside me, and as I envisioned him, felt myself surrender to his embrace, I felt that strange hardness move through my body, that hardness I had felt when I was really with him.

It made me sit up in a panic. I was breathing hard and fast, and there was the taste of blood in my mouth. Had I bitten my own lip? I rose and turned on the light at my vanity table. When I looked at myself, I thought the color of my eyes had changed from bluish green to Daddy's ebony. My shoulders looked bigger.

And I hadn't bitten my lip.

The taste of blood came from somewhere else, somewhere deep inside me.

I didn't understand why it should make me feel as if I had stepped into a fire pit and was going up in smoke, but it did.

I quickly turned off the light, and as Daddy had promised I would, I welcomed the embrace of darkness.

# 16

## Embrace of Darkness

I had convinced Ava that she had to take Marla to school in the morning, emphasizing that I couldn't do it, because a suspended student was not permitted to go on the property. I heard them get up and go to breakfast. When Ava looked in on me, I was still in bed. I sat up as soon as she stepped into my room.

"What time is it? Did you need me to do something?" I asked her.

"No. I just wanted to see what you were doing. I see you're taking advantage of this opportunity."

"I'm tired."

"You can sleep all day for all I care, Lorelei. I have to leave earlier to get Marla to school, thank you. We're leaving."

"I'm sorry, Ava."

"Right."

"Actually, I'm too nervous to sleep and too nervous to get up," I said.

"Don't overdo it," she told me, smirking. "Daddy can see right through a false face, and you know how he hates dishonesty among us. I'll be back after I pick up Marla at the end of her school day."

"Okay."

"Daddy and Mrs. Fennel will be home about then," she said. She hesitated a moment and then walked out to take Marla to school and go to her own classes.

I rose slowly and stood before my clothes in the closet, trying to decide what to put on. Every little decision, whether it was what to wear, how to fix my hair, where to sit, what to read, literally anything I had to decide, was agonizing. I knew it all radiated from the one big decision I had to make that day: to call Buddy or not. I had no doubt that if I didn't call him, he would surely eventually call me. I could leave my phone off, but later, if I forgot and turned it on while Ava or Daddy and Mrs. Fennel were home, it would signal a message they might hear, and they would want to know who was calling me.

The truth was that despite everything Ava had said, I wanted to call Buddy. I wanted to see him again. Maybe this was genuine love, or maybe it was simply a portal through which I could enter another world, the world I saw other girls my age enjoying. Ava and Daddy and even Mrs. Fennel held out the promise of a life in which I would enjoy everything anyone else enjoyed but ten times as much and forever. This was what my mysterious destiny would provide if I only lived up to my responsibilities as Daddy's daughter. For us girls, this was the heaven that awaited. Neither Brianna nor Ava seemed to have any difficulty believing in it. Even my younger sister, Marla, was more devout than I was when it came to the promise of our futures. Why wasn't I as trusting and as satisfied with the promise?

I wandered about the house like a confused particle

of matter that had broken off and was floating through
space with no clear direction or purpose. For a while, I
tried to amuse myself by tinkering on the piano, but the
long, deep silence before and after intensified my anxiety.
For a few minutes, I toyed with my phone, teasing myself
with turning it on and then quickly turning it off. The
tension inside me made it seem stifling in the house, so
I went out and around to the back, where I could sit on
the patio and capture the warmth and promise of the
strengthening late-morning sunshine.

We had nearly an acre of land, with the back being un-
developed woods. The excited twitter of baby birds caught
my attention. It was coming from a leafy oak tree off to
my right. I rose and walked to it to study the branches
until I spotted the nest. Moments later, the mother
swooped in with some worms in its beak. The baby birds
grew even more excited. While I watched and listened, I
recalled that afternoon when Daddy took me out to explain what Brianna had done when she had brought that
young man to the house. Once again, I felt the strong love
I had felt for Daddy that day. I remembered how safe he
had made me feel when he held me. There was nothing
in this world that could harm me as long as he was there
to protect me. But what, I wondered now, was the price
that I and my sisters ultimately paid for that security?
What did we really sacrifice?

What had my mother sacrificed, and Brianna's
mother and Marla's mother? According to what I had
been told, Ava's mother had lost her life, but what had
caused the others to give up their babies? What had they
risked for love and devotion? Did they feel so strongly

and so passionately about their lovers that they were blind to the costs? They didn't seem like teenagers who had sexual accidents. Maybe one of them was committing adultery. Maybe they all were. Maybe they were devout Catholics who had to have their babies but gave them away. Whatever the reasons, they suffered because of their passion.

Perhaps that was the difference between me and my sisters, I suddenly thought. They didn't know the answers, either, but I did know how powerful our passions could be. And I knew only because of what I felt when I was with Buddy. From what I understood, my older sisters had never had this experience, and Marla would surely not have it, either.

But I had had it, and I still had it, I thought. Why should I just throw it away without fully experiencing it? We were all special in our own way. Maybe this was what made me special. Determined now, I reached into my pocket and took out the cell phone to turn it on. The mother bird flew above me and off to the left to continue hunting for the food its babies needed. I watched it disappear, heard the babies crying for more, and then called Buddy. He really must have been keeping his phone close to his heart, because he picked up on the first ring.

"Lorelei?"

"Yes," I said. "Where are you?"

"I'm sitting in the rear of my uncle's house dreaming of you. I slept here last night," he confessed, "on the sofa where you sat. It helped me to feel close to you again."

"What about your classes? Didn't you attend any today?"

"Nothing else seems to matter to me."

"Now you're making me feel bad," I said. "You're going to ruin your college grades."

"Don't feel bad. I can make up any time I've lost. In fact, if you come to me today, I promise I'll work harder and be at the top of my class."

I laughed. It took only seconds of hearing his voice to wash away my tension. There was something honest and sincere about him, and that not only relaxed me but gave me a sense of optimism. For me, Buddy proved that all boys weren't what Ava portrayed them to be, prey or opponents. My conversations with Buddy didn't have to be coy, and I didn't have to be constantly on the defensive. There were lines I couldn't cross, but Ava would never consider a simple walk on the beach with a boy as something desirable. She was, like Brianna, always the hunter. There would never be a *we* in Ava's or Brianna's vocabulary, but did that mean there could never be one for me either?

"Will you come?" he asked.

I took a deep breath. The sun was warmer now, the breeze softer, the sky a deeper blue. Darkness and fury awaited me later in the day. For a while, at least, I could have something pleasant and wonderful. Perhaps, I rationalized, it would help me to be stronger for what was to come.

"Yes," I said. "I'm on my way."

"Prayers answered," he said. "I'll wait out front."

I hurried around to my car and, with only a moment's hesitation, started the engine and drove off defiantly. If my family had so many secrets, why couldn't I have one?

I was confident that I could keep it well. I had fooled Ava, hadn't I? Anyway, besides being something delicious and wonderful, this was exciting. Yes, my heart beat faster, but not out of fear so much as out of anticipation of that which would help me feel more complete as a woman. As I drove, I told myself I wasn't simply the blood slave Ava was. I didn't have her same hatred for and anger toward young men. *Love won't be poison for me. It won't, it won't.*

And then I stopped myself. Whom was I trying to convince? Was I going mad?

My stomach woke up a hive of bees inside. I slowed down.

*Turn around,* a voice within was telling me. *It's all too great a risk. Yes, you fooled Ava, perhaps, but you know Daddy will see right through you. He'll look into your eyes and know immediately. The disappointment he will feel will be too great. You'll lose him; you'll lose him forever.*

By the time I turned down the street toward Buddy's uncle's house, tears were streaming down my cheeks. I stopped before I thought he could see my car and pulled to the side. My body was shaking with fear. I was about to turn around when I saw him walking down the center of the street. He had been waiting closer to the turn. He was that anxious and excited.

*It's too late,* I told myself.

I wiped away my tears as quickly as I could, took another deep breath, and drove slowly toward him. He was waving and smiling and looked like a little boy. He jumped up and down to exaggerate his happiness, and I laughed.

*This is good,* I thought. *This has to be right.*

I stopped beside him.

"Why did you pull over down there? You were having second thoughts, weren't you?" he asked.

"Yes."

"Don't have third," he said, and nodded at the driveway.

I parked, and he hurried over to open my car door. When I stepped out, he didn't speak. He looked at me, and I looked at him, and then he kissed me. It was a soft kiss, but I could feel the desire in him and the love. His eyes were glossy with tears of happiness. Neither of us said a word. We didn't have to. We were speaking with our eyes, our lips, and our hearts. He took my hand and led me into the house.

He closed the door and still held my hand. Still, neither of us spoke. He led me down the hallway to a bedroom. I paused in the doorway. If I entered, I was crossing another forbidden line, and I knew that once I crossed it, it would be too late to turn back. My life would never be the same.

He looked at me with nothing but love and affection in his eyes, and I continued into the room. At the side of the bed, we kissed again. His lips moved down my chin and to my neck. I pulled my head back, and he unbuttoned my blouse and brought his lips to my breasts. Then he lifted me gently to the bed. For a moment, he stood looking down at me.

"I want to memorize every part of you," he said. "That way, you will never leave me."

"Everyone leaves everyone sometime," I told him in a whisper.

"Not us. We'll synchronize our heartbeats, and when yours runs out, mine will, too. It will be the same for you."

I smiled. He sounded like a hopeless romantic, a dreamer, a poet who had more faith in words than in anything else. Daddy once told me that dreamers and poets suffered more, however: "They create a world that cannot last, cannot be, and the disappointment for them is that much greater."

Maybe that was true, but right now, it seemed to me that the journey that would take us to that pain and disappointment was worth it. Wasn't all of life a journey that led to death? But we didn't stop trying to enjoy ourselves, to find something worth our effort. Daddy wasn't always right, I thought, and then had the shocking realization that my feelings for Buddy were causing me to challenge and question things Daddy had taught me my whole life. Before this, I had accepted everything as if it had rained down from some divine cloud.

Buddy pulled off his shirt and then gently undressed me. I thought he was out to kiss every part of me, every inch of my body, so he could do what he hoped . . . memorize me. When he was naked beside me, I could feel my blood carrying the heat from my heart through all of my veins. His lips grazed mine. His eyes were closed, and he looked as if he was trying to inhale the very scent of my being.

"We have to be careful," I said, knowing that soon I would lose all restraint.

"I will be," he promised, and showed me that he was prepared.

What neither of us was prepared for was the way my

body tightened as I accepted him. I saw the confusion in his eyes as the softness left my shoulders, my breasts, and my stomach.

"You're harder than I am," he muttered.

I had no explanation. In fact, I wasn't sure this wasn't what happened with every woman as she began to make love. It didn't matter to him. He wanted me as much as, if not more than, he had when he began.

And when we began, my mouth was filled with that taste of blood again. This time, it flowed back, down my throat and into my stomach. It wasn't unpleasant. It was sweet, and the stronger it became, the more demanding I was. He moaned in pleasure and then laughed at my enthusiasm, crying out playfully to complain that I was killing him. When I reached a climax, it felt as if my bones had thickened. I thought I was bigger, heavier, and I looked at him to see if he thought so, too, but he was in the throes of his own climax and reciting words of love, pledges and promises.

When it ended, he rolled onto his back, panting. He glanced at me, finally, with some surprise. "You're not even breathing hard," he said. "Although your skin is red everywhere."

"Is it?"

I sat up to look at myself. It was as though all my blood had come to the surface. I touched my legs to feel the heat. After a few more minutes, the heat slowly receded, and my normal color began to return.

"Is all of this something unusual?" he asked.

I shook my head. "I don't know, Buddy. I've never done this before."

He looked skeptical. "You're not having a virgin's reaction, if you know what I mean. It's all right," he quickly added. "I didn't expect you would, and I'm fine with that."

How was I to explain any of this to him, if I couldn't explain it to myself? He saw how I was struggling to find some explanation.

"Hey, don't sweat it. I hate people who make love and then sit around analyzing it all day. It is what it is, and for us, no matter what, it's wonderful. Short and simple." He waited for my agreement, and when it didn't come fast enough, he asked, "Right?"

"Yes, Buddy. It was wonderful, and I'm happy I came here to be with you." I reached for my clothes and began to get dressed.

"Are you all right?" he asked.

"Yes, Buddy."

"I didn't mean to move so fast, but—"

I looked at him and put my finger on his lips. "You mustn't apologize for passion," I said.

He smiled. "It was like it was all meant to be, even this secret rendezvous. Hey, we're like Romeo and Juliet. What's in a name and all that stuff."

I turned away. If he only knew how true that was. We didn't come from warring families, but we came from two worlds so different that we might as well. I could sense how my silence was making him nervous.

"You know I mean for this to be more, Lorelei. I wasn't looking for a one-night stand."

"I know."

"You're not saying anything," he said. "You're not angry, are you?"

"Oh, no, Buddy."

"Then what is it? Your father? Your sister? I mean—"

"Let's not talk about it anymore, Buddy. You were right. Just enjoy and live in the moment without doing an autopsy."

I saw the confusion in his face. "Autopsy? Nothing died here, I hope."

"No," I said. I smiled as warmly as I could. "Something was born here."

That pleased him. "Great."

"But let's leave it be for now," I said.

"That's fine, as long as I can see you and be with you."

What was I to tell him, to promise him? "We must not say things that will disappoint us in the end," I said.

"Why must there be an end?"

"There always is."

He shook his head. "I swear, I don't know what makes you so cynical, Lorelei. You're too young to be this cynical. Unless you've been hurt badly in a love affair. Have you?"

"I know you don't believe me, but this is my first love affair," I said.

"Mine, too. I mean it. Don't smile. I've been with other girls, yes, but I've never felt as strongly about any as I do for you."

I stopped smiling.

"Doesn't that make you happy?"

"Yes, but it frightens me, too."

"Frightens you? Why?"

"I told you. I don't want you or me to be deeply hurt by disappointment."

"Never happen," he said.

I stood up.

"I swear, you look taller," he said.

"Do I?"

I went to the mirror over the dresser and looked at myself. *He's right,* I thought. *I do look as if I've grown taller.* Was it just our imagination?

"Maybe you're just happy, fulfilled," he said. "You know, like a beautiful flower now able to blossom? Don't look at me like that. I've never said these things to any other girl. I swear." He raised his right hand.

"Okay," I said, laughing. "I'm convinced." I looked at my watch. "I have to go."

"To face the music for yesterday, huh?"

"Yes. I might not be able to see you again for a while, Buddy, and it might even be hard for me to call you."

"You can call me anytime, whenever you're able to call. I don't care how late or early it is."

"I'll try," I said.

"You look really worried," he told me as we started out together. "Are you sure I can't meet your father? I'm a charmer," he kidded.

"Not a good time," I said.

I paused when we stepped out of his uncle's house. The street was as quiet as these cul-de-sacs could be. Nothing was moving, yet I had the sense that we weren't alone. For a moment, I felt the way Daddy often did when that sixth sense of his was triggered by something. I stared ahead.

"Something wrong?" Buddy asked.

"No." I moved quickly to my car. When I reached for

the door, he reached for my hand to stop me and turn me around so he could kiss me again.

"The way you're talking, this kiss has to last a while," he said, and kissed me again.

"I will try to call you," I promised, and got into the car. He stood with his hands on the open window.

"I'm afraid to let you go. I have this sinking, sick feeling that I'll never see you again."

"No matter what," I said, "I'll see you again."

"You had better, or I'll find you, no matter where you are or how big your father might be."

I nodded. How ironic every word seemed to be. If he only knew how big my father could be, he wouldn't even think those words. I flashed a smile and then started to back out of the driveway. He walked after me, as if he really feared that he would never see me again. The look on his face was breaking my heart, but I couldn't stay any longer, and no matter how many promises I made, that look wouldn't go away. He would always hear the hesitation and doubt in my voice.

I watched him in my rearview mirror as I drove out of his uncle's street. I had come there with tears streaming down my cheeks, and I was leaving the same way. Really, how could I continue this love affair? Daddy was planning our move away. In a short time, Buddy would never be able to find me again. I truly would be like a dream he'd had. In time, I was confident I would fade. He'd find someone new, and whenever he did pause to try to remember me, he would smile and shake his head as he asked himself, *What was that all about, anyway?* He would rationalize away his disappointment by thinking of me as strange, weird, whatever would ease his pain.

But what about me? Wouldn't I go on to become Daddy's new Ava, and wouldn't that harden me so that I would never find anyone like Buddy again? Maybe I would come to believe what Mrs. Fennel taught us, that love was a disaster for us. Years from now, I might even persuade myself to be grateful for the separation. After all, I had come too close to a catastrophe. I had taken a drink from the poisonous fountain and, luckily, had survived.

For now, however, I had to throw off sorrow and brace myself for the cold waves of anger that I would soon face at home. Ava was right. I could look and act sorry, but I couldn't overdo my remorse, or I'd give it all away. I drove faster. There were still a few hours left before Daddy and Mrs. Fennel were to return. I decided I would take a soothing bath and do my best to relax.

When I pulled into our driveway, however, I was shocked to see Ava's car. What was she doing home so early? Where would I tell her I had been? Would she believe me if I told her I had to get out for a while because I was driving myself crazy with nervousness? One thing was for sure, I couldn't appear frightened about her being there and catching me away.

"Ava?" I called as I entered.

"I'm in here," she called back from the living room. She was sitting in Daddy's chair.

"Why are you home so early? I thought you said it was important for you not to miss those classes."

"That's what I told you," she said. "Sit." She nodded at the sofa across from her.

I sat.

"I can't believe that for one moment, one tiny second, you believed you could put one over on me, Lorelei. I'm the expert when it comes to gold-quality lies. How could you forget that I have the instincts? You're good, but you're not in my class yet. For your sake, I hope you will be soon, but as I told you a while ago, and as Daddy believed, you appear to lack some of that necessary instinct. We don't survive without it," she concluded.

I started to speak, but she put up her hand.

"Let's get quickly past your look of innocence, your amazed protestations, and your farcically asking me what I am talking about. Let's get right to the truth, huh? Daddy and Mrs. Fennel will be here soon."

I stared at her for a moment. The sharpness in her voice and the heat in her eyes were normally terrifying for me, but for some reason, I didn't feel as vulnerable and weak as I usually did when she was in a rage. I wasn't going to burst into tears and beg for her forgiveness. I wasn't going to plead for her to help me. And I could see by the way her eyes twitched that she saw something stronger in me as well.

"What did you do, Ava, follow me?"

"Of course, I did. I waited, knowing you were going to go to him. You were in that house quite a while. Enjoy it?"

"Matter of fact, yes, I did, very much."

"Well, I'm glad, because that will be the first and the last time you enjoy him," she snapped, leaning forward.

"Don't threaten me, Ava," I threw back at her.

She surprised me with a wide smile and then a short laugh.

"Threaten you? I'm not threatening you, you fool. I'm threatening him."

A thin sheet of ice slid down my back.

"I'm not going to guard the door or follow you around to be sure you don't go to him."

"Daddy won't let—"

"Daddy. Don't you dare mention Daddy to me. What you have done during the day and a half he and Mrs. Fennel have been gone would probably knock him off his feet, and you know how hard it is to do that," she said.

"And I'm sure you're going to enjoy telling him everything," I said, but it sounded more like me feeling sorry for myself than anything else.

"I would, yes, but if you cooperate, I won't."

"What do you mean, cooperate?"

"I know you're pretty smart, Lorelei. Daddy's probably right to think of you as one of his most intelligent daughters, so don't pretend you don't understand what I mean, what I want. It's perfect timing, actually. Daddy is ready for a feeding. We talked about this possibility."

I shook my head. "I can't."

"Yes, you can. In the end, it's a simple decision to make, isn't it? Daddy or him?"

I tried to swallow, but my throat felt as if it had turned to stone.

"Just think. We'll be co-conspirators. It will be a surprise for Daddy, but he won't care now. We're moving away. He'll forgive us for violating the rules."

I think my heart actually stopped for a few moments. She was sitting there describing the nightmares I had about Buddy.

She laughed at the shock on my face. "Think of how funny this will be," she said.

"Funny? How can you say that?"

"You can invite him to meet your father. Finally, you can do what I know you've always wanted to do, Lorelei, bring a boyfriend home to meet Daddy."

"You keep our little secret," Ava told me, rising, "and I'll help you today with Daddy and Mrs. Fennel. I'll tell them I was the one who called you at school to tell you I'd be late for dinner. I know Buddy was the one who called you, Lorelei. Don't try to deny it. But I'll take some of the blame off you this way."

Once I would have told her that I never lied to Daddy, but that seemed stupid now. I said and did nothing to lead her to believe I agreed and walked away. She left to pick up Marla at school. Daddy and Mrs. Fennel arrived less than a half-hour later, earlier than Ava and I had expected. The moment Daddy saw me, he knew something was wrong. I should have been at school and not home yet. He glanced at Mrs. Fennel and then asked me what was going on.

"I got suspended from school for two days," I immediately confessed. Was there any way to skirt the truth? I struggled to think of a way around it and came up with nothing else.

"Suspended? You? Why?"

"There's a strict rule about the use of cell phones

in the building. I used my cell phone in the hallway between classes. Actually, I was a little late for a class because of it. I'm sorry, Daddy. I just wasn't thinking. I shouldn't have left it on, but when it rang, I answered."

"Who called you?" Mrs. Fennel immediately demanded.

Choices bounced back and forth in my mind like Ping-Pong balls. Should I become indebted to Ava and accept her help? Should I try to convince them of the same story I had used on Ava and say it was a wrong number? I could even say that whoever called realized it was a wrong number and there was no one on the line when I answered. The only choices I had were lies. I certainly couldn't tell the truth now.

"Ava," I said.

Mrs. Fennel grimaced. "Ava? Why would she call you? What did she want?"

"She wanted to tell me she would be late for dinner," I recited.

Daddy's eyes narrowed. I tried to avoid his gaze and look only at Mrs. Fennel.

"Why was she going to be late?" Mrs. Fennel asked.

"She wouldn't say," I replied. "There wasn't time to ask her. Once I got caught and was sent to the principal's office, I was too upset to care. I knew how unhappy you would be about my suspension, Daddy. I'm sorry. It just happened."

"This is quite unlike you, Lorelei, to forget an important rule like that. Something very serious must have been on your mind."

"There was. I wanted to speak to Mrs. Fennel about it, but you were both gone."

"About what?" she asked. "What was distracting you to such an extent?"

"Things have been happening to me recently, things I described before," I told Mrs. Fennel, "only now they're more intense and more frequent."

"What things?" Daddy asked impatiently.

"For no apparent reason, muscles in my body start to harden."

Mrs. Fennel looked at Daddy. "I gave her something to make it easier," she told him.

He nodded. Whatever was happening to me was something they appeared to have expected. My using it was succeeding in deflecting their scrutiny.

"I guess that was heavily on my mind, and I didn't think about anything else," I continued. "Ava thought I was still at lunch and could take the call outside the building. It was all just an unfortunate accident."

"Where's Ava now?" Daddy asked.

"She went to pick up Marla. I'm not permitted to be on the school grounds during a suspension. I'm sorry, but you have to go to school with me tomorrow to meet with the principal. Anyone suspended can't return without one of his or her parents meeting with him. There's a message about it on the phone answering machine."

"This is precisely the wrong time for something like this to happen," Mrs. Fennel muttered.

"Go to your room," Daddy ordered. "I'll speak with Ava about this before I come to see you."

"Don't tell us how sorry you are again," Mrs. Fennel

warned instantly. "You know how I feel about that stupid word."

I nodded, lowered my head, and walked off to my bedroom. I knew from the stories I overheard at school that kids my age often lied to their parents. Some bragged about how successful they were, not even realizing that they were making their own parents sound gullible and stupid. In fact, the way they spoke about it made it seem as if they believed that kids our age who told their parents the truth about what they did were the stupid ones. For most of my life, I couldn't help but want to be more like the other girls and boys in my classes, but I never wanted to feel good about fooling Daddy and Mrs. Fennel.

Being a good liar, however, had become part of the job description. Clever liars mixed their fabrications with half-truths and thus muddied the waters, making it more difficult for their parents to understand what was true and what wasn't. Others left out the unpleasant things or things that would anger their parents. The stock excuse once they were caught was a simple "I forgot." From what I could see of some of these kids, they were very good at it. They could lie with straight faces, lie to their teachers, to their families, and even to their friends, without feeling a bit remorseful or guilty when they were caught. To me, that was like building relationships on a foundation of bubbles.

But too many famous, powerful, and influential people had been caught lying, and once they were exposed, they apologized and sounded and looked remorseful. They talked about the burden now on their shoulders to win back the trust of those they loved. They were so successful at it that lying was rapidly becoming a minor infraction and hardly a sin. Even those who perjured themselves in courtrooms could get good lawyers and get away with it. Why was it such a surprise, then, to see young people relying on falsehoods?

Even so, and with all of the reasons for me to be less conflicted about it, I still felt terrible about lying to Daddy. I saw the pain in his eyes, the disappointment. It was enough to make my heart feel like a pincushion.

I couldn't help but wonder what it was that both Mrs. Fennel and Daddy had expected when I had described how my body would suddenly harden. Neither seemed terribly concerned. Was this happening to me because of the things she fed us? Was it somehow part of the normal changes that occurred in a young woman? Nothing in my high school health class suggested such a thing, but I never felt that our teacher, who was also a part-time nurse, was comfortable discussing sexual maturing. It was probably a mistake to have boys and girls in the same class.

I went into my room, sat on my bed, and waited. I knew it wouldn't be long before Ava and Marla would be there. It suddenly occurred to me that Ava might have tricked me. The possibility brought the blood into my face. What if she acted as if she didn't know a thing about my story when Daddy asked her? I'd be trapped and have to confess to a bundle of lies. Maybe she and Marla had been plotting against me all along. Now that I thought more about it, I wondered why Ava would risk angering Daddy and Mrs. Fennel for me, anyway. Did she hate the fact that I had a boyfriend, someone I really cared for and who cared for me that much? Was her hatred of my succeeding in having something of a normal relationship so great that she would take the risk just to get me to destroy that relationship?

Where was the truth sleeping among all these lies, and if I found it, would I be able to wake it up? Did I want to? I didn't know where to put my loyalty at this moment. With Buddy? With myself? With Daddy? The house felt full of sticky cobwebs. Spiders and snakes crawled over everything. Never before had I felt as if I was living in a nest of vipers the way I did at that moment.

The moment I heard them drive up, I rose and looked out the window. They emerged from Ava's car, laughing the way they had been laughing when they had come home from school the day before. They looked closer than ever, real sisters hugging each other, bumping shoulders softly. I felt completely alienated from them.

Panic set in as a silence fell over the house. I felt a fluttering in my chest and a trembling in my legs. I took deep breaths and returned to my bed. The minutes that passed seemed more like hours to me. How well would Ava hold up in the cross-examination, even if she wanted to support the story? Would Mrs. Fennel frighten and threaten her until she told the truth? Would my bedroom door open and all four of them be standing out there looking in at me as if I was the biggest traitor the family had ever known, their eyes gaping, their faces distorted with rage?

Even before I knew the answers, tears began. Why shouldn't I cry? What other love had I known until then but Daddy's love? He had filled me with his poetry and his music, his vast knowledge and wisdom. I was as much part of him as I was of anyone or anything. He had cared for me, protected me, and placed his faith in me, as I had placed mine in him. In seconds, that might all be gone, and then what would I be? Who would I be? What would I have? The same fear of loneliness and abandonment I had felt all my young life came rushing back over me.

Anyone condemning me or judging me badly for having this fear would have had to have been abandoned first, would have had to have experienced life without family and friends, and would have had to have known nothing more about themselves than what they had been told. I had found the picture of a woman who could be my mother, but I had not found out anything about her. I had no grandparents, no real uncles and aunts, and no cousins. I was someone without any history except for the history I had been given. That had all supposedly begun the day I was plucked out of an orphanage. When I was sent away, I would have no name. Yes, before anyone condemned me for being so frightened and so upset about what might happen to me, he or she would have to stand in my shoes.

I heard footsteps in the hallway and knew from the sound that it was only Daddy who was coming to see me. I wiped away the tears from my cheeks and sat up straight, holding my breath until he opened the door.

"I swear, the two of you will be the death of me," he said. "Do you know why your sister was late for dinner last night and why she called you? Of course you don't. You said you didn't, but you'd never imagine."

I waited, yet to take a breath.

"She was afraid we would move away from here before she had helped you be your father's daughter. She went and answered one of those personal advertisements through the Internet. Frankly, I never thought of any of you doing that. There's a potential gold mine there. She had to meet the prospect. I guess I can't fault her for being clever, but I do fault the both of you for messing up, for being careless and getting yourself in trouble at school," he added, but not with the violent anger I had anticipated. "Mrs. Fennel's correct. This is not good timing for something like this, not that there is ever a good time for it for us."

I took a breath. "I know Mrs. Fennel hates my saying it, but I can't help it, Daddy. I'm sorry."

He nearly laughed. I felt my body soften and relax. "Well, Mrs. Fennel believes that in a world where no one could say he or she was sorry, fewer mistakes would be made. People would be more careful."

He stepped up to me, took my chin in his hand, and gazed at my face.

"You're too beautiful not to forgive, Lorelei. I know deep in your heart, you don't want to do anything that would hurt me, hurt all of us. Soon you will be fully mature, fully realize your potential and purpose, and then you will be unstoppable. This really is the wrong time to be making any mistakes. You're too close. I think you understand that now. Instinctively, you do."

I tried to nod, but he was holding my chin too tightly. I could feel the strength flowing through his fingers and into my face.

"I'll go with you to school tomorrow. We have a little more time here yet, and I want you to be all right, for all of us to be all right, until we leave."

"Where will we go, Daddy?"

"We're going to Louisiana," he said. "There are many new opportunities there for us since the floods."

He was still holding my chin between his thumb and fingers.

"So, I'm going to forgive you for this mistake, Lorelei. I want you to feel and appreciate my forgiveness," he added, and slowly lowered himself so he could bring his lips to mine. It was a kiss unlike any he had ever given me, a kiss that didn't awaken the daughter in me but awakened the woman. "There," he said. "Sealed with a kiss."

He let go of my chin and stood back, looking at me for a moment, a different sort of smile on his face, one I had not seen. It wasn't the fatherly smile he had given me so often and I had so cherished. It wasn't a smile of laughter or amusement, either. It was more the smile of an arrogant lover who was basking in the brightness of his own powerful sexuality. I really was reacting more like a woman than a daughter, and once again, I felt my body tighten and harden in places.

"Yes," he said. "You're too beautiful not to forgive. We'll talk again at dinner."

He stepped out and softly closed the door behind him.

I hadn't realized I had been holding my breath so long. My lungs nearly exploded. I glanced at myself in the mirror. The tears were gone, but in their place was a mixture of amazement and fear. What was I really learning about who and what I would become?

I tried not to think about it. Instead, I busied myself with myself. I took a shower, washed my hair, and brushed it out. As I was dressing, Ava came into my room.

"Well?" she asked.

"Well what?" I replied, and pulled up my skirt.

"Didn't I do what I promised? I saved your ass, Lorelei."

"You lied to Daddy, too. You took a big risk, too."

"So, what are you going to do, confess just to get me in trouble?"

I turned away from her and put on my blouse.

"I think you had better think hard about your future, Lorelei. If you don't do what I tell you to do, that future won't include Daddy or me or anyone in this family."

"Don't threaten me, Ava," I said, spinning on her but trying to remain as cool as I could.

She smiled that cool, arrogant smile. "I'm not threatening you, Lorelei. A threat is like a promise of something terrible that could happen. This is more like a prediction," she said. "You know, like when you're driving off a cliff and falling a thousand feet. You can predict you'll be dead in seconds."

I tried to keep my façade of strength and resistance, but she was still my older sister, still Ava, the one who could make me tremble.

"Put on those earrings I gave you. They go perfectly with that blouse," she said, and left.

I sat on the bed and stared at the floor. What would

happen now? I hoped that Mrs. Fennel would be so concerned that she would have Daddy move up our date to leave. Despite how I felt about Buddy, I wished it were tomorrow. I wished I would wake up and find my clothes had been packed and the car was idling outside. It would be a true getaway. We would disappear into that fog of mystery that kept all of our family secrets safely hidden. Daddy was right to think of it as being born again. The past would fall back and dissipate like smoke. Amnesia would be a blessing.

I rose and went to dinner.

It was as if nothing bad had happened. Daddy was very happy and talkative. He described our new home in Baton Rouge. It was an antebellum mansion. It surprised me to hear him say it had been in our family for nearly two hundred years. What family did he mean?

"What's *antebellum* mean?" Marla asked.

"Built before the Civil War," I said before Daddy could reply.

He smiled. "That's right. I've lived in many like it. It's a Greek Revival. You'll be impressed with the detailed work in it. And the two of you," he said, referring to Marla and me, "will have bedrooms nearly twice the size of the ones you have now. And don't forget, we'll have a new little girl. Another sister for you will be coming."

"I can't wait," Marla said. "It's boring here."

Daddy laughed. "Boredom won't be your problem, Marla. Will it, Ava?"

"Hardly," she said. Whenever Daddy spoke or she did, she looked mainly at me, searching for any hint that I was about to break down and confess.

"How much longer, Daddy?" Marla asked.

"Not much longer." He looked at Ava. "We still have a few things left to do here."

Ava smiled and said, "Yes, we do. Don't we, Lorelei?"

I glanced quickly at Daddy. He was gazing at me with a more studied look, searching for some hesitation.

"Yes," I said. Then I smiled. "I think I agree with Marla for once. I can't wait, either."

"Excellent," Daddy said. He reached for our hands. "My girls. No one anywhere, no other family, no father and daughter, will ever be, could ever be, as close as we are. Feel your pulses. Your hearts beat together as one heart with my heart. Others talk about the invisible umbilical cord that binds a child to his or her mother, but we are bound by the rhythm of life itself. When one of you is in pain, I am in pain, and more important, perhaps, when I'm in pain, you will be. That's what makes our unity, our devotion to each other, so special, so unique, and so different from anything you will see out there. Be sisters. Always be sisters," he said, "and you will always be good daughters."

Mrs. Fennel brought in our food. I looked to see if her face was still full of suspicion and anger toward me, but she didn't look any different from the way she usually looked. I wondered if she was going to take me aside after dinner finally to talk about the changes I had felt in my body and what they meant, but she said nothing.

Daddy wanted to spend a few hours after dinner as we often did. We gathered in the living room to listen to music. Despite what had happened earlier, he continued to be joyful. The prospect of a new home and a new daughter did appear to energize him. He lived what he preached. He was always being reborn. He did treat each day as if it were the first day of a new life.

He danced with all three of us, but this night, he chose to dance more with Ava. When they danced, they looked like lovers. He held her closer, kissed her on her cheeks and even her neck. She laughed and threw her head back. He spun her around, the two of them at times looking as if they were completely alone. I saw Marla had the same look of astonishment but also of envy on her face. I felt that, but I was also more intrigued with Daddy and how he held the three of us differently now from how he had at previous times. There were moments now when I would swear he looked twenty years younger. It was as if instead of drinking from some magic fountain, he could will himself back in time.

Tonight Mrs. Fennel did something unusual, too. She rarely showed her face in the living room after dinner when we were dancing with Daddy. She watched from the doorway this time, but she watched as if she wanted to be sure everything was going as it should. I tried not to stare at her, but I was curious about her reactions and searched her face for worry or concern, especially when she looked my way. There was nothing like that in her expression. She nodded to herself and eventually left.

Afterward, we all sat around Daddy, as usual, while he described something wonderful from his past, some memory stirred by our laughter and joy together. This time, he described his travels through China with a beautiful Chinese princess whose ancestors went back to the Middle Ages. Just as always, his descriptions of the countryside, the palaces, and the celebrations captured our imagination. He recited ancient Chinese poetry and showed us a little of a ritual dance. If anyone wondered how it was possible for three teenage girls to be so amused and entertained at home, they had only to participate in one of Daddy's special evenings.

When it was over, it left me feeling very sad. I was unhappy with myself, with my act of betrayal. How could I ever risk losing Daddy's love? What was I thinking? I think he saw the sadness in my face and made a point to kiss me and hold me longer than he did Marla and Ava.

"You don't worry about anything, Lorelei," he whispered in my ear. "I'll fix it all tomorrow, and we'll finish off wonderfully here. You'll do wonderfully. Sleep well."

It took all of my self-control not to begin crying. I held back the tears and retreated to my bedroom, but Ava was right behind me.

"How can you not see how much he still loves you, needs you?" she asked angrily. "How could you even think of risking that and hurting him?"

"Please, leave me alone, Ava."

"You fool."

"All right!" I cried. "I'm not going to see him again. We'll be gone, and that will be that."

"Oh, no, Lorelei. That won't be that. You will see him again. You owe me this, and you will do as I say. I know you'll never stop pining over him. Whether you care or not, he'll follow you everywhere you go, and you will be useless to Daddy and to yourself. Daddy will blame me."

I said nothing.

"If you don't do it yourself, I'll do it for you," she said. "And that you can take not as a threat but as a promise."

She left me to agonize over her words and my own feelings. I cried myself to sleep, but in the morning, I tried to look as fresh and as happy as possible. Daddy was taking Marla and me to school. He rarely came to any school we attended. He appeared only when it was absolutely necessary. But when he did come with me, I could see how quickly everyone was drawn to him. His elegant manner, heart-stopping good looks, and aristocratic self-confidence captured the attention of teachers and students alike. On those few occasions when any of the other girls in my classes had seen him, they told me things like, "Your father looks like a senator or a president. Is he a movie star? I think I've seen him in a magazine. Does he own a big company?"

"He's all of that," I would say, and laugh at their dumbfounded looks.

Dr. Phelps was no different. I could see how impressed he was when we entered his office. He looked and sounded almost apologetic. "This meeting is a mandatory formality," he began. "I have to do what the board requires."

"Of course you do," Daddy said, sounding generous.

"It was quite surprising having Lorelei sent to my office for anything improper. Until now, she has been an ideal student. Her grades are excellent, and her teachers only say laudatory things about her."

"Yes, it was surprising to me as well. She's been nothing less than an utter delight as a daughter. I know she's as upset about her behavior as you are, Dr. Phelps."

"I hope we won't see anything remotely like this again."

"Oh, I think we can safely say you won't," Daddy told him.

"Well, we don't want her to miss any more class time," Dr. Phelps said, rising. "I appreciate your coming in promptly."

"Not at all," Daddy said, standing up and offering his hand.

"What a beautiful ring," Dr. Phelps remarked.

"Yes. It was given to me a long, long time ago by someone I literally idolized. It's brought me lots of good luck ever since." He laughed. "Whether these things are true or not, it's comforting to believe in them, don't you think?"

"Absolutely," Dr. Phelps said. He sounded as if he were replying to an official military order. I half expected him to salute.

He walked us out of the office and said good-bye to Daddy.

"I'm letting you keep your phone," Daddy said to me. "You might have some need for it soon, and I have complete faith that you won't abuse it again. Ava certainly knows not to call you at school now unless it's some dire emergency, so there should be no chance of it, anyway."

I looked down. I knew I shouldn't have, but I couldn't look him right in the eyes and lie to him. I had no doubt he sensed it anyway, and I was afraid.

"Just go on and be a good student until we leave," he said. "Ava will be picking you and Marla up after school. I have some business to attend to this afternoon."

He kissed me softly, on the cheek but very close to my lips. Then he turned and left. I hurried to class, anticipating lots of busybody questions hurled at me every chance the gossips had. I knew girls like Ruta and Meg were gleeful over my suspension. In many ways, then, I really was like Marla in hoping that we would not be around much longer.

I was so involved with fending off the questions and nasty comments most of the day, as well as still smarting over how I had let Daddy down, that I didn't think much about Buddy. I checked my phone when I was able to go outside during lunch. As I expected, he had called and left a message. He was concerned about me and what had happened when my father found out I was suspended from school. I debated with myself about returning his call and perhaps telling him that he shouldn't call me again. I would tell him as firmly as I could that we could not see each other under any circumstances, but I was also afraid that I would break down and give in to his pleas. For now, at least, it was better to put it off for as long as I could.

But Ava had no intention of backing off on her demands. I could sense it the moment she picked up Marla and me. She couldn't wait for the opportunity to be alone with me. When we arrived at home and Marla and I started to get out of the car, she seized my arm and said, "No, you stay."

"Why is she staying?" Marla immediately demanded.

"Lorelei and I have to go somewhere to meet someone," Ava said. "Just go into the house."

"Why can't I go, too?"

"If you could, would I have wasted time bringing you home, Marla? This is Daddy's business. Just do what you're told," she said sharply.

Petulant, Marla got out, but she glared at me as if it was somehow all my fault. Had Ava told her about Buddy and me? The moment she was gone and Ava started to drive away, I asked her.

"Of course not," she said. "She's far too young to understand all of this, and besides, I couldn't trust that she would keep her mouth shut. She'd go to Mrs. Fennel, if not Daddy."

"How mean she's become."

"Mean? She's not mean, Lorelei. She's competitive. Have you forgotten Daddy's lectures about sibling rivalry and how it applies more to us than most? I told you, she's going to be breathing down your neck." She laughed.

"What's so funny, Ava?"

"I'm glad she came here after you and not after me. You're much easier to compete with," she said with a smile. "Which," she decided to add, "is not something of which you should be proud."

I was tired of her lectures and criticism. I just wanted to go home and go to sleep. "Where are we going?"

"Where do you think? We have to set up for the weekend."

"Must we do this, Ava? Isn't there any other way, any other choice? I'll do anything else you say. I swear."

"I know you would, and that's why we must do this. You can't remain this weak and vulnerable, even to me. In the end, years from now, you'll look back and thank me."

*I won't thank you as much as I'll hate myself,* I thought.

We drove on, Ava energized and excited and me sinking into myself as if my body had turned into quicksand.

"What this will do," she said as we turned toward UCLA, "is make you and me closer as sisters. I'm sure that's something you've always wanted." She turned to me when I didn't respond. "Something Daddy has always wanted," she tacked on.

"I know," I said.

But anyone listening would have wondered, as Ava was now wondering, if I saw that as something wonderful or something tragic.

Time, the real fortune-teller, would let us know sooner than we could imagine.

# 18

## A Plan

Ava sat silently for a moment after she had pulled the car into a parking space and turned off the engine. I was hoping she'd had a change of mind, that there was a complication she had not thought about until now. But she wasn't worrying about anything; she was planning details.

"All right. Here's how we'll do this. You'll arrange for him to meet your father this Saturday night. You can go out on your last date with him wherever you like and then bring him home. You'll tell him your father is returning at ten o'clock from a trip but is looking forward to meeting him, and if he wants to continue to see you, he had better do this. Do you understand?"

"What if I promise never to mention his name again? I'll tell him good-bye forever, Ava. I won't obsess over him like you think. I'll look forward to moving away and—"

"Stop it, Lorelei." She turned completely around to look at me, her face taking on the all-too-well-known look of distrust. "You know, I've always had my doubts about you, and despite how loving and kind Daddy's been to you, he's had his doubts as well. When I took you out to see how you would do with men, I was happy to see that you enjoyed the flirting, the seduction, and I did tell Daddy that I thought it was encouraging. But you are very different from me and from Marla. There are times I think you'll bolt out of the house and never come back. We all have the funds and charge cards Daddy has set up in our names, but I told him often that in your case, that might be a mistake." She paused and then continued in a reasonable, even sisterly tone. "Now, look at this as a wonderful opportunity to prove yourself. Once Daddy finds out what you've done and what you will do now, he'll have complete confidence in you. He'll forgive your stupid high school affair and write it off as the exuberance of youth or something, and you'll go on to fulfill your destiny."

"What is my destiny?"

"You're getting closer to finding out," she said. "Okay, I know what class he is supposed to be in right now." She looked at her watch. "I know where he goes next. You'll just be there waiting and catch his eye. I don't think you'll have any trouble doing that, do you?"

"No, but—"

"Take him somewhere to talk. Make it seem as though everything is fine, and you will be able to keep seeing him once he meets your father. I'll watch from a safe distance to be sure it all goes well."

"But what if he wants to go somewhere now to spend the rest of the day with me? What do I say?"

"Simple, Lorelei. I don't know why these lies don't come naturally to you. You say you took advantage of an opportunity to come here with me. I had to do something that would take an hour, and then you have to return home with me. You'll see him Saturday night. The more he waits, the more excited he'll be about your date, and the more vulnerable he'll be."

I nodded slightly and started to lower my head.

"Damn it, Lorelei," she snapped. "Stop looking like you're about to lose your best friend. Grin and bear it, and become Daddy's true daughter. If Buddy Gilroy looks at your face with that expression on it, you'll spook him and lose him, and then we'll both have to deal with bigger problems, problems you caused."

"Okay, okay. Don't yell at me," I said.

"Let's go," she said, and got out of the car.

She started walking away quickly, her annoyance with me palpable. I practically had to run to catch up to her, but when I did, she didn't slow down or speak. I followed her across the campus to the place where she wanted me to wait.

"All right. You stay here. It will only be minutes now."

"Should I just stay here in this place with him the whole time?"

"No, of course not. Do I have to plan every little second of this for you? Go to that coffee shop nearby, but keep looking at your watch so he understands you can't be with him long right now. I'm confident you can pull this off if you half try, Lorelei. Don't mess it up. The consequences will be bad for both of us but worse for you," she warned, and walked away.

I leaned against a wall. Ironically, I wasn't afraid of her as much as I was of Buddy. There was something special between us, and because of that, I was expecting he would surely see through me, see my deceit. What would I do then?

I saw the students begin filing out of their classes, but I didn't see him at all and had a fleeting hope that he had not gone to this class, that he had cut all of his classes again because he was too upset about not speaking to me or seeing me. Maybe he was back at his uncle's house. If I could postpone this now, maybe I could postpone it forever. Moments later, when I was about to give up, however, he appeared, and when he saw me, his face brightened.

"Lorelei, what are you doing here?" he asked, hurrying up to kiss me. "Not that I'm upset or anything like that. This is wonderful."

"Ava had to come here to do something she said would take about an hour. I realized it was an opportunity to see you and came along with her."

"Terrific."

"You have another class?"

"It doesn't matter. Nothing matters much when I put it up against seeing you," he said.

I looked at my watch. "I have about forty-five minutes."

"What's the rush? I could take you home."

"No," I said quickly. "Not yet. I'll tell you about that, about my plans for us."

"Okay, okay. Let's go somewhere where we can talk."

"How about that coffee place just off campus?"

"Perfect. Say, how do you know so much about everything here?"

"Ava," I said.

"Oh, right. I was hoping you were going to say you've been here many times watching me from a distance or something romantic like that."

I looked to my right and left, but I didn't see Ava. Even so, I felt her eyes were on me.

"So, how did things go when your father returned?"

"He was understanding, and he was wonderful in school today when he had to meet the principal. Things are back to normal."

"Well, he sounds like a neat guy."

"Neat? He's immaculate."

Buddy laughed. "I should have said cool. No one says neat anymore. I'm so excited about seeing you so unexpectedly like this. I can't think."

He took my hand, and we continued walking. It was another beautiful California day. The afternoons in spring were like this so often that people here took it for granted. I'd miss it when we moved away. The bright sunshine and deep blue skies washed away the darkness that could seep in from other places, troubling thoughts and fears. Daddy would say, "We're having a little bit of Eden today." No one could have put it better. I didn't know why Ava had told Marla she was the best at quoting him. I knew I was the best. I was confident that among the three of us, I clung to his every word the most.

"I take it you're no longer worried about Ava seeing us together or anything," he said as we crossed the street.

"No. I told her about my seeing you, how determined I was. She was the one who said I'd have to bring you to meet Daddy."

"Really? That's great."

We entered the coffee shop, and I ordered a tall chai tea. He got a coffee, and we sat at one of the tables outside.

"So, what's the plan?" he asked immediately.

"I can see you Saturday. In fact, Ava will bring me to meet you."

"Why can't I just pick you up? That way, I can see your father before we go out."

"He won't be there. He's returning between nine-thirty and ten, and the plan is that you'll bring me home and we'll spend some time with him."

"But I could do both. Why involve Ava?"

"She wants it this way," I said. "She likes to be in charge, and right now, I don't want to upset her."

"Oh." He thought a moment and then shrugged. "Well, that's great, actually. We'll get something to eat, spend some time at my uncle's, and then I'll take you home. I wish I could see you Friday night, too."

"I have something with my sisters."

"How come you've changed your mind about Ava and us? I mean, you were warning me off her as if she had the plague or something, and now—"

"I told you. I had a long talk with her. She understands now that you're not just any guy and that I'm going to see you no matter what she thinks or even what my father thinks. However, she likes playing the older sister looking out for the younger. It doesn't do us any harm to let her think what she wants, does it?" I tried sounding annoyed with him for asking so many questions, but he didn't pick up on it.

"No, I guess not." He nodded and smiled.

*Why can't he see the deception in my face?* I wondered. I was secretly hoping he would and that it would end there, but I guessed I was underestimating my skills at deception, or maybe his love for me simply blinded him.

"Where will we meet? Where should I tell you to have Ava bring you? My uncle's house?"

"That's fine," I said.

Finally, he looked a bit surprised, even skeptical. "That's fine? How much did you tell her?"

"I don't have to tell Ava much. She gets the idea," I said. "You've spent only a little time with Ava, but I think you know she's pretty worldly."

"Yeah, that's a good word for it. Worldly. Okay, you know what we can do then?" he asked, excited again. "I'll order in some food for us. For a little while at least, we can pretend we're living together. How's that?"

"Fine," I said.

"Wow, things are really changed. You don't seem nervous about anything anymore."

"Does that worry you?" *Please say yes,* I thought. *Find a reason to back out of this.*

"Hell, no. It makes me happier, happier than ever. What would you like me to order, Chinese, pizza?"

"It doesn't matter. Whatever you want," I said.

"Okay. I'll take care of it. What time should we meet? Can we meet at six? I'd like us to have some time together before I have to take you home and behave myself," he said, laughing.

"Six is fine," I said.

Ordinarily, if I had been in any way an ordinary girl, this would all have been exciting to me. I'd be as happy as he was. I'd do all sorts of things to prepare for the special night. I might have my hair and nails done and maybe buy a new outfit. I'd have a close friend in whom I could confide, and we'd giggle about what we knew would happen. If she didn't have a boyfriend of her own, she'd be terribly jealous, but she would also be happy for me and live vicariously through my revelations. If she had a boyfriend, we'd grow even closer, because we'd be sharing the passions we felt and the experiences we had. We'd talk forever on the phone, comparing kisses and sex and things we said to our boyfriends and they said to us. We'd spend hours talking and annoy our parents. We'd walk through the hallways between classes as if we had been chained together. Other girls would envy us and, because of that envy, compete for our attention, in the hope that we would tell them something secret, share a little of the romantic gold.

But none of this was true for me. In a few days, I would instead help engineer the most gruesome death for the boy for whom I had the deepest feelings. That smile would be gone forever from his face. I couldn't help but wonder when he would laugh for the last time, when he would smile or look at the world around him and feel wonderful. Would it be because of something I said or did? And what would be his final thoughts about me? Would they be angry thoughts or just utter shock? Would he be so disillusioned about life and love that he would welcome the darkness?

"Hey, you look sad about all this. Aren't you at least half as happy as I am?" he asked me, reaching for my hand.

I forced a smile. Then I looked at my watch. "We'd

better go back. I don't want to keep her waiting. Mainly, I don't want Ava to be angry about anything right now."

"From what you've said about her, neither do I," he said, rising quickly. "Where do you live? You've never told me," he said as we walked back to campus.

"In Brentwood, off Sunset. I'll direct you Saturday night."

"Great. We're close. More time for us," he said. "Where are you meeting Ava right now?"

"At the car," I said.

"I'll walk you there."

"No, let's just say good-bye here for now. Ava can be a bit of a pain, teasing and such. She might say or do something to embarrass us, me mainly, or she might have a change of heart once she sees us so happy together. She can be very jealous at times."

"I thought she was Miss Self-Confidence. Jealous?"

"Yes, jealous." He had no idea how true that was.

He shrugged. "Whatever you say."

He kissed me. *Surely, he feels the restraint in my kiss,* I thought, and waited for his reaction, but he just smiled and said, "I'll count the minutes until Saturday at six."

"Me, too," I told him, and walked quickly away.

Ava was already in the car when I arrived and got in.

"I can see that went well," she said. "Even though you didn't look as happy about it as I told you to look."

"I can't help being nervous. How can you be so sure Daddy's not going to be very upset, Ava?" I asked as we started away. "Even though we're leaving soon, it's still a rule violation, isn't it, and that's what the renegades do, right?"

"Leave that to me," she said. "If I'm in charge, he won't blame you for anything, but even if he's angry at first, I'll fix it. The bottom line, Lorelei, is he'll end up being very proud and satisfied with you. And isn't that what you really want, anyway?" She waited for a moment and then turned to me. "Isn't it?"

"Yes," I said, but felt sure that I was not skilled enough to cover up the doubt I was having.

"You'll feel better once it's over," she promised, nodding as though she were convincing herself.

My last hope was that either Daddy or Mrs. Fennel would see how worried and edgy I was the remainder of the week. They'd ask driving, penetrating questions of both me and Ava, and once they learned what was being planned, they'd put a stop to it, and that would be that. Twice during the time we were all home together, Ava warned me about wearing too long a face and snapping at Marla in front of Mrs. Fennel.

"You're endangering us both," she said. "Get hold of yourself. You're soon going to move to a new home and have a new sister. You should be full of the same excitement Marla is exhibiting. Stop moping and acting irritable, or you'll raise suspicions. You're just lucky Daddy and Mrs. Fennel have their minds occupied with other things; otherwise, we'd be finished. You'd be finished."

I promised to do better, and I did try, but I was eager to retreat to the sanctuary of my room. I spent hours looking at what could be my mother's picture and thinking. I went on the computer and found the address for the orphanage. What if I went there and pleaded for information? Wasn't there something, anything, about my past that would help me decide what to do and strengthen my resistance?

Whether Ava confided in her or not, Marla seemed the most suspicious, especially because of how short I was with her. She was full of questions when I took her to school. I tried to be as nonchalant and indifferent as I could, but she had Ava's perseverance and persistence.

"I know you two are planning something soon. I don't know why I can't be told. I'm tired of being treated like a little girl."

I gave her Ava's stock answer to everything. "Your time will come. Be patient."

"*Patient,*" she said. "I hate that word as much as Mrs. Fennel hates the word *sorry.*"

That made me laugh, and for me at the moment, the sound of my own laughter was like balm on a wound, soothing and relieving.

"Don't treat me like some cute little child," Marla snapped.

I pressed my lips together and then said the word. "Sorry."

"Oh!" she cried, and pounded her thighs.

It was the closest I came to laughing in those last few days.

Ava, whether to placate Marla or just to keep me busy, did plan something for the three of us for Friday night. With Daddy's and Mrs. Fennel's blessings, she took us to do some shopping first and then to have what Mrs. Fennel called "goat food" because it was garbage to her. Ava and I let Marla decide where we would go. To our surprise, she chose a steak house. Of all the food we ate away from the house, Ava enjoyed steak the most. I did, too.

All night, Marla tried to pry out of us what we were planning for Saturday.

"Why do I have to wait to find out? I should be just as trusted as either of you in our family now. More, even. I haven't made the mistakes Lorelei has made, have I?"

"See what I mean about her?" Ava told me. "I feel sorry for you when I leave."

I looked at Marla and saw the sparks in her eyes. Ava was right about her. I wished I could leave with Ava and not have to fend Marla off. Why hadn't I had the same driving, ruthless ambition when I was her age? Why didn't I have it now?

Marla watched us both very closely Saturday morning. The moment either of us moved from one room to another, she followed.

*She's going to ruin things yet,* I thought, or, rather, I hoped. I was tempted to make it easier for her to discover something, but Ava was watching me almost as closely as Marla was.

As was usual when a day for Daddy's feeding arrived, Mrs. Fennel moved about the house with more energy. It was as if nourishing him would nourish her as well. For his part, Daddy was mostly withdrawn, resting quietly in his suite. Mrs. Fennel brought him something for lunch, one of her magic elixirs created out of one of her secret herbal formulas. When we were younger, she often would have us drink one of them. It was sweet and syrupy but not appetizing to look at because of its greenish-blue color.

Late in the afternoon, Ava advised me to go to my room and spend time on my hair and my makeup and carefully choose something very sexy to wear, one of her hand-me-downs.

"It's like an assassin loading his gun," she explained, and laughed. I saw how much she was enjoying this. My nervousness and reluctance were obviously an integral part of that pleasure. She grew more serious. "You have to keep him turned on, Lorelei, even when you bring him up here. That's important. His blood should be hot with desire and passion. Make love with him as much as you can the whole time you're with him, but of course, be careful."

"Why is getting accidentally pregnant such a disaster for us, Ava? I know a number of girls at school who have gotten pregnant and had abortions. No one seems to make that big a deal of it."

"Some girls. Tramps," she said.

"It happens. People lose control."

"We don't," she said sharply. "We are always in control, Lorelei. That's the whole point. I can't believe you don't feel these things as deeply and as instinctively as I do. Honestly, you really do worry me. Doing this tonight will go far to bring you home."

"Bring me home? But I am home."

"Home to Daddy," she said, which only made things more mysterious and confusing. "Let's not talk about all of this now. Let's just do what has to be done and hope that afterward, you will answer your own questions."

"Is that what happened to you?"

"Of course. Go get ready," she ordered. "Daddy and

Mrs. Fennel expect us both to be preparing for tonight. They just don't know the target. Go!" she ordered when she saw I was still hesitating.

I hurried to my room. Marla swooped in like some buzzard moments after I began my preparations.

"What do you want?" I asked her. She was really annoying me now.

"I just want to watch. You're so lucky going out with Ava again, especially tonight."

I tried to ignore her, but she was making me jittery and uptight. Nothing was going the way I wanted it to go. My hair was difficult, and whatever I chose to wear seemed wrong. Finally, more curious about her now than she was about me and my night, I turned to her to put her in the spotlight instead of me. "Tell me something, Marla. Did you ever have a secret crush on any boy? Do you have one now?"

"Crush? No," she said. "Not like you mean," she added after a moment.

"How do I mean?"

"Love and all that gook."

"You really think that's what it is, gook?"

"What else is it? They nauseate me."

"Who does?"

"Girls my age who drool over boys. Every time they start, I have to walk away."

"Doesn't that get them talking about you?"

"I don't care what they say or think about me. Why should I? Why are you asking me these questions? Did Ava tell you to do that?"

"No. I was simply curious, that's all," I said, brushing

out my hair. Looking at her in the mirror, I saw her eyes narrowing with suspicion. *She looks more like Ava than I do now,* I thought. But how could that be? How could either of us really look anything like the other?

"Where are you two going? You can tell me that, at least. What city?"

"You'll have to ask Ava."

"I'm asking you."

I turned around. Ordinarily, I wouldn't enjoy doing this, but she brought out the meanness in me. "You're being impatient, and you're annoying me at the wrong time," I said. "Daddy's not going to like hearing about that."

She recoiled. "I don't care where you're going. Go and have a good time," she fired back, and left.

I sat looking after her a moment, wondering what it would have been like to have a little sister who looked up to me, idolized me, and took pleasure in spending time with me, instead of one who couldn't wait to put on my shoes and replace me in our daddy's eyes.

A little after five, Ava came to my room to inspect me.

"Good job," she said. "You put your heart into it."

I knew she was making a pun, teasing me, but I said nothing.

"Daddy wants to see you before we go."

"He does?"

"Don't act so surprised. He saw me before I went out the first time. There's nothing special about him asking for you now."

She had to make that point, perhaps to convince herself more than to convince me.

"Just be careful. Remember, we're doing this to correct your mistake, one made so soon after you brought that renegade here. This has to be a surprise, or it won't work. Understand? Lorelei!" she shouted, making me nearly jump out of my skin when I didn't answer immediately.

"Yes, yes, I understand."

"Okay. Go up to him," she said, stepping back. "Now."

I took a deep breath and walked out.

Mrs. Fennel was waiting at the end of the hallway. She looked at me as I approached her, and nodded. "This is for you," she said. She reached for my left hand and slipped a ring over my pinkie. It was identical to the ring Ava wore. "Wear it well," she said.

I looked at it, touched it, and then looked at her. She was actually smiling warmly at me.

"You've come a long way from the little girl who used to help me in my herbal garden. We're going to be proud of you, as proud as you will be of yourself. Tonight you will truly become your father's daughter."

I looked behind me. Ava was standing there smiling as well. Mrs. Fennel nodded again and went into the living room. I gazed at the stairway. Right now, it resembled a steep hill to climb.

"Go on," Ava whispered close to my ear. "Get his blessing."

I started up the stairway. My legs felt heavier and my breathing harder. *Get hold of yourself,* I thought. *You could bring the whole house down on you tonight.* I sucked in my breath, fixed my clothes, and primped my hair one more time before knocking on his door.

"Come in, Lorelei," Daddy called.

He was lying in his big bed with all the curtains closed and only a small lamp on. It threw a deep yellow glow over his face. His eyes were darker than ever. He pushed himself up on his pillow and beckoned for me to draw closer.

"Don't be alarmed," he said. "I'm simply conserving my energy for later. You do look breathtakingly beautiful, Lorelei. I can feel your sexual energy. It's fully blossomed within you. You're truly irresistible."

He held his hand out for mine and pulled me gently to him. Then he kissed me on the forehead. His lips felt so hot I thought they might burn me if he held them there much longer, but he didn't stop. He moved them down over my eyes, my cheeks, until they were at my lips, moving as if his lips were an artist's paintbrush and he was outlining the picture on his canvas. I had become his canvas in many ways, I realized. His lips grazed mine, and then he kissed me harder.

The feelings that flowed through me came as a frightening surprise. They were frightening because they filled me with unexpected pleasure. He had often sat me on his lap, had comforted me when I went to sleep and had bad thoughts, and had worn the mantle of my father and protector as I grew up. I had never dreamed he would touch me in places girls reserved for other men.

"Yes," he said. He was like the love chef sampling his newest creation. "I can taste your sex. You are so ready, and Ava has been a good influence on you, hasn't she?"

"Yes, Daddy."

"I want you to understand that what you are doing

tonight is carrying on a great history, enabling it to live. You bring immortality to me. You will truly be one of us now. Are you excited?"

"Nervous," I said, and he laughed. He had kissed me, held me, and looked into my eyes and had not seen what I had expected and feared he would see.

"That will come and be gone forever after tonight."

He touched the ring Mrs. Fennel had given me.

"These are all made out of the Patio stone. As long as you wear it now, you will be one of us and protected. Go now, my darling daughter, and begin to fulfill your destiny."

He released me and slipped back down onto the pillow.

"I have to rest a while," he said. He closed his eyes.

I stared at him for a few moments. I could see the paleness in his face. I thought I even saw lines where there had never been any. And then, suddenly, his eyelids opened again, and instead of the ebony black, there was a blazing red. It stabbed me with an electric sharpness that penetrated my heart.

I turned and hurried off like someone who had seen her own death.

# 19

## Judgment Day

"Did he give you his blessing? Wasn't it wonderful?" Ava asked me when we started out of the house.

"Yes," I said, and got into the car.

"And he gave you the family stone," she said, nodding at my new ring. "I hope you realize how lucky you are now, Lorelei, and what a privilege it is to make sacrifices for Daddy."

"You're not ever afraid? You were never afraid?" I asked her.

I thought she might become angry again and snap at me, but she was quiet. *She simply won't answer,* I thought. It felt like minutes of silence. "Of course I was afraid," she finally replied. "But I instinctively knew that once I had completed myself for Daddy, I would never feel that sort of fear again. We don't fear anything, Lorelei. We are aware of the renegades, but we don't fear them. We prepare ourselves, remain cautious and alert so we can defend ourselves, but even that has no fear in it. You can't imagine right now what you will feel once it's over. You don't have to try to imagine. I'll tell you, because I am sure you'll agree with me soon. You'll feel like a goddess, immortal and invulnerable. There are times when I feel the whole world is here for me and me alone. The air was created for me to breathe. The sun was created to warm me, and the night was created to protect me. Everything is for me, only me. When you are filled with that feeling of euphoria, that exaltation and rapture, you will see exactly what I mean. So, yes, I felt fear once, but it is so far back in my memory I can't remember what it was like."

What she said and the way she said it would probably make most people envious, I thought, but it didn't give me the relief I sought as we drove on. Buddy was out there waiting for his lover, believing I would give him the crown jewel of life, the most cherished and important reason to live—deep, long, and everlasting love. He longed for me, while I approached with deception and the promise of deep, long, and everlasting betrayal.

I wanted to cry, but I didn't. I was as cold as stone. Every part of my body was attached to strings I could not see but knew were there, strings that Daddy would pull, that he had been pulling all my life. I would dance the dance of seduction, and I would embrace Buddy with the iron grip my sex now could employ. He had no chance of escape. His own heart would blind him and bind him for deliverance into Daddy's waiting arms.

"The moment you drove over to his uncle's house that day," Ava said, "I knew this was perfect."

"You were always watching me? You always knew?"

"Of course, Lorelei. You're almost as important to me as you are to Daddy. You don't know how lucky you are to have it so easy the first time. I mean, it wasn't hard for me, but I still had to do a little work. You're getting a package wrapped and tied."

"Do we have to keep talking about it?" I asked, surprised at how sharp and defiant I sounded.

She glanced at me. "Well, excuse me," she said. "You're sounding like a spoiled bitch already," she added with a laugh. "I'll have to give you my whole wardrobe."

We drove the rest of the way in silence. Buddy stepped out of the house and waved the moment we drove up.

"Anxious, isn't he?" Ava said.

I started to get out, and she seized my arm. She glared at me with her full intensity, her eyes like daggers.

"Your whole life will be decided today, Lorelei. Make no mistake about that," she warned, and then let me go.

I got out quickly, the chill she threw over my body still clinging to my skin. As she pulled away and Buddy approached, I felt as if a thin sheet of ice were sliding down my torso and crumbling at my feet.

"Hey," he said. He took my hands, looked into my eyes, whispered "Welcome," and kissed me softly on the lips. He hesitated for a moment when he felt no reaction from me. I was still numb from Ava's ice-water words. "Everything all right?"

"Yes," I said quickly, and started for the house.

"I ordered pizza with some salad." He moved ahead to open the door for me.

Ordinarily, I would have been excited about getting what Mrs. Fennel called "goat food," but tonight I thought I would have little or no appetite for anything. Nevertheless, I quickly smiled and entered. He had music playing throughout the house.

"I thought I'd bone up on some classical music while I waited for you. I remember you mentioned how your father enjoyed it. This is Mozart."

"I know," I said. *"The Magic Flute."*

"Yeah, of course, you would know. When I went into the music store, I just asked for Mozart. You want to go in the living room or—"

"What's the backyard like? I've been in the house all day, and it's beautiful outside."

"Oh, it's great. He has a small pool, nice patio. C'mon," he urged, and led me through the house. We went out through the French doors in the den. There were light blue lounge chairs on a Spanish-tile patio. On the right side was a large barbecue grill and a sink. The pool was kidney-shaped, and there were a few tables, more lounges, and a small whirlpool. Five-foot-high ficus bushes provided lots of privacy, fencing in the property. There were some lemon trees on the right and also orange and grapefruit trees.

"Not bad, huh?"

"It's very nice, yes," I said.

"You want something cold to drink, beer, juice, water? I think there is some diet soda."

"Just water, thanks."

I sat on one of the lounges while he went to get me the water. The sky looked a few shades darker blue than usual, which made the scattered clouds a purer white. There wasn't much of a breeze. The clouds were puffy and thick and looked stuck in place.

Buddy brought me a glass of water. He had one for himself and sat at my feet. For a few moments, he was silent, sipping his water and looking at me.

"Is it my imagination, or are you a bundle of nerves?" he asked.

"It's not your imagination."

"Worried that your father won't like me?"

"Oh, he'll like you."

"How can you be so sure?"

"I know what he likes."

"So, why was there all that hesitation about me meeting him before?"

"Let's not ask any questions for a while," I said. "It's too beautiful and peaceful here. I feel as if I'm in a painting, and I like that feeling."

"Why?" he asked with a soft smile.

"It makes me feel all of this can go on forever," I said.

"Why can't it?"

I laughed. "You remind me of a little boy sometimes," I said. "So innocent, so trusting."

"Oh, and you're Miss Sophistication, I guess, huh?"

"I don't mean it to be a criticism," I said. "I wish we could all stay young and innocent forever."

He sipped his water. "We will."

"Oh, and how?"

"Love can do that for you," he said.

"Really? Why do you believe that?"

"Everything hard and difficult and even ugly seems far less so when you're in love. When I met you, as quick as all this seems to be, I felt as if my eyes were opened wider, my ears could hear more. All my senses were unclogged, sharper. Suddenly, everything I did was . . . not exciting, exactly, but more joyful, and that keeps you young. Does that make any sense?"

"Yes," I said.

"It was the same for you?" he asked hopefully.

"Yes."

"Then you won't laugh if I tell you I love you and want to be with you forever and ever."

"I won't laugh," I said.

He lowered his glass to the tile and leaned over to kiss me. This time, I kissed him back. He took the glass from my hand and put it down gently. We kissed again.

"I can't imagine ever being happier than I am at this moment. If I died tomorrow, I wouldn't feel cheated."

"But how can you be with me forever and ever if you die, Buddy?"

"You're here," he said, pressing his hand to his heart. "Locked in forever and always with me. If we never saw each other again after today, I'd see you everywhere in every woman's face and hear you in every woman's voice. You've possessed me."

"That sounds like—"

"Delicious torment. Don't stop."

He kissed me again. Half of me wanted to drive him away and save him, but the half of me that wanted him was stronger. His hands moved over me, tugging at my clothes. I felt myself tighten in anticipation. Ava's orders were to make love as much as possible before I brought him home. "His blood should be hot with passion and desire," she had said.

*It's all going the way it should,* I thought. Guilt, however, mixed in with my pleasure. I couldn't help being tentative, a little reluctant. He felt it and stopped.

"Want to go inside?" he asked.

"Yes," I said, and we reentered the house.

He led me to the bedroom in which we had made love. In moments, we were at each other, the hesitation quickly washed away by my own heat and passion. The intensity of it surprised me. He was surprised, too, but welcomed it as an indication of how much I wanted and loved him.

This time, however, I hardened faster in the places I had hardened before and became more aggressive. He started to laugh and then pretended to cry out for mercy. *Maybe he's not pretending,* I thought, but I couldn't stop. I kissed him more demandingly than he kissed me, rushed him to undress, and became impatient with how long he was taking to undress me. When we were naked, I rolled him over and mounted him.

"Wait!" he cried. "I'm not prepared."

"It's all right. We'll be fine," I said, too impatient to wait.

My hunger made him ravenous. With all abandon gone, we made love until he begged for mercy, laughing but astonished.

"I don't know if you were loving me or trying to kill me," he said, half joking. He paused, studying me a moment. "Do you work out or something? You have real muscle definition."

"I work out," I said, reaching for the blanket to cover my nudity.

"I'd better start working out harder myself to keep up with you."

He rose and put on one of his uncle's robes that was hanging on a closet door. He looked at his watch.

"Our food should be here any moment," he said. "I need some nourishment after that." He sat on the bed and took my hand, gently playing with my fingers. "Why should I be so lucky? I keep asking myself that."

"Maybe you're not."

"I love it when you're modest." He sighed and looked around. "My uncle's returning next week. We'll lose our love nest for a while."

Longer than a while, I thought.

"I'll figure something out," he quickly added. "Don't worry."

"I'm sure you would," I said.

"Will, not would."

We heard the doorbell.

"That's the food. Don't move. I'll bring it all in here. We'll spend all our time in bed until we have to leave. Consider this our honeymoon."

I said nothing. It was all going the way it was supposed to go.

"What do you want to drink now?"

"Just some water again," I said.

"Coming right up. Whew," he said, laughing. He dug his wallet out of his pants, smiled, and then went out to get our food.

"You want any help?" I called.

"Don't you move!" he shouted back. "I know a good thing when I see it."

I looked around. My body felt as if it was cooling down, the madness of my lovemaking dissipating. Outside, a cloud moved over the sun, and an ominous shadow washed over the window, darkening the room for a few moments. I felt a chill, like what someone might feel if he or she knew he or she was being watched. Was Ava there spying on me?

I heard him returning, proclaiming how delicious it all smelled.

"We're making a mess here," I said after he had brought in the food and set up plates on the bed. He threw off his robe and sat next to me, putting pillows behind our backs. I didn't think I would have any appetite, but, maybe because of our lovemaking, I was suddenly ravenous. He laughed at how fast and how much I was eating.

"I had better watch my fingers," he joked.

I paused, recalling Ava's description of Mrs. Fennel when she ate. "Watching her eat is like watching a starving dog eat," she had said. Just a suggestion that I would be anything like Mrs. Fennel was enough to ruin my appetite. I pushed the plate away.

"Hey, I didn't mean to stop you."

"I've had enough," I said. "I'll help you clean up."

"No, you won't. I invited you. You just stay here, comfortably." He rose and began gathering things. He saw me glance at the clock. "We're fine. Don't worry. We have plenty of time," he said.

"Okay."

*Let him cherish and enjoy every moment,* I thought. Maybe I would feel less guilty. I tried not to think of it. Instead, I imagined what life was going to be like in a new home, in a new place, and with a new baby sister as well. Like Marla, I had no loyalty or affection for the school we were in now. I didn't mind moving away, but I also had no illusions about what would await us somewhere else. Close friendships with other girls would always be forbidden. Most likely, I wouldn't be going to school much longer, if at all, anyway. Daddy might find something for me to do in Louisiana until it was time for Marla to take my place. Maybe he'd send me to college as he had sent Ava.

Buddy hurried back and dove onto the bed. The whole frame strained.

"Buddy, you'll break it."

"Unc would understand," he said.

"Understand? Why? Did you tell him about me?"

"No. I haven't told anyone about you."

"Really? Why not?"

"Superstitious."

"What's that mean?"

"My grandmother lived with us when I was just a little boy. She always warned me, warned everyone, not to be too proud and not to brag about what you had; otherwise, the Evil Eye would find you and take whatever it was away from you. I can't help it. I'm not shy or overly modest. I'm just . . . superstitious. Besides, most of my friends are idiots and wouldn't understand how strong my feelings are for you. They'd mock me, tease me. Who needs it, right?"

"Yes."

"What about you? Tell any of your friends about me?"

"No. I don't really have any friends."

He pulled his head back. "I can't believe that. Not only do you have friends, but I'm sure you have a trail of boys sucking up your shadow."

"I don't," I said.

"Why not?"

"Maybe I've outgrown them."

"I'll believe that more than anything else. It doesn't matter," he said after a moment of thought. "You have me. I'll be not only your lover but your best friend, and I'll fill every free moment of your time seven days a week, three hundred and sixty-five days a year."

I laughed. "Not even married couples do that, Buddy."

"We're more than just any married couple could be. We're . . . soul mates."

I looked away. Ava was right. This wasn't hard, but that didn't make it any easier for me to do.

"So," he said, lying on his back and putting his head on my lap, "tell me about your father. I'd like to know as much as I can about him before I meet him."

"What do you want to know?"

"What's he like? All I know is he's away a lot. He likes classical music, and oh, yeah, he's immaculate," he said, laughing. "I'm just teasing," he said when I didn't laugh. "If you don't want to talk about him, that's fine."

"Of course I don't mind talking about him. I love talking about him. If anyone is sophisticated, it's Daddy," I began. "He's always aware of the newest fashions. He speaks four languages, plays the piano, goes to concerts and the theater in London, New York, and Paris. He knows the richest, most successful people, here or in Greece or Rome. And he's handsome, devastatingly handsome. People who first meet him think he's a member of some royal family. No one is more elegant than Daddy."

Buddy sat with his mouth open.

"What?" I asked.

"Do you always call him Daddy?"

"What else should I call him?"

"Holy smokes. It sounds like I'm going to meet a Greek god or something. Now you do have me nervous."

"Sorry. I guess I do go a bit overboard when I talk about him."

"That's okay. It's wonderful to think so highly of your parents, I guess. I mean, I look up to my father and my mother. My father's a pretty bright guy, and he keeps himself fit."

"Oh, Daddy looks years younger than he is."

Buddy nodded. Then he paused, tilted his head, and gave me a coy smile. "He doesn't walk on water, does he?"

"No, but I think he could," I said, and he laughed.

"I do love you, Lorelei. I've never seen or heard a girl talk like you. You're special."

"That's what Daddy says."

"He's right. I guess he is a genius, and if he's so intelligent, he'll immediately see how deeply and sincerely I care for you and approve of me. Hey," he said after a moment. "You don't look happy about that."

I brushed his hair off his forehead. "No matter what, Buddy, I'm very happy I met you, got to know you."

"Great, only don't make it sound like the last scene in *Casablanca* or something. There's always tomorrow when it comes to us, Lorelei. Tomorrow forever."

"Tomorrow forever," I repeated.

He shook his head. "Looks like I have to do more convincing." He sat up to kiss me.

This time, I tried to control my passion so he could take the lead in our lovemaking. I wanted it to be softer and gentler and take longer, too. I tried to tell myself that this was the way Ava wanted it to be, but I felt it was more. With each caress, each kiss, we seemed to tighten and solidify the connection between us. This was the reason making love was the most intimate thing you could do with someone else, I thought, but only if you did it like this, with concern and care and not selfishness. In those precious minutes, you visited each other's very soul, and if it was real and meant to be, you were like one person ready to share every joy and every sadness.

When we were finished, I was crying softly.

He smiled at my tears and kissed them away. "I hope those are tears of happiness," he said.

"They are, but they are tears of sadness, too."

"What? Why?"

I didn't answer. I rose and reached for my clothing instead.

"What are you doing? It's only a little past eight. We're only twenty minutes away, and you told me we had to be there no earlier than ten."

"I want to go home now," I said. "Just get dressed."

"What's wrong?"

"Get dressed," I repeated.

He started to dress, but he looked very unhappy. "Did I do something wrong, say something wrong?"

"No." I turned to him. "I wish you had," I said, and walked out of the bedroom.

"Huh? Why?"

"I'll wait for you out back," I said.

Before he could reply, I left. I wanted to be alone for a few moments to argue with myself.

*What are you doing? Are you mad? Daddy is waiting. What possible excuse can you give, and what good would even the best excuse do? You would have failed, and Daddy would be in grave danger. Mrs. Fennel and Ava would be furious.*

Ava was right. This was too easy. But it shouldn't be this easy. I shouldn't be delivering someone as wonderful and good as Buddy. I should be delivering the type of young man Ava delivered and Brianna delivered—lustful, selfish, deceitful men who had hoped to use them for pleasure and leave them. I didn't have to use any guile or any seductive tricks to capture Buddy. Besides, he had captured me as much as I'd captured him. It couldn't be. It wouldn't be.

*You're the one who won't be,* my other self replied. *That's what won't be if you don't bring him to Daddy. You will be cast out and be less than an orphan.*

"What's going on?" Buddy asked, coming up behind me.

My heart was pounding. Thoughts and words became jumbled in my brain. A hot flush came over me and was quickly followed by a chill that almost made my teeth chatter. My body was in turmoil, a part of it in rebellion, a part of it opposing that rebellion.

I took a deep breath.

"We don't have to wait here any longer," I said. "We can wait for him at my house."

"Oh. Yeah, I suppose we could. That makes sense. You're a character. You scared me, jumping up like that. Talk about your impulsive person."

I turned and looked at him. "It occurred to me that you should have more time."

"More time?"

"To meet my younger sister, our housekeeper, and even Ava. That way, you'll be more comfortable when you meet Daddy."

He nodded. "Sure." He leaned toward me to kiss me.

"Let's go," I said, walking away and into the house.

He followed quickly. "You certainly can be confusing," he said when I opened the front door. "First, you were adamant about keeping me away from your house, your father, and now you can't wait to bring me to him."

I turned to him. "Yes. I know. I'm sorry."

"Nothing to be sorry about. I'm just amused. You're full of surprises."

We headed for his car.

*I'm sorry,* I repeated, but only to myself, and under my breath, I whispered, "I don't think I have the strength not to bring you to him."

# 20

## Tomorrow Forever

Buddy couldn't stop talking as he drove. I knew that my abrupt decision to leave immediately disturbed him, even though he agreed it made sense to go to my house and spend some time with my sisters before my father arrived. Try as I would, I couldn't pretend to be as enthusiastic as he was about our future relationship. I knew most of his effort was going toward getting me at least to sound half as excited as he was.

"Now that I'm going to meet your family, you've got to meet mine. Maybe next week, we can take a drive down to Long Beach. You'll love my mother. She's pretty hip and very pretty, if I may say so myself. Most of my friends tell me she looks more like my older sister than my mother. She dresses in up-to-date fashions, likes a lot of the music I like, and has a bubbly personality."

"Bubbly?"

"Yeah, you know. She's always up, and if something unpleasant happens, she always seems to find something positive to say. You know the type."

"No, I don't," I said.

"Why not? Your father doesn't sound like a depressing

guy. May I ask if he's seeing anyone? Romantically? I know he's had some tragedy, with his first wife dying and the mother of your younger sister deserting him."

I didn't answer. It was much darker now. Twilight had thinned away, and shadows found every vaguely lit place to invade and occupy. To me, it felt as if they were closing in on us. A sliver of the moon flashed between buildings and trees. For some reason, when the light from cars passing us in the opposite direction illuminated the inside of Buddy's car, I looked at my reflection in the window and, instead of myself, saw the face of the woman who could be my mother. I imagined her whispering, *How are you going to live with the sound of his scream?*

When we made a turn onto Sunset, he asked me what street he should turn on to get to my house.

"Just keep going," I said.

"Yeah, but with this traffic, I'll need some heads-up. Don't suddenly shout 'Turn here!' " he warned.

"I don't want you to turn. Just keep going."

"If we keep going, we'll be in Pacific Palisades, and then we'll be at the ocean, Lorelei."

"Good."

"Good? I don't get it. You were in a hurry to get home only a little while ago. Now, what's going on in that pretty head of yours?"

"I want to see the ocean at night."

He shook his head but smiled. "Women," he said. "Can't live without them and can't live with them."

"You have no idea how right you are," I said. I was thinking it and didn't realize I had spoken.

"What's that supposed to mean? Man, you're like a *tangram* all of a sudden."

"What's that?"

"A Chinese puzzle. Pretty hard to figure out most of the time. It's a dissection puzzle consisting of seven flat shapes, always seven, called *tans,* which you have to put together to form shapes. You're given a specific shape only in outline or silhouette, and you can't overlap any of the pieces. My father likes to do them. He picked it up when he was stationed in Hong Kong. I'm not bad at it," he said. "Makes Dad proud and happy that his son takes after him, I guess."

"You sound like you have a very nice family, Buddy."

"Good as any I know and better than most I know," he said, nodding. "Which is why they'll love you."

*No, they won't,* I thought, but this time, I didn't say it aloud.

We drove through Pacific Palisades and came out on the Pacific Coast Highway.

"Where should I go?"

"Any place you can park where we can look out at the water," I said.

"Not that easy around here."

We drove until he found a place to pull over.

"Now what?"

"I wanted to see the moonlight break out over the water. Not that long ago, I walked on the beach in Santa Barbara with my father, and we stopped to look at the moonlight. It was a fuller moon, but this is pretty, too."

"Why did you get so sad on me so suddenly, Lorelei?"

I tried to hide my face from the illumination of

passing cars, because I could feel the tears on my cheeks, but he saw them and reached for me.

"Lorelei, what's wrong?"

"I can't take you to see my father, Buddy. Ever."

"What? Why not?"

"It wouldn't work out well for either of us."

"Why are you saying this now? What are you talking about? You're not making any sense."

"My father is a very different kind of person."

I paused to think about what I had said. All my young life, I had thought of Daddy as a person, because almost all the time, he was no different from anyone else. He was talented and very intelligent. He had great charm and was very good-looking, but no one, least of all me, who loved him so much, could look at him and not think of him as a person. Despite everything, I couldn't think of him as being a creature of darkness. What I had seen him do frightened me, but as difficult as it would be for anyone to believe, I had accepted it, almost the way someone whose father was a convicted criminal might accept his father, love him, no matter what crime he had committed.

Tonight, now that I had been brought to the point of doing what my sisters called fulfilling themselves and giving Daddy what he needed to survive, I was forced to see him as who and what he really was and not what I wanted him to be. My sisters were able to live with it and go on to fulfill whatever destiny was out there for them to fulfill. That was still a secret for me to learn about myself, and about them as well, but it wasn't enough right now to comfort me, despite what they might think.

After all, they had not fallen in love with someone, cared deeply for someone, and been asked to deliver him to Daddy. Ava had put me in this position. In a real sense, she had blackmailed me by threatening to tell Daddy I had developed a relationship with a young man, something expressly forbidden. My desperate need to keep Daddy's love had brought me to this moment, had me bringing Buddy so close.

I did not understand what it was inside me that had caused me to turn around. I felt confident that whatever it was, however, was what made me different from my sisters. Ava had sensed it, and if I thought back hard enough, I think Brianna had sensed that about me as well. Ava implied that what I was to do with Buddy was my only way to show that I wasn't significantly different enough for Daddy to disown me.

"How different a kind of person can he be, Lorelei?" Buddy asked. He thought a moment. "Is your father into organized crime or something like that? Is that why he's away so much and why you have hesitated to bring me around until now?"

His suggestion seemed a perfect means of escape for both of us. "Yes," I said.

"Oh." He sat back like someone who had just been told he had terminal cancer.

"I'm sorry. I shouldn't have gone this far with you," I said. "This is all my fault."

"No, no. Look. I'm not in love with your father. I'm in love with you."

"It can't be, Buddy. He won't permit it, and he's . . . dangerous."

"Dangerous? Is he a Mob hit man or something?"

"Something," I said.

"Well, I don't get it," he said, his voice more full of anger than confusion now. "Why did your sister bring you to my uncle's house? What was all of this about her agreeing to my being brought to meet your father?"

"She's done things he wouldn't approve of, too, and I basically blackmailed her."

Lying and deception were coming so naturally to me, I thought. I really was so good at it that I'd even believe myself. It made me realize that although there was something in me that made me different from Ava and Brianna, there was also much in me that made me the same.

"Well . . . I don't care if your father's a criminal."

"Your wonderful family will," I said.

"This is crazy. You spoke so highly of him back at my uncle's house, Lorelei. You made him sound terrific."

"I know. I guess that's the father I wish I had, Buddy. I was fantasizing, just as I've been fantasizing about us and everything turning out wonderful."

"It will," he insisted.

"I've lied to you too much. There can't be love without trust."

He was silent for a moment. I hated doing this to him. I could feel the pain in his heart in my heart, and although I couldn't see his eyes clearly in the darkness, I knew they were glossed with tears, just as mine were.

"Well, what are you going to do, go out with another criminal, marry another hit man? Is that what your father would approve of?" he said, raising his voice. "What is it, one of those Sicilian things? Is he a made man? Does he work for some godfather?"

"I don't know what will please him. I know he wouldn't approve of you and me. He'd feel threatened, and Daddy doesn't like feeling threatened," I said, hoping I sounded frightening enough to scare him away.

"Okay. So, let's just keep ourselves secret until we figure something out."

"It wouldn't matter, anyway, Buddy. We're leaving soon," I said.

"Leaving? When?"

"When Daddy says, but it should be less than a few weeks."

"Daddy, Daddy. How can you call someone like that Daddy?" he asked, his anger raw now because of his pain.

"It's who I've known him to be all my life, Buddy. He does have some very nice qualities. He loves me and my sisters very much, and as you just said, he has had some terrible disappointments in love himself."

"How'd his wife die? I mean, really?"

"I told you the truth about her. I know you're very upset, and I'm sorry. I don't want to hurt you any more, Buddy. That's why I decided we shouldn't do this. Trust me. I'm right about it."

"I fell in love with you, Lorelei. I'm still in love with you no matter what," he said defiantly. He started the car and turned us around. "I imagine you still will permit me to drop you off at your house."

"Yes, thank you," I said.

"Where are you going to go? Where's your father's next territory?" he asked sarcastically.

"We're going to Louisiana, but I'm not sure exactly where yet."

"Yeah, I heard Louisiana has always had a big organized-crime population."

I was silent. He drove fast, angrily.

"Jeez, I feel as if I was with a schizophrenic today," he said. He looked at me as though he was really wondering if I had some mental illness.

"Listen to me, Buddy. It's all my fault. I thought I could have a normal relationship with someone, but I realized I was fooling myself and hurting you. It's less painful for us both this way."

"Yeah, I know. You keep saying that. How can you live this way? Don't you want to have a normal relationship?"

"For now, it has to be this way," I said.

"Yeah, well, don't forget to write me when you can have a normal relationship."

Of course, I understood why he was so angry, but I thought it was better that he be mad at me now than what would come later. We rode in silence for a while.

"Better tell me this time where to turn."

"It's not much farther."

"So, is your father home or not?"

"Not yet," I said.

"At least that was true," he muttered.

"The next road on the left," I said, and he slowed down to turn.

"So, after I drop you off now, I won't see you again? Is that it?"

"I don't know," I said.

"You don't know?"

"Maybe you won't want to see me again now, Buddy."

"From what you're telling me, I shouldn't. Unless I just want to have some good sex," he added. He was quiet a moment and then said, "I'm sorry. I'm just . . . frustrated."

"I know."

"God, you're calm about this."

"Turn up here," I said when we reached our driveway. It led up a small incline. "You can stop here," I said when we reached the top. Our house was just off to the left.

"Here?"

"Just in case," I said. I opened the door. "Good night, Buddy," I said. "Thanks for . . ."

"For what?"

"Everything," I said, and got out.

He watched me walk toward the house and then turned around and left. I stood there until his car lights were gone, and I looked at the house. Most of the lights were out, as they usually were in anticipation of an arrival. I felt my legs begin to tremble. It was as though we were having an earthquake and the ground beneath my feet was shaking.

At first, when I entered the house, I saw no one. Then Ava stepped out of the living room with Mrs. Fennel and Marla beside her.

"What are you doing here now? And alone? I saw him bring you to the edge of our driveway."

"I couldn't do it," I said, and turned quickly to the hallway and my bedroom.

She was right behind me. "Are you mad? What do you mean, you couldn't do it? Don't you realize how important this is? Get on the phone, and call him back immediately," she ordered.

I entered my room, trying to close the door behind me, but she was quickly there preventing it. She shoved me forward, and I spun around to face her. "Stop it, Ava."

"Daddy is depending on you, on us," she said, her eyes wide with rage.

"I couldn't do it, Ava. I love him."

"Love him? How could you love him, love anyone?"

"I don't know, but I do."

She nodded. "You really are a mistake. I was right," she said, with a cold smile creasing her lips. "Your life is nothing now. When Daddy finds out about this, you'll be worthless to him. He'll give you to the renegades."

I opened the dresser drawer and took out the photograph. "This very well might be my mother," I said, showing it to her. "I saw pictures of women who could be Brianna's mother and Marla's mother, too. Maybe my mother isn't dead and gone like your mother. Maybe I have a real father, too."

"Where did you get that?"

"I found it in Daddy's room."

"You fool!" she said. "You are a traitor. You really are as good as any renegade. Just stay here and wallow in your misery while I go back out there to bring Daddy what he needs. Thank goodness I had the instinct to train Marla faster."

She turned and left. I sat on my bed and stared down

at the picture with my name written on the back of it. Any moment, I expected to hear Mrs. Fennel's footsteps in the hallway, or Marla's. Maybe they would both come to chastise me and threaten me, but minutes passed, and I heard nothing.

I had no doubt that Ava was right. Daddy would disown me now. He and Mrs. Fennel would send me away. There was no point in waiting for it to happen, and besides, an idea floating beneath the surface of my conscious thoughts popped up. I should go find the orphanage and speak to the administrators to see if I could get information about myself and my parents. I had the address.

The idea kept me from sobbing myself to sleep. I began to pack a small bag and made sure I had all of my credit cards and my checkbook. I could get by for a short time with what I had. Choosing what to take in a small bag was difficult. Daddy had given me so many things, had brought beautiful gifts back for me from his travels. Each thing I looked at brought back a cherished memory. I had intended to keep myself from crying by doing all of this, but it had only brought on a flood of tears. How could I not cry? This was the only world I had known all my life. Daddy was the only one who had shown me real love. I hated to think of how much he would hate me now and wanted to run from that as much as from anything else.

When I had put together what I wanted, I slipped out of my room quietly. The house was still as dark as it had been when Buddy brought me home. I was anticipating Mrs. Fennel or Marla waiting out by the front door, but neither was there. Marla wasn't watching television, either. There was, in fact, a heavy silence in the house. Before I reached the front door, I heard a creak on the stairway and turned to look.

Daddy was coming down slowly, gathering shadows around him to thicken the darkness he already carried. He grew taller, wider, his eyes luminous, two circles of red in pools of yellow. His hand on the banister looked the size of two or three hands, the fingers long, with long nails. The sight of him stopped my heart. I could feel the taste of blood in my mouth and realized I had been biting down on my lower lip. Suddenly, to my utter surprise, Ava stepped out of the living room. What was she doing there? Why hadn't she gone out on a quick hunt?

"Oh, hi, Lorelei," she said, smiling. "Everything is perfect now. Don't worry. Daddy understands."

A terrifying thought exploded in my mind. I shook my head and backed toward the door. "No," I said.

"Yes," Ava said.

I heard a car coming up the driveway. Daddy moved faster down the stairway. I opened the door and rushed out to see Buddy returning.

"Oh, no!" I screamed into the bright headlights. He stopped the car and opened the door.

I could feel the wave of icy air hit my back. Daddy was in the doorway. I charged forward as Buddy stepped out.

"Hi," he said, not realizing anything. "Your sister called and explained, and—"

"Get back in the car! Hurry!" I shouted at him.

He froze in place and then looked past me. I could

see the shock in his face. I didn't have to turn around to know why. I lunged at the passenger door and shouted again for him to get into the car.

He did, but he looked too frightened to do anything more.

"Start the engine. Back out of here. Go!" I shouted, and punched him in the right shoulder hard enough to shake him out of his daze.

He fumbled with the key. The engine started, but as he put the car into reverse, a great shadow rushed over the windshield. It threw us both into complete darkness for a moment.

"Back up and drive out!" I cried.

He did, and when he turned to go down the driveway and away, we heard a piercing scream that sounded as if all of the metal in the car, all of the metal around us, was being peeled away. The car bounced. Buddy nearly missed the turn and sent us off the road, but somehow, he managed to keep the wheels from being caught on the edge. The car felt as if it were being heaved down the remaining portion of the hill. When we reached the end, he couldn't stop. We shot out into the heavy, fast traffic of Sunset Boulevard. Drivers hit their brakes. One car turned off the road. Another slammed into the rear of the one in front of it. Another hit that one. Horns blared. Buddy spun to his left and accelerated until we were away from the mess. Then he slowed down. He checked his rearview mirror and started to pull to the side of the road.

"No, don't stop," I said. "Keep going."

He looked at me. His throat was probably still too tightly closed for him to speak. He nodded and drove on.

Finally, he took some deep breaths and asked me what he had seen.

"Your own horrible death," I said.

"What?"

"Why did you come back?"

"Your sister called me and told me you were crying hysterically. She asked me why you hadn't brought me home and what you had told me. I didn't see any reason not to tell her, so I did. She said you were being too dramatic and that your father had heard you crying and told you that you were ridiculous and you should have brought me to see him. She thought it would be a wonderful surprise if I would just return, so I did."

"I should have realized she wouldn't give up."

"Give up what? What was that, Lorelei? I mean, I thought I saw a gigantic man with arms connected to his hips with . . . it looked like wings, bat wings, and his eyes . . . who or what was that?"

"That was my daddy," I said. "I was supposed to be the one who brought you to him, not Ava. It was my time, my turn to be his best daughter."

"I don't understand. Bring me to him for what?"

"Nourishment," I said.

"Nourishment? What is he, a cannibal?"

"No. He doesn't want all of you, just your blood, what's in your blood."

"What are you saying? Your father is . . ." He shook his head. "You're not telling me that your father is a vampire, are you?"

"We've never used that word, and I've never heard anyone else say it."

"You were supposed to bring me to him? That's why you were seeing me now, making love to me?"

"At first. But I couldn't do it, Buddy."

"Why not?"

"I do love you, and that's something we're not permitted to do."

"Not permitted . . . you're not . . . I mean, do you drink blood, too?"

"No. I eat strange things that Mrs. Fennel makes for us. I think there's something in it that you wouldn't eat or like, but I don't feed on people."

"I'm in a nightmare," he said. "Soon I'll wake up."

"I wish that were true."

"You have a piece of luggage with you," he said, nodding at my bag. "Where were you going?"

"My first home," I said.

"Where's that?"

"It's an orphanage in Oregon. I want to locate my mother."

"Your mother?" He thought a moment, looked into his rearview mirror, and jerked his head back as he asked, "That isn't your real father, is it?"

"I don't know," I said. "Ava told me he was her real father. I used to think, to hope, she was saying that only to make me jealous and it wasn't true for her, either, but she often looks like him, maybe more so now than ever."

"Jealous? Jealous of what?"

"We all want Daddy's love, Buddy. We all compete for it."

"Do you know your real mother's name?"

"No, but I have what might be her picture," I said, and took it out to show him.

"Well, we should just go to the police now, okay?"

"No," I said. "That would be stupid."

"Why?"

"They won't believe you, and Daddy will charm them to death. You'll look like a fool."

"But you'll testify now, won't you?"

"No, I can't do that."

"Why not?"

"Because as hard as I try, I can't stop loving him," I said.

# 21

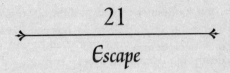

## Escape

"Do you think he'll come after us?" Buddy asked. "I mean, is he still interested in me?"

"No. Daddy doesn't go out to feed. His daughters have always brought what he needs to him."

"Daughters? How many daughters does he have?"

"I don't know, Buddy. I know only my older sisters, Brianna and Ava, and my younger sister, Marla."

"And they're all supposed to do this?"

"Yes."

"Have you done this?"

"Tonight was to be my first, my beginning."

"Hurray for me."

"I tried to keep you away."

"Yes, you did. Where did you say this orphanage was?"

"It's in Oregon, not far from Portland. I have the address. Take me to the airport. I'll get the earliest flight I can to Portland."

"What are you going to do if you can't get any information or you find out your mother is dead or something?"

"I don't know," I said.

He was quiet a moment, and then he said, "I'm going with you."

"No. You had better stay away from all this now. I know it's probably impossible to do, but you should just try to forget it, forget me."

"You saved me tonight. I can do this for you, Lorelei. I want to very much."

"But you'll miss more college, and your family will wonder what's going on."

"I'll take care of that. Don't you worry about me. Oregon's not far. The whole thing won't take more than a day or so."

"Yes, but—"

"Look, you just said you love me. To me, that's enough reason. I meant all the things I said to you. I admit, this is all very weird and something I'd rather forget, but you're in trouble now. Maybe there's some scientific explanation for what I saw and what's happening, and maybe there isn't, but afterward, we can try to get some help and stop it. Okay?"

"I'd rather you not come, Buddy."

"I knew you'd agree," he said, ignoring me and smiling.

I was too tired to argue any more, and I did want to get started as soon as possible. We drove to Los Angeles Airport and parked the car in short-term parking. We had to wait only an hour before the next flight. Even after we had our tickets, I asked him again if he really wanted to come along.

"More than you can imagine," he said.

It wasn't until we boarded and sat together that I accepted the fact that he was really going with me. There was no turning back now. I watched him close his eyes and sit back. The emotional shock of what he had seen and what had almost happened to him had finally settled in. He was exhausted. We both were. Moments after takeoff, I leaned against his shoulder, and he rested his head against mine. Despite the noise, the captain's little speeches, and the flight attendants passing out drinks and snacks, we both fell asleep quickly, neither waking up until the announcement of our impending landing.

We spent a longer time on the tarmac than expected. The anticipation tired us out even more. It was still dark by the time we deplaned, so I suggested we should check ourselves into the closest motel. I saw how he was dragging himself along, and I was feeling sapped of energy, too.

"We can get a rental car after we get some rest," I said.

He agreed. We chose the motel and made the call for a pickup.

"You haven't called anyone yet, Buddy. Shouldn't you?" I asked.

"It's all right," he said. "No one will miss me for a day or so."

The desk clerk at the motel asked if we wanted a room with separate beds. I quickly said no. If there was anything I wanted now, it was to fall asleep in Buddy's arms. He smiled. I think he wanted the same thing, to have me fall asleep beside him, to enjoy the comfort and the companionship we both needed to get through this horrible experience.

But despite our exhaustion, we both found it difficult to fall asleep quickly. For a while, we just lay there in each other's arms, lost in our own thoughts. It wasn't until now, now that I had stopped running, that I gave thought to Daddy and his reaction to what I had done. I could easily imagine him sitting there listening to Ava as she described my relationship with Buddy, how she had tried to stop it, and finally how she had hoped I would come to my senses and stop it myself with what was to be my first delivery.

I could almost hear Mrs. Fennel agreeing with every accusation Ava made about me, saying she had sensed the same weaknesses in me and blamed herself for letting it get this far. But it would be Daddy who would accept all the blame, telling them he had been blinded by the love he had for me and I had for him.

"In every way, she seemed so perfect," he would say.

Of course, by now, Ava would have found a substitute for Buddy. She would luxuriate in Daddy's praise and gratitude. Now she would surely be crowned his best daughter ever, for she had saved him in a crisis. Ironically, despite all that had happened, I still felt a pang of envy. I could easily envision Daddy's grateful expression, the flow of love and affection that came from his eyes, and the wonderful kiss of gratitude and love that came from his lips. I still wished it had all been directed at me.

Buddy's eyes closed, and he finally fell asleep. I did, too, but only a few hours later, I had the feeling someone was nudging me awake, and I opened my eyes. Buddy was still asleep, and there was no one else in the room, but I didn't feel we were alone. I rose and went to the windows. The curtains were closed as tightly as we could close them to keep out the daylight. Slowly, I pulled one aside so I could peer out at the motel parking lot. It was nearly empty, with only two vehicles in sight, and there was no one walking about. Traffic rushed by on the street facing the motel, yet I couldn't shake the feeling.

In fact, I realized my body was as tight and as hard as stone. What I was feeling reminded me of the times Daddy would stop what he was doing and suddenly become very quiet, listening hard. We'd all hold our breath until he relaxed again.

"What is it?" Buddy asked, waking and seeing me at the window.

"I don't know."

"You don't know?" He sat up. "Is there someone out there?"

"I don't see anyone."

He rose and stepped beside me to look out. "Seems pretty quiet out there."

"There's something," I whispered.

"Okay. I'll call for the car now, and we'll get started. You want to shower or something?"

"No, you go on," I said.

I remained by the window while he called for our car and then went to shower.

"How about something to eat?" he asked, coming out of the bathroom.

"After we get started," I said, and went in to throw some cold water on my face and brush my hair. I got dressed while he did the paperwork for the rental car, and then we left the motel.

"You still feel spooked?" he asked.

"Yes," I said. "I wish you hadn't come along."

"Well, I did, so stop saying it. I'm going to see you through this," he said firmly. "We'd better eat something." He turned into a roadside restaurant.

I could feel his eyes on me as I looked at everyone closely.

"Hey, you think they've put the word out on you? Are your father's kind everywhere?"

The waitress came over for our order. Nothing interested me, but I ordered a rare hamburger. Buddy ordered one, too, but medium, with French fries and a salad.

"How about some lemonade? They claim it's freshly made."

"I've never had lemonade," I said.

"Never?"

He ordered it for us and then reached across the table to take my hands. I was still looking out the window at the people coming to the restaurant.

"So, are your father's kind everywhere?"

"I don't know, Buddy. Sometimes it seems that way. He has contacts everywhere he goes in the world," I said. "And even if he doesn't, Daddy often knows things no one else could possibly know, and so does Mrs. Fennel."

"Who is this Mrs. Fennel, anyway?"

"She's my father's sister."

"Yeah, you mentioned you were living with your father's sister, but how come you never called her your aunt?"

"I didn't know she was my aunt until recently."

"Huh?"

"Our lives are twisted in secrets, tied up like a ball of string, Buddy."

"I can imagine."

"No, you can't," I insisted. "That's why I wish you hadn't come along."

"Look," he said, still holding my hands. "You didn't do what you were supposed to do last night. You cared about me. You took a great risk. I have to believe it was not just for me but for yourself as well. It was for us. You're different from whatever lives in that house. I couldn't love you if you weren't."

I said nothing. His words were comforting and beautiful to me, but they didn't change how I felt. My body was still tight. My heart was still thumping with anticipation, and I was still drawn to watch everything that moved around me. He continued to ask me questions, to keep me talking, expecting it would relax me or maybe to relax himself. I gave him as many answers as I could, hoping that he would finally realize that he was possibly in even greater danger than he had been last night if he continued to accompany me. If he had simply gone home, he would surely have been safe. Neither Ava nor Mrs. Fennel, and especially not Daddy, would have pursued him and given credence to the stories he might have told. They would have simply left, and it would have been forgotten. But not now. Now he was here, still part of who and what I was.

Our food came. The danger and the flight made him ravenous, whereas I barely picked at my hamburger and didn't touch the bun.

"How can you not be hungry? Don't you like hamburgers?"

"I've had this so rarely," I said. "Meat was always the only thing we enjoyed outside of what Mrs. Fennel fed us."

"What did she feed you?"

"I couldn't tell you what it was, exactly. She used herbs in combinations only she knew. You would probably spit out the first bite."

He ate and nodded and looked at me oddly.

"What?" I asked.

"You'll think I've just gone crazy after all that's happened, but you look older to me. I don't mean aged or anything. You just look older."

"I feel older," I said. "It's like whatever was childish in me died."

"Well, I can understand that. I think the same thing happened to me last night."

He finished eating. We paid our bill and got back into the car. Buddy had asked the rental attendant for a map of the state when the car was delivered, and we both studied it for a few moments to make sure to choose the best route.

"Not that I know much about Oregon," Buddy said, "but from the looks of it on the map, this town isn't much." He sat back. "Come to think of it, I remember when we first met, your sister asked me if I was from a small town."

"She was trying to find out if you were possibly a renegade," I said.

"Renegade? What's that?"

"People like my father who don't follow our rules. They endanger us all. They're actually our worst enemy, because they invade our territory and try to take control."

"No kidding?" His expression changed. "She decided I wasn't one of those renegades, right?"

"Yes," I said. I nearly laughed. "I don't know why that should give you any sense of relief now, Buddy. You've kept yourself a target by coming along with me."

He shrugged. "No sense talking about it now."

He drove on. Because we had started so late in the day and because of the time it took us to reach Hearts-port, it was twilight by the time we found Dunning Road. The road began as a solid macadam street, but after a good mile and a half, it became gravel.

"You sure about this address?" Buddy asked. "I haven't seen any houses since we turned, and this isn't looking like anything that's been developed, especially when you think how long ago you were there."

"It's the address I have," I said.

We continued almost another mile until we saw a large, two-story house with a cupola at the crest of a small rise. It had stone cladding, a small stairway to the front door, and a double slanted roof. From this angle, the dormer windows looked like eyebrows. The grounds around the house were not very neat. There were patches of grass here and there and wild bushes.

"That's a pretty old house," Buddy said. "I know a little bit about architecture because of a class I took. It's what's known as Second Empire."

The downstairs windows were dimly lit, but the upstairs windows were dark.

"If I didn't see that sign there," Buddy said, nodding at the sign that read, "Lost Angels, An Infant Sanctuary," "I'd think we were at the wrong address for sure, or it was a place nearly deserted. Maybe it is. Maybe someone bought it, and it's no longer an orphanage."

"Then why the sign?"

"I don't know. Whoever bought it might think that's cool. I mean, look at it. The gardener must be legally blind."

There were no signs of life around the house, no cars, no one outside.

"I feel this is it, Buddy."

"So, I guess we'll go in to see what's what," he said.

"No."

"No?"

"I don't want you going in with me. Wait in the car."

"Are you sure? I mean . . ."

"I'm sure," I said.

I couldn't tell him why, exactly, but the feeling I had had back at the motel was much stronger here, and those famous instincts Ava often accused me of not having were alive and behaving like sirens and alarms.

"Well, I don't think I should let you go . . ."

"Please, Buddy. I agreed to let you come along with me this far. Please."

"Okay, if that's the way you want it."

"I do," I said. "If I need you, I promise I'll come out to get you."

He nodded.

"Lock the doors," I said when I opened mine and stepped out.

I heard the click and looked back at him. He was sitting forward, his face caught in the dim glow of the slowly brightening half-moon. His face looked made of wax and in danger of melting away completely.

I walked up the gravel drive to the front steps. Just as I reached the top, the door opened, and Mrs. Fennel stepped out of the shadows and into the dimly lit front doorway. I gasped and drew back. She smiled.

"We expected you sooner," she said.

Ava came up to stand a foot or so behind her.

I took another step back, glanced at the car, and considered running back to it.

"There's no need for you to run away, Lorelei. No one is going to hurt you," Mrs. Fennel said softly.

"Even though you've done a lot that could hurt us," Ava added.

"Now, stop," Mrs. Fennel said. "You know what your father told you."

Ava smirked. "We won't hurt you, but that doesn't mean we'll leave him alone," she said, nodding toward the rental car.

"There's no need to threaten her," Mrs. Fennel said. "I know my girl. Come on in, Lorelei. You want to know so much, and you've come so far."

She stepped back. Ava disappeared inside. I looked back toward Buddy. He had never seen Mrs. Fennel, so he wouldn't know that they had beaten us here. I hoped he hadn't seen Ava standing next to her. I was afraid for him, but what drew me back up those stairs was my own need to know about myself as much as anything else. Mrs. Fennel kept her smile.

When I reached the doorway, I heard the sound of women laughing.

"Those are just other daughters and sisters," Mrs. Fennel said. "They all know you're coming. Everyone's waiting for you."

She put her arm around my shoulders and closed the door behind me.

"You know, this is a wonderful second chance for you, Lorelei. I can tell you, few of us would have enjoyed such an opportunity. Your father really loves you."

The house was old, but nothing looked worn or as untidy as the grounds did. There was no dust, no cobwebs. Everything looked as it might have looked the day the house was built and furnished. The floors glittered like immaculate hospital floors, and the wood of the walls and ceilings looked polished. I followed her through the short entryway and hallway and then heard the sound of babies crying.

"Feeding time," she said. "Don't look so surprised. This really is an orphanage of sorts," she added. "Come. Look."

We stopped at a doorway on the left. Inside was a nursery with ten infants in bassinets. Two women wearing nurses' uniforms were tending to them.

"Go on, look at them, Lorelei. Each one is perfect and will be quite beautiful."

The nurses turned and smiled at me.

The one on the left reached into a bassinet and took out an infant who wasn't crying. She looked asleep. The nurse held her so I could see her face. She did look perfect.

"Wouldn't you love to have a daughter like that?" Mrs. Fennel asked.

I didn't answer.

The laughter in the other room grew louder.

"Oh, come on," Mrs. Fennel said. "They're so anxious to see you."

I followed her across the hallway and into a large living room. Five young women sat on settees. I didn't recognize them from the pictures I had seen in Daddy's closet, but when the fifth turned to me, I gasped.

It was Brianna.

"Hi, Lorelei. You have grown beautifully. She's perfect, isn't she, Mrs. Fennel?"

"Perfect."

Ava, who was now sitting in a large cushioned chair on the right, continued to glare angrily at me. The four other women were as beautiful as Brianna, two with rich, radiant black hair and two with auburn. All of them, including Brianna, were dressed in black gowns very similar to the one Daddy had brought for me from Paris. Ava laughed at the expression of surprise that I was sure I wore.

"Dresses look familiar?" she asked. Her expression soured again. "I didn't wear mine tonight. Thanks to you."

"Ava," Mrs. Fennel said with a tone of warning. She smiled again and nodded at one of the women with black hair. "This is Sophie, Ava's mother. Don't they look more like sisters?"

"I thought . . . she died in childbirth," I said.

"You weren't ready for this sort of truth when we told you that story, Lorelei," Mrs. Fennel said.

How much had been fabricated? I wondered.

"Here you are," I heard, and turned to see the woman in the picture with my name on it, the woman I had thought was my mother, enter the room. She didn't look any older than she had looked in the picture and certainly no older than any of the other women. She carried a dress in her arms that looked just like the dresses the others were wearing. "Look at how she's grown, Mrs. Fennel."

"Yes," Mrs. Fennel said.

"It's not fair," Ava said.

I looked at her, confused. What wasn't fair?

"Stop it, Ava. Your father has decided," Mrs. Fennel said.

Ava pouted.

"You know who this is, don't you?" Mrs. Fennel asked me. "You took her picture from your father's closet." She shook her head. "Don't look so surprised. Of course, I knew you had, and your father knew you had, too. You could keep no secrets from either of us."

"Is she my mother?"

"Yes."

"Then Daddy is . . ."

"Is really your daddy," Mrs. Fennel said, nodding. "He's all their daddies," she added, with a sweeping gesture toward Brianna, Sophie, and the other two.

I shook my head. It was all overwhelming.

"Maybe you're telling her too much too quickly," my mother suggested.

"No," Mrs. Fennel replied. "It's what Sergio wants. He believes that if she's told the truth now, she'll stop resisting."

"I don't understand," I said. "You said she was my mother."

"I am your mother, Lorelei, and your daddy is my daddy, too."

"But that's . . . incest," I said, and they all laughed, Ava the loudest.

"Those kinds of rules, biological or otherwise, don't apply to us," Mrs. Fennel said. "Now you know. You have your father's blood, just as they all do. It's how we go on. This is your destiny, to have your father's progeny."

I shook my head.

"Don't try to understand everything at once," my mother said. "For now, you're to put on this dress. Mrs. Fennel brought it along."

"Why?"

I saw how all the others were smiling. Only Ava continued to sulk.

"It's what we think of as a bridal dress. Daddy is going to be here soon. You're moving to the head of the line."

"It's not fair," Ava insisted, rising to her feet. "I've done everything right, and she hasn't, and she's moving ahead of me."

"A mistake has been made, and your father believes this is the way to correct it. You should be thinking of him, not of yourself," Mrs. Fennel said sharply.

Ava glared at me and then sat again.

"What are you saying, Mrs. Fennel, that they are all Daddy's daughters and Daddy's wives?"

"Well, we don't have formal weddings here," she said, and they all laughed again.

I looked at Ava. Why did she want this more than I did?

"You probably noticed that your mother doesn't look a day older than she did in that picture," Mrs. Fennel said, as if she could hear my thoughts. "And Brianna . . . not much of a change in her, either. As your father promised you many times," Mrs. Fennel said, "you will have more and do more than any other young woman."

"But you're older," I said.

Mrs. Fennel laughed. "I'm older," she said to the others, and they laughed, too. "Yes, I'm older, Lorelei. I've passed my prime, but we're talking in terms of centuries, not decades, and I have a long time to go yet, a very long time. Besides, do you know anyone who looks my age who has my energy and strength?"

I looked at my sisters. "Do they all need what Daddy needs every month?"

"No. Only the males feed, Lorelei, but the females provide for them and give birth to our new ones. That's their destiny, and that's your destiny now."

"Put on your dress," my mother said, thrusting it at me. "It's getting late."

I didn't move.

"You can go out and tell your young man that everything is fine and he can leave. We'll let you do that," Mrs. Fennel said when she saw my hesitation.

"He'd better not be out there when Daddy comes," Ava warned.

Everyone stared at me, waiting. Some of the babies began to cry louder.

Mrs. Fennel's smile began to fade as I remained

hesitant and took a step back. Her eyes narrowed into that more familiar face of suspicion and anger. "You don't want to do this, do you?" she asked me. "You don't want to be one of us, after all? There is something wrong with you."

"Wrong with me?" I shook my head. In my way of thinking, there was something right with me.

"There is no long window here, Lorelei. If you refuse your destiny now, you could end up never being one of us, never being accepted. You might even become hunted, and not only by us."

"Don't beg her," Ava said. "Let her go. We don't want an impurity in our family."

"What family?" I asked. "This isn't a real family. Daughters who are wives and mothers of other daughter-wives."

"Lorelei," my mother said. "Please."

I backed away, shaking my head. No one moved. They all stared at me as if they couldn't believe what they were seeing. Only Ava looked pleased.

"You can't have any sort of real life out there without your father," Mrs. Fennel said. "You have his blood running through your veins. Anyone you're with will sense something is very different about you, and if you ever did have a child with another man, you could never be sure of what and who that child would be, especially if it was a boy."

I shook my head again.

All of the babies sounded as if they were crying now. I backed farther away from her. Still, no one moved. No one looked interested in preventing my escape.

"Lorelei," Brianna said.

"Lorelei," they all chanted.

I turned and ran to the front door, expecting them to follow, but no one did.

No one was chasing me, but I didn't hesitate. There were no clouds, but a shadow moved over the light.

*Daddy's almost here,* I thought, and charged toward the car.

Buddy saw that I was fleeing and started the engine, but he had forgotten to unlock the doors. I tugged madly at the handle. I could hear the babies screaming. It was a piercing sound, cutting through my brain. I put my hands over my ears. I felt myself weakening and sinking to the earth as if I were actually melting away.

And then darkness rushed in.

# Epilogue

———◆———◆———

I woke in the car. We were bouncing over the gravel road, because Buddy was driving so fast. I heard the tiny stones being kicked up into the wheel wells. Buddy didn't know I was conscious. I could see how terrified he was. I groaned and sat up.

"What happened?" I asked.

"You fainted. I got out and got you into the car as quickly as I could and drove off. What happened in there? Why did you come running out like that?"

"Did anyone come after me?"

He shook his head. "But I wasn't going to wait around to see."

"Good."

We reached the smooth macadam portion of the road, and he picked up more speed.

"So? Who was in there? What did you find out? But more important, what made you run to the car like that and faint?"

I wondered how much I wanted Buddy to know. I had no doubts in my mind about what his reaction would be if he knew I was literally my father's daughter.

I was no orphan, and I had no parents who were normal human beings.

Lying had already become second nature to me. So much about the way we had lived depended on good and credible fabrication. Deception and darkness were our true guardians. None of us could survive if we didn't develop the skills to be crafty and cunning. This was what Daddy meant when he had told me that darkness was our friend. He didn't mean only the darkness that comes with night. He meant the darkness we could draw over our true faces, the darkness in which we could hide our true feelings, and the darkness through which we navigated during everyday life to avoid exposure.

I realized now that there was so much I had inherited from Daddy. I used to be jealous of Ava, who we were told was Daddy's actual daughter. The resemblances I saw between him and her often disturbed me, because I wanted those resemblances, too. The very fact that I had not been told until now that he was my father, too, underscored how important it was for us to ration the truth. I didn't know whose idea it had been to keep me and Marla believing we were simply orphans, but I saw the purpose. For however long we believed it, we were grateful and willing to be obedient and loyal and, of course, to make the sacrifices necessary always to protect Daddy. I didn't know when Ava had been told the truth or why she was an exception, but I was sure it had to do with what Daddy and Mrs. Fennel sensed about her. Even I sensed something more about her, something that brought her closer to Mrs. Fennel. It occurred to me that perhaps Marla had been told the truth just recently, and that was what had given her the self-confidence and the edge.

It all seemed to make sense to me now. Daddy was like the queen bee in a hive. He didn't give birth, but he was the only one who could propagate his kind. All who surrounded him lived to defend and nourish him. This was what Ava and Mrs. Fennel always meant when they emphasized that I shouldn't think of myself but only of my family. They reminded me of this whenever I felt sorry for myself because I wasn't permitted to do the things girls my age were doing.

The compensation for this undying loyalty and sacrifice was true, however. I had just seen it. Yes, we would enjoy youth and beauty for decades, even centuries, longer than any normal human being. Yes, we would have anything we wanted, go anywhere we wanted, and satisfy all of our senses, our desires. We would never be frustrated or disappointed, unless we had what I thought I had, a longing to be loved and to love someone.

Whatever capacity for love my sisters possessed had to be directed toward and reserved for Daddy. He demanded all of it, for it was only then that he could be confident that they would never betray him or desert him or fail to provide for him. There was no girl anywhere who was more of a Daddy's girl than we were and would be forever.

"Well?" Buddy asked.

"Daddy and Mrs. Fennel knew I would be coming there. They called ahead to warn them."

"Really? But what was it like in there?"

"It's a very special little orphanage. Daddy obviously

does a lot to support it, so whatever he asks for, they are sure to do."

"What did he ask for?"

"He asked that they not be cooperative with me. They were nasty to me, in fact," I said, thinking only of Ava.

"But why did you run out of there and faint?"

"I was persistent, probably too persistent, and one of their attendants frightened me."

"Frightened you? After what you've been used to seeing? He must have been something else. What did he do, come after you with a knife or a gun or something?"

"I didn't want to wait around to find out. It was very unpleasant for me, Buddy. I'm glad you didn't go in with me, too. You would have lost your temper or something, and it would have turned out even worse."

"Yeah, but you fainted."

"I'm just tired, I guess, tired and weak. I should have eaten more. This has been terribly stressful."

He nodded, but he didn't look as if he believed everything completely. "Do you think I should take you to see a doctor?"

"Oh, no. I'm fine now."

"So, what are you going to do now? Will you speak to the police back home?"

"Maybe. I'll think about it on the way."

"Good," he said. He reached for my hand. "I'll be right beside you, no matter what, Lorelei."

"I know you will."

"I'm sorry you came all this way and didn't find out what you needed to find out. Maybe, once you see the police and the police contact this orphanage, they'll have to tell you things."

"I hope so," I said.

"Well, it's late now. First thing I should do is get you something substantial to eat. Then we can see about a flight back, huh?"

"Yes, that sounds good."

"You look tired," he said.

"I didn't get much sleep, and this was quite an added ordeal."

He nodded and smiled. "Some warm food will help. Got to get you used to eating something other than that gruel your Mrs. Fennel gave you."

"Yes. I want to avoid all the things she gave me," I muttered.

We were back on a main highway leading to Portland.

"Hey, see that roadside restaurant up there on the right?" he asked after a few miles.

"Yes."

"Look at all the trucks in the parking lot. Truckers know the best places to eat. My father always said that. Whenever we went on long rides, he would look for trucks in parking lots, and it always proved to be good."

"Looks fine to me," I said.

We pulled into the parking lot and parked next to a tractor-trailer.

"Okay?" he asked.

"Yes, fine. Let's go eat," I said.

The restaurant resembled an old-time diner with a long counter and booths with red leather seats. There was even a jukebox at the far end. It was crowded and busy, but there was an empty booth on the right. A short woman with bushy white hair and thick-framed glasses greeted us and took us to the booth. She handed us menus.

"I can't believe how hungry I am," Buddy said.

"Tension builds your appetite," I said. "Mrs. Fennel used to say . . ." I stopped myself. "Order me the meatloaf special. I'm going to the bathroom to wash up."

"What do you want to drink?" he asked as I slid out.

"Oh. One of those lemonades."

"Done deal," he said, and I went to the bathroom. I splashed cold water on my face and looked at myself in the small mirror above the sink. What Buddy had observed earlier looked accurate to me, too. I did look older. It was as if I had aged a few years. Whatever innocence had once been in my eyes was gone and replaced with a cold, hard look. I had the face of someone who might not laugh for quite a long time, if ever again.

When I stepped out of the bathroom, I looked toward our booth. Buddy had his head in his hands, his elbows on the table. I was sure that this was the worst nightmare he had ever had and one that seemed not to have an ending. I told myself I had given in too easily when he had insisted on going with me. There were many reasons he was in danger now, and it had all begun with one thing. Ironically, Ava and Mrs. Fennel had been right. It was love that had brought Buddy here. Love could be poison when it involved us.

He looked up and smiled as I started for the table. "You all right?" he asked.

"Yes, I'm okay."

"I ordered for you," he said. The waitress had already served the lemonades. I sipped mine. "Better than before, right? This is really homemade."

"Yes," I said, smiling.

"I told you. Truck drivers know exactly where to go to eat on the highway. They have the instincts for it."

"I'm sure they do."

"I'm going to wash up, too," he said. "Be right back."

"Okay."

He slipped out of the booth but paused to kiss me on the cheek. "I do love you, Lorelei," he whispered.

"I know you do, and I love you."

I watched him walk toward the men's room, and then I looked out the window at our rental car. I saw the driver of the truck next to it start to get into his cab. As if by reflex rather than thought, I got up and walked quickly out of the restaurant and to our car. I opened the door, took out my bag, and knocked on the truck driver's passenger-side door. Then I opened it.

"What's up?" he asked. He was an African American man who looked to be about fifty, with graying black hair. He was tall and slim and had a white mustache.

"Would you give me a ride?"

"A ride? Where to?"

"Where are you going?"

He laughed. "Just anywhere but here, huh?"

"Yes."

"Hop in," he said.

I did, and closed the door. He put his truck in gear and started out of the parking lot. I looked back at the restaurant. Buddy had not yet returned to our booth.

"So, don't tell me you're running away from home?" the truck driver said.

"No. I think I'm running toward it."

"What's that mean?"

"Just that where I belong is somewhere out there," I said, nodding at the road ahead.

He laughed. "You young kids today," he said, shaking his head. "What's your name?"

"Lorelei."

"That's a beautiful name. My mother and father decided to call me Moses. Hey, maybe I'm taking you to the Promised Land."

"Maybe," I said. "I guess I'll find out soon enough."

Ahead, the road seemed to stretch toward forever. The lights of the truck parted the darkness and drove it back. That gave me hope. Maybe I could be just as comfortable, if not more so, in the sunshine.

"Can't imagine what would put a girl as pretty as you on the road," Moses said.

"No. You could never imagine it."

Moses laughed. It was melodic and beautiful.

I heard myself laugh, too.

It was like hearing the laughter of someone I once knew, someone who was truly going home.

Pocket Star Books
Proudly Presents

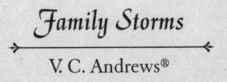

*Family Storms*

V. C. Andrews®

Available in paperback
March 2011
from Pocket Star Books

Turn the page for a preview of
*Family Storms . . .*

# Prologue

⟢————————————————————⟣

"We gotta move," Mama said.

I had just closed my eyes and curled up as tightly as a caterpillar in the heavy woolen blanket. Over the past few months, I had grown immune to the variety of unpleasant odors woven into it. Most nights, I think I held my breath as much as I breathed, anyway. I was always anticipating that something terrible would wake me, so I never slept much deeper than the very edge of unconsciousness. My ears were still open, my eyelids fluttering, and the dreams that came tiptoed in on cat's paws.

It had begun to rain harder, and the wind blowing in from the ocean made it impossible to stay dry under the cardboard roof Mama had constructed from some choice cartons she had plucked out of a Dumpster behind the supermarket. In the beginning, I would tremble with embarrassment while she sorted through the garbage. Now, I stood by quietly, watching and waiting, as disinterested as someone who had lost all memory. I had learned how to shut out the world and not hear other people talking or see them gaping at us as they walked by. It was almost as if it were all happening to someone else, anyway, someone who had borrowed my fourteen-year-old body to suffer in and endure.

"Where will we go, Mama?" I asked.

"Home," she muttered.

"Home? Where's home?"

She didn't answer. Sometimes I thought she hoarded her words the way a squirrel hoarded acorns, because she was afraid the day would soon come when she would have nothing left to say. Lately, she was saying less and less, even to me. If I pressed her to talk, she would take on the look of terror that someone in the desert would have if she were asked to share her last cup of water. Consequently, I wouldn't talk very much to anyone, either. We both said only what was necessary. Anyone who watched us for a while would think we were actors in a silent movie.

I blocked my face from the drizzle and sat up. Mama was already stuffing her bedding into her suitcase, forcing it in as if it were screaming and fighting not to be locked away. She closed it and paused. The rain fell harder, but she stood there with her face fully exposed to the rain, as if we were in bright sunlight, coating ourselves with suntan oil on the Santa Monica Beach the way we did years ago when Daddy was still with us. I knew she was looking at the ocean, expecting some boat to be rushing in to rescue us. A number of times over the past few days, she had told me she expected that to happen, as we wandered up and down the beach searching for a good location to set up her Chinese calligraphy. Most people who bought any wanted their names in Chinese calligraphy and took Mama's word for it that she was doing just that. She could have been spelling out *toilet* for all they knew.

While she painted with expert strokes, I sat at her side and wove multicolored lanyard key chains that I sold for two dollars each. I usually began the day with a few dozen I had managed to do during the night. Between the two of us, we made enough to eat two, sometimes three, meals and occasionally have enough to buy some new article of clothing or old shoes from the thrift store. We had been doing this for nearly a year now, ever since we were evicted from our apartment and then from the hotel. Daddy had deserted us nearly two years before that.

Occasionally, someone would ask me why I wasn't in school. I would say I was on vacation or we were between locations and I'd be starting a new school soon. Most knew I was lying but didn't care, and when policemen looked our way, it seemed they either looked through us or didn't care, either. Sometimes I thought maybe we had become invisible, and they could walk right through us. Maybe it was painful to look at us. It was already past very painful to *be* us.

In the beginning, when Daddy first left, Mama had managed to keep us afloat, working first as a restaurant hostess and then as a waitress, but her depression led her to more and more drinking, and she had trouble holding on to any employment. Occasionally, she would sell one or two of her works of calligraphy to one of the arts-and-crafts stores. One of the better-known bars, the Gravediggers, had one prominently on a wall to the right of the bar. Mama told me it spelled *heaven*.

"The Gravediggers will take you to heaven," she joked.

Although I had never met her, my maternal grandmother was the one who had taught Mama calligraphy. They had lived in Portland, Oregon. My grandparents had Mama late in life, and my grandfather, who was a fisherman, had died in a fishing accident during a bad storm. Just like us, Mama and her mother were left to fend for themselves. Both of my maternal grandparents had died before I was born, so I had never seen my grandfather in person, either. All I had were the few old photographs of her parents Mama had brought with her. She told me they were taken when she was only ten, but her parents looked as if they could easily be her grandparents.

Mama said the struggle, which was what she called their lives after her father died, was responsible for aging and killing her mother. Her father didn't make a lot of money and had very little life insurance.

Despite our own struggle, Mama would say that my daddy's desertion of us was no great loss. I knew she was just speaking out of anger. At least we ate and had a roof over our heads when he was with us. We never really expected to have much more. Daddy had barely graduated from high school, enlisted in the army, where he learned some mechanical skills, and gotten a job as an appliance repairman when he was discharged. That was what he was doing when he met my mother at a bar in Venice Beach, California.

Mama had left Portland with a girlfriend right after high school, because her English teacher and drama club coach lavished so much praise on her acting skills that she thought becoming a movie star was inevitable. She had been in every one of her school drama productions since the eighth grade.

Of course, after endless rejection and only very minor acting opportunities, she blamed her teacher for ruining her life. "He got me full of myself until I couldn't see anything else, Sasha," she would say. According to her, he was right up there, just behind Daddy, as the cause of all our troubles. "Beware of compliments," she told me. "Half the time, people you know tell them to you so you'll like them more, not yourself."

Both she and her girlfriend were waitresses in the bar where she had met Daddy. Her girlfriend was already going hot and heavy with someone she had met there, and according to my mother, "The writing was on the wall. I knew I'd be on my own very soon, and with what I was making, that was nearly impossible. The real possibility of my having to go home to Mama Pearl was looming. That's why I fell in love so quickly with a spineless, unambitious clod like your father."

She admitted or, rather, used as an additional excuse the fact that Daddy was very handsome, with his crystal-like cobalt-blue eyes, firm lips, and wavy light brown hair. I had his eyes but Mama's hair, which Mama said made me ever more beautiful than she was.

"When I first met him," she said, "he looked like he could be a movie star himself. He had a sexy smile, the kind that could unlock anyone's chastity belt."

"What's a chastity belt?"

"Never mind that," she said. "He was built like a Greek god in those days, too, but I mistook his silence for strength. It took me a while to realize that most of the time, he was silent because he simply didn't know what to say. He never read anything, parroted whatever sound bite he had heard on television, and rarely went to a movie. When we first met, he had never been to the theater. Now that I think about it, Sasha, I must have been out of my mind."

She eventually told me he had gotten her pregnant with me, and when he proposed, she thought maybe she should settle down and become a wife and mother. She tried to make it sound as if I wasn't just a mistake. She said she was surely not going to be the famous movie star she had hoped to be, and she was just not tall enough to work as a model.

"Becoming a mother seemed to be the right thing for me to do. Besides, I needed you. I needed someone else. Your father wasn't much company."

There was no question, however, that she had once been very beautiful. Her half-Asian look was quite exotic, and she once had silky, long black hair down to her wing bones. Both men and women turned their heads to look at her when she sauntered down the street. I was proud to be walking beside her then. She walked like an angel, practically floating, her soft smile imprinting itself on the eyes of men who surely saw her often in their dreams. I wanted to be in that aura that rippled around her so I'd grow up to be just as special.

"If I would have had the sense to hang out where more well-to-do young men hung out, I'm sure I would have hooked a real catch instead of a mediocre clod. Almost as soon as we married, your father began cheating on me. He was never much help with taking care of you. He hated having to stay home, so he would pretend he had to meet someone for a little while, maybe to get a better-paying job, and then not return until the wee hours and sometimes not until morning, bathed in the scent of another woman."

"Why didn't you return to Portland?" I asked. "You said Mama Pearl's sister still lived there. Wouldn't she have helped you?"

"She had her own troubles and was fifteen years older than my mother. She was an old lady, and my mother's family wasn't happy she had married my father. His family wasn't happy he had married my mother. Everyone expects their children to make them happy," she added, with a maddening laugh that always ended with her starting to cry, making me feel bad that I had asked anything.

By then, I was almost eleven. Daddy had recently deserted us, but I was tired of hearing my mother complain about my father. It wasn't that I wanted to defend him, either. Even when I was only seven, I realized my father was not like the fathers of other girls at school. For one thing, he never came to a single parents' night and never seemed at all interested in my schoolwork. Sometimes I thought he wasn't interested in me, period. Once, when he and my mother were having an argument, which was most of the time, I heard him say, "Children are punishment for sins committed earlier."

"That makes sense when it comes to *your* parents," Mama told him. He never talked about his parents or his sister, and none of his family ever called or was interested in him or any of us, for that matter.

Mama and Daddy's fights usually ended with Daddy pounding a table or a wall and sometimes breaking something and then running out of the house with curses trailing behind him like ugly car exhaust.

I'll never forget the day we were evicted from our apartment. I was twelve, nearly thirteen, and home from school because I had a bad cough. We had no medical insurance, so Mama would always try to cure me with some over-the-counter medicines. More often than not, she would just tell me to take a nap or sit in the sun. She was in and out so much those days that she hardly noticed when I was sick, and she was not taking very good care of herself, either. I knew she was with different men frequently and drinking too much. I hated when she came home late at night and began babbling and crying. She would stumble and bang into things. I would bury my face in my pillow and refuse to help her.

Eventually, her good looks began to fade like a week-old rose. Her hair lost its rich, soft look, until it no longer flowed. The ends were always splitting, and she wasn't keeping it clean. She finally decided to cut it herself to make herself look better. When she was done, it looked as if someone had hacked it with a bread knife, but even if she hadn't done it while she was high on cheap gin, she wouldn't have done a good job.

It wasn't only her hair and complexion that grew worse. Her figure seemed to stretch and bulge like the walls of a water-filled balloon. She couldn't get into her jeans and had to wear baggy skirts. Because we didn't have a car and she couldn't afford taxis, she walked so much in old shoes that her feet were always aching or blotched with ugly blisters. She took to wearing oversize sneakers.

I remember once looking out the window and seeing a woman walking up the street, her eyes glassy, her gait uneven, and thinking, *How sad. Look at that bag lady.* When she drew close enough for me to realize it was my mother, I was stunned.

But I was frightened more than anything. The little there was of my own world was falling apart. I had long since stopped having friends over to visit, and no one was inviting me. My attention span in school was bad. I dozed off too much and took little or no pride in my work. My grades were tanking. My teachers said I had attention deficit disorder, which only made me feel more different from the others. Teachers were constantly asking me to bring my mother to school. We had no phone by then, so they didn't call, and letters were useless. She considered everything a bill and read nothing.

Now that I think back, I realize my mother was really the one who was stunned. One morning, she must have woken and realized just how bad off we were and how helpless she was. Instead of the realization driving her to be more vigorous in search of solutions, it caused her to retreat to gin and whiskey. It almost didn't matter what it was, as long as it was alcoholic and could jumble up her thoughts and fears to the point where nothing seemed to bother her.

However, to this day, I don't think of her as an alcoholic. I believe she really could have stopped if she had wanted to. She didn't have the courage to stop. It was ironically easier to look into the mirror and see someone she didn't recognize. Otherwise, she would have committed suicide.

I suppose if we could have afforded psychoanalysis back then, she would have been diagnosed as a borderline schizophrenic. Something that had begun too subtly for me to realize right away had been happening in her head. At times, I thought she was talking to someone else. At first, I thought that occurred only when she was drunk, but I quickly realized that it was happening even when she was stone sober. I think the person she was talking to was herself before I was born, and even before she met Daddy. From what I heard and could understand, she was warning her younger self not to leave home, that if she did, this could be how she would be.

Of course, it made no sense to me, and if I asked her what she was doing, or whom she was talking to, she would look at me angrily, as if I were intruding on a very private conversation.

"None of your business," she might say, or, "It's not for your ears."

*Whose ears is it for?* I wanted to ask. *There's no one there.*

But I kept quiet. I was too frightened to push much further, anyway. Who knew what that might cause to happen? And enough had already happened.

She wasn't home when the police came to the apartment the day we were evicted. The landlord had followed all of the necessary legal steps, but Mama had ignored it all. I was home because I was sick with a bad cough. I opened the door and looked up at two burly sheriff's deputies. One took off his hat and combed through his hair with his fingers, as if he were searching for a lost thought. He looked sorrier than the other for what he was about to do.

"Your mother here?" he asked.

"No," I said.

"Where is she?" the other deputy asked.

"I don't know," I said, and coughed so hard and long that they both stepped back, fearing infection.

"Jesus," the first deputy muttered.

"Do you know when she'll be back, at least?" the second deputy asked me.

I shook my head.

"We'll wait in the car," he told the first deputy, and they turned and went to their vehicle parked right outside our first-floor apartment. At the time, I didn't know why they were there. I thought maybe they had found my father and needed to tell my mother.

After I closed the door, I went to the front window and waited, watching the street. Finally, I could see her coming. She didn't look drunk. She was walking fast, swinging her arms, with her purse wrapped around the front of her body like some shield. She told me she did that to avoid having it grabbed. "Not that I ever have much in it," she added.

The deputies saw her heading our way and got out of their vehicle to approach her. She stood listening to them and then just nodded without comment and continued to the front door. When she entered, she saw me standing there and shook her head.

"You can thank your father someday for this," she said. "Pack only what you really need. We can't carry too much. I'm not spending money on a taxi."

"Why are we leaving?"

"We can't live here anymore. The landlord got the police on us."

"Where are we going?"

"To a hotel nearby," she said.

It sounded good, but when we arrived, I saw how small it was. The lobby was barely bigger than our living room had been, and what we had was one room with two double beds and a bathroom.

"What about a kitchen?" I asked.

"We'll eat out when we want hot food. This will have to do for now," she told me.

Her best hope was that "for now" was forever, only I didn't know that. I didn't know how serious was the dying going on in her head. Because we slept in the same room, I woke up often to hear her nighttime chats with her invisible second self. Most of the time, it was done in whispers, but I often caught a word or two. None of it ever made much sense to me. *Maybe she's just dreaming aloud,* I thought, and went back to sleep.

She was doing it now as we trekked up the beach. The raindrops had become more like pellets. I kept my head down and just lifted my eyes enough to see her soaked old sneakers, pasted with sand and mud, plodding forward awkwardly.

"Where are we going?" I cried. I was tired and would have gladly just slept in the rain.

She didn't answer, but from the way she was moving her arms and hands, I knew she was talking to her imaginary self. I could see the top of a bottle of gin in her shabby coat pocket. There was no one else on the beach but us, so there was no one to appeal to for any help. I was feeling worse than ever. The only way I realized I was crying was by the shudder in my shoulders. My tears were mixed in with the rain.

Mama suddenly turned and started toward the sidewalk. I hurried to catch up. She carried her suitcase limply. It looked as if it was dragging. Even though I was exhausted myself, I wanted to help her, to take it from her, but she wouldn't let go of the handle.

"I'll carry it!" I cried.

"No, no. This is all I have. Let go," she said.

The way she looked at me sent a sharp pain through my heart. *She doesn't recognize me,* I thought. *My own mother doesn't know who I am. She thinks I'm some stranger trying to steal her things.*

"Mama, it's me, Sasha. Let go, and I'll help you."

"No!" she screamed, and tore it out of my grip. We stared at each other for a moment in the rain. Maybe she realized her momentary amnesia and it frightened her as much as it had frightened me. Whatever, she turned and surged forward.

I sped up to keep up with her. We were at a traffic light on the Pacific Coast Highway, and it turned green for us. She stepped into the road, and I caught up with her to walk side-by-side. We were nearly to the other side when I heard the car tires squealing and looked to my right.

The vehicle struck Mama first and literally lifted her over my head before it struck me hard in the right thigh. I saw Mama slapped down on the pavement, just before I fell and slid in her direction.

That was how my life began.